ESCAPE from the PAST

First published in 1997 by
Saga Publishing, an imprint of
Gary Allen Pty Ltd
9, Cooper St
Smithfield
NSW 2164

text ©1997 Anne Infante
The author asserts the moral right to be
identified as the author of the work

National Library of Australia
Cataloguing-in-publication data

Anne Infante
    Escape from the Past
    ISBN 1 875169 67 9

    I. Title
    823.914

Printed in Australia by
Bookworks Printing Pty Ltd
2/17 Laser Drive
Rowville
VIC 3178

Cover design by
David and Traci Harding

Typeset and produced in Australia for
Gary Allen Pty Ltd by
Allan Cornwell Pty Ltd,
25, Churchill Rd,
Mt Martha,
Vic 3934.

ESCAPE from the PAST

Anne Infante

SAGA

With grateful thanks to she of the keen eye and meticulous attention to detail, my editor, Lynne Wilding

also

Warm thanks to Selwa Anthony for her encouragement and kindness, for believing in me, and for taking a chance.

Author Biography

Anne Infante was born in Sydney, Australia, and raised in Papua New Guinea. She has been writing for her own amusment as long as she can remember. She was involved in amateur theatricals for many years and later became known as a folk singer, running her own club, The Barley Mow, and singing in National folk festivals in Australia and New Zealand. She has performed in and co-written folk programmes for ABC radio and appeared as a regular guest in the ABC TV series *Around Folk*. She has become equally well known as a songwriter and has to date recorded three albums of her own songs and two cassettes of positive affirmations for children and adults. Anne began writing seriously in 1987 and has had five crime novels published by Collins Crime Club in the UK. This is her first mainstream novel.

Anne lives in Brisbane, Australia, and shares a house with her mother and three cats.

PART ONE

Brisbane Valley
1880

Chapter 1

A bright half moon slid up from behind the mountain
ridge, striping the forest with silver-grey bands and deepening the shadows in hollows and gullies and thickets.

One slim silver moonbeam penetrated a tangle of spindly aca-
cias and picked out the profile of a rider, waiting motionless in the
shelter of a huge blackbutt. The light ran down the taut line of his
young jaw but the rest of his face remained hidden under the
broad brim of his hat.

Directly above, a mopoke, startled by the sudden brightness,
gave its distinctive warning cry and, with a flurry of wings, flapped
further into the trees. The rider's horse snorted with alarm and
threw up its head.

Its master tightened the reins with one strong hand and qui-
eted the fretting animal with the other. Soothed, the horse dropped
its head to lip at a clump of rough grass. The rider let the reins go
slack on the animal's neck and continued his vigil.

Behind him and to his left was a tall outcrop of weathered rock
known as The Citadel. If necessary, he could withdraw into its fis-
sured depths and remain concealed from anyone passing along
the track which ran through the narrow valley below. Not that
there'd be much risk of travellers at this hour of the night; that was

why Buck had chosen the time and place.

The moon broke free of the tall mountain pines and the rider moved, backing his mount into the shadows. There were other men here, standing or squatting on their heels, as silent as the bush itself. Among the trees were horses, watched over by a small jockey-like figure.

'Well?' The oldest of the group, a man with long light brown hair and a fine handlebar moustache, asked quietly. His voice had a soft American drawl.

The rider slipped from the saddle.

'No sign. Damnation! We can't wait.'

The youth glanced at the sky. 'Past ten,' he said and pulled a silver watch from his pocket although he could tell by the position of the moon that he was right. His coat fell open, revealing a dandy's waistcoat, floral print, with a fancy silk lining.

The others moved closer. 'We can't go with two men short.'

The American gave a soft laugh. 'We could make it. It'd be a challenge.'

Flash Johnny Francis, of the watch and fancy waistcoat, said, 'Buck, can't we wait another ten minutes?'

Buck Buchanan, the American and the group's leader, nodded. 'I allowed for some extra time; but no more'n ten minutes. We go without them if we have to.' He jerked his head towards the horses. 'Someone go tell Limpy.'

Flash remounted and returned to his post, anxiously scanning the valley for the missing men. His heart beat faster at the thought of going without them but the timing was critical. Buck's plans were always immaculately thought out and had to be followed exactly; and they still had a long ride ahead of them.

The horse sensed his increased adrenalin and stamped nervously. He patted its neck and murmured gently to it, then smiled to himself. Of course they could do it. They had four good men, even without the O'Meally brothers; five, if you counted Limpy Patterson, who might be a cripple but could ride and shoot as well as any of them. His confidence returned. They were all fine bushmen, all *wild colonial boys*, most of them born and bred in this tough, uncompromising land. They could out-ride, out-fight and out-shoot anyone in Australia, couldn't they? They were Buck's Boys, Buchanan's Raiders, as hard as the ranges they rode with such consummate skill.

The sound of a horse being swiftly ridden alerted him and he drew back a little, his eyes and ears straining in the night. The rider below left the valley road and began to pick his way up the rough track which led steeply into the foothills of the mountain range.

Flash gave a soft whistle. It was answered from down the track and within minutes the horse and rider broke free of the scrub and came up beside him. They joined the others in the protective shadow of The Citadel.

Flash said, 'It's Red.'

'What kept you?' Buck rasped out, then, 'Where's Billy?'

Walter O'Meally shook his head and the mop of red curls which had earned him his nickname, Red, fell across his forehead. Impatiently, he brushed them back. 'He's not coming.'

'Why not?'

The others were mounted now and gathered around the newcomer. There was a growing tension.

'He's gone to see Rose.'

Wild Jack d'Arcy groaned aloud. 'The fool! Tonight of all nights.'

'He couldn't help it, he got a message,' Red said defensively. 'George Carew's gone away to Brisbane and has forbidden Rose to see my brother again.'

'So he runs straight there to hide behind a woman's skirts.'

'You will not call Billy a coward, Red snapped the challenge back. 'He's no need to hide and is as brave as any of us here. But he was desperate to see Rose. He doesn't know how much time he has before Carew returns.'

'Meanwhile, we are fast running out of time ourselves.' Buck moved forward. 'We'll go ahead with the plan. Limpy can take Billy's place tonight.'

James MacLeod, a big, quiet man, muttered, 'Aye, but he canna run like Billy, if we hae to quit the place in a hurry, and who's to hold the nags for us?'

Buchanan laughed again. 'Perhaps you'd like to stay with the horses, Scotsman?'

'Oh, aye, and where would ye be without the Scotsman to help you transfer all those beautiful nags from Squatter McIntyre's yard to our ain?' He chuckled. 'Well, lads, are we going, or no?'

Sub-Inspector Frederick Arthur Stapleton emerged from a side door onto the verandah of Bellara homestead. Louvred shutters, beautifully crafted from glowing red cedar, protected the verandah doorways at night. A full seven foot high, they were still folded back to allow access as, this evening, Squatter McIntyre was entertaining the district's new senior police officer.

To honour his host, who was the acknowledged leader of Bell's Creek society, Frederick had donned evening dress, rather than his uniform. The sub-inspector was aware that, as he'd so recently arrived in the colony, his elegant black trousers, tail coat, starched white shirt and fawn waistcoat were the height of fashion, being of the latest English cut; although God alone knew how long he'd be able to maintain any sense of style so far from home. From his observation, Australian fashion seemed at least two years behind England and the Continent, due to the immense distance which necessitated many slow months of travel on even the fastest clipper ships before the latest fashion journals could arrive in this farthest of countries.

Frederick found some comfort in the fact that he was an attractive figure, either in civilian dress or his navy police garb. He was tall and slim, his body finely muscled. His thick black hair was parted at the side and cut short in military style and he wore no beard, preferring only his moustache and side whiskers. At the moment his well-shaped black brows were drawn together in a frown as his grey eyes stared rather despondently across the shadowed gardens and well-tended sweeping lawns of McIntyre's spread. Frederick strolled along the broad verandah which was sheltered by a curved iron roof, supported by graceful pairs of white posts turned out of cedar logs, making it an ideal place to entertain in hot weather. He looked up at the blazing canopy of stars. Among the bright clusters he could pick out the great glowing Pointers and they guided his eyes to the constellation called the Southern Cross which, he'd been told, always pointed to the South Pole. It was one of the few constellations he could name in this alien southern sky and he found himself nostalgically wishing for the familiar Pole Star or a glimpse of the Plough or the Great Bear.

He shook his head, dismissing the unwelcome surge of home sickness. He'd known it wouldn't be easy, leaving his home and family and embarking on a whole new life in the colonies, on the other side of the world.

He lit a cigar and leaned against the verandah rail. Although the moon riding up the sky was still only showing half its face, its brightness was turning the garden and the wide paddocks beyond to silver and dimming the stars. The night was very still with only the occasional harsh cry of a night bird. Close by a dog barked then fell silent.

Stapleton set his jaw. He was determined to stick it out, to learn the new ways and new customs and make a success of his life here, even though the heat and isolation could be almost unbearable at times and Australia seemed to be inhabited by every biting or stinging insect and plant sent to plague mankind. As if to prove his point a mosquito whined near his cheek. He struck at it and missed, then waved his cigar in the air, hoping the pungent smoke would deter the persistent insect. He had few bitter thoughts about the past. He preferred to see the succession of blows as opportunities to break from his ordered pattern of existence and embark on *his colonial adventure* as he liked to put it. A fresh start in a new land which, as he well knew, was brimming with wealth and the possibilities of advancement.

What there was of local society had welcomed the handsome young English officer and he had been inundated with invitations to dine or to attend the sudden rush of dances, shooting parties and other entertainments which were hastily arranged for his benefit. He was openly courted by hopeful mammas with daughters of marriageable age but — Caroline still lay like a bruise across his heart. He was always polite and pleasantly attentive but it was clear he simply was not interested, which made him even more of a challenge to various frustrated young ladies.

If only father had lived. If only Roger had not squandered the family fortune at the gaming tables. If Caroline had stood by him instead of declaring she could not marry a poor man, her family expected her to make a suitable match — and Henry Morrisey was a prize catch. If only he hadn't fought that senseless duel and half killed the man: his colonel had no choice, he knew; he'd disgraced the regiment. The only reason he'd been allowed to resign his commission was that Colonel Fitzgibbon had been a friend of his father and was sympathetic about Caroline. No, *if only* was a fool's game. He refused to play it. That was all behind him, he'd make his name in the new colony and go home a hero one day. Yes, that was a better way to think. Not only a hero but a rich man.

Then Caroline would see what her selfish ambition had lost her.

The door to the verandah opened and his host, also in black evening dress, with a shiny black silk waistcoat, stepped out to join him, followed by a servant carrying a heavy silver tray which he placed on a low table.

Andrew McIntyre was a thick-set man of medium height in his early fifties. He had a strong broad face and grizzled sandy hair. He favoured mutton-chop whiskers and his beard was neatly clipped into two points. He pulled out a large white handkerchief, wiped his damp forehead and smiled at the younger man.

'Thought we'd have coffee out here if the damned insects'll let us alone. Yes, Jones, you can pour — and we'll have a brandy. Bring out the decanter.'

He motioned his guest to one of the comfortable canvas chairs which seemed to have been designed for lounging at one's ease while surveying one's acres. The sub-inspector had been pleasantly surprised by the grace and style of Bellara, with its spacious, high-ceilinged rooms, stained glass fanlights, polished floors, fireplaces with carved red cedar surrounds and elegant furniture. He'd not expected such a degree of luxury in the bush. The house was built on a knoll overlooking wide rolling acres that ran down to the creek which gave the little township its name. The homestead was low-set, the verandah being only two steps up from the garden. Stapleton relaxed into the chair and accepted a cup of coffee. McIntyre lit a cigar and the two men shared a companionable silence.

The servant reappeared with the decanter, served them, and went back into the house.

Frederick sipped the brandy. It was excellent. He said so.

'I can afford the best,' his host told him frankly. 'Couldn't always, b'God. I battled for years; drought, stock losses, disease, farmers trying to take my land. It's a tough country and a man needs to be tough to survive here. I'm a survivor. Now I own the biggest station in the district, wool prices are high, exports booming; and I can indulge my passion for breeding racehorses.' He winked. 'In the bottom paddock I've a nice lot of yearlings, waiting for branding before they go to the Brisbane market.'

Frederick stretched out his legs and crossed his ankles. 'You serve a superb meal, sir. I've enjoyed this evening.'

'Thought you needed rescuing from the women. You're a nine day wonder; the girls don't get much excitement so you've been a fine excuse for everyone to outdo her neighbour in entertaining the dashing newcomer.' He broke into a slow chuckle.

'To tell the truth, it's a little embarrassing.' Frederick ran a finger along his moustache as if seeking comfort from its luxuriant growth.

'They'll settle down, give 'em time. How're you getting along at the police camp?'.

'I hope, well, sir. The native police are interesting and Sergeant Mallory is helping me acclimatise. I spent two years with the Indian army so I've had experience with handling natives. These are somewhat different but they seem a dedicated bunch.'

'The ladies are lucky there's been little criminal activity of late or you'd not have been available for their parties. You'd be up country somewhere, miles away from the town for weeks on end, chasing law-breakers.'

'That would suit me very well. I'm eager to see some action. I believe there was some local trouble before I arrived.'

The squatter leaned forward and topped up both brandy glasses. 'Local lads, looking for adventure. You see, boys brought up out here, on the farms, in the bush; well, it has to be said they don't receive much education, if they get any schooling at all. They've no respect for the law — indeed, I believe they feel themselves to be above it; they boast of being hard men, they know horses and firearms and judge a man solely on how he sits his mount or handles his weapon. They've a natural contempt for any who fall below their own rigid standards. Such boys are easy targets for manipulation by older men, more experienced in the ways of crime.'

Stapleton raised an eyebrow. 'One might say you were speaking of Fagin.'

McIntyre laughed. 'No, for these boys aren't starving or homeless, merely tired of their humdrum lives and ripe for a spree. They delight in thumbing their noses at anyone in authority and are such superb bushmen even your black trackers have been outwitted by them.' He looked amused. 'You should know, Stapleton, that police officers and bush larrikins are natural enemies.'

Stapleton smiled slightly. 'You give me a keen desire for the chance to come to grips with these lads. I'm held to be a pretty fair shot myself and a not contemptible rider.'

'In that case, I hope to show you some good sport very soon.'

Frederick thought the statement cryptic and looked a question at the squatter. McIntyre merely smiled gently and asked, 'More coffee?'

The six horsemen stopped at a noisy, fast running creek and dismounted. They made their preparations in silence with the ease of long practice. Although the night was warm they donned dark coats and scarves, muffling the lower part of their faces and pulling their hats well down. Buck Buchanan folded his yellow fringed buckskin coat and strapped it behind his saddle. Flash Johnny Francis buttoned his coat to the neck. The moon would not betray them by fingering some light spot or trademark clothing. All the men checked their weapons.

They remounted, a dark, anonymous group, and picked their way among the she-oaks. The creek bank was rocky; there would be few tell-tale tracks for the new sub-inspector's police to follow.

Half an hour later they reached the boundary fence of Squatter McIntyre's station.

Chapter 2

'N ow there's a bonny sight.' The Scotsman gazed across the paddock at the small herd of young horses who were staring with nervous curiosity at their unexpected visitors. 'Good of the man to leave them here for us; handy, so to speak.'

Limpy Patterson looked around with a knowledgeable eye at the preparations already under way. 'Branding tomorrow,' he said softly.

'We'll relieve them of the necessity.' Buck swung down from his saddle. 'Jack, take our nags and tie them under the trees. Limpy, keep watch. Red, Flash, get the sliprails down. Keep it nice and quiet. Let's go, boys.'

Buck and the Scotsman went over the fence towards their quarry. The horses shifted in alarm and one gave a whinny.

'Easy, easy,' Buck cooed, soothing the animals with gentle sounds. He reached the group and went among them, patting, stroking, gentling the yearlings. He slipped a rope around the neck of a dappled grey and began to walk it towards the sliprails, murmuring, 'Come, boy, come with Uncle Buck. He's got a nice, comfortable paddock waitin' for you.'

He had reached the open gateway when a shout froze him in his tracks.

A shot whistled over his head and a voice yelled, 'Stay right there. We've caught you, you thieving bastards.'

On the homestead verandah, the squatter was regaling his guest with tales of the lawless days of the past.

'We had our own native police squad.' He smiled reminiscently. 'Paid for and maintained by myself, George Carew and a couple of the squatters out further. Had to, you see. It was just before separation and the New South Wales Government was not prepared to spend any more than they needed, protecting a territory they'd shortly lose. Police numbers were minimal, what few patrols we had couldn't hope to cover the territory effectively. Then the blacks raided us here, at Bellara, and killed one of my men. So we took the law into our own hands.'

He pulled out his watch and tapped it. 'Won't be long now, I think.'

'What are you expecting, sir?'

'A little surprise, my boy, a little surprise.'

In the distance a muffled popping noise broke the stillness.

'Good God! That was rifle fire.' Frederick came to his feet as the station dogs began barking in earnest, drowning out the far sound.

McIntyre stubbed out his cigar.

'Our horses are waiting outside. Shall we ride over and watch the fun?'

At the first shot, the Scotsman and Red O'Meally, who had followed Buck in among the horses, dropped to the ground.

Limpy Patterson screamed out, 'We're rumbled,' and fired into a nearby stand of eucalypts where their attackers had been hiding. Flash Johnny Francis, his blue eyes blazing with excitement, crouched by the sliprails, his revolver cocked, coolly watching for a target. Wild Jack d'Arcy ran, bent double, along the fence to join him.

'They won't fire near the horses,' Flash said urgently. 'We'll keep 'em busy and give the lads a chance to get away.' He raised his gun and fired into the trees; d'Arcy followed his example. Behind them came the crack of Patterson's rifle.

In the paddock the horses were whinnying in fright, rearing and stamping, moving in an agitated group. The Scotsman, his heart pounding with shock at the unexpected attack, rolled to his elbows and began to crawl clear of the herd. He could see the grey, ghostly in the moonlight, and the dark figure of Buchanan hugging its neck, keeping it between himself and the trees.

Red O'Meally crawled alongside the Scotsman and raised himself cautiously, sighting along his revolver. He fired and there was a startled shout. A bullet sang past his ear and buried itself in the ground. 'Bastard!' He snarled and felt a stab of fear as he ducked his head. The acrid smell of gunpowder filled his nostrils as the Scotsman fired his own weapon. Red reloaded, thinking furiously, Damn Billy! Damn him to hell! He should be here with us, with his mates. The shifting horses, hooves flailing, were still dangerously near. The Scotsman shouted something and Red strained to hear him above the din. He read the mouthed words, 'Cover me!' He nodded and they began to give each other covering fire as they crawled desperately towards the gate.

A bullet buried itself in the ground, too close for comfort, and a little spray of dirt spurted into Red's eyes. He swore and blinked angrily to clear them.

An urgent voice called, 'Don't fire at the herd, you fools,' then, 'Give yourselves up, you can't escape.'

Buck's buoyant laugh rang out. 'I wouldn't wager on that, boys.' He let go his iron hold on the grey, turning it towards the trees, and slapped it hard on the rump. The horse bolted towards the eucalypts. Buck dropped to the ground outside the fence.

The voice called again. 'You won't get away. Surrender now!'

'That's Big Mick Harrison, McIntyre's overseer,' Jack groaned. 'It's a trap. We've walked into a trap.'

A bullet thudded dully beside him and Flash gasped out, 'I'm hit. The bugger got me.' His hand went urgently to his left shoulder where a sticky warmth was spreading across his shirt. He thought hazily, Feels bad. Dear God, I'm done for. He gritted his teeth against the pain. He wouldn't give in, wouldn't let the others see how afraid he was. If he was dying, he'd die game. He rasped out, between laboured breaths, 'That was good shooting.'

A flurry of shots was exchanged. There was an agonised scream from one of the squatter's men. The grey had turned and was now running, terrified, across the line of fire.

Buck knelt beside Flash. 'Come on, lad, I'll get you out safe.' The wounded boy tried to stifle a groan as the pain bit into him and Buck's face set in harsh lines. He knew he was responsible for this shambles. He was the general, the others followed his lead unquestioningly, confident that he'd see them through.He cursed himself for a blind fool. He'd been taken in like a raw boy, not seeing the danger. He should have known it was too easy, too convenient. He should have been expecting a trap. He'd grown too complacent, too cocksure. He'd behaved like a crass idiot and led his men into a disastrous situation; he might even have got his courageous young friend killed.

He put an arm around Flash, hoisting him to his feet. The lad winced and gave a sharp moan but stumbled with Buck towards the horses.

The American glanced back at the others fighting gamely to break away. 'Save yourselves, boys,' he shouted above the noise of the conflict. 'Save yourselves.'

Stapleton and McIntyre rode hard across the moonlit fields towards the sound of the fight. On a rise above the bottom paddock, they reined in.

The scene laid out before them was all silver and violet with the trees throwing stark black bars across the grass. In the paddock, terrified horses were circling, screaming in fright. The grey was running parallel to a tree break. Dark figures moved towards the bush cover. The firing had temporarily ceased.

McIntyre spurred his horse down the slope, shouting, 'They're getting away. After them!'

Stapleton drew his revolver from its holster and followed. This was just the sort of action he'd been waiting for. This was his chance to show that he could do the job and do it well. These colonial louts might elude the local police but Frederick was a man trained for military combat and he'd seen his share of fighting. He urged his horse on, grateful for the chance to come to grips with McIntyre's *bush larrikins*.

The two men reached the eucalypts. Several station hands lay groaning on the ground; others were grabbing for their horses' reins. The body of the overseer lay in a swelling pool of blood.

One of the wounded men grunted out, 'Harrison. They've killed Big Mick Harrison.'

'Follow me!' Frederick waved an arm to the squatter's men. Those who were uninjured quickly mounted. They left the shelter of the trees and galloped across the clear space beyond, following the sound of hooves. Four riders were visible through the bush ahead, crouching low in their saddles. Suddenly they veered off the narrow track and scattered through the trees.

'They've split up.' Frederick pulled his horse to a sudden halt. He had three men with him; a European station hand and two Aboriginal stockmen.

'We'll do the same,' he ordered. 'Follow as best we can. You, there,' he pointed at one of the stockmen, 'ride as fast as you can to the police camp and bring back Sergeant Mallory and a detachment.'

The man rode off. The station hand shook his head.

'We can't follow the bastards, we haven't the men. There were a dozen of them, at least.'

'I counted only four ahead of us.' Frederick looked around. Under the trees the bush was dark, filled with dim, mysterious shapes moving in a rising wind, and he could no longer hear the raiders' horses. 'Where did they go?' He wondered aloud.

'Tricky devils.' The other stockman pointed. 'I go along there, pick 'em up further down.'

Frederick motioned to the remaining man who reluctantly rode a little way into a grove of bunya pines then shrugged, pushing back his hat to scratch his receding hairline.

'We haven't a hope of catching them. There are dozens of ways they could have gone. And they're well armed,' he added.

Frederick compressed his mouth in annoyance. Their quarry, melting soundlessly into the bush, had simply vanished.

He swore helplessly and turned his horse around. 'We'll wait for the sergeant and the native police,' he said optimistically.

As they rode away, Frederick's mount gave an agitated cry and he stroked her glossy black neck. 'Easy, Diamond,' he told her.

Standing in the middle of the bunyas, Buck slid his fingers along his horse's nose. As the sub-inspector's mare neighed, he tightened his grip, checking an answering whinny from his own animal. The soft thud of hooves slowly died away.

Buck looked up at Flash, slumped over his mount's neck. He looped both pairs of reins through his arm.

'You all right, boy?'

'Bearing up, old fellow, quite well, considering.' Flash said faintly. 'Just get me home and put me to bed, will you?'

At Bellara homestead, Sergeant Mallory clicked his tongue disapprovingly. 'No chance of tracking them tonight, sir. We'll come back at dawn and pick up the trail.'

McIntyre was scowling, his broad face flushed with anger. He thumped the verandah rail hard with clenched fists and growled, 'They'll be back in their homes like rats in their holes.'

'We can try to ascertain who the men might be, sir. I'm bound to say, if we'd been informed you were expecting trouble tonight, we could have been waiting for them.'

'It was my trap,' the squatter said violently. 'I set it. I baited it; and we were ready for them.' He swung away and began to pace furiously along the verandah.

'You'll excuse me, sir, but that was the job of the police. Better to have let us handle the situation.'

McIntyre turned on him, his fists raised, the dull red flush in his cheeks deepening alarmingly. Frederick wondered if the man would burst a blood vessel. He looked to be in a complete rage.

The sergeant stood quietly, his stolid calm contrasting with the other man's agitation. McIntyre shouted, 'Blast you, Sergeant, there was a time when I owned the police.'

'That would be over twenty years ago, would it, sir?' Sergeant Mallory said doggedly. 'Luckily, things are different now and we've adequate men to take care of raiders, especially this little lot.'

The squatter slowly lowered his fists and tried for a more reasonable tone. 'There were a dozen of 'em, my men said so. You've got six men in camp.'

The sergeant looked at Frederick. 'Will you be coming back to camp now, sir?'

'Yes, I'll ride with you.' He held out his hand to McIntyre. 'Goodnight, sir. Thank you for an — interesting evening. We'll be back in the morning.'

Red O'Meally rode easily, splashing down the creek bed, leaving no trace of his passing; Jack d'Arcy followed close behind him. They left the water at a rocky beach and brought their mounts to walk side by side. They had shed their dark coats and mufflers and were now dressed like any other bushmen in flannel shirts, waistcoats and trousers of tough, serviceable material. Both had knotted bright 'kerchiefs around their necks and wore broad-brimmed bush hats.

Jack broke the silence. His dark eyes were sombre as he said, 'Earlier tonight, Red, what I said about Billy — I'm sorry, I know he's not a coward.'

Red flashed him a smile, his teeth gleaming white in the moonlight. 'It's all right. I was angry with him, too. I tried to stop him going. He should have been with us tonight.'

'I doubt it would have made a difference. They were waiting for us. It was a trap, Buck led us right into it.'

His companion rubbed a hand tiredly over his short red beard and smoothed his thick moustache. 'It looked safe enough. We all knew McIntyre was sending the horses to Brisbane. We had to move quickly.'

'It was too easy.' Jack tugged angrily at his own dark moustache. He hesitated, not wanting to voice his suspicions, to criticise Buck. He was always fiercely loyal to his friends and his leader; but the doubt had been growing since the ambush and he needed to express it. He said evenly, 'McIntyre talked openly at the Squatters' Arms. He knew what he was doing, saying he had the nags in the bottom paddock and they'd be branding tomorrow. He was making sure the information was heard and he knew, if there was a raid, it had to be tonight.'

Red stared. 'Does that mean he suspects Buck?'

'I don't know. Buck works at the Arms. If Squatter McIntyre suspects him, he might have some evidence against him, against others of us.'

'We got away, didn't we? Buck's taking care of Flash. A bullet in the shoulder won't kill him.'

'He can't take him to Doc Evans and risk word getting out about the wound.'

'Buck knows how to dig out a bullet. He'll take Flash to his place.' Jack shuddered.

'Perhaps it was as well Billy wasn't with us,' Red added. 'With his mind in a turmoil over Rose, he could have been injured, even killed.'

'That would suit George Carew,' d'Arcy said. 'He wants Rose to marry Robert Leicester.'

'Rose is the prettiest girl in the district,' Red countered. 'She can have her pick of the boys.' There was a brusque note in his voice and Jack looked at him in surprise. 'You were never one of her suitors.'

Red gave a quick grin. 'No, it's my brother she dotes on. It's him I worry for. He'll get himself into trouble one day.'

Jack sighed. 'I doubt if George Carew would like any of us for his Rose. He'll see her settled with that staid banker, saying it's for her own sake, her future security; whilst all the time he's thinking that a banker son-in-law would be an asset for a farmer. I've heard him say every farmer needs a friend in the bank, in case of lean times.'

They broke from the cover of the trees and cantered through a small open valley. The land here was settled and fences cut across the pasture.

'Carew's run.' Jack turned his horse to follow a long fence line. 'Well, as much as I hate the thought of your brother marrying Rose, if it was between him and Robert, I'd have to cheer for Billy.'

'You still love her?'

Jack reined in and looked squarely at his friend. 'I've always loved her.' He smiled faintly. 'I've never understood what she sees in Billy.'

He reached out his hand and the other man clasped it. 'I'll leave you here, Red, and make my way home over the range. That should fool 'em. Keep safe, now. Remember, they can't know it was us.'

'No.' Red nodded. 'You keep safe as well, Jack.'

Chapter 3

The police camp was half an hour's ride to the south of Bellara homestead. The force consisted of the sub-inspector, Sergeant Mallory and six native troopers and was responsible for maintaining law and order over a vast tract of rugged country. Their jurisdiction stretched from the Great Dividing Range to the D'Aguilar Range, and incorporated the wild Blackbutt Range and settlements along the Brisbane Valley.

The only police presence for hundreds of miles, the camp was really a small community, as the native police were mostly married men and their wives and children lived with them. Sergeant Mallory's wife, Grace, and their two daughters also lived at the camp, in the sergeant's quarters.

As the two men rode along the dusty, moonlit track, Frederick said, 'How do you read the situation, sergeant?'

Sergeant Mallory was sitting very straight in the saddle. His rigid expression and the firm set of his broad shoulders under his blue police jacket betrayed his continued irritation with the squatter. Normally a placid man, now his eyes snapped and even his full chestnut beard seemed to bristle as he said curtly, 'Sir, Mr McIntyre should be told he can't take the law into his own hands. The man lives in the past, thinks he owns the police. It's a great annoyance.'

'Yes, I think you made that clear. I agree, it was a stupid act, designed to impress me I think, with his expertise. His men seemed incompetent; they swore they'd been attacked by a dozen or more ruffians.'

The sergeant snorted. 'Perhaps half that number, sir.'

'Yes, I think so, too. I counted six, although with all the confusion and the shelter afforded them by the trees, I couldn't swear to it. They kept in the shadows, where they could. There were certainly four riders ahead of us before they separated and disappeared into the bush.'

'We'll be lucky to catch them,' Mallory said bitterly. 'A right shambles, if you ask me. Although,' he added thoughtfully, 'I'll make a wager on who they are, sir, and I'll be close to the truth, you can be sure.'

'Why do you say that?'

'One of the squatter's men said he heard a Yankee voice after they challenged the thieves. There's a man, Buchanan, works at the Squatters' Arms. Turned up here more than a year back, an adventurer, you might say; and the local lads look up to him, being older than them. He's filled their heads with amazing tales of his life in the wild west of America.'

'He's not the only American in the district,' Frederick countered. 'There are the Anderson brothers with their gold mine up on Cooyar Creek and Joe Clayton, the saddler, is from Texas, so he tells me.'

'But Buchanan works at the Arms, which is where you'll find McIntyre most nights, since his wife was carried off with the fever. They say he's been boasting about those yearlings, being the first return, you might say, of his new venture into horse breeding.'

'You think Buchanan took the bait and persuaded some of the local boys to join him? Which of them, in your opinion, would go on such a venture?'

'The ones most likely are the O'Meally boys and Johnny Francis, him they call Flash. They're often in his company. Of course, they're friends with Jack d'Arcy and he fancies himself a cut above the law.

To tell you the truth, sir,' the sergeant continued, 'I've had my eye on those lads for a good while, since these outbreaks began. It's no coincidence, I'll be bound, that our rash of trouble started a few weeks after Buchanan came to town.'

'Mostly horse thefts?'

'No, the Andersons were robbed last year, coming into town with gold from their diggings, which points to them not being involved; and more than one farmer has lost prize stock. We came across a hidden valley some months ago on this side of the Blackbutt Range, when we were tracking some missing stock from Rendell's station. The far end of the valley was more like a narrow gorge and had been fenced across to make a holding yard. There was evidence cattle had been recently held and branded there but the place was deserted. It was quite near James McLeod's shack, if you take my meaning, sir.'

'The man they call the Scotsman?'

'The same, sir. McLeod is a quiet man, keeps himself to himself, likes living out in the bush. He's a fencer, works on all the local properties; he'd know the stock as well as any. They probably know we found the valley because it's not been used since — but there are any amount of secret places in these ranges. We could look for months and ride straight past without knowing.'

The roofs of the camp buildings came into view between the trees and the men cantered for home.

As they dismounted and the trooper on duty ran to stable their horses, Frederick said, 'You seem to have collected quite an amount of information on the likely offenders.'

'Yes, sir. I thought it would be useful to observe various individuals, build up a case against them.'

'I'd like to have that information from you. After we learn what we can at Bellara, I'll get you to pay a visit to your suspects. See if they betray themselves in any way.'

Sergeant Mallory thought that was about as likely as snow falling at Christmas but he saluted and went to his quarters to get a couple of hours sleep before dawn.

The sub-inspector stood, deep in thought. The native trooper, on his way back from the stables, looked at him curiously. Frederick came out of his reverie and beckoned the man over.

'I'm going out again. Saddle Black Diamond and tell Trooper Jacky-Jacky to join me.'

Ten minutes later, Frederick and the trooper left the camp, riding hard towards Bell's Creek.

William O'Meally rode slowly home like a man in a dream, following the line of Carew's fence as it ran down a gentle slope to angle sharply away north. His coat had fallen open revealing a dark grey waistcoat and a grey scarf, hastily tied around his neck. His hat was pushed back on his red-brown curls and his deep brown eyes, lit by tender memories, shone with a soft warmth. Under a drooping moustache, his mouth curved in a gentle smile, then straightened as, for a brief moment, he remembered the raid. He felt a pang of guilt, then dismissed it. They'd have managed perfectly well without him. Squatter McIntyre's yearlings would now be penned in a certain secret valley, watched over by the Scotsman and ready for branding when the search for them had been called off — and it wouldn't be Bellara's brand they'd be wearing.

Then he forgot the others in the blissful memory of his own night's events.

Rose had been waiting, as they'd arranged, in the side garden, with its high hedges giving them cover from prying servants' eyes. William had caught his breath at the sight of her sweet face framed by soft golden hair which tumbled down her back, free from the restraints of ribbons or bonnet. Her deep blue eyes sparkled with tears and an embroidered shawl slipped from her shoulders as she'd held out her hands in a joyful welcome. Her grief at her father's decree that she was not to see *that young larrikin* again, had made her cling to him more closely than she'd ever done before. His heart had risen on a wave of ecstasy as he'd held her in his arms and wiped her tears away and then kissed her soft mouth which was so willingly turned to meet his. As their kisses became more urgent, Rose had taken him by the hand and led him stealthily up the steps, along the verandah to her own room.

In the glowing lamp light, William had stared, bemused, thinking the room more like a bower, with its feminine frills and floral prints. The furniture was delicate, painted white and set with flower prints and gleaming inlay. The wash stand held a pretty porcelain basin and jug, decorated with roses on a green background. It was as dainty and beautiful as Rose herself and he felt clumsy and out of place until she tugged at his hand, smiling at him and rousing him from his stupor. They'd sat side by side on her fourposter bed with its frilled coverlet and curtains, whispering their love so that Mrs Moore, the Carews' housekeeper, wouldn't hear them. And they'd kissed again until neither of them could have stopped the inevitable result, even if they'd thought of doing so.

Afterwards, lying in each other's arms, with only a single candle to give them light, they'd made a solemn vow.

'You belong to me now, Rose,' William said tenderly. 'We'll have to wait, bide our time, but I'll not let your father separate us.'

'Neither will I.' Rose snuggled against him. 'He wants me to marry Robert Leicester but I never shall. I've given myself to you, my darling and, whatever father says, you are my husband now although there was no one but God to bless us.'

William's confidence soared. Although he was only eighteen, he knew there'd never be another woman for him. Rose was his heart's delight, his soul mate. Her love made him feel invincible, a god among mere mortals. Nothing was impossible, as long as Rose loved him and looked at him with eyes so full of trust and adoration. He wouldn't let her be taken from him. They'd be together always, be happy always.

He pulled her even closer, smiling into her eyes, stroking her soft hair. 'We'll go away together,' he promised. 'I'll find a way. I'll have to make some money, then we'll go to Brisbane and get properly married, in the eyes of the law. Then your father will have no power over us.'

Rose shivered. 'He is a hard, stern man. If he knew you had been here tonight, that we'd lain together, he'd find a way to punish you, send you away.'

William kissed her. 'He will never know, I swear it. I'll protect you, Rose.'

Her eyes shone in the soft candlelight. 'I know you will and I trust you, William. I'd trust you with my life.'

He pulled himself reluctantly out of her arms. 'When does your father return?'

'In two days. Will I see you tomorrow?'

He swung his legs over the side of the bed and stood, looking down at her.

'I must go. If I fall asleep, we'll be discovered and I must be seen to have slept in my own bed tonight.' He bent over her and kissed her again, lingeringly. 'I'll come tomorrow night, love. Wait for me in the garden.'

She slipped out of bed and stood beside him. In her white cotton shift, her hair tousled from their love-making, he thought she had never looked more beautiful. With a supreme effort of will he pulled on his trousers and found his shirt and scarf.

Carrying his hat and boots he trod quietly to the door, pausing for one last, long kiss.

'I'll wait for you,' she whispered. 'I'd wait for you forever, William O'Meally.'

Buck Buchanan had a shack behind the Squatters' Arms. It was small and plain, made from roughly hewn timber planks, below a sloping roof of wooden shingles. The inner walls were lined with sacking and the furniture was sparse and serviceable rather than elegant but it suited him to live there. He had the freedom to come and go as he pleased, when the publican didn't need him, and no one any the wiser. He'd ridden straight there, leading Flash Francis' nag, for the lad had lost a lot of blood and was barely able to keep himself in the saddle.

Buck tethered the horses and carried Flash inside. He laid him on the bed and stripped open his coat, revealing a deep bullet hole in his left shoulder. It was still sluggishly bleeding. He lit the fire and hung a kettle of water over it, then gathered some clean rags.

Lifting the wounded boy, he got him out of his coat, waistcoat and shirt. 'You'll never wear that again,' he muttered and tore the shirt into strips.

When the water was boiling he worked swiftly. To his relief, as he began to probe the torn shoulder, Flash gave a moan of pain and fainted. Buck dug out the bullet and threw it into the fire, then cleaned the wound and packed it with an antiseptic powder before covering it with a thick wad of cloth to stop the bleeding. Then he bound the pad firmly into place with the torn shirt strips.

He held up the floral waistcoat, and gave a soft laugh at the sight of the ripped and bloodied garment. Bundling it together with the coat, he carried the clothes and the remains of the shirt outside and buried them by the stables before he attended to the horses. All his senses were pleasurably alert to the imminent danger and he whistled a polka under his breath as he returned to the tiny cottage.

Buck hung up his dark coat and shrugged into his yellow buckskin. He found a shirt for Flash and dressed him in it, knotting his brightest 'kerchief around the boy's neck. He couldn't provide a fancy waistcoat, which might look suspicious to anyone with a knowledge of the young dandy's style of dress; the 'kerchief would have to do.

He took a bottle of whisky from the cupboard and drank deeply, then set two glasses on the table. He filled them both, and lit two cigars, leaving them smouldering in the ashtray.

Flash groaned and he went quickly to the bed. In the distance the beat of horses' hooves was growing louder. Two nags, Buck thought, coming fast.

He lifted Flash's head. 'Drink this.' He held the whisky to his lips and the youth took a long swallow.

'What's happening?' He asked weakly.

'Troopers coming. You were hit but I've made it look all right. Couldn't save your pretty waistcoat, though. Now, listen, we've been here all night, dicing. You got drunk and you're sleeping it off. Have another pull.' He held the glass steady while the boy drank, then he sprinkled whisky liberally over them both.

The horses had pulled up outside. He could hear the scrape of boots on the gravel path. He tossed a pair of dice on the table and divided a pile of coins, dropping a couple on the floor for artistic effect.

There was an imperative knocking at the door. Buck cast a hasty look around. It wasn't perfect but it *might* fool them. He took another long pull at the whisky bottle to steady his nerves, splashed some on the table as an afterthought, took a deep breath and strolled over to the door.

Chapter 4

S till with his thoughts on Rose, thrilled at her willing surrender to him and her unashamed passion, which had matched his own, William reached the bottom of the hill and turned away from the fence line. He rode south down the rough bush track that would bring him out above Bell's Creek and connect him with the western road that was his way home. His spirits soaring, he urged his horse to a canter, then to a gallop. There was no danger; both knew the track by heart.

In the shifting moon shadows as a rising breeze stirred the leaves, he didn't see the rope stretched taut across the track. It caught him hard across the throat, bruising his windpipe and pulling him backwards out of the saddle. He fell heavily to the ground, choking and fighting for breath.

His attacker was on him before he had time to recover. Dazed from the fall, William tried to see the man's face but he had some sort of hood over his head with holes cut for the eyes. He was bigger than William and stronger, and the boy was suddenly aware he was fighting for his life.

Yet...there was a familiarity about the bigger man.

George Carew, William thought, Rose's father has laid a trap for me. Anger gave him an added strength. As he'd often found in wrestling bouts with Red, his smaller size could be used to advantage. The air was filled with the sound of shifting, scuffling feet and the angry grunts of the two men as they desperately battled each other. William managed to slip clear of the other man who flung himself after him, bringing him face down in the dirt. William, winded, gasped for air as the other's strong hands tried to close around his throat. He felt his forehead cut open on a stone and blood ran into his eyes.

Each man struggled furiously for the advantage. They rolled over one another, their breathing hard. William's attacker, a dark nemesis, never uttered a word, making only a soft grunt as William landed a fist against his jaw.

He wants to kill me, leave me for dead, as if I'd been set on by robbers, William realised. A stab of fear went through him, followed by a hot anger that spurred him to greater effort. With a furious exclamation he dragged himself to his feet. The other grappled with him but William broke free again and kicked savagely at the man who dodged away, giving him breathing space to stumble towards his horse. Country Lass shied as he reached her but he caught the reins and grabbed frantically for his rifle which was in its saddle holster.

As he drew it out, there was a thump in his back as if he'd been hit by a man's hard fist. He fell forward, vaguely aware of the crack of a revolver. He was losing consciousness fast. He had the impression of a horse galloping away, then everything went black.

The mare, quiet now the fight was over, came up to him, nudging him to get up. William lay without moving and Country Lass, puzzled, began to lip delicately at his coat.

Stapleton hammered on the door, calling, 'Open, in the name of the law.' He heard a lock turning, the door scraped back and a tall man in a yellow jacket with fringed sleeves stood, swaying unsteadily, in a pool of lamplight.

'Wha's matter? Wha's happening?' His voice was slurred. He

Escape from the Past

listed towards the sub-inspector who turned his head from the reek
of whisky fumes.

Buck leaned heavily against the door. "S open.' He peered blear-
ily at the men. 'You're the police. Pub's closed.'

'I'm Sub-Inspector Stapleton,' Frederick told him briskly.

Buck held out an unsteady hand. 'Delighted, sir, make y'r
'quaintance.' He belched. 'Scuse me; a little drunk. Come in, sir,
come in and have a whisky with me and my pal.'

Frederick stepped past him into the room. He found it hard to
equate the American with the description of the rogue given him
by Sergeant Mallory. The man looked like some damned actor in
his buckskins, with his hair around his shoulders, no doubt aping
the famous American army scout, William Cody or the late General Custer. And he obviously couldn't hold his liquor. He was nothing but an effeminate fraud. His home was like a pig sty. Frederick
glanced distastefully around the dark room, lit only by a single
lamp with a grimy glass and the crackling fire's leaping flames.
The furniture was roughly made from dark timber, the bed just a
slatted frame with a thin mattress. He frowned. There was grog
spilt all over the table, money on the floor. It looked as if the American and his friend had been having a riotous night. They couldn't
have been on the raid at Bellara. He scanned the table, the dice
and the money. They'd obviously been dicing and had been very
evenly matched by the winnings on both sides. Then his eyes narrowed.

Buck, watching him closely, gave a vacuous grin. 'Pub's closed
but I got whisky. Pour y'self a drink.'

Frederick stiffened. 'No, thank you, sir. Have you been here all
evening?'

'Tha's right, 'spector.'

'And your friend will verify that?'

Buck lurched to the table and swallowed some more of the grog.
He flung an arm around Stapleton's shoulders and said confid-
ingly, "S Flash Johnny Francis. Lad's a bit under the weather. Can't
hold his liquor, not like me. Passed out. Don't tell anyone. Thinks
he can drink, y'see.'

36

Frederick detached himself and walked over to the bed.

'Mr Francis, are you awake?'

Buck thought urgently, Don't fail now, Flash, stay with us, boy. He sat down, knowing if he went to the bed it might look as if he was anxious. He began to roll the dice noisily back and forth across the table's bare wooden surface and said with heavy amusement, 'Told you, can't hold his grog. Sleep for hours, I reckon.'

'Mr Francis!' Frederick shook the boy.

Flash, cool as ever in the face of danger, opened his eyes and stared blankly up at him. 'Who're you? You playing too?' He ran his words together and brought his right arm up to rub his eyes, focusing them in a puzzled way on the sub-inspector's face. 'Don't 'member you joining the game. You play without me, ol' fellow, I'll jus' get some sleep.' He closed his eyes.

Frederick shook him again, his hand on Flash's left shoulder. The boy mustered all his strength to prevent himself from crying out with the sudden shock of pain. He pushed Frederick's hand away and, gritting his teeth, raised himself on his right elbow.

'Tha's a boy,' Buck applauded. 'Come back and play. Have another drink.'

'Have you been here all night, Mr Francis?'

Flash met the sub-inspector's keen gaze unflinchingly. 'No, sir, arrived at nine o'clock 'xactly.' He said. 'Been here since nine o'clock. You ask Buck. If you wan' game, happy to accommodate you, sir, but jus' now, beg your pardon, mus' go back to sleep.'

Buck was giggling in a helpless, inebriated way. 'Told you,' he repeated, 'Flash can't drink. Won't be able to ride home in that state. Sleep here tonight, sick as a dog in the morning.'

Frederick hesitated. He glanced at the trooper who was standing to attention inside the doorway, looking rigidly ahead. Francis gave every indication of being drunk and incapable, Buchanan was lounging in his chair, innocently throwing the dice, playing one hand against the other. Neither had acted as if he was afraid of the unexpected police visit.

Flash began snoring loudly, his mouth open. The reek of whisky was disgusting. Frederick made up his mind.

'Sorry to have bothered you. We'll be on our way.'

''S no bother, 'spector. Sure you won't join us? Night's young.'

'It's three o'clock in the morning.' Frederick told him shortly. 'Goodnight, Mr Buchanan.'

Buck gave him a drunken grin. 'Night-night, 'spector.' He stood at the door and watched until the police were out of sight, then went thoughtfully back to Flash.

'Are you still with me, boy?'

Flash opened his eyes and gave a shaky grin. 'Was I all right?'

'Game as Ned Kelly,' Buck assured him.

'We fool 'em, Buck?'

'I don't know, but they've gone for now. I think our new sub-inspector's suspicious. He's no fool but he could see no evidence to warrant a search. However, he'll be watching us closely.'

He pulled the covers back over the boy. 'We'll have to get you away somewhere. It won't do to have you still here in the morning with a bullet hole in your shoulder. Get some sleep now and I'll ride for the O'Meallys' farm. The brothers will help. They've got a dray. We'll get you out of the district until your shoulder's healed.'

'Thanks, Buck, you're a real friend.'

Buck locked the door as he left the shack. He wasn't going to have the police walking in on the sleeping youth and discover the host had gone and the guest had been shot. If they returned and knocked, hopefully they'd assume both men were dead to the world in a drunken stupor.

He was alert for watchers as he saddled his horse. He led the big bay stallion out of the shed and mounted, frowning. Damnation! He couldn't risk being absent from the hotel in the morning. Someone else would have to go with Flash. Red would be the least suspicious choice. He could say they'd taken produce to the Brisbane market.

He began to canter, whistling his favourite tune, *The Brown Jug Polka*. Yes, that would fool the police. If not, they'd need hard evidence to refute the story and he was sure they had none of that.

Chapter 5

Kitty O'Meally had no reason to love the law. Her late husband's father, Liam, had been transported in 1814, when only a lad of sixteen, for political activities against British rule in Ireland. He had barely survived his horror passage on the death ship *Surrey* . Penned for long months below decks with foul air and water, no exercise and short rations, many had died en route and been casually disposed of over the ship's side. The *General Hewitt* and the *Surrey* had been private transports, contracted by the English Government. When they'd arrived in New South Wales, conditions on board had been so appalling, even for those harsh days, that Governor Macquarie had instigated an inquiry to be conducted by his medical officers. The inquiry had found that ships' captains and doctors were generally negligent and Macquarie had advised the government that action must be taken. After that, a Surgeon Superintendent travelled on each transport and conditions began to improve. Kitty, listening to Liam O'Meally's stories, wondered how any of the convicts had survived the cruelty of the English.

'Like slaves, we were treated,' he would declare vehemently. 'No, worse than slaves. The captains made a profit on them poor black wretches so it was to their advantage to keep them alive; but there's no profit in convicts, Kitty me girl. T'was no sorrow to the British Government if a few of Ireland's sons were lost along the way.'

Kitty had seen English cruelty at first hand. The fruits of Ireland's farms, she was told, were not for the Irish but their British landlords, who didn't even live there. When the potato famine of 1846 drove the people to death by starvation, it was partly because they were not allowed, on pain of prison or death, to touch the other crops. Many died because of the greed and unconcern of the *strangers* across the water. Her father and little brother had been victims of the famine and her mother, fearful for Kitty's life and her own, decided to emigrate to what might be a British colony, but was a wild, free land, she'd heard, where folk could farm unmolested and own their crops.

Kitty's mother, Maggie McGuire, had found a job as a kitchen maid in Sydney town. She enrolled Kitty in a small Catholic school and they seemed to be settled. But Maggie longed for a farm in the country, and one day in 1851 she'd swept ten-year-old Kitty into her arms and danced her around their tiny room, laughing and singing and finally telling her that gold had been discovered in the new colony of Victoria. There were riches for all, gold lying about in the streets for anyone to pick up and they were going south to make their fortunes.

Kitty loved the life in the tent city that sprawled across the Ballarat district. There were Irish here in their hundreds and the nights were filled with music and singing, dancing and, inevitably, talk of rebellion. The diggers were being harassed daily by police enforcing the licensing laws; even chasing the diggers down the mines to collect what Tom O'Meally, Liam's son, called an *exorbitant and unjust fee.* Tom was a fine young man, tall and handsome, with fiery red hair and an eloquent way of talking that made him respected and admired. He was a natural leader and was often in the McGuire's tent, talking nineteen to the dozen with Maggie, whom he'd adopted as an elder sister, while Kitty listened in silence, adoring her wonderful young hero.

Every day, the cry of, 'The traps. The traps!' would echo across the diggings making the miners scatter to avoid detection. Tom taught Kitty a popular new song, which went:

'Oh, the traps, the dirty traps,
Kick the traps when e're you're able.
At the traps, the nasty traps,
Kick the traps right under the table.'

A man called Charles Thatcher was also writing wonderful songs about life on the goldfields and many of them were sung at the McGuires'. Mr Thatcher was soon being called the minstrel of the goldfields, with good reason.

However, Ballarat had not come up to Maggie's expectations. Gold couldn't be found in the streets but only through hard, dirty labour, digging it out of the ground. She quickly decided there were easier ways to get gold and took a job as a barmaid in one of the many hotels that sprang up over the goldfields. Popular with the customers, she was soon squirreling away coins and little dull yellow nuggets she got as tips, in an empty syrup tin she kept under her bed.

'Soon, my darling,' she crowed to Kitty as she fingered the tin's growing contents, 'soon we'll have that farm.'

Trouble between the law and the miners escalated and Tom O'Meally made his stand at the stockade at Eureka. Wounded by a bullet through the lung, he sought shelter with the McGuires and Maggie nursed him back to health. Kitty often sat with him, amusing him with tales and songs and, when he was strong enough to travel, Maggie and Kitty bought a pony and trap and smuggled the wanted man out of Victoria.

On a small rise overlooking rolling farm land, a steep wood shingled roof lifted tall red brick chimneys above Glendale Farmhouse, home of the O'Meallys. The surrounding land was cleared except for occasional stands of eucalypt and pine. In the fields, crops of corn and maize, potatoes and barley, stood out clearly under the bright moon.

The farmhouse was square in shape, built of hardwood felled

and prepared on site, its box-like appearance softened by verandahs on three sides. Behind it, a large vegetable and herb garden separated the kitchen, also square and pyramid-roofed, from the main house.

In the small parlour, which was lined with pine boards hung with pictures from the pages of illustrated magazines, Kitty O'Meally kept a vigil by a low fire. Her rocking chair, made by Tom's own dear hands, creaked as she rocked, keeping herself busy with mending a torn shirt of William's. A lamp on a nearby table showed the strain on her face. Her features still bore a trace of the once pretty Irish girl, but were prematurely aged from the lonely years of running the farm and bringing up two spirited boys, mostly on her own. As she worked she softly crooned an old Irish ballad to keep up her courage.

After a while she put down the shirt and smoothed her greying hair, tucking back a strand that had escaped from its bun. She stood up, neatened her calico blouse and shook out her brown skirt. She threw a long, warm woollen shawl around her shoulders and walked across to the door, mechanically straightening one of the bright wool rugs which were scattered over the floor. To brighten the bare floor boards Kitty and her mother had woven the rugs on Maggie's old loom which stood in a corner of the room.

Kitty left the house and walked down the front path, listening intently to the night sounds. Above her, among the leaves of a wattle, the moonlight silvered a sleeping butcher bird, its soft grey feathers fluffed out and its head turned back to rest on its shoulder.

Sensing her presence, while still sleeping, it twitched and opened its beak. Kitty looked up, thinking, I could put out my hand and pick you from your perch but don't fret, little one, for I'll not do it.

She'd woken from an uneasy doze some time before, a mother's instinct warning her of danger. Walter and William hadn't returned home and it was very late. She knew they'd gone out on some lark; she could tell the signs of nervous anticipation in both her boys, although they tried to conceal it from her. Now she peered anxiously down the road and prayed to the Holy Mother to keep them safe. Whatever they were up to.

Kitty thought it was no wonder her boys were on the wild side and contemptuous of the law. They'd been brought up on her memories and Tom's and Grandfather O'Meally's all their lives.

The boys had never known Maggie, who'd died falling from a bolting horse on her beloved farm, three years after the flight from the diggings. They'd bought a property near Bathurst, west of Sydney. Tom had stayed with them to plough and fence and clear their land, although it was obvious he'd never be fully strong again after his wounding. Kitty had grown into a beautiful young woman and Tom had fallen in love with her. After Maggie's funeral he'd come upon her crying her eyes out and he'd taken her in his arms and whispered, 'Marry me, Kitty, for I want to look after you.'

Liam O'Meally had moved in with them and for a while they'd prospered, selling their produce to the Bathurst miners, for there was gold here, too. Then a digger from the Ballarat fields had recognised Tom and told some of his friends that one of the Eureka heroes was there. Word spread. The police got wind of it and once again Tom and Kitty were on the run from the law, this time with their infant son Walter and Tom's father in tow.

'Holy Mary, Mother of God, keep my boys safe and return them, unharmed, to me. Forgive them whatever they may be doing this night for they've learned all their lives to rebel. Punish me, if need be, but not them, not Walter and William. Amen.'

Walter had inherited his father's height and fiery hair. William, smaller and darker haired, like his mother, had Tom's passion and clever way of talking and his gentle manners. Kitty sighed. It was a sin, she was sure, to favour one son above the other but, while her prayers named both boys impartially, it was William, her youngest, she worried for.

She heard the welcome sound, faintly at first, then growing louder. Horses! 'No,' she corrected herself, 'one horse only.' She opened the gate and ran a little way down the road.

Walter urged his tired mount on. He saw Kitty's small, upright figure clearly outlined under the moon, and his nerves jolted. He pulled up and leapt from the saddle.

She stared down the road. 'Where's William?'

Walter was breathing hard. 'Hasn't he come home yet?'

'He has not. He left with you.'

'He didn't come with us. He — went visiting Rose.'

She clicked her tongue angrily. 'He'll get himself into trouble over that girl. What sort of time is this to be meetin' a girl, anyhow?'

Walter followed her through the gate, stumbling a little. She turned back and stepped close to him, her eyes widening as she turned his face to the light.

'Glory be, son, what happened to you?'

'I'm in trouble, Ma. We — weren't exactly on lawful business tonight. We fell into a trap and shots were fired. I think a man's been killed. I was injured myself, getting away.'

'You took a bullet?'

'No, I rode into some low branches and came off Tara. Luckily he waited for me.' He grinned and patted his horse's neck. The animal was sweating and agitated.

'The police, are they after you?'

'Don't know. I don't think so. I've been riding for hours, trying to lay a false trail.'

'Get inside, boy, and clean yourself up.'

'Tara needs stabling. He'd give me away in his condition, if they came.'

'Leave him to me. Do you think I can't rub down a horse? Get inside and muss up your bed so they'll think you were in it all along — and William's, too.' She gave him a little push. 'Don't stand there gawping at me, boy. Inside with you.'

Long after Walter had fallen asleep, Kitty sat in her rocking chair, her shawl pulled tightly around her, rocking backwards and forwards, her fingers clicking her rosary beads.

'Holy Mother, he should be home by now. If he's not careful

he'll be caught by George Carew, a vindictive man and a Protestant with no love for William. He thinks my son's dirt under his feet. And what's that crazy boy doing anyhow,' she appealed to the Virgin, 'falling in love with an English Protestant's daughter? You're a mother yourself, now, so you'll understand me. I've nothing against Rose, she's a sweet girl and a pretty one but she's not Catholic and she'll never become one with a father like Carew. He's a stern, religious man, even if it's the wrong religion.

'Holy Mother,' she begged, 'make my boy fall right out of love with Rose so we can all be comfortable again. And please don't let him be up to anything with the girl tonight.'

The sky was brightening with the soft flush of dawn; the kookaburras, always the first to wake, began a noisy chorus in the tall blue gum beside the shed. A whipbird gave its long drawn out whistle, followed by a loud crack.

Chunk, chunk, its mate said immediately.

Kitty thought of the sleeping butcher bird in the wattle by the path and, as if it could read her mind, it started carolling a wonderful liquid call. The morning was suddenly full of bird song.

Kitty got up and pulled back the curtains, letting the dawn into the house. She opened the windows, then her heart quickened as she heard a horse coming swiftly towards the farm.

'Pray God it's William.'

She stood still, hands clasped nervously against her bosom. The horse stopped by the gate and the rider dismounted. Minutes later there was an urgent knocking on the door.

The police. Kitty waited. To rush to open it would let them know she'd been awake and expecting them. Then she heard a soft voice.

'Red, are you there? It's Buck. Open up.'

Kitty stiffened. She knew that the American was a friend of her sons. She didn't approve of him and strongly suspected him of leading her boys into trouble — they spoke of him as if he was their leader. She opened the door.

'Mrs O'Meally.' Buck took a step back. 'I apologise for disturbing you so early, ma'am. Is Walter at home?'

Walter, his hair dishevelled, came out of his room in his night shirt, rubbing his eyes and yawning. But the sight of Buck made him instantly alert.

'Buck! What's the matter?'

Kitty stood reluctantly aside and Buck came into the house.

'It's Flash. He's got to get away. I'm sorry, Mrs O'Meally. There was a spot of trouble last night and we need your help. I've come to borrow your dray to take Johnny Francis somewhere safe,'

'If it's trouble, Mr Buchanan, I'll be bound you were the cause of it,' Kitty snapped. 'You've no business larking about at your age, encouraging lads younger than yourself to be up to all kinds of mischief.'

Walter put a hand on her shoulder. 'Ma, it's for Johnny, a mate. He needs our help.'

Kitty frowned direfully. 'I don't let my friends down. I'd never be able to look Mrs Francis in the face again if I refused to help her boy. But if he'd not been influenced by those who should know better...' She gave Buck a straight look.

'Ma!' Walter protested.

Buck shook his head. 'No, your mother's right, Red. It was my fault and I'll make sure Flash doesn't pay for it. Can we use the dray, Mrs O'Meally?'

'You'll be driving?' She asked, watching him closely.

'I can't. I had Stapleton at my place only an hour ago. He's suspicious but cautious, in case he makes a fool of himself. If I'm not in the hotel today he'll know I was involved and he'll find out, soon enough, who I was with.'

'You stay and keep him busy here; I'll drive Flash.' Walter gave a laugh. 'They won't catch me in a hurry.'

Kitty said, 'I want you to look for William.'

Walter had gone into his room to dress. He called back, 'William will be with Rose. George Carew is out of town so he's taken this chance to be with her. He didn't tell you, so you wouldn't worry. He'll be home soon. He wasn't in this, so they've nothing on him.'

'The police will come here,' Buck warned. 'They'll be checking on all the lads who are my friends.'

'Let them come.' Kitty put her hands on her hips. 'I've outwitted the police before and I can do it again. You get young Johnny away safe.'

'Thanks, Ma, you're a wonder.' Walter came into the parlour and kissed her cheek, then he and Buck went out to the shed.

Kitty went to the back door and walked through her vegetable garden to the kitchen. Tom had built it away from the main house; in case of fire, he'd said. She went in and started to light the stove. A short time later she heard the dray being driven out of the yard.

Chapter 6

F rederick sat in his arm chair, reading. It was too late to go to bed, dawn was not long away; and he'd had little chance to read since his arrival at Bell's Creek. He'd brought a tin trunk full of books with him from England, his favourite form of relaxation being to settle down after dinner with a cigar, a glass of port or brandy and a favourite volume.

For a while he lost himself in Edward John Eyre's discoveries in Central Australia, as documented in his *Journals of Expeditions* which had been published in London in 1845 and had fascinated Frederick since boyhood. He wondered if he'd get his chance to see the great sandy desert, to experience the vision of the wide, rolling ocean from the massive limestone cliffs of the Great Australian Bight, or encounter as yet undiscovered tribes with their strange customs. Mr Eyre had frequently enriched the prose of his journals with almost lyrical descriptions of the vast country which had so moved him that Frederick was similarly inspired.

The light in the room was increasing, diminishing the candle flame and he snuffed it out and put down the book. He donned his navy blue uniform jacket and buttoned it, running a finger around the inside of the high, stiff collar. Inappropriate, he thought, to dress a man in a dark, hot, tight-collared uniform in the tropics. Then he surveyed his reflection in the mirror over the mantelpiece, and acknowledged that, in spite of its drawbacks, the police uniform was smart and he looked suitably dashing with his long black side whiskers and drooping moustache.

He found himself staring into his own eyes as his reflection grew sharper in the rapidly strengthening light.

Why hadn't he challenged Buchanan and Francis? He had the power under the law to demand — what? They'd both given a convincing performance. Could a badly wounded man have acted the drunkard so perfectly or looked at him so frankly?

He wanted to begin his career as an officer with the Queensland Native Mounted Police with strength but also understanding. He'd do himself no good being over-zealous and officious, setting these people's backs up. He wanted their cooperation — indeed, he knew it was essential. They were a tight-knit community, he was the interloper. They could hide a wrong-doer from him out of sheer perverseness. He'd already seen that Australians were an independent, free-spirited people, not generally given to subservience. Many of them, he knew, were not sympathetic to the police and resented their authority, until they were attacked or robbed. Then, he thought grimly, it would be a different matter.

There'd been no evidence in Buchanan's tiny cottage that either man had been doing other than he claimed. He'd checked the out-houses; the horses had been stabled and were comfortably munching through a pile of hay. Buchanan's place smelled like a brewery and Francis, although lying down, had seemed merely tired, as he claimed. He'd pulled himself together when Frederick had persisted and answered his questions rationally enough for a man under the influence.

Frederick frowned at his image. What was niggling at him? Had he been taken in like any fool newcomer by a clever pair of rogues?

A knock at the door made him shrug and turn away from the mirror. He went outside onto the tiny verandah. Four native troopers, neat in their navy coats, caps and white trousers, sat astride solid, perfectly groomed horses. Mallory's mount was tied to the verandah rail alongside Black Diamond who was looking bored. A thoroughbred, Frederick had brought her from England, anxiously nursing her through rough seas and stifling tropic calms. Now he wondered if he should not have left her in her lush English meadows rather than have dragged her across most of the seven seas to a land of heat, dust, flies and rough, razor-edged grasses. She tossed her glossy head and snorted, as if in agreement.

He trod down the steps then stopped as if rooted to the spot, one eyebrow raised.

'Sir?' The sergeant prompted. 'Time to go; it's nearly dawn.'

'Damnation!' Frederick swore. 'I've just recalled; the cigars, the ashtray. I must have been blind.'

'Sir?'

'There should have been a pile of ash; or at least, evidence that there had been earlier, if the ashtray had been recently emptied. But it was clean. Men in their condition would hardly have emptied the dish then wiped it clean.'

Frederick experienced an uncomfortable sinking feeling. That damned Yankee scoundrel had fooled him completely and, what was worse, he'd now betrayed his stupidity to his subordinate. The sergeant had a superior smirk on his face. Frederick would have to eat a portion of humble pie, even if it choked him.

His lips compressed angrily. 'I was not convinced that an American accent must automatically point to Buchanan. I apologise, sergeant. He's made a fine game of me.' He swung himself into the saddle. 'However, if Francis was shot, we'll know it soon enough. A bullet wound is not something you can easily hide. Mount up, man, I'll tell you about it as we ride.'

At Bellara, the troopers spread out around the recent battle ground, looking for tracks and signs of broken bushes, twigs, leaves torn from their branches; any of the multitude of clues, invisible to Frederick, that the raiders had passed that way.

Soon they were gesticulating, nodding in agreement. Frederick and Mallory joined them. Yes, definitely six men had been here.

One had been shot and lost much blood, very bad wound. One had half carried him to his horse, here. He'd led the injured man's horse — see the difference in the tracks? Then he'd dismounted and stood, here, among the bunyas, for a while, holding both horses. Here, the sub-inspector's and the other horse came very close to the hidden men, then went back.

Frederick groaned. 'We were right on top of them.'

'You wouldn't have known, sir. You could have hunted all night with them standing within a stone's throw. They enjoy making fools of the police.'

'Yes, so I've seen.'

Trooper Weearunga claimed the European officers' attention.

'Four fellas split up, go this way.' He pointed out the different directions. 'Not hurt, ride fast.'

'Divide and follow the other men; but I want to know where this pair went.'

A shadow passed, darkening the bush, and a chorus of cicadas gave a couple of false starts then broke into full cry, a high-pitched, deafening drone.

Trooper Bob Jildaree sniffed the air. 'Hurry,' he said worriedly.

Mallory looked up at the rapidly building clouds and swore.

'These two,' Frederick said again. 'We'll come with you, the other troopers must track the four unhurt men.'

'Get Billy Wirral, the squatter's stockman,' Mallory ordered. 'He's a good tracker. One man for each raider.'

'Yessir.'

'Weearunga, we'll follow you. Show us where these two fellas went.'

But at the creek the black tracker shook his head.

'They ride in water, up or down?'

'If we search the banks, both sides, both directions?' Frederick suggested.

'Water come up since last night. Big rain up country, comin' here soon.'

'We'll try,' Frederick decided. 'You and I will go downstream. Sergeant, try upstream. If you find nothing, follow us.'

'This is called Rocky Creek,' Sergeant Mallory pointed out. 'These men are bushmen; they won't leave the water where there's mud or sand. It'll be on hard, bare rock — and there's plenty of that.'

'Do your best. I want these men. If Francis was wounded and Buchanan took him back to his place, there'll be some sense in our going downstream and searching the far bank for tracks.'

The sergeant nodded and coaxed his horse into the stream, then began to ride up the rising water.

Rose Carew lay in bed, hugging herself with joy, her body tingling with desire as she remembered the previous night.

A pair of magpies was chorusing on the lawn outside her window as a pink flush spread across the eastern sky. Rose felt like singing a similar joyous anthem.

She'd been told by her aunt in London what to expect on her wedding night.

'Remember, my dear, men are little more than animals, driven by their lusts and passions. Women, thankfully, don't know about such things.'

'But — may a woman not feel passionate love for a man, Aunt Alice?'

'Perhaps common women allow their baser natures to override their intellect but women of quality, my dear Rose, most assuredly do not. Don't allow stupid romantic notions into your head and don't expect to enjoy a man's — ardour. Be thankful if your father finds you a husband with some consideration for you, then he may be gentle with you in your innocence.'

Rose, suddenly frightened, asked, 'Is it not — pleasurable — to love, Aunt?'

'It is pleasant to be the centre of attention, to be courted by a gallant man; but the physical act of love cannot be pleasurable for a woman, as it is for the opposite sex. A well-bred woman accepts that such — contact — is inevitable, indeed, necessary for the procreation of children. But to take pleasure in it? Her husband would be shocked by such a suggestion.'

'So we may not enjoy the act of love with our husbands.' Rose's eyes were wide. Her aunt made men seem brutal, pleasure seeking monsters who delighted in unnatural acts of lust which their poor wives had to endure to produce children.

'Only a whore would enjoy such an act. You, my dear Rose, when you go to your marriage bed, will permit your husband his rights without resistance. You will allow him to take his pleasure, lie quietly until he has finished and accept that, however difficult, painful or unpleasant, it is the lot of women. We can be thankful that we do not desire to inflict brutish behaviour on others.'

It sounded dreadful and Rose had decided she would never be married or allow a brutal, lustful man near her. She didn't want to be used as a plaything to give a beast pleasure. She simply wouldn't agree to any such thing.

She smiled at the morning and touched her soft breasts. How her body had come alive when William had kissed her in the garden. It had seemed to have a life of its own which surged through her blood until her ears were pounding and her breath came unevenly. If she hadn't kissed him back she'd certainly have burst and his hunger seemed to fuel her own.

Was this Aunt Alice's horror? Rose laughed. She was wise at last. This was love, common to both sexes and could be desired and enjoyed by both equally.

'Oh, William,' she breathed, 'my dear, precious love.'

She got out of bed and danced around the room in her shift, her feet bare, her arms above her head. She flung back the curtains and the sunbeams poured through the window and seemed to dance with her.

'William, William, William,' she chanted, 'I love you, love you, love you.'

She sat down at her escritoire with its pretty shell inlay and pulled out her diary. She dipped her pen in the ink well and began to record this most wondrous event.

"Is it possible that there are women who are so well-bred that they could lie with the man they love and not know this exquisite joy?" She wrote. "His tenderness and gentle care of me have made me love him even more, if that were imaginable. My whole body raged with an unquenchable fire as he embraced me and when we made love, or, as poor Aunt Alice would prefer to say, when I *endured* the physical act of love, I thought I would die of ecstasy. And he felt the same. All the time we kissed and caressed and came to such a peak of desire we cried out, and were engulfed then swept away in a flood of abandonment as our bodies perfectly flowed together. I could not have imagined such a delightful thing could ever be experienced by a mortal, or that it could be feared or thought of as dreadful or horrid."

She nibbled the end of her pen, then, with a little gleam of naughtiness in her eye, wrote: "Aunt Alice would say that this passionate enjoyment of a man makes me a whore, but I do not feel that I am. I am a woman in love; with the unbounded happiness of being loved and desired by the object of my adoration.

"Oh, night, come swiftly and bring William back into my arms so I may once again experience that pure bliss."

Chapter 7

Frederick was smarting. On the way to Bellara he'd told Sergeant Mallory about his visit to Buchanan's and the sergeant, while remaining correctly non-committal, had made the sub-inspector feel like an inexperienced, inept bungler.

The Native Mounted Police was the only military body in the Empire where the officers rode behind the men. At first Frederick had wondered if it was because the Europeans feared treachery from the native troopers but was assured that, no, it was because the blacks had such superb bush skills, a white officer would very likely, albeit unwittingly, destroy any tracks. Also, the blacks had unbelievable homing instincts and were never lost. Most of the country they were required to patrol had no landmarks, buildings, fences or roads. Europeans often became confused, unless they had the ability of a pigeon, and lost face with the blacks if they showed themselves unable to find their way. It was vital, he was warned, that European prestige be upheld.

At least, while riding behind, he could talk to Mallory without fear of being overheard by the troopers. He'd told the sergeant how he'd left Buchanan's shack without taking further action.

Mallory said, 'Was that wise, sir?'

'Obviously I thought so at the time,' Frederick snapped. 'I gather you'd have had me pull the man out of bed on no visible evidence and strip him down.'

'Sir, these people respect a man who makes strong decisions. They'd more likely have admired you for standing by your belief, even if you'd been heavy handed, and proving yourself right.'

'And what if I'd been wrong?'

'You'd have been a laughing stock, sir. They'd have known they could outwit you.'

'So, either way I'd have lost. If I'd found evidence of his guilt, the whole community would have closed ranks and made it ten times more difficult for us. As it is, they've made me look like a damned fool of a new chum.'

Mallory thought the new officer had just proved that he was a damned fool of a new chum but he continued to stare woodenly ahead between his horse's ears. Better the man learnt his painful lesson now; he'd be wiser next time and less inclined to give law breakers the benefit of the doubt. Since the inquiry into the massacre of two shepherds at the Dawson River in 1858, the native police had been given wide powers. They had been told to carry out their patrols with a strong hand and punish, with necessary severity, all future outrages upon life and property. And here was his senior officer treating probable murderers with kid gloves.

He's too soft for this country, Mallory thought uneasily. The sergeant wished he'd been at Buchanan's. He'd have put the fear of God and the law into the robbers.

Frederick knew what Mallory was thinking. Now, following the trooper along the creek, it seemed he might have made another unwise decision. Weearunga was leaning down, riding half out of the saddle, scanning the banks but finding nothing. Frederick prayed there'd be something soon.

At last Weearunga made a gutteral sound and lifted his hand in warning. Frederick reined Black Diamond in. He wasn't going to add the possible accusation of destroying precious tracks to his list of blunders. The trooper dismounted, leaving his horse to stand patiently in the fast running water, and walked carefully up the bank, his head turning this way and that. Then he squatted on the ground to examine some just visible mark.

There was a splashing noise behind the sub-inspector and he turned to see the sergeant coming down the creek.

'No good upstream, sir. There's no sign.'

'I think Weearunga's found something.'

The trooper was back in the saddle. 'Two fella, come out here, go east.'

'Our two men?'

'Not wounded man and that other fella; two different men.'

Frederick cast a reluctant look at Mallory who said deferentially, 'I'd stick with this pair, sir. If the wounded man was Johnny Francis and the Yankee was with him, they'd have followed the creek clear through to the town and lost their tracks amongst a score of others.'

'I agree. Weearunga, we'll take these tracks.'

As they followed the black tracker, Frederick asked, 'Tell me about these men, sergeant?'

'Well, you know about Buchanan. He's the oldest, going on thirty. The rest follow his lead. The O'Meally brothers, Walter and William, are in and out of trouble. Mostly no more than you'd expect from a couple of wild lads brought up by an Irish mother and father who filled their heads with a lot of talk against the law. Their father, he's dead now, sir, was wanted in Victoria for his part in the Eureka rebellion — that was twenty-five years ago, in '54'

'But surely — I remember reading that the leaders of that rebellion were acquitted.'

'You know your history, sir. The juries were sympathetic to the miners and refused to find them guilty. But Tom O'Meally shot a man and was wanted for murder. He'd been farming in the Bathurst district after the Victorian trouble and was spotted by an old acquaintance. Came up to Queensland and settled at Bell's Creek.'

'And continued to elude the police?'

'No, sir, the case was reopened when the Victorian police heard he'd been seen in New South Wales. The evidence against him was strongly suspect; reviewed in a more rational light it was agreed he'd acted in self-defence and the matter was dropped. Tom died seven years later of pneumonia. Had a bad lung, from a gunshot at Eureka. Kitty O'Meally and the boys stayed on. All that was well before my time, of course, sir. The boys mostly get up to their tricks because they lack a father's guidance. They want to impress their peers as being big men. William's turned eighteen, Walter is twenty.'

'I see. Who else do you think is involved?'

'John Francis,' the sergeant replied promptly, 'better known as Flash Johnny Francis, as I said. He's the youngest, only sixteen, but thinks he's a cut above them all; talks flash, always wears a fancy waistcoat.'

'Always, sergeant?'

'I've never seen him without, sir. It's his trademark, so to speak.'

'He wasn't wearing one last night, just a coloured handkerchief around his neck.' Frederick realised the implication of that as he saw Mallory's rigid expression.

'Must have had a very good reason to take it off, sir.'

'There was no sign of such a garment in the room. We'll pay another visit to this Flash Johnny of yours.'

'It would be wise, sir. I'd also see John d'Arcy. He's a friend of the O'Meallys, the same age as William. He's called Wild Jack d'Arcy, you can imagine why. He's a larrikin, like all the rest, up to any and all mischief. Sees himself as a game one; rides a great brute of a stallion I wouldn't like to put my leg over, usually hell for leather. Quick tempered, wild with the girls, too, although I'd make a bet that he favours Rose Carew above all of them. So does the young-est O'Meally boy,' he finished drily.

'Is there trouble between them?'

'There might be if Rose was the kind of girl to flirt with the boys; but she's head over heels for William O'Meally. Won't look at any of the others, even Robert Leicester, at the bank, who's her father's choice for her. There must be resentment amongst the lads, though, for all they're friends and have been brought up to-gether.'

Frederick had met Rose and her father at a dinner at the Rendell's station. He'd gladly accepted George's invitation to dine at the Carew's the following week. Rose was the prettiest girl he'd seen so far in Bell's Creek and he'd been happy to renew his acquaintance with her. He could imagine that the rivalry between her suitors might become quite heated.

He returned to the problem at hand. 'There were six men,' he said positively. 'Buchanan, the O'Meallys, d'Arcy, Francis — who else, by your reckoning?'

'Could be one of two others, sir. Alan Patterson's one of their group. He's a small man, trained as a jockey. He was all set for a great career until his mount rolled on him and his right foot was amputated. He has a wooden one in its place, just like the real thing, but he walks with a limp. His nickname's Limpy.'

'But, if he's a cripple...'

'He can still ride and he's one of the best marksmen in the district. The other man I've got my eye on is the Scotsman, James McLeod. I told you about him, sir. He's older than the other lads and he's a drinking companion of Buchanan's, on the rare occasions when he comes to town. He knows the ranges like the back of his hand and I don't think he'd turn down the chance to make a dishonest pound or two.'

'Then I wonder which of the rogues we're tracking?' Frederick remarked.

'I'd say the O'Meallys. They'd likely come this way and it's two horses.'

The trooper, ahead among the trees, gave a shout and beckoned. The two officers spurred forward eagerly.

Weearunga was quickly out of the saddle and kneeling on the ground over a man's body. A pretty bay mare grazed quietly nearby.

Mallory dismounted and ran to see. He called back, 'It's William O'Meally, sir. He's been shot in the back. We've got one of our raiders.'

Kitty had finished her breakfast and was washing her crockery in a big, yellow china bowl on the kitchen table, when the sub-inspector and Weearunga arrived. She heard the horses and came out of the kitchen, wiping her hands on her apron. Seeing her, the men rode along the fence and dismounted by the side gate.

'Good morning,' she called. 'And what can I do for you this fine day?'

Frederick touched his hat to her and introduced himself.

She dimpled at him, giving him a sunny smile. 'I heard Mr Bolton's replacement had arrived at last. Poor man, he was shot up country. I expect you knew that.'

Frederick was well aware how his predecessor had died.

'You'll need to take care, Mr Stapleton,' Kitty said cheerfully. 'Will you step inside and drink a cup of tea?'

'I've come to speak to your sons, Mrs O'Meally.'

'Well, now, I can't oblige you. William's not at home and Walter's gone to Brisbane town this very morning with produce for the markets.'

'That's a long trip to take alone. We've had reports of bushrangers on the Brisbane track recently.'

'Oh, he didn't go alone. Young Johnny Francis offered to go with him, help with the driving.'

'I see. Where's William?'

'He's off on my business — which is none of your business.'

'Where were the boys last night?' Frederick asked.

'They were here, with me.'

'You're sure of that, ma'am?'

'What sort of a question is that? Of course I'm sure. You can look in their room, if you like. I've not made up their beds yet.'

'So they didn't go out at all?'

'Haven't I told you? They were at home with me all night, Mr Stapleton.'

'Suppose I told you there was a raid last night at Bellara and your two sons were involved?'

Kitty shook her head. 'I see what it is, now. It's always the way. Some of the lads get up to mischief and the police come running around here, blaming my boys. Well, if you're so sure of your facts, produce your evidence.'

Frederick said, 'We'd better go inside, Mrs O'Meally.' He followed her into the kitchen, a large, cheerful room with whitewashed walls and a floor of wide wooden slabs split from ironbark logs. In one wall an iron stove stood in a deep recess, its fire warming the kitchen. On one side of the stove a basket was piled high with wood; on the other, pots and pans gleamed on a tall metal rack.

The door of the baker's oven was open and the appetising aroma of freshly baked bread assailed Frederick's nostrils, making him feel unaccountably like an intruder at the hearth. He glanced at the table. Under a red-checked cloth was the unmistakable shape of a fat round loaf.

Frederick pushed down his unwanted discomfort and looked at Kitty. Surely her eyes were over-bright and her hands were gripping each other too tightly? He kept his eyes fixed on her face as he pulled out a chair for her. With a sinking heart but a smile on her lips, she sat down. He sat opposite her.

'You look very serious, Mr Stapleton. What's all this nonsense about?'

'We found William O'Meally this morning,' Frederick said evenly. 'We were tracking the raiders from McIntyre's station. William was lying on the path. He'd been shot in the back; no doubt while fleeing from the squatter's men.'

Kitty went white and pushed her fist against her mouth.

Frederick went on, 'He'd been there for some hours, so we know he wasn't here last night.'

Kitty closed her eyes. She thought she was going to faint and grasped the edge of the table, feeling its solid strength. Her shocked mind swung desperately back and forth. Oh, Holy Mother, save us. Save my boy. Why did I let Walter go? I need him now. Heavenly Father, don't let it be true, don't let William be hurt. Make this man be lying. Oh, God, it is true, I can feel it. Oh, William, my darling, darling son.

She put up a trembling hand to the small gold cross which always hung on a dainty chain around her neck. A present from Tom. 'To keep you ever safe from harm,' he'd said. But it wasn't herself that needed protection now, it was William. And the only protection she could give him was her strength and courage.

She opened her eyes and met Frederick's gaze. 'Is he — dead?' she managed.

He was taken aback. For a moment she'd seemed on the verge of breaking down. She might even have sobbed out a confession. He'd have sworn she was close to weeping. But even as she'd seemed most vulnerable, she'd managed to pull herself together and face him almost defiantly. He said curtly, 'No, but he was in a very bad way and unconscious. Sergeant Mallory has taken him to Doctor Evans.'

Kitty got up. 'I'll go to him right away.'

'Wait.' Frederick stood, blocking her path. 'I want you to tell me when your sons left last night and who they were to meet.'

Kitty drew herself up to her full five feet and four inches. 'Walter was at home with me all night. William went out but only to see Rose Carew. I know nothing of any raid and neither do my boys. Yes, I lied about William but it was to save him from trouble with Carew who hates him. He would do him some mischief if he knew he was meeting Rose at night. That's the plain truth of it. William must have been set upon on his way home from Carew's.'

Frederick felt his anger rising and set his jaw. The wretched woman wasn't going to get away with her ridiculous story. He knew the truth of the matter and he'd let her know he knew she was lying through her teeth. He said in a harsh voice, 'I don't believe you, Mrs O'Meally. The tracks we were following point to William's involvement. At least one of the thieves was shot and I believe John Francis was also wounded. Will I tell you what I think? I was at Mr Buchanan's house last night and he and Mr Francis did their best to convince me they'd been there all along. But I don't believe them, either. I believe that, as soon as I left, Mr Buchanan rode here to get Walter's help and they've taken Mr Francis away somewhere.'

Kitty fought to keep her expression calm although inside she was raging to get away from this man and rush to William. A sudden panic gripped her. Perhaps the new sub-inspector was smarter than she'd thought, to have realised young Johnny had been smuggled out of the district. But he didn't know it all. Walter had promised her that William hadn't been with the others last night and he'd not been lying. She could always tell when her boys weren't being straight with her. So Stapleton couldn't prove anything against William and she'd fight for her dearest son every step of the way.

She allowed a little scornful smile to curl her lip. 'It's no matter to me what you believe; you'll have to prove it.'

'I intend to,' Frederick said stiffly. 'We've found the tracks of the dray. I'm sure they'll go straight to Buchanan's. We will search his house and, I promise you, we'll find the evidence we need.'

Kitty glared up at him. 'You're a fool, Mr Stapleton. Did it never occur to you that, if my William was out with the lads and got himself shot, they'd never have left him to die in the bush? They'd have brought him to me or got him away somewhere safe to tend him. You've a lot to learn about the loyalty of these people. We don't abandon one of our own.'

'These men are thieves and murderers. They'd have saved their own skins.'

Kitty clicked her tongue. 'Believe what you like, you'll be proved wrong. Now, get out of my way.' She pushed past him to the door.

Caught off balance, Frederick was forced to step back. He recovered quickly and followed her, angry at her temerity in shoving him aside in such a brusque fashion. He snapped, 'The tracks from your own door will prove me right, Mrs O'Meally.'

Nearby in the deep undergrowth a strange throbbing sound had begun. Kitty cocked her head on one side.

'Then you'd better hurry along, Mr Stapleton,' she said, a note of satisfaction in her voice. 'Do you hear that sound? It's the bush pheasants, them the blacks call coucals. They sing like that when rain's coming.'

She flung the door open. The wind was whipping up little eddies of dust and dry leaves, and dark clouds were massing on the horizon. In the distance thunder rolled. Weearunga was astride his horse, looking anxiously towards the sky. Frederick swore and ran down the path.

'Do you want to know what I believe, Mr Stapleton?' Kitty called after him. 'I believe all your precious evidence will be washed clean away. Then where will you be?'

He flushed. As he turned Black Diamond to go after the trooper, her taunting laugh followed him.

Chapter 8

R ose sat on the verandah overlooking the front garden and the long drive lined with stately pines. Her sewing box was open on the table beside her and she had some half-finished mending in her lap, but her mind had wandered from the task and her thoughts were racing ahead to the evening.

She twisted the carved ivory thimble around on her finger and gazed across the rolling acres of the farm. She could see horses ploughing, contouring the hills with deep red furrows of new turned soil. Closer to the farm house, a small flock of sheep grazed and in the next paddock, the dairy herd spread out across the grass.

The air was heavy and insects buzzed persistently in the garden. The wind which had been gusting earlier had dropped and the morning was hot and humid and still. Storm clouds gathering in the distance were billowing like giant fleeces over the sky, supported on swiftly moving black bases. The light was rapidly darkening.

There was a loud crack and a bolt of lightning split the sky. The first heavy drops of rain began to fall, pock-marking the dust on the path and raising the sweet scent of damp earth. Then, as the thunder growled and a run of long lightning bursts shimmered across the clouds, they let go their burden in a torrent of water.

Peering through the grey curtain of rain, Rose could see a horse and rider making haste along the drive, riding under the trees in a vain attempt to escape a drenching. Who could be coming to visit in such a downpour? Then she caught her breath.

'Father!'

George Carew waved at her as he rode around the verandah to the stables. Rose felt her breathing quicken. She thought, He's back early. And William is coming tonight. How can I get word to him? Her mind began to weave urgent plans. She mustn't allow her love to be caught anywhere near the house. She could have wept with frustration. She had so wanted to see him again.

Then a new, frightening thought came. Could they have been seen together and been betrayed to her father? Was that the reason for his unexpected return? She picked up her sewing, a nervous pulse beating in her throat, and folded it into the workbox which she carried inside.

Mrs Moore had come into the sitting room. Rose forced herself to smile.

'Father has returned, a day early. He'll be soaked, poor thing. We'll take tea now, Mrs Moore.'

The trooper stood in the road, rain splashing off the peak of his cap as he shook his head. The track was rapidly turning to the consistency of porridge, rivuletted with little flows running off into the bush on either side. A waterfall gushed down an embankment, spilling out across the road.

Frederick swore. That damned woman had been right. The rain bucketing down reminded him of the sudden storms of India. The sky seemed hell bent on emptying itself of all the water it could possibly hold, and all in the one spot.

Weearunga was waiting for instructions.

Frederick motioned him to remount. 'We'll ride to Bell's Creek,' he shouted above the noise of the drumming rain, 'to the Squatters' Arms.'

The road, heavy with mud which clung to the horses' hooves, made the going slow. By the time they dismounted outside the hotel, Frederick was wet, tired and bad tempered.

He sent the constable to the stables and went into the bar, his waterproof coat making a little stream of water on the bare wooden floor. The licencee, Daniel Reilly, resplendent in a brown and yellow checked suit and matching waistcoat, stepped from behind the counter.

'You caught the downpour, sir. It's not a day to be out riding but I expect duty calls. Have a whisky, on the house, or a rum. That'll warm your insides.'

'No, thank you; as you say, duty calls. I've come to see Mr Buchanan.'

'He's down the cellar with the kegs. I'll just whistle him up.'

The trapdoor to the cellar was open. Frederick stood, shaking the rain off his hat as Reilly bent down and put two fingers to his mouth, giving a shrill whistle.

'Come on up, Bucko, there's someone here to see you.'

Frederick experienced a shock of surprise. He was sure the American would not be there. He set his mouth in a stern line.

Buck's head appeared and he came up the steps, looking an inquiry. Reilly said non-committally, ''Tis the police,' and jerked his head towards Frederick.

Buck came over, grinning ruefully.

'Say, I had a mighty sore head this morning. I seem to remember you callin' around in the middle of the night but I can't recall much about it. Hope I don't need to apologise for anything.'

'How long have you been here, Mr Buchanan?'

'What? I started at my usual time; I wasn't that bad. The second cup of coffee usually sees me all right.'

'And you haven't been out at all today?'

'Been in the cellar all mornin', shifting those damned kegs around.' Buck looked at Reilly. 'Dan'll bear out my story, sub-inspector.'

'Yep.' Reilly nodded. 'All morning he's been down them stairs, working like a navvy.'

'And Mr Francis, what time did he leave last night?'

'Flash? Slept like the dead until I woke him this morning. We had breakfast and he went off — must have been around seven, perhaps later. He'd promised to drive with Red O'Meally to Brisbane. Red picked him up in the dray around then, I reckon. Flash has left his horse stabled here until they get back.' He gave Frederick a puzzled look. 'Is there a problem, sir?'

'William O'Meally was shot last night and left for dead along the northern track.'

The reaction was all he could have hoped for but Buchanan seemed more shocked than afraid or wary.

'What, Billy? Shot, you say? My God, man, how did that happen?'

'You can't tell me?'

'Well, how would I know? I didn't see Billy last night.'

There was a note of complete sincerity in his voice. Frederick thought, You've made a fool of me once, you're certainly lying now. 'He was shot in an ambush at Bellara Station. William O'Meally and his friends were stealing Mr McIntyre's horses.'

'No, that's not true.'

'How do you know that, Mr Buchanan? You were gaming with Mr Francis all night.'

'I hear things; all of the lads drink here, they talk to me, ask my advice, me being older than themselves. I reckon I know where Billy was last night.'

'That would be hearsay only and not evidence unless it could be proven.'

Buck lowered his voice. 'What if I told you Billy was with a girl last night?'

'Which girl?'

'Hell, I can't tell you that. She'd be in trouble if it got around. I'm not draggin' her name into this.'

'In fact, Mr Buchanan, whilst I admire your defence of your young friend, even if it is misguided, you can't say for certain where the boy was last night. We followed two riders from Bellara. The tracks led straight to William.'

'Terrible lot of thieves and vagabonds around,' Daniel Reilly cut in helpfully. He'd been hovering as close as he could to hear the conversation. 'Poor Billy's likely met one of them wild blacks or some wicked bushranger.'

Buck said hoarsely, 'Where's the kid now?'

'He's with Doctor Evans, if he's still alive. When he's fit to be interviewed, he'll be charged with horse stealing and murder. Good day, Mr Buchanan.'

Buck stood, pulling at his moustache in a worried way as Frederick strode out of the bar. It seemed the man was hell bent on convicting Billy and how could Buck say Billy wasn't on the raid without betraying himself and the others? As it was, Stapleton was clearly suspicious of Flash and, as he'd already made up his mind about Billy, next he'd assume Red was involved.

Buck frowned, deep in thought. He had to find a way to account for all the gang members' whereabouts and give Billy an alibi without betraying Rose. It wouldn't be long before that stiff-necked English policeman was contacting the Brisbane hospital and hearing that Flash had been admitted with a gunshot wound.

He shrugged. Hell, it was his responsibility so he'd better think of something, and fast.

Behind the bar, Daniel Reilly watched his American cellar man with bright, inquisitive eyes.

Rose and her father were drinking tea in the sitting room. He'd changed into dry clothes and towelled his thinning fair hair and beard. He was glad to be in the comfort of his own home, out of the blasted weather. He'd brought Rose various gifts from Brisbane town and had watched, with enjoyment, her obvious pleasure in his purchases. She was looking beautiful today, he thought, with that soft flush in her cheeks and her eyes glowing. She'd seemed jumpy when he'd arrived; probably nervous, being left alone without a man to protect her. But she was better now. In fact, he couldn't remember when he'd last seen her so happy.

His heart warmed at the thought that she must be glad to see him. He loved his daughter, as much as any man of his stern temperament could but, although she was only seventeen, she had a strong will of her own which had caused many a conflict between them. It never occurred to him that she was a reflection of himself and had inherited his independence.

She'd always been wilful, even as a child. It seemed he only had to forbid her to do something to push her headlong into that very thing. He still felt a pang of fear when he remembered some of her exploits. There was the time he strictly forbade her to approach a new, half-broken stallion he'd purchased, only to find her astride the great white beast not half an hour later, plunging up and down across the paddock, crying out, 'I can master him; I can!' When she'd been thrown it had been a miracle she hadn't broken every bone in her body; but, no, seven-year-old Rose had picked herself up, dizzy but undaunted and marched right back to the rearing animal. If George hadn't swept her up under one arm and carried her, kicking furiously, out of danger, heaven knew what might have been the outcome. When he'd set her on her feet she'd looked angrily up at him and shouted defiantly, 'He's *my* horse, Daddy, I want him and I'll ride him. I *will* !'

Whitey was her horse now. 'Not a lady's mount,' the critics in the district said to each other, 'it's a wonder she can hold him, he's so strong.'

George worried that Rose had grown too wild. Motherless since she was ten, she needed the gentleness of a woman's guiding hand. He'd hired Mrs Moore in the hope that Rose would form a friendship with the housekeeper. He thought her a good, sensible woman but Rose had never liked her and resented the suggestion that she could somehow take the place of her adored mother.

Meanwhile, she was forming unwelcome friendships with the local boys and particularly William O'Meally, that wild Irish lad who was quite the wrong sort of match for her. William was more fit to be a servant, a stable-hand, than coming visiting as if he was an equal.

No, George shook his head, Rose was worth better than a local larrikin. He wanted to see her marry an educated man with good prospects. He wouldn't always be here to take care of her. He fingered his beard reflectively. The grey hairs were coming on fast. His brows slowly drew together. He was still a fine figure of a man but lately a day in the saddle made his bones ache as never before. He was getting old and he'd have to face it and think about slowing down. But he had to make sure his girl was looked after.

Rose saw him frowning and her ready smile broke out. She immediately hid her face behind a pretty pink silk fan on ivory sticks he'd bought her, her eyes laughing at him from over the top. 'It will be perfect with my pink party frock. I love all the things you brought me, Father.'

Perhaps he should send her to England for a season, to stay with his sister Alice. She could give the girl polish, rid her of some of her wildness, teach her how a well-bred girl should behave; introduce her to men of wealth and position. Surely then she'd recognise the advantages of the marriage her father planned for her. In England, she'd forget all about William and her heart might even warm to Robert Leicester.

Leicester was a good fellow of solid worth, making something of his life. When the young man had arrived at Bell's Creek, George had invited him to dinner but Rose hadn't liked him very much.

'He's so dull,' she'd objected and wrinkled her pretty nose. 'He seems to think he's of very great consequence but he certainly doesn't know how to entertain a girl.'

When Carew broached the subject of marriage Rose had laughed. 'Marry Robert? Never! I'd be bored to tears in a day.'

George put down his cup and watched Rose lift the teapot to refill it. Perhaps it wasn't a good idea to send her to London. Alice hadn't had a noticeable influence over her when Rose had visited her two years ago. She'd written that Rose had quite worn her out with her arguments and impossible attitudes.

"She is not interested in fashion or polite society," Alice had told her brother, "and her tongue is so blunt I live in constant dread of her offending suitors with her very definite points of view. I have given her what guidance I could and make allowance for her youth, but she seems determined to go her own way and make her own judgements rather than accept the advice of older, wiser heads. She is also far more at home on a horse than in a ballroom, and I blame that dreadful country of yours for that. Heavens, man, have you *no* society in that outlandish place? And, on being taken to a showing of the very latest fashions, she actually laughed aloud and said she found them grotesque and restricting. She would rather, she informed me, wear a comfortable skirt in which she could easily ride — then she confessed that she always rode *astride*. I'm sorry, George, I can do no more with her."

Yes, George thought, remembering that letter, Alice would not welcome another visit from her turbulent niece; neither could he impose upon Richard and Constance who had two daughters of their own to find husbands for. They would certainly not welcome a visitor, even for one season, who would outshine their girls in beauty.

Rose broke into his thoughts.

'I was surprised to see you back early, Father.'

'A nice surprise, I hope.'

'Of course.' She smiled, thinking, Oh, William, we've been robbed of our night.

'I finished my business early. I'd have been home last night but the coach lost a wheel and we were so late arriving at Bell's Creek that, instead of riding out here, I put up at the Squatters' Arms for the night. I wanted to see Robert first thing this morning so it saved me valuable time.'

'You were in town last night?' Rose held her breath. She and William could have so easily have been caught. They'd been lucky.

'I was indeed. Would you have preferred me to come home?'

'Not if it was more convenient for you to stay in Bell's Creek, Father.'

He sipped his tea, thankful that at least he'd made it clear to Rose that he would no longer tolerate her friendship with William O'Meally. And she, realising he was adamant, had simply said, "Yes, Father" and had, for once, refrained from argument. Perhaps she was finally getting some sense.

He cast a covert look at his daughter. It was true, she was maturing. She even seemed different from when he'd left for Brisbane. He couldn't put his finger on the change but for some reason he suddenly thought of her as a woman rather than a little girl.

The farm dogs began barking and George excused himself and went out to the verandah. The rain burst was over and the clouds were rapidly retreating, pulling a freshly washed blue sky behind them. Two men were riding up to the house, both in waterproof coats but probably pretty damp, poor fellows.

The new police sub-inspector and one of his black troopers. George raised his brows. Now, why the devil had they ridden all the way out here in such a storm?

Chapter 9

Rose didn't cry out when Frederick broke the news about William but it took all her strength to remain outwardly calm. She thought the sub-inspector was watching her too closely and knew she'd turned pale but was determined not to betray her lover.

She sat with her head bent to hide her distress from the men as they talked. She was filled with a bitter loathing towards the sub-inspector who had remarked indifferently that he didn't know whether William was alive or dead. The man was callous and cruel. Now he was saying that William had been ambushed stealing horses from Mr McIntyre's farm. How could he tell such a wicked lie? She wanted to scream at him, hit him with angry fists, cry out, 'It's not true. William was with me last night, safe in my arms.'

She bit her lip, forcing back the passionate confession that could save him from the police. Father would deny it, refuse to believe her. They'd say she was making up a tale for William's sake. Then father would use her championing of him to prove she was too much under his influence. He'd send her away, perhaps overseas to Aunt Alice. And when she was gone? He'd do everything in his power to destroy William. She wouldn't be able to help her lover.

When she was allowed to return, he'd be gone and she'd never be able to find him again. Her father was well capable of ruining the O'Meallys and driving them away.

The horror of it brought furious tears to her eyes that were lowered so meekly. If father was capable of that, he might do even worse. He knew her determined nature. What if she returned to find William had met with some *accident* and was dead?

She glanced surreptitiously at her father. She thought he was pleased, even delighted to hear of William's predicament, sure that he must have been in the raid.

George said complacently, 'I'm not surprised to hear of it. He's the makings of a young criminal. No doubt, if he recovers, he'll hang.'

What could she do? Rose sought for an answer. She couldn't say William had been in her bed. She noticed Frederick's eyes turn to her and her heart skipped a beat. She was used to men looking at her with undisguised admiration. She recognised the glimmer of approval in his eyes. There might be a chance to charm him, win him over. She'd have to play her part skillfully, smile at the hateful man, act towards him with friendship.

She had to do something to help William. If not, her father had said he would hang.

Rose felt her throat constrict but she lifted her head proudly and returned Frederick's stare. 'Will you have some tea, sub-inspector?'

'Tea would be very welcome, ma'am, thank you. I have some questions for you. I hope they will not be too distressing but they must be cleared up.'

'Questions for my daughter?' George frowned. 'She's not implicated in any of this, man.'

'Of course not, sir.' Frederick reached for the cup Rose handed him. He observed that, although she'd changed colour, her hand was steady and her smile friendly. She was showing no more signs of upset than were natural upon hearing of the wounding of a friend, but not an especially close friend. Are the stories that she's in love with the boy greatly exaggerated or is she a consummate actress?

he thought as he raised the cup to his lips.

'Well, sir,' George barked, 'What are these questions?'

'Perhaps I could speak to Miss Carew alone?' Frederick put down his cup.

'Alone, sir? Nonsense! If you are questioning my daughter I intend to stay and support her. Has someone been spreading stories about her?'

'Really, sir, it would be better if...'

'Well, I'm not moving.' George leant back and crossed his arms. 'Rose has no secrets from her father so ask your questions, sir, and get it over with.'

Frederick gave a slight shrug. Rose said, 'Father is right, there is nothing which he cannot hear. Please ask whatever you need.'

She certainly has courage, Frederick thought. 'Very well, Miss Carew. I'm told that you and William O'Meally have formed an — attachment.'

She continued to meet his eyes, her head erect, a smile on her lips. 'We have known each other since we were children and we are neighbours. Of course we are friends.'

'No more than friends, Miss Carew?'

'Perhaps more than casual friends. Consider, sub-inspector, the young people of the district have grown up together, we are a very small community, always meeting at each others' houses, at parties and dances. There is only our group from which to choose escorts and dancing partners; because of this, we are perhaps more like family than friends. I am sincerely fond of William, as I am of his brother. Mrs O'Meally has always been very kind to me and I am deeply sorry that this dreadful thing has happened.'

She's lovely, Frederick thought. Lord, I hope she's not too deep in with that boy. His resolve faltered but he steeled himself. 'Miss Carew, please think very carefully before you answer my next question. Mrs O'Meally has said that William was not at McIntyre's last night but was, in fact, visiting you.'

'That's not possible, sir.' George broke in angrily. 'I have lately thought it unwise for Rose to encourage that young man as he's clearly growing too fond of her; so I've forbidden her to see him again. She promised to obey me and I trust my daughter. She would not see O'Meally behind my back.'

Frederick continued to watch Rose. She was certainly becoming agitated — but that would be normal enough for any girl accused of conducting a clandestine affair. He found himself profoundly hoping that was the only reason for her sudden flush.

'Well, Miss Carew?'

'I'm afraid Mrs O'Meally has been misinformed,' Rose said firmly. Forgive me, she thought, forgive me, my love. How can I say you were here and risk the consequences of father's fury? There must be another way to clear your name.

'So, William O'Meally was not here last night.' Frederick persisted.

'Father has told you, sir. He asked me not to see William again and I agreed.'

'Miss Carew, I need to hear you say that William was not here last night.'

'For heaven's sake, man, she's said that.'

'It's all right, Father. If you insist, sub-inspector then no, William was not here last night.'

As she spoke her denial, Rose felt wrenched apart inside. She had tried not to lie but this man had demanded a clear statement. Well, he had it and he still appeared dissatisfied. Now she would have to use all her wits to save William from the gallows.

'Perhaps,' she said, hanging her head as if embarrassed, 'perhaps William was with another girl last night and Mrs O'Meally assumed — William is popular with all the girls. Because he was not with me cannot be proof that he was stealing horses at Bellara.'

Buchanan had said William was with a girl. He'd seemed positive. Frederick finished his tea.

'Of course not, ma'am and we'll be doing all in our power to get at the truth. I'm sorry I had to embarrass you and your father.'

Rose said quietly, 'We understand. You were given information and were obliged to act upon it.'

'Thank you, Miss Carew.' Frederick rose. 'I must be off. Miss Carew. Sir.'

George followed him to the hall where his coat was hanging.

'The storm's over, now. You'll have an easier ride back.' The farmer faced him worriedly. 'Look, Stapleton, I don't want that story about Rose and O'Meally to go any further. For God's sake, man, be discreet. You wouldn't want to harm a young woman's reputation and she denied he was here.'

'She did indeed.' Frederick folded the coat and smiled. 'No need for you to worry, sir. I'll be conducting my inquiries with great care.'

At the Squatters' Arms, Daniel Reilly looked up in surprise at the big man who had just entered.

'This is a rare visit, Scotsman. What brings you to town?'

'I've come for ma supplies,' McLeod said shortly, 'and for a drink wi' ma friends, if it's any o' your business, Daniel.'

'I hear you've been fencing up at Nanango.'

'Aye, there's plenty o' work around for them wi' a mind to look for it.'

'What's your pleasure?'

'I'll have a whisky, make it a large one.'

McLeod took his drink and crossed to a table where Limpy Patterson was deep in conversation with Wild Jack d'Arcy.

'Have you heard?' Jack hissed.

'Aye, rumours are flyin' about thick and fast. What's the truth of it?'

'Flash stopped a bullet. Buck brought him back here and Red got him away to Brisbane this morning. Stapleton's nosing about but all's well.'

'What o' young Billy?'

'Someone bushwhacked him last night.' Limpy said. 'Left him for dead on the track up by Carew's.'

'He's alive,' Jack cut in, 'but bad. Hasn't regained consciousness. They've got him over at the doc's with an armed trooper by his bed.'

'Who'd have jumped the lad?'

'He was coming back from Carew's. Could have been Robert Leicester, in a jealous rage.' Jack guessed.

'What? That staid and sober gentleman?'

'Whoever it was put a bullet in his back,' Limpy growled. 'Couldn't fight him face to face like a man but took him from behind. Cowardly mongrel.'

'Buck reckons George Carew came in on the coach late last night and took a room at the hotel. He was here this morning.'

'Aye, he'd have every reason to see William out o' the way; only, our man must have known where to find the boy, must have known where he'd be last night, to have laid for him at all.'

'Carew might have guessed,' Limpy said. 'He could have planned it this way, knowing if he went out of town Billy would try to see Rose.'

Jack stirred restlessly. 'I was at Doc Evans when Stapleton came in from the Carews. Heard him tell Mallory that Rose denied Billy was ever there last night.'

'Aye, well, what do ye expect the poor lassie to say? That she waited until her father's back was turned to spend the night in the arms of her lover?'

'That's a foul thing to say!' Jack scraped back his chair.

'Och, sit still, Jack. It's the truth; we heard it from Red himself. I know ye fancy Rose but she's no more a saint than any high spirited lass wi' a mind of her ain. She's no demure wee creature who'd take tamely to her daddy's strictures. Carew knows that — or he's a right fool if he doesna.'

Buck came over to the table and sat down. 'You come up with any ideas to get Billy out of this?' He asked quietly. 'I've been working on one or two angles.'

'He's innocent,' Jack objected. 'They won't hang him.'

'And what's to stop them?' Buck asked seriously. 'Rose has denied he was with her, so what will the police think? We know for sure he wasn't at McIntyre's but we can't speak out or we hang ourselves. If Billy says he was not with Rose — and he will, of course, to save her reputation — then our hands are tied. We need to give the boy an alibi. I told Stapleton that Flash and I were together all night; what about the rest of you?'

'I dinna need an alibi,' the Scotsman said dourly. 'It's well known I keep mysel' to mysel' and it would look strange if I said I was wi' any of ye. They'll need to prove I was at McIntyre's and the storm's taken care o' that.'

'I already told them Jack and I were together,' Limpy said. 'I didn't know what else to say.'

'They haven't asked me yet.' Jack grinned. 'I'll back you up, Limpy. We'll tell a good tale; they'll never prove us guilty.'

'So, it's only William and Walter they've no alibi for.'

'Mrs O'Meally told Stapleton the boys were at home with her all night until he gave her the news,' Limpy said. 'I met her coming into town and she told me what had happened. She's with Billy now.'

'We'll have to see Red as soon as he returns, before the police can get to him,' Buck decided. 'He'll give his brother an alibi and Kitty'll back them up, for sure.'

Limpy said, 'It might help to find out who else knew of Billy's visit last night.'

The Scotsman downed the last of his whisky and stood up. 'Well, we all knew of it,' he said softly, 'but we know where we all were, don't we?'

Frederick quietly entered the small sick-room at the back of Doctor Evans' surgery and motioned the native trooper to wait outside. He drew up a chair and sat opposite Kitty who eyed him angrily over William's inert body.

'Is there any improvement?' He asked.

'Yes, you'll want to be sure he'll be alive enough for you to arrest him and take my boy to trial for something he never did,' she countered bitterly.

'We're making inquiries, Mrs O'Meally. The trouble is, none of William's friends has, so far, admitted to seeing him last night.'

'Are you trying to make out my son went horse stealing on his own?'

'I'm sure he did not. I was dining at Bellara last night and rode to render assistance when the fight broke out. I saw six men and the black trackers confirmed it. It's my belief that you know who the other men were or, at least, have a very good idea. If you will not tell me, what can I do? All his friends have alibis and William does not. Rose Carew denies seeing him.'

'Well, so she would, you being such a simpleton to ask her in front of that father of hers.'

'She was emphatic.'

'You've no proof my boy was at Bellara.'

'One of the raiders was certainly shot fleeing from the property; possibly more than one. William had a bullet in his back. We followed the tracks of two horses that led us straight to William. For a magistrate, that will be proof enough.'

'You cannot hang an innocent man.'

'That is entirely up to yourself, Miss Carew and his friends. If someone knows the truth they need only come to me.'

'Whoever he was with will come forward,' Kitty said. 'They'll not let you hurt my boy. Is it not enough that the police killed my husband? Those bastards shot him through the lung when he was doing no more than defending the rights of others. They spread evil stories that he'd murdered a man, although they later changed their minds. My Tom died of an infection he was not strong enough to fight, owing to the damage you police did to him. Are you not content with taking my man that you now wish to take my son?'

She was panting with anger, emotion flushing her cheeks.

'Get out of here, Mr Stapleton, and leave my son and me alone. I promise you, you'll not get him easily.'

Frederick went outside. Sergeant Mallory came up to him. 'd'Arcy confirms Patterson's story. More, he swears William was with his brother last night.'

'We'll speak to Walter as soon as he returns, before any of his friends can warn him to change his story. One thing bothers me, sergeant. The black trackers were fairly certain only one man was shot at Bellara, the blood stains were clear. That was the man we were following. They were sure the other four were unhurt and the wounded man was helped by a friend, also unhurt. There were only six men. Was it William O'Meally who was wounded and not John Francis at all? I'd have been prepared to swear, with hindsight, that Francis was the wounded man. There was the absence of his waistcoat — and he never actually stood up, you know. Remained in bed all the while.'

'We'll know soon enough, sir.' Mallory said, 'When Walter and Johnny return, we'll soon see if Flash Johnny Francis has a bullet hole in him.'

But at dusk on the following day Walter O'Meally drove into Bell's Creek with an astonishing story and lost no time in seeking out the police himself.

They'd been held up by bushrangers on the Brisbane track. They'd fought the bastards off but Johnny Francis had taken a bullet in the shoulder. Walter had got him to hospital in Brisbane where he was recovering. Evidence? The sub-inspector could examine the dray. It was peppered with shot. Walter could give a description of the robbers and show exactly where they were bailed up.

Frederick had no choice. He duly despatched a patrol to the spot. They found a few spent rifle cartridges but nothing else. The storms had extended as far as Brisbane.

Meanwhile, Buck took Walter aside and gave him the news.

Chapter 10

I n the administrative block attached to his living quarters, Frederick listened to Sergeant Mallory questioning the troopers.

Corporal Charlie Moon was rapidly describing something in a mixture of pidgin English and his own dialect. As he finished, Mallory turned to the sub-inspector.

'One man walked with a limp. His track was not like a normal man's. It was Limpy Patterson.'

'I do not see how they can be so specific.'

'It's a gift they have, sir. Corporal Moon's prepared to swear to it. Patterson and d'Arcy have made up their tale of a possum hunt. That means Jack was likely one of the thieves as well.'

'What about the others?'

'The two hiding in the bunya grove must have waited until the coast was clear then made their way to Rocky Creek. Their tracks could not be found beyond the point where they entered the water.'

'Why are the troopers so sure one was wounded?'

'There was a blood trail at first, clear to them; and the horses were close together, too close for the normal riding situation. At times they were almost touching, as if one man was supporting the other.'

'So, this was definitely not the pair we were following, which must have included William O'Meally?'

'Weearunga is quite sure ours was a different pair. Our men rode fast and separately, one following the other. However, he does not believe one could have been William, owing to his injuries and Doctor Evans says William was involved in a fight at or around the time he was shot. He opines it was earlier, as William must have been instantly felled by the bullet. Weearunga also found evidence of a struggle and that the boy's head was cut open on a stone.'

'It doesn't prove O'Meally was not on the raid. He and his companion may have fallen out on the way home and decided to settle the matter. I'm inclined to believe that is what happened.'

'Sir, we've equally strong evidence that the other story is true; that William was with Rose and was waylaid by a rival or a robber on his way home.'

'I disagree. He is one of that group of boys. He would have surely been with his mates on such an enterprise, proving his mettle, as you say these boys love to do.'

'George Carew was away that night,' Mallory reminded him, 'leaving the way open for Rose and William to be together.'

Frederick felt unreasonably annoyed and spoke sharply. 'Miss Carew clearly stated she was not with O'Meally and I believe her. She seems an honest young woman who feels as she ought and is obedient to her father's wishes. I see no need to create a scandal for an innocent girl of excellent character by pursuing this line of questioning. A clandestine affair would, I am sure, be repugnant to her.'

Mallory reflected that this was not the Rose Carew he knew. He said stolidly, 'Nonetheless, sir, the accusation has been made and she'll have to go before the magistrate and tell her story.'

'I'll be most strongly recommending that her reputation and delicate feelings be considered and that she is not subjected to any more of this unpleasantness. We'll have to find enough evidence to convict William O'Meally.'

The sergeant experienced a sinking feeling. So far the sub-inspector had been unmoved by the blandishments of the district's unmarried ladies. Surely he was not falling for Rose Carew. That would make the situation tricky in the extreme. The new senior officer would certainly be reluctant to consider any evidence pointing to the girl if she had engaged his affections.

'What of the other raiders, sergeant?'

Mallory brought his attention back.

'Sir, two rode into the bush and managed to conceal their tracks. Probably by dismounting and driving their horses ahead of them whilst carefully sweeping away all trace of their passing by means of a leafy branch or some such thing. Two rode into the creek and their tracks were lost in the water; the two we were following, I'd say. Both Walter O'Meally and John d'Arcy would go that way to reach their homes.'

'Equally, so would the O'Meally brothers.'

'There were only six men, sir. Our evidence points to Buchanan and Francis, Patterson and d'Arcy, as he gave Limpy his alibi; Walter O'Meally, who clearly got Johnny Francis away before we could question him again and, from the direction of one of the riders, I'd go bail the Scotsman was involved. One of McIntyre's men described a man of McLeod's build.'

'Perhaps the troopers were mistaken in Patterson's prints. I do not see how they can be absolute about it and now the rain has prevented further investigation. William O'Meally must have been there and lied to his mother about seeing Miss Carew. I believe we can be sure of at least three things: that there were six scoundrels, that one was wounded and bled heavily and that William O'Meally must have been shot during a falling out of thieves along the track. You'd better interview Patterson again; see if he has any explanation. Someone else may be found to corroborate his story.'

'I'll do that, sir.'

Mallory saluted and left, his emotions in a turmoil. Surely the sub-inspector couldn't seriously expect to refute the troopers' findings in his obvious desire to place William at the scene? All Australia knew the reputation of the Queensland Native Police. Only last year they'd been called upon by the Victorian Government to track down the bushranger Ned Kelly, much as the Victoria police disliked having to admit they needed help — and it was said that Kelly himself had a morbid fear and hatred of the Queensland black trackers. A party had gone down under Sub-Inspector O'Connor last March and were reported to be closing the net on the outlaw and his gang, succeeding where all others had failed.

On the parade ground a lad was waiting, holding the reins of a small mottled grey pony. The sergeant recognised Rhys Evans, the doctor's young son.

'Me dad says to tell you William's awake and fit to answer questions.'

'Good lad. Cut along to my quarters and see if Mrs Mallory has a cake for you.'

A smile broke out over the boy's freckled face. 'Thanks, Sergeant Mallory.'

The sergeant turned back to the administration building. He was sure the sub-inspector would want to interview William himself. Mallory would request that he, too, be present. He was beginning not to trust his senior officer.

Limpy Patterson looked Mallory straight in the eye and said, 'You don't say so?'

'It doesn't surprise you, Limpy?'

'Not very much, sergeant; after all, I know horses. It's my trade. Was my trade,' he corrected himself. 'I know race horses and that's what Squatter McIntyre's hoping to breed; the next Queensland champion. He invited me over to look at the yearlings, ask my opinion.'

'When was this?'

'Well, now, when was it?' Limpy stared thoughtfully at the sky, rubbing his ear as if to aid his memory. 'My gosh, sergeant, I do believe it was the day of the raid.'

'Do you know, somehow I was sure you would?'

'Now, sergeant, that's not a very Christian idea you've got in your head. Go and ask McIntyre. I've nothing to hide. After all, Jack and I were out after possums that night.'

'I'd say you and d'Arcy cooked up the whole story between you,' Mallory said darkly.

'The only thing we cooked up was a good possum stew.' Limpy grinned. 'I dare say you'd find my tracks all over Bellara if you were to look.'

Frederick was writing his report, uneasily aware that his first case as a police officer was going completely awry. He couldn't bring six men before a magistrate with no evidence other than his sergeant's suspicions. The Brisbane General Hospital at Herston was certainly treating Mr Francis for a gunshot wound to the left shoulder he'd purportedly got in a bushranger attack. Thanks to the expert treatment by his friend who had stopped the bleeding and dressed the wound, he was making a good recovery. No, there was no record as to when Mr Francis might have received the wound — Mr O'Meally had given a clear account of the attack and the hospital staff were rushed off their feet at the moment with an epidemic of influenza — why would they query Mr O'Meally's statement? Injuries such as gunshots and stabbings were routine and occasioned no special interest.

Even Andrew McIntyre, who had every reason to want the thieves captured, had admitted inviting Patterson to inspect the yearlings and yes, they had been in the bottom paddock. At least that had silenced Sergeant Mallory who had been officiously insisting it was Patterson, not William O'Meally, who was the sixth man.

The suspects were all sticking to their stories, cheerfully inviting the police to prove them wrong.

'Damn these people,' Frederick swore, 'do they think I'm such a johnny raw they can pull the wool over my eyes like this? I am determined to teach them a lesson. I'll bring *someone* to justice over this, I swear it.' In the back of his mind the thought flickered that, as William must have been one of the raiders, it wasn't right that he should get away scot free and continue to force his unwelcome attentions on Rose — Miss Carew.

He went over the evidence again. He'd been confident that, if the dray's tracks had led from the O'Meally's farm to Buchanan's shack, it would implicate Walter, Buchanan and Francis. But Buchanan, cleverly mixing a little truth with the lies, had openly admitted that Walter had driven there so, even if he'd proved it before the dratted rain had melted the tracks away, it would not have mattered. Everyone was giving him such plausible stories — and laughing at him behind his back, he supposed.

He'd gone immediately to interview William. The boy was in a weak state but spoke lucidly. He claimed he had no memory of that night. He rather thought he'd been at home with Walter, who had suggested going out quite late in the evening, only he couldn't now recall why.

This had been Buck's idea. 'He's too sick to remember any fine details of a lie so get him to say he's lost his memory; the cut on his head will point to the truth of that. It'll work wonders on the jury, if he goes to trial. Wounded in a foul attack, loss of memory; he'll win their sympathy. It'll come out that he was forbidden to see Rose and they'll be even sorrier for him. Let him become the victim of all this.'

The only thing the prisoner seemed sure of was that he had not been with Rose Carew. Frederick was glad to hear it. He'd known she could not have looked at him so candidly and lied.

However, he strongly doubted that William had lost his memory.

He's been put up to it by the others, he mused. The prisoner had been refused all visitors but his mother; it must have been her doing. Either she'd concocted the idea or relayed the suggestion from one of his mates. He'd rather have denied even Kitty access to the boy but he couldn't appear a brute. It would be reasonable to not admit his friends but how could he deny an anxious mother?

The woman had changed her story yet again. William had been in despair over Rose and Walter had suggested they ride into Bell's Creek for a drink at the Squatters' Arms. Walter, having to get up early to drive to Brisbane — Mr Stapleton would remember that's where he'd been bound — had left his brother there, drowning his sorrows.

'You told me he was with Miss Carew.'

'Ah, Mr Stapleton, a mother's fond dream, it was, no more. I hoped he might have gone to his dear Rose but all the time he was lying out there in the bush, his life's blood pouring into the earth.'

'Why didn't you tell me straight away that your sons were in Bell's Creek so we could seek witnesses?'

'I was confused. All I knew was you were blaming my boys for something they never did. I thought it best to say they were with me.'

It was maddening. Buchanan was now confirming the brothers were in the hotel and had stopped to play a game with himself and Francis. The other patrons had been strangely forgetful. They often saw the O'Meallys there — yes, they possibly had been in that night. If Buck said so, it must have been so.

'I seem to recall,' Daniel Reilly had said slowly, 'me memory's not what it was, sir; but I'm inclined to think I did see them two young 'uns on that very night.'

'You didn't mention it before.'

'Ah, well, you didn't ask me before.'

Frederick put down his pen and called for Black Diamond to be saddled. He rode into Bell's Creek and tied the mare to the rail outside Doctor Evans' surgery.

Rose Carew was leaving the building, carrying a basket. She looked charming in a sky blue skirt and jacket, a white lace blouse and a pretty straw bonnet with ribbons which exactly matched the clear blue of her eyes. Frederick noticed her crestfallen face and saluted her.

'Miss Carew.'

'Why, Sub-Inspector! I hope your inquiries are progressing well, sir.'

'I'm doing my best, Miss Carew.'

'I was taking some food to William but was told I am not permitted to see him. Would it be very wrong of me to ask you to allow the visit?' She smiled prettily. 'You may search my basket. He is so sick and it would please me very much to be able to help in some small way, for his mother's sake.'

'I think I must open your basket but, yes, you may see him. I'm not a hard man, Miss Carew, and he has confirmed he was not with you that night. Not that I required any such confirmation,' Frederick added hastily.

She blushed. 'You are too good, sir. See, it is only some pasties and bread and cheese.'

'Made by your own fair hands? He is a lucky fellow.' He hesitated. 'Miss Carew?'

'Yes, Sub-Inspector?'

She gazed innocently up at him and he felt his heart turn over. She would not be mercenary or cynical like Caroline; she was sweetly unspoiled by worldly ambition. She would stand by her man, delight in his successes, comfort him in times of need...

He said, 'I — would like to visit you again, as a friend, not an inquisitor. I must have given you reason to dislike me and would like the chance to redeem myself.'

'I don't dislike you, sir. You must do your job, after all.'

'You are generous, ma'am. I should like to know you — and your father — better.'

'You will be welcome whenever you come.' Rose gave him her gloved hand and he held it for a moment longer than was strictly polite. She withdrew it and went into the building.

In the sick-room Rose clung to William, passionately kissing his face.

'My darling, my darling.'

'Where's that damned black guard?'

'I sent him out. I told him the sub-inspector permitted me to see you alone.'

'You're a wonderful girl, Rose.' William struggled to sit up. 'I must tell you, must warn you ...' he began to cough with the exertion and Rose pushed him back against the pillows.

'Hush, dearest, I'm quite safe. In fact, I believe Mr Stapleton is determined to protect me. I am trying to turn his interest in me to our account. If I could make him my friend, take him into my confidence...'

'Rose, you must promise me not to tell them we were together. I've said I was not with you. Walter will save me — he's given them some story. We must put our trust in our friends. I couldn't bear it if your father sent you away, kept us from seeing each other again. My sweet girl, when I'm well and this is behind us, we'll go away, I swear it.'

'Oh, yes, William, yes. I long for you, to be in your arms again. I will not tell them, to have them make our love something shameful and wicked. It is wonderful and good.'

'If they make me stand trial, even then, you are not to try to help me. I'll not see you put through the pain of it, them making you describe what happened between us, how we made love. We can come through this by other means. Promise me, Rose.'

She held his face between her hands and kissed his mouth tenderly.

'With all my heart. I love you and only you and I will do as you ask and wait for you.'

'And I'll come back to you, whatever happens. I swear it.'

There was a discreet knock at the door.

'The guard. He's back.'

The trooper entered to find Rose calmly explaining the contents of the basket to William.

Later Frederick asked him, 'What passed between Miss Carew and the prisoner?'

Jacky-Jacky shrugged. 'She give 'im basket of tucker, sir.'

'Nothing more than that?'

'I didn't see nothin' else, sir.'

Ten days later William was sent to Brisbane to face trial for horse-stealing and murder. The jury was not convinced by the alibi given by his brother and the fact that Kitty had changed her story twice. He was found guilty and sentenced to hang.

PART TWO

Brisbane
1996

Chapter 11

Sally Cooper sat, cross legged, eyes closed, on a cushion on the floor, listening to the familiar sounds of her immediate environment as they took on a new clarity. She gently moved her mind through the house. The soft monotonous click of the kitchen clock; an unexpected crack — house settling; an odd tapping, shuffling sort of noise — what on earth? — she frowned, concentrating. Oh! The blind in the bedroom moving in the breeze.

Don't analyse. Her meditation teacher's voice jumped into her head. 'The purpose of the exercise is to still your thoughts, move right out of your left brain. Let the sounds flow over you; hear them but don't think about them. Gradually you'll notice your breathing becoming slower, your mind will quiet down and those worrying thoughts will begin to fade, be less dominant. Eventually, you'll realise you haven't actually thought anything for minutes at a time.'

Minutes at a time? Sally thought dismally. I'd settle for seconds at a time.

She determinedly dragged her mind back to listening.

Like a recalcitrant puppy. The idea was irresistible. Pulling at its lead, digging its feet in, sitting down and refusing to budge or following enticing scents while she tried to haul it back to heel.

Damn! Another thought. She opened her eyes.

The phone shrilled, startlingly loud in the still room. Sally jumped at the unexpected noise then uncrossed her legs and ran to answer its imperious summons.

'Hello!' She trilled artificially. 'You have reached Sally and Tim. We can't come to the phone right now but if you'd like to leave us a message and your number, we'll call you back as soon as we can. Please speak after the beep.'

She waited.

'Beep!'

'That was the most unconvincing beep I've ever heard,' Juliet Ryan told her. 'If you don't want to answer the phone, why don't you simply plug in the answering machine?'

'Forgot. I was doing my meditation.' Sally drove impatient fingers through her mop of short, fair hair then flicked her fringe back into order and admitted ruefully, 'I think I must be trying to sabotage myself because Kaitlin's always reminding us to turn off our mobiles, plug in our answering machines and lose our beepers before we practise.'

'How's it going, oh, ye of the quiet mind?'

She glanced down at her slim figure. Her T shirt bore the slogan, 'A quiet mind is MAGIC'. She began to twist the hem into a knot, a frown in her expressive grey eyes. 'It's frustrating. Do you know, some of our group say they can sit without a single thought in their heads for half an hour at a time or longer?'

'Of course, you have to consider that they may be brain dead to start with,' Juliet soothed.

'Sadly, they're highly motivated achievers. They reckon it's the meditation that does it, curse them.'

'That's the wrong attitude. Not very spiritual.'

'I don't feel spiritual. I feel — dissatisfied.'

'Poor Sal. Anyway, I've got something that'll amuse you.'

'What?'

'St Helena.'

'Napoleon.'

'It isn't word association, you idiot. I'm talking about *our* St Helena, Moreton Bay. Dread prison island of the last century.'

'What about it?'

'I'm doing some research on early prisons for a thesis and I'm going over on Sunday on a tourist jaunt. Want to come? Or do you and Tim have something excitingly erotic planned for the weekend?'

'Don't I wish! I don't know, Jules...'

Sally glanced across the living room. A long low coffee table in front of a comfortable old sofa was stacked with Tim's books and papers. Under the table, a rainbow of Manila folders, each colour categorising the different subject within, had splayed across the green carpet like a bunch of bright flowers. Tim was all set up for a weekend of hard study. He'd hardly notice if she wasn't there.

Juliet broke into her thoughts. 'Do you good to get out of each other's hair for a while so Tim isn't invited. Oh, come on, Sally, just us girls together. A nice trip down the river and across the bay, a tour of the island and a barbecue lunch. It'll be a fun day out — and you can remind me of anything I miss later when I'm sorting my notes.'

'A sort of back-up memory? Thanks.'

'Say you will or I won't give you a moment's peace. I'll ring you in the middle of your meditation every day.'

'Blackmail. All right, I'll come.'

She wrote down the details, smiling. Juliet Ryan was her oldest friend and had the uncanny ability to sense when she needed someone to listen, to divert her, to just be a companion in times of need. And Jules was a good listener, like her brother Peter, who'd devoted his life to helping others by becoming a priest.

'Sad, really,' Sally told the telephone as Jules rang off. 'I always thought Peter was a hunk. I had a crush on him for years, at school.'

She toyed for a moment with the thought that, if Peter hadn't got religion and taken the cloth, he and she might have — it was possible; he'd liked her quite a lot. Then, of course, she wouldn't have met Tim. Well, she might have met him but they wouldn't have got together and drifted into a relationship.

Drifted was the word. They'd started as friends sharing a house, then, celebrating Tim's excellent uni results, had drunk a little too much, kissed a little too long and ended up in the same bed. After that it seemed less trouble to sleep together.

Sally wandered over to the sofa and sat down, plumping up the cushions behind her back. She'd made their covers from remnants of bright, tough cotton that matched Tim's folders. She smiled to herself, remembering how she'd accused him of using the multi-coloured files to brighten up his medical studies.

'Does it make them less dull?'

He'd looked at her seriously over his glasses. 'I don't find medicine dull, Sal. It's exciting. I really love it.'

She ruffled his hair. 'It was a joke.'

But he'd already gone back to his book.

She hugged a cushion to her chest, annoyed by her restlessness. Everything was all right; what more did she want? She was engaged to a good man, she enjoyed her job and living in this lovely old house with its narrow corridors and fretwork above the doorways. It had been a dream of a find. So close to the city — and the landlady had laid new carpet throughout before they moved in. Tim reckoned she'd been afraid they'd catch their feet in the worn old carpet that had been here when they'd viewed the house and sue her for damages. Sally was just grateful the rent hadn't increased and, although Tim complained green wouldn't have been his choice, it made Sally feel she was walking barefoot on grass. She ran up new curtains in a cheerful floral print for the living room and reminded Tim of the blessings of the indoor laundry and good paintwork.

She looked around the sunlit room. They'd gradually decorated it with souvenirs and books and knick-knacks. A pair of tropical prints reminded her of their Christmas holiday at the beach. In spite of the differences in their temperaments, they were making something good with their relationship.

It might not be a match made in heaven but it was all right; nothing to set the world on fire — just good friends, good sex — if only Tim could lose his tendency towards protectiveness, worrying if she was late coming home, or overseas as part of her job.

The travel perks had made her go for the job with a travel agent. She enjoyed the independence, the freedom. It was a career, not just a job. She was good at it, good with people. She didn't like having to explain her movements too much.

It was all right, as long as she and Tim remained friends and kept a space between them.

His insecurity was understandable. His father was a bully, despising the weak and gentle. It amused him to bark at Tim and watch him jump. Sally deplored his tactics but understood Tim's reluctance to stand up to his father.

'It only makes him worse and I don't see him enough to bother. I don't want to spend hours in mindless arguments. I left home to get away from that. I won't give him the satisfaction of a quarrel. Anyhow,' he finished with a grin. 'you give him enough of a fight.'

'He likes me better for it.'

'You enjoy a scrap, I don't. He can snipe at me all he likes. I just ignore it.'

Sally reflected that perhaps Tim knew how to get his own back, after all. Giles was always trying to get a rise out of him without success. Tim had perfected the art of non-attachment. She shook her head. She'd never have Tim's forbearance. She was perfectly happy to scrap with Giles.

'When are you two going to get married?' He'd asked one evening. They'd been invited for dinner with the family. It was before they'd even thought of becoming engaged. 'It's clear you're shacked up together.'

'Dad.' Amanda, Tim's sister, implored.

'All right, having a relationship. Is that the modern term for sleeping together?'

Amanda had looked a mute appeal to her mother.

'It's their business, Giles,' Ellie had said placidly.

'What our son does is the family's business. He and Sally have been living together as man and wife for two years. Time they stopped playing at life, made a commitment and settled down. The children have to be thought of.'

'Whose children?' Tim had asked, puzzled.

'Well, you're planning to have kids, aren't you? You want them to grow up bastards?'

' *Dad*! '

'Keep your hair on, Mandy. What else do you call kids whose parents aren't married?'

Sally smiled at the embarrassed teenager. 'It's all right, Mandy, Giles has a right to his opinion. Tim and I are really just friends. We haven't any plans to have children.'

'Just friends? Lovers, we used to call it.'

'Dad, it's really up to me and Sal.' Tim kept his eyes on his wine glass. 'I'm still studying and Sal's got her career. We're fond of each other, good mates.' He spoke patiently, refusing to meet Giles glare.

'Oh, mates, is it? A good sight more than mates, if you ask me.'

Sally said clearly, 'But no one did ask you, Giles. We're happy doing our own thing.'

Giles Horan was never short of admiration for someone who could stand up to him and hit straight from the shoulder, as he put it. He liked Sally, thought her full of pluck. He'd have enjoyed having her in the family, another daughter. In spite of that, he'd frowned at her and burst out angrily, 'Doing your own thing! I'm sick to death of hearing about young people doing their own thing. It's the excuse for everything these days. Drugs, broken marriages, street kids. It's bloody selfish, if you ask me. Doing your own thing means ducking your responsibilities.'

Tim raised his eyes and gave Sally a straight look. She swallowed back a retort. He was right, there was no point in adding fuel to an already uncomfortable situation. She was making things difficult for Ellie and Mandy. Giles gave her far more leeway than he did his family. And his beliefs were set in concrete. He didn't want to change. He'd never admit he was wrong.

She smiled back at Tim, liking the way his soft brown hair flopped over his forehead and his glasses made his eyes seem large and dreamy. He was hating all this bickering.

Tim drank his wine and set the glass down again, fiddling restively with the stem. Sally winked at him. 'You may be right, Giles,' she'd said serenely, 'but you're upsetting Tim and Mandy and my tongue's hanging out for another drink. Pour the wine and let's drop the subject.'

'I'm upsetting Tim,' Giles replied grimly, 'but I don't seem to be upsetting you.'

Sally tilted her head and considered him. 'I don't see any reason to be upset. After all, you really are entitled to your opinion and you can't make us do anything, you know. We'll live together if we choose to and not get married if we don't want to.' She'd seen he was still glaring at her and added pertly, 'So there.'

Giles met her gaze in silence. She could irritate the hell out of him then open wide those pretty grey eyes and wrinkle her mobile face and charm the bloody birds out of the trees. She looked great tonight, in a dark blue dress with a long skirt and a sash under the bodice — old fashioned, like they wore them these days. Her hair was too short, more like a boy's, but shining like gold. Tim was a bloody fool if he didn't get on and marry her. She had guts and — my God, the cheek of her! She was giving him back look for look, a smile dancing in her eyes.

He suddenly saw the humour and his great shout of laughter had made his wife and daughter jump.

'All right, missy, hold out your glass. But don't think I've done yet.'

'I hope you haven't.' Sally had passed her glass across to him. 'If Tim and I did get married, you'd have nothing to fight me over and you know you enjoy a good slanging match.'

'You're equal to me, at any rate.' Giles sent Tim a disgusted glance but seeing Sally's quelling gaze, held his peace.

Sally knew Tim wasn't the weakling his father branded him. Hating rows, over the years he'd developed a quiet disposition, enabling him to slip away when his father began to voice his strong opinions; or simply let them flow over his head. Tim would be a gentle, dedicated doctor, Sally was sure. He'd probably be adored by his patients. He'll worry about them the way he does about me, she thought and sighed. At first it had been nice to have a caring man in her life who seemed concerned about her, willing to look after her. Lately it had begun to pall, even to be a little irritating.

She turned the diamond and sapphire engagement ring around on her finger as if suddenly wondering how it had got there, then shrugged and went back to her cushion on the floor. Another ten minutes then she'd give it away for today. She sat down and crossed her legs.

'Damn! I forgot the answering machine again.' She said, then thought, Oh, let it go, what does it matter anyway? I'm not getting anywhere with this.

She closed her eyes and let the sounds grow around her. Tiny noises suddenly becoming prominent in the still house. Tim would be home soon and she hadn't done anything about a meal. She'd flexed off work early, promising she'd cook dinner tonight.

Why don't we go out somewhere? We haven't done that for ages. We're acting like an old, married couple, set in our ways. When did that happen? Can't remember. Was it when we got engaged? Something changed, took the spark away — what little spark there was.

She opened her eyes. 'I'm thinking again.' The words echoed in the quietness.

Sally began to breathe deeply, slowly sinking herself back into nothingness. Her lids fluttered down and shut out the late afternoon shadows on the wall.

But, if you're in love, getting engaged should make it better, shouldn't it? If you're in love. Of course she was in love with Tim. She was. In love with Tim. She was a lucky girl, Tim was a wonderful man. Everyone said so. All her girl friends said it. Only Peter hadn't. He'd warmed her heart by saying gently, 'You're a wonderful girl, Sally. Tim's a lucky man.'

The pain had eased a little then. She'd been hurt that everyone thought she was the lucky one and Tim was so wonderful.

That's disloyal. Of course Tim's wonderful. Why else would you be marrying the man?

I'm terribly unhappy.

Sally's eyes flashed open. Where had that come from? Some deep place inside her had opened a crack and let out one of the thoughts she'd got firmly buried and under rigid control; never, never to see the light of day.

'I'm terribly unhappy.' She said it quietly, testing the sound of the words and her stomach twisted. She felt her chest tighten and caught her breath. Behind her eyes hot tears were prickling.

'No!' She said loudly. 'No!' Then the words came screaming out of her mouth of their own accord. 'I'm terribly unhappy, terribly unhappy. Oh, Tim, I'm so terribly unhappy.'

When Tim came home he found Sally curled up on the sofa, weeping with gut-wrenching sobs from a part of her he'd never known. He pulled up short at the door, thinking, What on earth! Then he took quiet control. He gave her a mild sedative and made dinner, frying eggs with chips on the side and tossing together a green salad. He racked his brains for anything that he might have done or said to cause her distress but instinct held him back from asking for an explanation. He wouldn't push her. She'd tell him when she was ready. He watched her as she ate in silence, her gestures mechanical.

That night they slept in separate beds.

Chapter 12

The wide brown mouth of the Brisbane River dropped away to stern as the small tourist boat lifted its bow to meet the bay's choppy swell. Sally, sitting in the open stern, was wet by flying spray and shook the salty drops from her hair.

'We'll get drenched if we stay here. Let's go inside, Jules. It'll be warmer, too.'

Earlier, the morning had not looked promising for an outing on the bay. Cool, gusty winds were driving showers before them, sharply spattering the city as the girls drove down to the river jetty. The sky was overcast and the forecast didn't offer much better odds for the rest of the day.

When Juliet called to collect her, Sally, in blue jeans and a warm, long sleeved checked shirt, had opened the door to her friend.

'We're not still going, are we?'

Juliet was rugged up in a green duffle coat, her thick dark brown hair confined in a long plait down her back. She grinned. 'Absolutely. The weather won't be bad enough to stop the boat.'

'It'll be cold,' Sally wailed, 'and wet.'

There was a twinkle in Juliet's blue eyes. 'Bring a jac' said unsympathetically.

Escape from the Past

They moved into the shelter of the boat's interior. There was a small bar section and display area and rows of seats facing the bow. Sally put on her denim jacket and Juliet said, 'Very country. All you need is an akubra and a horse.'

'There are books for sale.' Sally wandered over to the display of books and memorabilia. 'About St Helena. This looks interesting.' She picked up a slim volume. 'By James Carew, stories of some of the prisoners on the island. It's not expensive; I think I'll get it.'

She fished a five dollar note from her purse and paid for the booklet.

'You can't bury your nose in a book.'

'Of course not. You should have a look at this display for your notes.'

A printed notice gave a brief history of the island which had been a men's prison from 1866 to 1932. A brutal and feared destination in the early years and virtually escape proof owing to its isolated location, by the turn of the century it had become a self-sufficient prison farm, exporting produce to the mainland. Various workshops had been established where prisoners could learn a trade. In the last years it had gradually been dismantled and the remaining prisoners relocated to the Boggo Road gaol in Brisbane.

The company that ran the tours had put together a collection of photographs of the island and its prisoners; men with close cropped hair, many with moustaches, as was the fashion in the eighteen hundreds and some with flowing beards. All had sad, resigned faces. Something about them made Sally shiver.

'What is it?' Juliet tucked her hand into her friend's arm.

'I don't know. Rabbits running up my back. I just had the oddest feeling.'

Juliet looked closely at her. 'Are you all right?'

Sally laughed. 'Of course. It's — these men. Just for an instant I felt their despair as if it was mine.'

'You'd better give up on the meditation. It's making you hypersensitive.'

'I don't think it's having any effect at all. A bit disappointing, really. Look at these photos. Dice, dominoes, gambling chips and cards; all hand made — I bet gambling was illegal in the prison — and a canvas belt to hide the cards. Here's a photograph of a hand-made rope. Oh, no, a man used it to hang himself. A William O'Meally.' There was a catch in her voice.

'You're taking this far too seriously. These men were here because they deserved to be. They were maximum security prisoners. Murderers, rapists, bushrangers, muggers...'

'They weren't all,' Sally said distressfully. 'Some were only boys, maybe a bit wild, probably petty criminals, but they didn't deserve this.'

Juliet looked at her in surprise, her head tilted to one side consideringly. 'How on earth do you know that?'

'I don't know. I just felt it.'

'You still look a bit odd. Come and sit down before people think you're a loony. I'll get you a coffee from the bar.'

She pushed Sally firmly into a vacant seat. 'Stay there. I'll be back soon. I'd no idea you were so easily upset.' She shook her head wonderingly.

Sally flushed and said quickly, 'I'm not, normally. Sorry, Jules, I'll sit here quietly like a good girl and I promise I'll stop being weird; and I'd love a coffee.'

Juliet gave her a relieved smile and went to queue at the bar.

Sally settled back and watched other passengers around the display. She remembered the booklet and, pulling it out of her jacket pocket, began to flick through the pages.

It was illustrated with a number of old photographs. One caught her attention. A handsome young man with a thick moustache, short curly hair and a strained expression. She stared at the picture, shock waves flowing through her body. The man's eyes were hypnotic, wide set and dark shadowed, staring out of the page with such intense desperation she felt her heart stop.

Breathe, she told herself, breathe. It's a trick of the black and white photography. I've got to stop over-reacting. I'm not this impressionable; it's probably because I'm worried about me and Tim.

She forced her gaze away from the young man's face and began to read what the book said about him. William O'Meally had the distinction of being the most escaped prisoner from St Helena. He'd been sentenced to hang in 1880 for horse theft and murder but this was later commuted to life imprisonment when the murder charge was changed to manslaughter. Unable to be broken, he'd fled from this most escape proof of prisons no less than five times. On three attempts, he'd actually reached the mainland claiming, each time he was recaptured, that there was something he must do to see justice done. Just eighteen years old when sent to St Helena, after so many fruitless bids for freedom, he finally hanged himself in 1882 from a tree on the island, with a rope he'd made himself.

Sally closed her eyes. William O'Meally. It was his rope in the photograph. She suddenly felt ill.

She heard a low cry next to her and opened her eyes to see a dishevelled young man. Gaunt and unshaven, dressed in old-fashioned clothes, he stared at her with shocked eyes. The sight of him was so unexpected she jumped and looked around for Juliet who had nearly reached the counter.

She stared back curiously at the man beside her. She hadn't previously noticed him among the passengers but he looked vaguely familiar. He seemed half starved and filthy; his moustache was bedraggled and his dark curls were shaven close to his head. His clothes looked and smelt as if he'd slept in them for days.

Could he be a stowaway? She dismissed the thought immediately. Stowing away to where? A bay island? Ridiculous. She felt uncomfortable under his scrutiny and turned away.

The strange young man grabbed her arm in a vice-like grip. She tried in vain to free herself. The last thing she needed was some vagrant making a pass at her.

'You're a female!' He sounded appalled. 'You may be wearing trousers but for certain you're not a man.'

Not wanting to make a scene, Sally tried again to pull away but he held on grimly.

'By God, they would not send a woman to that inferno.'

His voice was as rough as a file and he looked near to collapse. She wondered if he was mentally deranged and began to feel decidedly alarmed. At the same time, she couldn't shake an odd sensation of familiarity. Her scalp began to prickle. There was a frighteningly nightmarish feeling to all of this. Even the boat seemed oddly ethereal. Sally felt as if she'd slipped into a waking dream. The situation was becoming bizarre, out of control. She had to get rid of this man.

She took a deep breath to steady her jangled nerves and said firmly, 'If you don't let me go I'll call someone to take you in charge.'

He gave a harsh laugh, which ended in a bout of coughing, and released his hold on her.

'What do you call these, ma'am? It seems I am already taken in charge.'

He held up his arms and she recoiled from the horror of his manacled hands and feet.

The protest that rose to her lips was suddenly stifled by a flash of relieved insight. 'Oh, now I get it.' She almost laughed aloud. No wonder she thought she knew him. She'd probably seen him in TV commercials. The other passengers hadn't appeared to notice her startling companion. Presumably they'd all been on this trip before and were now surreptitiously watching her to see if she'd work it out.

'You really had me going for a minute. I honestly thought you were a lunatic. This is some sort of pageant, isn't it? To amuse the passengers?'

'Ma'am? I do not completely understand your speech.' He was looking her up and down, a concerned frown in his deep brown eyes which were red-rimmed from lack of sleep. 'Do they think you a lad in your strange trousers and jacket? Could they not have realised you're a female?'

Sally noticed the slight tremor in his body, the hoarseness in his voice. She thought, this is a great performance. He could really be exhausted. At the same time she felt uneasy. He was too convincing. It was making her uncomfortable. She said briskly, 'Stop it, I've sussed you. You did a marvellous job but you can drop the act, now. Do you do this every trip? Are you an actor?'

'Can you not see I'm a prisoner, like yourself, pray God have mercy on us both?'

She was embarrassed. Surely he wasn't going to keep this up all the way to the island. It was becoming un-funny.

'I told you, drop it. I'm perfectly happy to talk to you but don't try to keep up the charade. What's your name, anyway?'

'I am William O'Meally.'

Sally started. Why hadn't she realised? That's who he'd reminded her of. He was made up to look like that tragic young prisoner. Of course, they'd use their most famous escapee in the pageant. She felt her anger rising. It wasn't fair. Why couldn't they allow him dignity in death instead of making him a joke for the tourists? She was fed up with this pantomime. She glared at the man and said tartly, 'Oh, yes, I've read about you.'

'I've no doubt of that,' he said frankly. 'I've escaped four times from their so-called escape-proof hell. The newspapers have reported the story.' He leaned closer. 'I shall escape again and see justice done, I promise you. Please, you must help me and save yourself also. I tell you, the island is a hell-hole and not fit for a woman, whatever you may have done.'

His breath was hot against her cheek and she could smell the rank, stale smell of sweat and the sourness of unwashed clothes. She gave an audible gasp. His eyes were *bloodshot*. It was real dirt on his skin. His face had an unnatural, grey pallor. That wasn't make-up. She felt panicky and looked desperately around.

Across the cabin Jules was chatting to someone at the bar, people were laughing, enjoying their day out, looking at the photographs and notices, watching the water foaming against the boat's sides. What's happening? Sally thought. It isn't real, any of this. I'm hallucinating. Her stomach jolted sickeningly. That man beside her was surely too solid for some crazed phantom in her mind. He was suddenly more substantial than her surroundings.

The cabin had begun to take on an unreal, shimmering quality, as if a mist was rising before her eyes.

I'm having a nervous breakdown. She was pleased at her comparative calmness. This will pass. Jules will be back in a minute. I'll snap out of it and when we get back home I'll talk to Tim, get him to recommend a therapist. People survive breakdowns. I'll be fine.

The sounds of the boat; the passengers' voices, the chink of glasses and cups, the throb of the motor, were becoming fainter; other sounds were taking their place. A man's strong voice, raised against the wind. And the shimmering mist thickened and swirled, blotting out the other tourists.

'Pull, you men, pull.'

The creak of oars in rowlocks. The splash of water, suddenly very close to her. A strident shout.

'Hey, you, O'Meally, who the devil do you think you're talking to?'

Sally jerked her head back. Where the hell was the launch? What was she doing in an open boat with sailors in old-fashioned jackets straining at the oars, driving the boat through the ocean swell? Around her, waves rose like mountains as the mist curled back across the sea. She shrank onto the hard bench, terrified.

A man in a dark blue uniform was holding a heavy looking rifle menacingly against the young man's head. Despite his weariness, William looked up and said with cheerful insolence, 'I'm just telling myself what I'd like to do to you if I were not stuck here in chains, Sergeant. I don't think you'd enjoy my little plans.'

'You're a mouth, O'Meally, too cocky by half. They'll take you down a peg or two when we deliver you. Things have changed on the island, me boyo. Mr McDonald's gone and you've got Captain Townley to deal with now. He'll soon knock the impudence out of you. He'll have you in the dark cells for a month and order you flogged until your bones are laid bare. Then you'll change your ways, mark my words.'

'At least in solitary I'll be saved the need to look at the likes of your ugly face.'

The guard showed stained teeth in a snarl. 'Shut your mouth, O'Meally, or I'll shut it for you.' He shouldered his gun and moved away.

Sally, disoriented and frightened, heard the youth whisper.

'There are worse than him on the island and you'll not fool them in that disguise for much longer, girl. You cannot stay a prisoner here. The guards will discover your secret and some of them are brutes. They'll not respect you; likely they'll take you for their own sport, do you understand? They'll have free access to your cell at night. You're a pretty lass, for all your strange ways.' He faltered. 'I — I have a lass of my own with golden hair like yours.' He continued imperatively, 'You can't prevent their abuse. As soon as they take you to be searched tell them you're a woman and demand to see the superintendent. Then they'll have to send you back to Brisbane town.'

She was strangely affected by the urgency of his voice, She whispered back, 'Please tell me, who are you?'

'I told you. I am William O'Meally. Has this dreadful experience turned your brain?' He peered anxiously into her face. 'No, for your eyes are clear, thank God. Whatever happens to me, save yourself. Give up your masquerade.'

His voice was strangely compelling. Sally felt an odd sense of comfort in his presence. He seemed so worried for her. She thought, he'd be really handsome if he wasn't in such a shocking state. Even like this, he's attractive. The story she'd read about him flickered into her mind. How could he be William O'Meally? That poor boy was dead. But he looked exactly like the photograph, as far as she could tell in his filthy condition; and his speech was old-fashioned, its rhythm strange to her ears. She looked down. The ugly metal shackles were real enough. The manacles had severely bruised his wrists. He was real and alive to her and she wanted terribly to help him. They were fellow conspirators in a violent, confusing, alien world

He looked so anxious, Sally said impulsively, 'Yes, I will. I'll do as you suggest.'

A smile spread across his tired young face and she thought how vulnerable he looked. She touched his hand and her fingers felt the cold iron at his wrists.

He dropped his voice lower. 'Help me, ma'am; you are my only hope. I have been imprisoned for another's wrong and I must see justice done. I nearly reached home this time but put my trust in a friend who betrayed me to the police. Please say you will help me when you return to the mainland.'

'Of course.' Sally nodded vehemently. 'I'll do whatever I can for you.'

'Promise me. Say you promise.'

'I promise.'

'Good.' He smiled with relief and she felt his fingers turn under hers and squeeze her hand gratefully. 'I am in your debt.'

The guard had returned, unnoticed by them both. Without warning, he brought the butt of his rifle down hard onto William's temple, knocking him sideways. Blood gushed down his face and he raised his manacled hands to ward off a second blow.

Sally screamed, 'No, no, William!' Again she was assailed by a sickening feeling of disorientation. That strange sea mist was rolling back over them, shining and pulsing like a live thing. Sally clung to the hard wooden seat but her fingers scrabbled in mid air. She saw William's eyes, glowing in his gaunt face. They were wide with sudden confusion. She reached for him but he seemed insubstantial, his image hazy and shadowed, dissolving even as she touched him.

'Where are you? Wait.' Her hand closed on thin air. 'Oh, please, don't go. William!' She closed her eyes to shut out the dreadful, churning scene.

The steady splash of oars was drowned out by the chug of the tourist boat's engine. Juliet said worriedly, 'Whatever's the matter, Sal? I've got your coffee.'

Sally's eyes flew open. She stared uncomprehendingly at her friend for a second or two then burst into hysterical tears.

Chapter 13

Sally dried her eyes. 'I'm sorry. Have I made a complete fool of myself?'

'Don't be silly. Hardly anyone noticed.'

Juliet had helped her back to the small stern area which had been deserted by the other passengers who'd moved inside to escape the weather. She'd sat with her arm around her friend's shoulders, a look of deep concern on her face as Sally spilled out her story.

'I was screaming out. I must have scared the life out of everyone.'

'Sally, you weren't screaming. When I came back you were asleep, muttering something. That's all. Then you burst into tears.'

'It was William O'Meally, the boy in the photograph. He was sitting right next to me.'

Juliet shook her head firmly. 'He certainly was not. No one else saw him, I didn't see him. You went to sleep reading about him and had a vivid dream.'

'He was real. I can still feel his fingers on my arm. He hurt me. He smelt awful, too, and looked as if he hadn't eaten for days. His face — I can *see* the sweat and the stubble.'

'A dream. More like a nightmare. All this metaphysical stuff you're doing; obviously it's affecting you on an unconscious level, making you more aware of details.'

Sally opened her mouth to protest then stopped. William's voice echoed in her mind. 'Help me. Say you promise.' He'd sounded so sincere, so urgent. Could it have been just a vivid dream? She was here on the launch. The eyes that watched her with such anxiety weren't William's wide-set brown eyes but Juliet's bright blue ones. She reached out a hand and Juliet clasped it warmly. She could feel the other girl's cool skin and the pressure of her fingers. This was real. How could the other have been real as well?

'Kaitlin talks about heightened awareness,' Sally admitted slowly.

'See? It's possible. You had an experience of heightened awareness and dreamt in extraordinary detail. Simple explanation. Either that or you're telling me you talked to the ghost of a man who died over a hundred years ago.'

'He was no ghost.' Sally rubbed her arm in memory of the young man's hard grip. 'I could touch him.'

'Well it wasn't him in person or he'd be a little old — *very* old — man, barely able to stand up. I gather he wasn't?'

Sally began to laugh. 'No. He was young and extremely good looking and intense, and attractive, in spite of his filthy clothes.'

'Just as you'd expect him to be, and that's what you dreamt.'

'I really was asleep?'

'Cross my heart. Your eyes were closed and you were mumbling. Until you started crying I'll bet no one took the slightest notice of you. I told the only pair that seemed interested that you'd had a fight with your boyfriend and you'd be okay.'

'Thanks, Jules. For a minute I thought I was going mad.'

'You've been mad for years. I'm used to it.' Juliet smiled and patted her shoulder.

She sighed. 'I expect it is because of Tim. You were right there.' The thought crossd her mind that it wasn't really Tim. It was herself. Tim was perfectly content with their relationship. She was the one who was worrying at it like a dog with a bone, discontented for no obvious reason. She'd made a complete fool of herself the other night, breaking down like that. What was the matter with her? Tim had been wonderful about it. Since then he'd looked at her sideways a few times but hadn't pressed her to explain. He'd probably put it down to 'woman's troubles'. She owed him an explanation but wasn't sure she had one. It was all so nebulous. And now, this! She felt a tug of anxiety.

Juliet watched Sally's expressive face, reading her thoughts with the ease of long friendship. She said quietly, 'You've got to sort that out. You're not having a row, are you?'

'Tim never quarrels. He slides out from under any time there's a sign of one. Because of Giles. He's a bit of a pig, really, and he dominates his family. The original male chauvinist. Tim's oversensitive; he learnt as a kid to avoid trouble.'

'I don't know Tim's parents well but I must say I didn't warm to Giles Horan the couple of times we've met.'

'He's okay if you stand up to him but his family never does. Ellie is complacent and Amanda mutters a protest then collapses when Giles senses a promising lead and takes her up. It must be frustrating for the poor man. I seem to be the only one who can handle him.'

'That's because you don't see him very often,' Juliet said wisely. 'It'd be a different situation if you lived with him all the time. You might shut up to avoid the constant arguments, too. You be careful, Sal. What if Tim turns out to be like his father?'

'Tim? I can't see it.' She chuckled.

One of the boat's crew came out of the cabin. 'We'll be docking in a few minutes. Are you coming ashore?'

'Yes, of course.' Sally got to her feet. 'I'm fine now. Come on, Jules, let's go and look at your island.'

The fifty or so passengers disembarked and walked across the jetty and down a long stone causeway which stretched over the wide mud flats to the island. The causeway, like all the island's constructions had been built by prisoners.

The first thing that struck Sally was the extreme quiet. Apart from the chatter of the tourists, the only sounds were the ocean, an occasional bird call and a sharp breeze whispering over the island.

The clouds were dispersing before the wind and patches of pale blue sky were letting sun shafts through. The ground, once covered by dense scrub, had been extensively cleared during the prison's history and previously cultivated fields were now home to rough grasses and tall weeds. As the sky cleared, all around the green island Moreton Bay sparkled deep blue in the morning sunshine.

The passengers were divided into two groups and led at a brisk pace to view the various ruins. There was a quarry close by the jetty, now filled with fresh water which reflected grassy banks and a low rock wall. A well preserved lime kiln of red-brown bricks was flanked with great charcoal-grey blocks of beach-rock from the quarry.

'Next stop, the cemetery,' their guide said.

'Would you rather not?' Juliet asked.

'I'm all right.' Sally walked quickly after the others. 'I know he hanged himself and he's buried up there. Anyway, you were right, Jules, it was a dream — or a nightmare.'

On the southern shore, on a sweep of high ground overlooking the bay and the distant mainland, there were two separate cemeteries behind neat white fences. The smaller one had headstones of marble and granite which bore the names of civilian children and one young woman for, until 1890, the warders' families had lived on St Helena and there had been children, even a small wooden school. These headstones had been relocated to their present position some years earlier owing to the erosion by the sea of the original site and the loss of headstones tumbling down the cliff into the water.

The other burial ground was larger with some forty sandstone crosses in rows. There were many gaps where crosses had been souvenired in previous years. Others had fallen and were lying among the sparse weeds which struggled in the sandy ground. The crosses had no names but were distinguished by chiselled numbers; the prisoners' sole identification.

'That one,' the guide pointed, 'belongs to the prison's most celebrated escapee, William O'Meally. He got away five times in the two years he was a prisoner. Ended up by hanging himself from a tree with a rope he made himself.'

One of the group said, 'So he did escape.'

'He was a lifer. In those days you wouldn't want to be a prisoner on St Helena. Attitudes were different and punishments could be brutal. He took the only way out.'

A woman looked around at the peaceful green island set like a jewel in the blue waters of the bay. 'It's beautiful,' she said. 'Surely the scenery alone would be some compensation.'

Stupid bitch! Sally thought savagely, surprising herself.

'I doubt the prisoners thought so,' the guide said drily.

Sally was staring at William's stone cross. 'And he — the prisoners are actually buried here? These crosses haven't been relocated?'

'No, this is the actual site of the prisoners' cemetery.' He touched the sandstone marker and said apologetically, 'We don't believe there'd be anything left of the bodies by now — there's a heavy lime content in the soil.'

Sally nodded slowly. That would put any fantasies to rest, she was sure. A young man had come briefly to this place, had not accepted its regime but had finally come to lie here to be dissolved into the soil of the island from which he'd tried so determinedly to escape. Poor William.

His voice echoed in her mind. "I have been imprisoned for another man's wrong and must see justice done."

And she had promised to help him.

'It's too late for justice now, William,' she whispered to the cross. 'You went to heaven's judgement a long time ago. I hope somehow it balanced out for you somewhere along the way. What's done is done and I came here a hundred and fourteen years too late.'

She shut her eyes briefly. William's haggard face rose against her closed lids and she felt a pang of regret for a young life wasted.

'Have you done your mourning?' Juliet asked softly.

'Yes.' She smiled at her friend. 'Just saying goodbye.'

They turned and followed the rest of the group.

The tree where William O'Meally had finally ended his unhappy life was a huge Moreton Bay fig. They paused under its spreading branches to see where, according to history, the young man had died. Sally felt a wave of sadness and shuddered. She moved away, a lump in her throat. It wasn't right, couldn't be right, that such a tragedy had taken place.

After that she found a sameness about the ruins. All but one of the original wooden structures had fallen into decay or been dismantled by the last of the prisoners who must, she thought, have been delighted to have the privilege of actually tearing down their gaol. All that was left were stone walls, crumbling chimneys, the remains of the huge baker's oven, badly damaged by a large fig tree which had seeded itself in the ruins. Now grass grew where cells and corridors had been and iron bars rusted in broken windows.

You ought to see it now, Sally told William silently. You wouldn't have any trouble escaping this lot. Lift the bars out and stow away on a tourist boat.

The sun was now quite hot and she sat down on the grass in the shade of a stone-block wall of the blacksmith's shop. She was worn out with the heat, the long walk and the memory of the distressing experience — she was still reluctant to admit to herself it was only a dream — on the boat.

Juliet joined her. 'Aren't you coming to see the rest?'

'I'm tired and all the ruins look the same. I think I'll sit here for a while.'

'There's a display in a building further up the road — artifacts and photographs.'

'I don't really want to see any more. I'll wait here for you.'

'All right.' Juliet stood up. 'It'll probably do you good to have a rest. I'll see you soon.'

Sally leaned back against the wall and idly watched the other passengers walking further up the rise. A bird was singing in a tree behind the ruined building and, as the group's voices receded, the island became very still.

The sunlight seemed to be creating a curious shimmering effect and she rubbed her eyes. What a strange trick of the light. She couldn't hear the bird any more but a different sound grew in her ears, becoming so loud it seemed directly behind her.

Escape from the Past

She hastily got to her feet. She knew that sound. It was a forge. The rush of fire, the sharp hiss of steam as red hot metal was plunged into water, the clang of hammer against iron, the shouts of men.

She spun around. The empty windows gaped, sunshine poured down into the roofless ruin, a rusted buggy frame stood outside the door.

It's happening again, she thought, close to panic. I'm hearing things from the past.

A man came around the corner. He had a thick moustache and was dressed in a shirt and trousers of a coarse dirty-white cloth, patched, and printed with faded numbers and the prison's name. His cheeks and chin were clean shaven and for a moment she didn't recognise him. Then she caught her breath.

'I'm asleep,' she said forcefully 'asleep in the sun against the ruin of the smithy. This is a dream. I can wake up any time I want to.'

'It's you.' He stopped in front of her. 'Did you not do as I told you?'

Her scalp began to prickle as she stared at him and her heart thudded painfully. Fear tightened her throat but she forced her voice to sound calm. 'Hello, William,' she managed. 'What are you doing here?'

He gave a short laugh. 'You have a strange humour. And where else would you expect to find me?'

She hesitated, confused. It was insane to believe she was having a conversation with a man who'd been dead for over a century. And yet, he was waiting, one eyebrow raised quizzically. She said feebly, 'They were bringing you back in chains — now you seem to be walking around free.'

'Ah, I understand your meaning. It's true, I'm to be punished and no doubt it will be severe.' He grinned but there was no humour in it. 'But they cannot pass their foul sentence until the visiting justice comes again so I'm merely reprimanded and sent to clean myself up and get back to work.'

If it's a dream, Sally thought rationally, it's what Kaitlin calls a lucid dream, where you watch yourself dreaming. It can't hurt me. I should go along with it, see what happens. That wouldn't be crazy, would it? Her panic slowly subsided.

'Can't you just walk out?'

'What, over the stockade wall and the guards watching from their towers, allowing me to stroll away?'

Sally remembered there had once been a high stockade wall surrounding the prison cells, workshops and exercise yards, with guard posts set strategically to prevent escapes.

'What will they do to you?' She asked bleakly.

The poor, frightened lass, William thought. She's in such trouble and yet she's concerning herself with my fate. 'Are you worrying for me?' His eyes softened. 'That's kind. I doubt they'll be satisfied to cut my rations or deny me my sugar and tobacco. The justice will bring the government's flagellator, him we call Annie the Artist, for the pretty stripes he puts so neatly across a man's back.'

Sally gave a cry of protest. 'But — that's wrong. Wicked!'

William shrugged. ''Tis the rules. I don't make 'em.' He saw her horrified expression and immediately regretted his bluntness. I've upset her. I'd do better to heed that brute of a guard and keep my trap shut. She's a woman with delicate senses. What's she doing here? She's not the look of a criminal. More like a lady with her fine skin and soft hands, in spite of her queer speech and garb. Doubtless she cut her hair for a disguise or she's lately had the fever. He rubbed his chin reflectively. She's a strange one. But that ring she's wearing, that's quality. By the looks of it, she's engaged to be married.

He had a sudden idea. It might be better for her to learn what she's in for if she remains here. Perhaps, if I do scare the wits out of her, she'll save herself. She should be worrying for her own sake, not for mine.

He said, 'It's not so bad. I can take a beating from *Annie*.'

In spite of her revulsion, Sally was puzzled. She asked, 'Why *Annie*?'

'It's a name we call him, a joke. To let him know we don't fear what he can do, that he's no more strength in his arms than a girl, d'you see?' William smiled ruefully. 'Unhappily, it's not true. He's a brute of a gentleman. Annie'll give me fifty of his best and I'll spend a month in the black hole under the ground on bread and water. After all, I'm giving their little paradise a bad name. But they won't break me and I'll be leaving their tender care yet again as soon as I can arrange it.'

'William, you can't keep this up. Isn't there another way?'

'Not for me. My sentence was for all my life so there's no sense in waiting for it to be over. It never will be. It's natural for a caged wild thing to want to be free.'

'But — they punish you. It's horrible.'

'Ma'am, they cannot punish me worse than the day they tore me from my sweet Rose and sent me here. You'd do better to think of your own plight. For the Lord's sake, tell them you're a woman.'

Sally felt overwhelmed. She couldn't even begin to explain it to him. He had enough to contend with. She said merely, 'They know. I'll be leaving this afternoon.'

His eyes gleamed triumphantly. 'Then you can help me.'

They had been talking in low voices, for fear of being overheard. In the distance the sound of men shouting came on the breeze followed by the crack of rifle fire.

William paused, listening intently, then he relaxed.

'It will be a fight broken out in the yard again. This is a violent place and every day some poor devil's nerves are tried past breaking point. The warders will soon end it.' He grabbed her wrist urgently. 'Now, listen to me. I prayed for a miracle and you've appeared and you swore you'd help.'

'What can I do?'

He took an envelope from his pocket and thrust it into her hand.

'I wrote it before I was captured but I never got to post it. It's for my brother, Walter. He's the only one who can do anything for me now. When you are back in Brisbane town, you must get it to him. He'll know what to do.'

'How...?' Sally bit her lip. She'd been going to ask how on earth she could post a letter to someone who'd been dead for years. Her fingers closed around the envelope. William was gazing at her en-treatingly. She wasn't about to destroy his hopes. She'd take it, to please him. The thought flickered, What's the harm? It's only a dream. She tucked the letter into her bag. 'All right, I'll take it.'

'I'll not forget you. You've done me a great service.'

The noise of the smithy was hardly discernible now. The shout-ing from the prison yard had stopped. In the distance an echo remained of cattle lowing and a bell clanging with a hollow sound. The bird had recommenced its loud melody in the tree nearby.

This time Sally recognised the sudden sense of unreality, of the world slowly turning upside-down, dissolving before her eyes. I'm about to wake up, she told herself. No need to panic. In a few min-utes everything will be normal again. Just hang on.

She felt her wrist suddenly freed. William stared at her, a star-tled expression in his dark eyes. He slowly reached out and touched her face.

'What — what is happening?' He asked hoarsely. 'This is not the same — and yet, the walls, the blacksmith's shop — I recognise its shell. What has happened to make it such a ruin?' He looked wildly around. 'Where is the prison? The stockade walls?' He swung back to her. 'Who are you? Are you making this happen? Have I caught some madness?'

The odd shimmering was around them both. Sally tried to speak but her voice made no sound. William cried out, 'Where are you going? Wait!'

She felt his hands clutching at her but only very faintly.

'My God, you must be a ghost or a witch. Holy Mother, protect me!'

With a last desperate effort he brought his face close to hers and she could feel his shock and despair.

'Whatever you are, from heaven or hell, help me, for I'll accept aid from the devil himself to change my situation.'

Chapter 14

S ally ran up the long road as if she was being pursued by all her greatest terrors. She found the tour group examining prison relics in what had once been the chief warder's quarters and touched Juliet on the shoulder.

The other girl turned, her welcoming smile vanishing as she saw Sally's flushed and frightened face.

'It's happened again?'

'Yes.' She fought to control her breath. 'I'm going crazy, Jules, I know it.'

'Hang on.' Juliet quickly led her outside. 'We've got to get you away from here. Something's triggering your imagination in a really strange way.'

'I want to go home.' Sally's eyes filled with tears. She pushed a trembling hand against her forehead.

'We can't until the boat leaves but we'll go down to the jetty. They'll serve lunch soon then we'll be back in Brisbane before you know it.'

Sally clung to her, her eyes staring. 'I'm losing my mind, aren't I?'

Juliet said seriously, 'I shouldn't think so, because you're aware of having these attacks. I'm no expert and I may be wrong but I

think, if you really were crazy, you wouldn't be able to tell the difference between reality and fantasy.'

Sally hugged her. 'Thank goodness you're here. You're so sensible.'

'Well, you seem quite normal to me; just frightened. I honestly
think you're overstressed and you've fallen asleep and had a couple of wild dreams. When I left you you were looking exhausted
and leaning up against that wall — I bet you just drifted off again
and took up where you left off before. I've done that — heaps of
people must.'

'Yes, that's true.' She was comforted by Juliet's prosaic explanation. 'It must have been that.'

'Tell me what it was about this time. Same man? Your handsome prisoner?'

'Yes.' Sally described the incident as they walked down the road
to the jetty where the ferry was waiting.

Juliet frowned. 'He gave you a letter?'

'I put it in my bag. It was so real, I swear, if I looked, it'd be
there.'

'So, look.'

'I'm scared. What — what if the letter is there?'

'Then I imagine you're set for life. Think. You can sell your
story to the magazines, give exclusives to TV shows — "How I talked
to a prisoner from 1882 — and he gave me a letter".'

'It's not going to be there, is it?'

'I'd say not.' Juliet's eyes twinkled. 'But I don't know how you
can resist the urge to look. That should convince you it was all a
dream.'

Sally stopped. 'It's silly. I almost wish it was there.' She opened
her bag and rummaged for a few minutes, then looked up.

Her mixed emotions pulled her face into what Juliet thought
was relieved disappointment. 'Not there?'

'No.'

'You do surprise me!' Juliet linked her arm in Sally's. 'Come on,
we'll get a coffee and wait for the others. Better still,' she scanned
her friend's face, 'a glass of wine would be more the ticket.'

'That's interesting.' Kaitlin's voice was calm. 'Sounds like a past life thing to me.'

'Past life?'

'People sometimes get very strong feelings, vibrations, if you like, for a particular place or time in history. I don't know where you stand on past lives but I believe it means they were actually in that place, at that time, in a former existence.'

'You think I was a prisoner on St Helena?' Sally asked.

'Either that or you knew this man William. You connected with him again as soon as you saw his photograph and had a vivid memory of a past life experience. Have you seen him again?'

'No, not since we left the prison.'

'It was probably triggered by the island. I have a friend who does hypnotherapy. She could regress you and see what turns up, if you want to take this any further.'

'She'll think I'm a nutter.'

'She won't.' Kaitlin laughed. 'This sort of thing is far more common than you'd think. Look at the number of articles you read in women's magazines these days, even in scientific journals. There are all sorts of well-researched cases of past life memory: go and look in your local library. There are dozens of books on the subject.'

'Do you think it's important?'

Kaitlin hesitated. 'Honestly, Sally, I don't know. I think, myself, that finding out about past lives for mere curiosity is a waste of time and doesn't necessarily help you to deal with the present. It's more an ego thing, you know, wanting to know if you were Cleopatra. So many people claim to have been that particular lady, it's become highly suspect. As far as I'm concerned, if you haven't dealt with issues in the past, you'll get them again in a way that's relevant to you in the present. What matters is, do *you* think it's important? This has been thrust on you and you've been thoroughly upset, I can tell by your voice, even through the phone.'

'I don't know what to do. I can't stop thinking about him.'

'Well, it's entirely up to you. If you think it would help to know if you were with this man in a former life, then call me. Take your time and go with your feelings. If you decide to see Chris, I'll come with you and hold your hand.'

'That would be a help. Thanks Kaitlin.'

'Don't thank me,' Kaitlin said frankly, 'you couldn't keep me away. I'm fascinated.'

A car drew up outside and a door slammed. Sally jumped.

'I have to go. Tim's just come back from the shops.'

'Haven't you told him about this?'

'Not a word and I'm not going to. He'd think I was psychotic or something and want me to have treatment.'

'You'd thought of doing that anyway.'

'Well, it hasn't come to that yet and I couldn't stand him watching me all the time and worrying.'

'It's your life, Sally. Call me when you've decided what to do.'

Tim's key turned in the lock and the front door opened. Sally hung up the receiver and went into the kitchen. A few minutes later Tim came in with a bag of groceries.

'Who's cooking tonight?'

'Why don't we eat out, Tim?'

'Can't. I've got to study.'

'We could hurry back.'

'We wouldn't. We'd want another wine and another coffee and we'd linger on until I was all mellow and randy.' He paused. 'Speaking of which ...'

'I'd rather not.'

He pulled out a chair and sat facing her, his elbows on the table. He watched her for a moment without expression, then asked quietly, 'When are we going to sleep together again?'

Sally turned to the stove. She wasn't ready to deal with this yet. 'I don't know.'

'Look at me, Sal.'

She moved back to the table and sat opposite him.

'It's been four days.' His voice took on an edge. 'I don't know what's going on. I accepted you were upset about something the other night, although you wouldn't talk about it, but you look fine now. I — need you, Sally. I lie awake just thinking about you and I want you back.'

'I know.' She reached out a hand and rubbed his arm. 'I'm sorry, Tim, I just need my own space at the moment.'

'Is it something I've done?'

'Of course not.' Was it? She didn't know. 'I need more time to sort myself out. I'm a bit stressed, that's all.'

His eyes were grave. 'You need a thorough check-up. Why don't you make an appointment at the clinic and let them run some tests?'

Sally felt her stomach muscles knot together. 'I'm okay, Tim, I don't need a check-up.'

'I think you do. I'm worried about you.'

Her tone was sharp. 'Don't. Don't worry about me. I'm quite capable of looking after myself. It's up to me if I want to go for a check-up.'

'Look, love, I can see you're showing signs of stress, anxiety. I should know.'

Sally got up, feeling an urgent need to escape. She took a hasty step towards the door, then swung angrily back to him. 'What makes you such an expert on my feelings? A few text books?' She was shouting, unable to stop herself. 'Just let me sort it out my way, will you?'

He dropped his eyes but not before she saw the sudden hurt in them.

'All right, Sally, I didn't mean to interfere. I'm sorry.'

'Don't be sorry.' She felt exasperated to the point of fury. Why did he always have to be so — accommodating? No wonder it infuriated Giles. 'I don't want to sleep with you; you're worried. Why the hell should you be sorry?'

There was some relief, at least, in banging the kitchen door as she ran out and she slammed it as hard as she could.

In the privacy of her room she stood for a moment, rubbing her arm; then, with an almost morbid curiosity, pushed up her sleeve and pressed her fingers once again into the long dark bruises.

Half an hour later she found Tim still in the kitchen, making a sauce for the spaghetti bubbling on the stove. He looked at her, waiting for her to make the first move.

Sally crossed the room and put her arms around him.

'I'm sorry, Tim.'

'I know.' He stroked her hair and kissed her forehead. As she felt his arms tighten around her, she pulled away.

He gave her a resigned look and turned back to the stove. 'Dinner's nearly ready.'

His voice was casual and Sally felt like kicking herself for wounding him.

'Will you set the table?'

She rang Kaitlin later that evening. Tim was studying in the lounge room so she went into her room and used her mobile.

'I've decided to see Chris,' she said as soon as the other woman answered.

'All right, I'll set it up and call you back.'

'Use my mobile.' She gave the number. 'Whatever time she can see me, as soon as possible.'

Kaitlin called back after a few minutes.

'Tomorrow, one o'clock. Can you get time off work?'

'I'll take it,' Sally said grimly. 'This is an emergency.'

Sally heard a gentle voice reaching through the mists of her brain.

'Three...two...one...that's excellent, Sally, you're wide awake now and feeling very relaxed and happy. Open your eyes, dear.'

She stretched, feeling peaceful and totally comfortable. Her eyes fluttered open to see the face of the hypnotherapist smiling at her.

'Is it all over?'

'You sound as if I'm a dentist.' Chris switched off the tape recorder. 'Yes, it's all over and the patient will recover.'

Sally glanced around the elegant decor which was ultra modern and uncluttered, an expensive professional suite. She'd expected fringed curtains hiding mysterious doorways, soft lamp light, or perhaps even candles — and the exotic suggestion of incense. She'd been surprised to find the hypnotherapist's rooms at the top of an inner city high-rise with a commanding view across the roof tops to the river. She'd been greeted by an efficient woman of fifty in a fashionable suit, sheer black stockings and high heels, whom Kaitlin had introduced as Chris.

Chris had seen Sally's expression and grinned.

'I'm sorry, I left the scarves and gypsy skirt at home.'

'Oh, dear, yes, I was expecting something like that.'

'I'd scare my clients away,' Chris told her. 'Most of them are professional business people. I don't just regress people, you know. I often treat people for stress and anxiety disorders, panic attacks, phobias — but,' she'd taken Sally's hand comfortingly, 'this is much more fun. Now, let's see what we can find out about you.'

Now Sally smiled up at her. 'Was I all right?'

'That depends on what you mean. You went under very well and told us quite a bit about yourself, one way and another. Did you know you and your Tim were once brother and sister? However, there was no William O'Meally and no St Helena Island in there.'

She ejected a cassette from the recorder. 'It's all on here — it's up to you whether you want to listen to it or not. Depends on your curiosity. However, these, what should I call them, dreams? visitations? They're not past life events as far as I can tell and you say he's not a ghost. I think the only other possibility is, as your friend thought, remarkably vivid dreams brought about by emotional strain and an over active imagination. We can certainly work on that if you'd like; but possibly, even after this session, you'll find yourself very much improved anyway.'

'Thanks, Chris.' Sally picked up the tape. 'Do you really believe all this past life stuff?'

'I should do,' Chris said soberly. 'I hear enough of it and I can't think of any other explanation for the things people know about past events and times. Some say it's simply information picked up and stored in the subconscious over a lifetime, but that doesn't explain children's experiences. Anyway,' she smiled, 'whatever I believe, what I do helps people so that's the only reason I need.' She saw Sally and Kaitlin to the door. 'Best of luck in your search, dear. Let me know if I can help you in any way.'

Search? Sally thought as they rode the lift to the ground floor. What search?

Chapter 15

Sally sat on the sofa and turned the cassette over in her hands. She had a curious reluctance to listen to it. Perhaps Kaitlin had been right and it was an indulgence of the ego to want to go back — perhaps it showed an inability to deal with the present. She was intrigued by the idea that, encapsulated in this thin plastic sheath, was a part of her she had no memory of, even a past relationship with Tim as his sister. Or possibly he'd been her sister; Chris hadn't said which of them had been the female.

Kaitlin had driven her home without mentioning the session at all. She'd offered to chauffeur her in case she might be upset by anything that came up and need help to get home. Sally couldn't remember a thing about it and was at once glad and sorry.

I could simply put the tape on and hear what it was all about, she thought. I don't even know if I believe in past lives but, if I listened to it, I'm sure I'd know if I was making it up, imagining the whole thing.

She got up and went to the phone. Juliet answered promptly. 'Sally! Tell me all about it.'

'There's nothing to tell. Chris was highly professional and lives, like a witch, at the top of a glass tower. She wore a smart city business suit and she didn't swing a watch or a crystal in front of me and tell me I was getting sleepy. We just sat down in super comfortable arm chairs and she told me to relax while she talked — and that's all I remember until I came to and she gave me a tape of the session.'

'Fascinating.' Juliet murmured. 'So, what's on the tape?'

'I haven't heard it.'

'Oh, Sally, how can you be so un-curious?'

'She told me all I wanted to know. I don't have any past connection with William and I was never on St Helena — or, if I was, it didn't come out. She also mentioned in passing that Tim and I had been brother and sister in a former life.'

'Are you going to put the tape on?'

'I don't know. It might trigger even worse dreams. She agreed with you; if it wasn't a past life memory and he wasn't a ghost, then it was probably all just a dream.'

'But you're still not convinced.'

'I didn't tell you before, I don't know why. Where he gripped my arm on the boat, I've got a bruise.'

'Sally!'

'A clear mark of his fingers,' she continued flatly. 'It hurt then and it's still tender. At first I thought I must have gripped my own arm, in my sleep, until I noticed the marks go the wrong way. *Someone* sat beside me and no one else saw him but he held my arm so tightly the marks are still there.'

'Did you tell Chris? Kaitlin?'

'No. I don't know what to think. A ghost couldn't do that, could it?'

'Are you sure you didn't do it to yourself?'

'I'd have had to twist myself in knots — and my hand is smaller.'

Juliet was silent. Then she said, 'Gosh!'

'Gosh it is.'

'Look,' Juliet hesitated, 'it's just a thought and I know he's only my brother — but Peter is really good at this sort of thing. I mean, listening, helping out — and he's interested in psychic stuff. He might have a clue as to what's going on. He's done a course in psychology as well.'

'I don't think so.' Sally felt her cheeks redden. 'I wouldn't know where to start.'

'I don't want to push you but it sounds more serious than I thought. Promise me you'll at least think about it.'

'Okay, I'll think about it.'

'Do you want to come over later for a cuppa?'

'Why not? Tim's always studying these nights; and I need to pay the rent. I forgot this morning. I could stick the cheque under the door of the real estate office on the way over.'

'After dinner, then. See you soon.'

Sally remembered she hadn't even made out the rent cheque. She replaced the receiver and found her handbag, unzipping the special inner pocket where she kept her cheque book. As she pulled it out, an envelope which had been tucked in behind it dropped into her lap.

She picked it up, her heart racing. She didn't remember putting the letter there; it must have been an instinctive desire to keep it as safe as possible in the most secure place. She hadn't thought to unzip the hidden inner pocket when Juliet had challenged her on St Helena.

Now she held the envelope gingerly. Square, cream in colour, it had two pale red one-penny stamps stuck in the right-hand corner. She looked at them wonderingly. The address was scratched with a fine nib dipped in black ink. Mr W.T. O'Meally, Glendale Farm, Bell's Creek, Queensland.

She was holding William's letter.

Sally sipped at a mug of coffee, her eyes fixed on the envelope on the kitchen table. Several times she'd reached out to touch it, feeling the rough quality of the paper, stunned at the enormity of the events which had left her in such a predicament.

It's not possible, her mind repeated numbly. William wasn't real. 'Remarkably vivid dreams', Chris said. Not real. She shut her eyes as tightly as she could. If this was another dream she'd will the letter away.

When she cautiously opened her eyes the envelope with its penny stamps was still there, challenging her to prove it false. The afternoon sun had worked its way around to the kitchen window and was highlighting dancing dust motes. She felt its warmth on her shoulders. The table was reassuringly solid under her hands.

She wasn't asleep.

'*It's true!*' Fear and excitement flooded through her, overpowering all other emotions. She gave a loud gasp and pressed her hands to her mouth, then dropped them again to snatch up the letter.

'William.' She breathed his name with awe. It had actually happened. The letter was the proof. She hadn't dreamt it, wasn't having a nervous breakdown. She was beautifully and completely sane — and totally vindicated.

'Wait till you see this, Jules,' she crowed. 'William was real. Somehow he was alive and talked to me.' She paused. 'Why me? How come he picked the very time I was on St Helena to start appearing?'

She remembered something she'd read in the booklet and ran to fetch it from her room. She leafed frantically through it, quickly scanning the pages. When she found the date she'd been looking for she sat back, breathing hard. Now she knew the answer to her question, what was she going to do about it? William had certainly seemed alive on the boat and again on the island but cold reason told her otherwise.

I promised, she thought unhappily. I promised William I'd help him. He trusted me to post his letter for him. I can't and now he's dead. A slow tear slipped down her cheek. Would it have made a difference? That was the source of the terrible weight she felt inside her. If the letter had been delivered then, in 1882, would it have saved William from hanging himself?

'It wasn't my fault. Everything got mixed up and I don't know how.'

She fingered her arm. The bruises were fading. Soon there'd be nothing to show how a young man, wild with despair, had gripped her and made her promise.

A promise was important to Sally. She always followed through on her commitments. It was a matter of trust.

'What did you write to Walter?' She asked. 'If I hadn't bumbled into your life, would you have somehow got this to him? Would it have helped you?'

She gently moved the envelope with a finger. William was long dead and Walter too, but they might have descendents and this letter rightly belonged to them. But how could she explain it? She couldn't say she found it tucked in an old book or in a junk shop — it was obvious the paper and the stamps were new. The letter was in mint condition, albeit a little crushed and marked from being hidden in William's clothes. So well hidden it had avoided detection in the customary search undergone by every prisoner on arrival at St Helena.

She picked up the envelope and turned it over. She had to know or she'd go crazy wondering if she'd inadvertently caused William to take his life by her inability to fulfill her promise.

It wasn't difficult to ease the flap open. She drew out a single sheet of paper, closely written in a flowing script. She took a deep breath and began to read.

Red,

I cannot write much. I am on the run. I escaped again from that place of torment and this time I came so near to you. I sought refuge with Jack d'Arcy, and he rode to find you, or so I thought, but the troopers came instead and I barely escaped out the back window.

Red, I figure that Jack betrayed me to the police, and it must have been him who laid for me and put a bullet in my back that night, after he parted from you. He always wanted Rose and had made up his mind to put me out of the way forever and have his chance with her.

You must find out the truth of this and take the evidence to Stapleton. Look after my sweet Rose and move heaven and

earth to bring me back to my dear love.
We are all in your hands, now. I know you will not fail.
Give my love to our dear ma.
Your brother,
Billy.

Sally felt the colour drain from her face, leaving her cold and sick.

'It would have made a difference,' she whispered. 'If the letter had got to Walter and Jack had been made to tell the truth.' She stopped. What truth? She had no idea. The booklet merely said William had been sentenced to hang but had instead been sent to St Helena for life and had been the island's most famous escapee. The dates of his five escape attempts had been listed. After the last attempt, he'd hanged himself.

He'd had something he must do, to see justice done. Was this something to do with his false friend, Jack d'Arcy, who, instead of riding to Walter, had gone to the police?

Sally bowed her head in grief for the sad young man whose world she'd been briefly thrust into in ways she still couldn't fathom.

I failed him, she thought, and I couldn't help it. He wasn't just betrayed by Jack but by me as well.

Had he waited, confident she'd get his message through, putting his trust in her? How could he have understood the extraordinary turn of events. She didn't understand it herself.

'I'm sorry, William, I'm so sorry.'

Suddenly Sally lifted her head. She'd given her word to help him. Perhaps she still could — if there was any possible way — she was going to give it her very best shot.

Chapter 16

P eter Ryan gave Sally a brotherly peck on the cheek and drew her into his living room. It was a comfortable room, neat, but not intimidatingly so, with deep lounge chairs, a worn rug with a floral pattern, a small TV set, a crucifix on the wall. A bookshelf was crammed with well-read volumes.

Sally sat gingerly on the edge of a chair and glanced at him. It always surprised her how like Juliet he was with his thick dark hair, humorous blue eyes and the crooked smile they both shared. He was wearing casual clothes, grey corduroy trousers and a long sleeved T-shirt with the slogan 'Good God!' in bright red letters.

He grinned at his sister who'd driven over with Sally.

'Go and make us a cuppa, will you, Jules?'

'Peter.'

'Sorry, sis. A little priestly confidentiality, please. If Sally wants to tell you she can do it later.'

He settled himself opposite her as the door closed behind Juliet.

'Jules has filled me in so far. I must say you're looking well, in spite of all the trauma.' He gave her an encouraging smile.

'You look great yourself.'

'I love my job. It's hard work, frustrating as hell, sometimes, but immensely satisfying.' He paused, then said quietly, 'May I see the letter?'

'Oh!' Sally jumped and unzipped the pocket in her handbag. 'Here it is.'

Peter took it carefully, his face absorbed. 'Intriguing.' He turned it over.

'I opened it,' she said defensively. 'I had to know.'

'Of course you did. I don't blame you. This is fascinating. There's no doubt about it, Sal, the paper quality, the ink, the stamps! Two single penny stamps, you see? In those days, it cost a penny for city postage, tuppence for the country.'

'You honestly think it's from 1882?'

'Absolutely. It's a bit of a hobby of mine, old manuscripts.'

'Then, how?' She spread her hands.

Peter smiled. 'Relax, Sal, you're not going crazy. Your William may be a ghost.'

'He was solid.'

'Ah. Jules told me about the bruises. Could I, would you mind?'

She extended her arm and he leaned forward, holding it gently, touching the yellowing marks. 'I see. Interesting, but not proof he was real.' He released her and sat back.

Sally, feeling a sense of an ordeal overcome, relaxed into her own chair. 'I didn't know priests believed in ghosts.'

His eyes twinkled. 'We're very modern these days. I've seen too many bizarre things to be dogmatic about anything. There's a very well documented case — a young English psychic, Matthew Manning. Do you know of him?'

She shook her head.

'When he was a teenager he had an encounter with a ghost who lived in his family's house. This entity manifested items from the past. A loaf of bread, an old beeswax candle, beads, other objects. The bread was dated at about seventy years old. It couldn't have been faked and there were enough people to testify as to the authenticity of all these happenings. Matthew wrote a book about his experiences, *The Link*.'

'So a ghost could bring something forward from the past?'

Peter noddded. 'Presumably it might. We don't understand the powers of the mind and how time may be transformed. Even now we don't understand how Jesus did the things he did so we call them miracles, although he himself said that all he could do we could also — and more. That was his clear promise. We say "yes, Lord", but we don't believe it, despite the fact that his own disciples, ordinary, mostly poorly educated country blokes, learnt how to do these things too. They somehow got the secret at last. Now we have members of the clergy saying the age of miracles is over.' He held up the letter. 'What would they make of this, eh?'

'Have me certified, probably,' Sally muttered. She was pleased that she could actually joke about it. She'd been reluctant to tell Peter but his sympathetic interest and lack of judgement of her actions had put her at ease.

'The interesting thing about your letter,' he continued enthusiastically, 'is that it's new, as if it was written yesterday. The items Matthew's ghost delivered were old. The bread was seventy years old and hard as a rock. Now, did he send it forward through time or did he know of an old loaf in the back of a cupboard somewhere or in a museum and simply transport it through telekinesis to the Mannings' house?'

He leaned forward. 'You, on the other hand, met and talked to someone from the past and brought back a letter which is brand new. Gosh, Sally, what a find! There's a miracle, if you like.'

'I'm glad you're enjoying it.'

He became immediately serious. 'You're not, are you?'

'No. I feel I've let William down; that I got in the way, somehow, and stopped Walter receiving the letter. It might have made all the difference. The message never got through, you see, and it was my fault. I didn't do it deliberately but it was just another piece of appalling bad luck for William.'

'It's affected you deeply.'

'He was so intense — so vitally alive, in spite of the horror of his life. He sat there, cheeking the guard, and got a rifle butt in the face for his trouble, but he didn't care. He enjoyed deliberately goading the brute. Then, later, he was kind, not savage at all. He cared about what might happen to me. He thought I'd be raped by the guards and he couldn't stand it. He was a gentleman. I felt, with him, I'd always be safe — although he couldn't even save himself. Oh, God, Peter, I wish I hadn't interfered. I feel so guilty.' Sally covered her face with her hands and sobbed.

Peter got to his feet and went to the kitchen where Juliet was drinking tea and reading a book.

'I didn't want to disturb you. It's all ready. Is Sally okay?'

'She's feeling profoundly guilty. You were right to bring her to me, Jules.' He flicked her cheek with an affectionate finger and said, in the footballers' vernacular, 'You done good.'

He picked up the tray she'd prepared and went back to Sally who was drying her eyes.

'My housekeeper, Mrs Adams, swears by a good strong cuppa.' He poured the tea. 'Drink up, Sally.'

They shared the tea in silence for a while then Sally touched her arm.

'And the bruises?'

'Jules tells me they were definitely not self-inflicted. If the experience was as strong as you say, no doubt William might have manifested them as he did the letter — or you yourself could have caused them to appear in the same way many devout Christians experience the stigmata.'

'Religious hysteria?'

'If you like. Profound faith manifesting a sign of that faith. You believed passionately in William, whether he was a ghost or a dream.'

She put down her cup. 'Tell me the truth, Peter, what do you think?'

'I'm in the truth business,' he said soberly. 'I think one of two things has happened. The first is that you met the ghost of William O'Meally and one of you manifested the bruises and the letter; the other — and, I warn you, it's even stranger, is that there was a fluctuation in time which opened a brief passage enabling you to meet.'

'Science fiction?' Sally stared.

'There is a theory of parallel universes. Time, after all, is prob-

by us for our convenience here on Planet Earth.
...t and into space and time, as we comprehend it,
...tly. There's a convincing argument that all of crea-
tion, past and present, is happening at the one instant and we simply view it through what we call time — a series of minutes, hours,
days, events — so we can experience it and react to it.'

'But time takes *time!*' She objected. 'You can feel it passing.'

'Ah, we think we can,' Peter agreed, 'but you know yourself —
everyone knows — the experience of time flying or standing still,
depending on whatever activity we're engaged with. In the dentist's waiting room or anticipating a longed-for event, time crawls.
Watching a great movie or on a date, time can rush past. Then,
look at dreaming. We can be deeply involved with a dream that, in
the dream state, may last for hours and even days. In reality, the
dream may last only a few seconds, although we can remember the
time it took.' He nodded. 'Yes, we certainly don't understand about
time — not enough to start making any rules about it.'

As Sally digested this, Peter, his eagerness mounting again,
reached across to the bookshelf and picked out a novel.

'Here's a whole story, you see, of someone's life — all in my
hands at the one instant in time. But, if I want to understand it, I
have to start at page one and read, word by word, page by page, to
the end. You can use the same analogy with a videotape or a reel of
film.'

'I see.' She nodded slowly. 'We could all be living, past and
present, all at the same time, but shielded from each other in some
way.'

'Exactly. So it should be feasible that occasionally, because of
location, coincidence of dates, whatever reason, the barrier slips.

'Which would mean, he wasn't a ghost but our times just over-
lapped?'

'Exactly. The real question here is, why?'

Sally sighed. 'I know why. Your "coincidence of dates" — and the
place. I worked it out. We were on the way to St Helena on the
same day, one hundred and fourteen years later, that William was
being returned in a whaleboat, after his fourth escape attempt.'

'That explains part of it.' Peter ran a hand through his hair which had fallen forward into his eyes in his excitement. 'But the tourist boats go over regularly, almost on a daily basis, unless the weather's bad. Why hasn't anyone else reported the same sort of thing and why were you the only person on the boat to see the man? Why you, Sally? What's your link?'

'I don't know.' Sally bit her lip. 'Did Jules tell you I'd seen a hypnotherapist?'

'Chris Young? Yes, I know her. She's one of a group I meet with. Call it another hobby.'

'She didn't find any connection.'

'What were you doing while William was having his life on St Helena?'

'I don't know. I don't remember anything about the session and I haven't played the tape.'

He leaned forward again, 'It would be interesting to know where and who Sally Cooper was in 1882. You're the link, Sal, you must be. Somewhere, somehow, you're the link.'

Sally lay in bed, tossing and turning, fighting for the oblivion of sleep. She stared miserably into the darkness, the image of William's dark, pleading eyes boring into her very soul. She imagined him waiting, trusting that she'd posted his letter and that his brother was even now receiving it. Off the mail coach, she thought hazily, at Bell's Creek, wherever that was. She turned over and thumped the pillow into a better shape. She'd given William her word. She'd decided to do something, but what? For her own curiosity she'd like to know more about him. The girl he'd mentioned in the letter, Rose. He must have been thinking of her when he'd told Sally he had a lass of his own with golden hair. What had happened to her? To Walter? Had the law finally caught up with Jack d'Arcy? She couldn't help William but she could find out for herself. Someone must know the history. Perhaps the man who wrote the booklet, James Carew.

At least she'd feel she was doing something.

Escape from the Past

The curtains were open and the light from the pale city sky made William's envelope glow strangely on her small bedside table.

'Oh, William.' she breathed, 'what did you do after I disappeared? You were so shocked. Did you wait and wait and finally give up in despair? Oh, God, I wish I knew.'

Chapter 17

Near St Helena's southern shore the steady tramp, tramp of boots went on unceasingly as the line of men walked round and round in the silo pit, trampling down the sugar cane. William, bored by the monotony of it, let his mind drift. Surely it wouldn't be long now and he'd be away from this cursed place for good.

A sharp wind sloughed over the island, tossing the heads of trees in the bush which was invitingly near to a man desperate enough to risk a break. That was how he'd got away the time before last, only to be recaptured the next day.

At least the wind cooled the men's hot faces. This was a hated job at the best of times, the grinding boredom of it got on all their nerves as the slow hours passed. In the summer heat it could be unbearable and tempers flared at the slightest provocation.

William grinned. He'd better get used to it for now. He could hardly hope to be assigned one of the soft jobs. He'd not endeared himself to the authorities and prison was, after all, there to punish a man for his sins.

'What are you grinning about, O'Meally?' The warder growled.

'A little cheerfulness never hurt anyone, you should try it yourself now and again.'

'Keep your trap shut.'

'It was shut nice and tight until you got me to open it.'

The warder smiled maliciously. 'I'd put you on report except that you're in enough trouble already. The Kate will be arriving in three days, then you'll get your desserts.'

'A kangaroo court, will it be? With Judge Lash presiding?'

The warder glared. William had stopped to answer him and the column of men had halted, taking a welcome breather.

'Get moving, O'Meally, and stop holding up the work.'

The line walked on. Behind William a deep voice muttered, 'You're lucky it won't be Judge Lynch presiding, you young fool. Things have changed here since you were last a guest at Queensland's inferno.'

'I heard,' William hissed back, his lips barely moving. 'McDonald's gone, then?'

'We've been blessed with Captain Townley,' the other man said bitterly. 'Thinks he's God Almighty because he was police magistrate at Ipswich. Man's mad for discipline and comes down mighty heavy on the most petty breaches of the rules.'

'I haven't met the gentleman. Chief warder gave me a caution and told me I'd be having an appointment with the visiting justice.'

'Then you've a treat to come. Man's a right bastard.'

'Grogan!'

'Here, sir.'

'Shut your mouth or I'll make sure it's shut for you.'

'Shutting my mouth, sir!'

The column moved around. On the opposite side of the pit from where the warder was standing, Tom Grogan whispered, 'You weren't gone long, Billy.'

'Damned black trackers. Nearly got away from 'em, though. Might have made it but for a man I thought was my friend.'

Ahead of William a young prisoner moaned. William surreptitiously nudged him in the back.

'Steady, lad.'

'I'm thirsty,' the boy gasped.

'Put something in your mouth to suck.'

'I ain't got nothin'.'

'Hold on. Won't be long now and it'll all be over, for today.'

Grogan said, 'Tell me, what went wrong?'

They passed the warder in silence. As their backs turned to him, William said briefly, 'I was betrayed to the police by Jack d'Arcy, whom I loved as a brother. I reckon it was him that jumped me and left me for dead, like I told you. He'd do anything to get me out of the way. He loves my girl, Rose. I'll make him pay if it takes me all my life.'

'You'll not make him pay a farthing with you here and him free as a bird.'

'Well, that's about to change.'

'What, lad, you've a special pull with the Almighty Himself?'

'It seems I have.' William lowered his voice even further and mumbled, 'I got a letter off the island.'

The boy in front of him cried out in distress and the warder snapped, 'No talking amongst the prisoners. You, Ludlow, shut your trap or I'll put you on report.'

The lad snarled, 'Does he not say anything else but "shut your trap" and "I'll put you on report"?'

'He's had no education, poor fellow,' William muttered sorrowfully. 'We must have pity on his ignorance.'

'I hate his guts. He's a devil.'

'He's not the only one in this evil place. Keep quiet and keep your head down.'

'Billy,' Grogan said softly, 'a letter, you say?'

'It seems I do have a special place in the Almighty's heart because He sent a woman, or maybe she was an angel, dressed like a man with such strange clothing — a new city fashion, I'll be bound. She'd been took for a man but I warned her of this place and she confessed to her disguise. Even now she's back in Brisbane town, posting my letter. Red will see d'Arcy brought to justice.'

'And what was the name of this angel of yours?'

'I don't know, but angel she must have been and I'll be in her debt for as long as I live.'

Escape from the Past

'I can't stand it no more!' Prisoner Ludlow gave a demented wail and flew at the warder, scrambling to the edge of the silo pit and dragging the man down onto the grass. Thankful for the diversion, some prisoners leapt after him to prevent him doing the warder an injury which would get the boy into serious trouble. Others threw themselves onto the ground and stretched out.

William sat down next to Tom Grogan and smiled affectionately at the older man with his fierce shaggy grey eyebrows and craggy, pockmarked face. Tom's sparse hair was compensated by a flowing grey beard. 'Who's the lad?' William asked.

'He's new. He was an apprentice butcher. Hacked his employer to death with a meat-axe because he didn't like the way he was treated. Name's Robert Ludlow — we've renamed him "Meat-Axe".'

'He won't like the way he's treated here, then, and he won't have a meat-axe handy.'

'Oh, he will. Remember the ways of officialdom, Billy. He's only on hard labour temporarily, for swearing and spitting at the chief warder. Tomorrow he goes back to work,' Grogan winked, 'in the butcher's shop.'

William gave a chuckle. 'Makes sense, that.'

The excitement was dying down, the warder emerged from the press of men holding down the young prisoner.

'You've done it now, Ludlow. You'll be up before Captain Townley and he'll invite you to join O'Meally's flogging party.'

'Have some compassion, man,' Grogan said. 'Can you not see the lad's demented?'

'My wages aren't enough as it is,' the warder growled. 'I don't get paid extra for compassion.'

He turned to the men and shouted, 'Line up, we'll go back to the stockade. Keep a hold of that man and don't let him go.'

'Or put an axe in his hand first and let him rid the island of one more bastard,' William suggested.

Marching beside him, Tom Grogan said through the corner of his mouth, 'If they ever catch the bastard who did for you, Billy, woe betide him if he's sent to St Helena. I'll kill him with my bare hands — and enjoy doing it.'

146

Chapter 18

S ally zipped William's letter into her bag and left the house. She drove across town to the leafy bay-side suburb of Wynnum, checking with her street directory every now and then as Brisbane's south side was unfamiliar territory to her.

Her supervisor had been sympathetic when Sally had rung in to say she wasn't well.

'I thought you looked a bit red-eyed and peaky. It's probably one of these wretched viruses or 'flu. Colette's coming down with it, too. You've got sick leave owing, Sally. Take a couple of days off — come back when you're really better.'

'I feel guilty. We're so busy, and if Colette's sick...'

'We'll cope, better than if you were here and feeling awful. Look after yourself and we'll see you soon.'

'Thanks, Fran.'

She turned into the Esplanade at Oyster Point and counted the house numbers, pulling up outside a small, low-set bungalow. Dwarfed by its high-stilt neighbours, its verandah and wide windows were positioned to catch the bay breezes.

Sally got out of the car. Separated from the road by a grassy tree- lined bank and a concrete bike track, mangrove mud flats lay shining in the bright autumn sunshine. The air smelt of mud and rotting fish and a salt breeze whipped the hair back from her face. Several rowing boats rested on the mud; further out a dozen white sails shone against the long bulk of Moreton Island, a hazy blue smudge on the horizon, as yachts tacked back and forth across the distant grey-green water. Small bright blue and orange crabs sidled about the mud like glittering jewels and various birds searched the flats for shell fish and other delights. Among the long-legged, curved-billed water birds, a pigeon wandered about, its throat shining an irridescent, metallic pink and green. Seagulls stood around or dipped in shallow pools, waiting for the tide to deliver its rich harvest.

Across the bay Sally could see the low green shapes of islands. St Helena, directly in front of her, was easily recognisable. Its long grassy slopes ran down to the shore and she could make out the stone ruins and the causeway. So close. The prisoners must have often gazed across to the mainland, she thought, so tantalisingly near and yet so far.

She turned away, a lump in her throat, and crossed the road to the bungalow.

James Carew was tall and slightly stooping. He shook Sally's hand and invited her in. Taking off his reading glasses, he carefully folded them into a leather case which he placed on the dining room table next to a pile of manuscripts, photographs and books.

'I'm pleased to help a fellow enthusiast,' he said, brushing aside her apology for taking up his time. 'Fascinating place, St Helena. I have it right on my doorstep, as you'd have seen.'

He moved to the table. The bungalow was built on an open plan, the lounge room at the front and the dining area running off it along the left wall.

'We'll sit at the table. I've got everything together for you.'

'I've given you a lot of work.'

'I've enjoyed it. I've been rummaging since you rang, and it wasn't difficult.' He smiled and went into the kitchen, which opened onto the dining room, and continued to talk to her across the servery counter.

'Coffee? Good, I'm ready for one. No, it wasn't work for me

because I've already researched poor William extensively. He's my special interest because he's by way of being a relative of mine.'

Sally's knees threatened to give way and she sat down at the table.

James went on, not noticing her shock. 'William's brother Walter married Rose Carew who was a cousin of my great-great grandfather Anthony. I've got both family trees here so you can have a look.'

He brought the coffee to the table and handed her a mug, laid some papers in front of her, then went back to the kitchen.

'See, George Carew, Rose's father, had a brother and sister in England, Richard and Alice. Alice never married, Richard married Constance and Anthony was their son.'

He came back to Sally and put a milk carton and jar of sugar in front of her.

'Help yourself. My grandfather came out to Australia in 1928. He was a bit of a tearaway and the family more or less told him to go and make a nuisance of himself anywhere but in Dorset, preferably as far away as possible. So, out he came, and became very respectable. He settled in South Australia, got into wine making and the rest of the family is still there. I got interested in family history, came up to trace my relatives, loved the place and stayed on.'

'Who was alive then?' Sally was tracing the neat geneologies with her finger.

'Quite a number of cousins. See, here, Walter and Rose had four children. Thomas and Michael died in the first world war, Michael in 1915 at Gallipoli, Thomas a year later at The Somme. They had children. Margaret, known as Maggie, never married. George married a girl from Perth and they went to live there. Maggie, being the oldest surviving child, inherited the family home at Bell's Creek and lived there with her parents. When they died she stayed on until 1962. She was seventy-five by then and the property was too much for her, fallen into a dreadful state. Maggie came down to Brisbane and moved in with family until she died in 1964.'

'So, descendants of the three sons are still alive?'

'Yes, scattered about. Why the interest in William's family, if you don't mind me asking?'

'I just wondered about them,' Sally said. 'I didn't know you had a connection. When I bought your booklet and read his story I rang your publisher. They gave me your number but didn't tell me anything about you.'

James looked at her, a puzzled expression on his face.

She said hurriedly, 'Was it true, that there'd been an injustice?'

'Yes, I think there probably was. He claimed to have been falsely accused, that he only kept going AWOL to find out who laid for him and shot him, setting him up to take the fall for the gang. Rose claimed she was his alibi. A little late, as it turned out, by confirming a story she'd already denied to the sub-inspector on the case. She wasn't believed. Apparently there'd been an attempt to steal some valuable race horses and William was blamed. There was a gang, he was probably part of it, but the rest weren't caught. William was shot, apparently by one of the others, only it never came out who and why, and the police picked him up. As his was the only body in the frame, they threw the book at him. He would have hanged if the local sergeant hadn't appealed in a comprehensive report on the handling of the whole affair. As it was, he was sent to St Helena and hanged anyway, by his own hand.'

'So he did escape in the end.' Sally remembered the tourist's words on the island.

'Yes, the final escape, poor bloke. He didn't have much to live for. On top of everything, Rose married his brother.'

Sally's mind flashed to the letter in her handbag. William had begged his brother to look after Rose and do everything in his power to reunite them. Oh, William, she mourned silently, even Walter betrayed you in the end. He took your lass with the golden hair. You must have been so miserable. If I hadn't got mixed up in your life the letter might have been delivered and you'd probably have got home to Rose.

'Did he ever make it back to see justice done?' Sally's voice was bleak. She was hurting with grief and guilt.

'No, although he escaped five times. The last attempt was a bit odd. He disappeared for a number of hours but claimed he'd never left the island. A lot of escape attempts were made by prisoners bolting into the bush or hiding in the sugar cane. Most of them were caught or gave themselves up after a few hours, hungry and covered with sandfly and mosquito bites. It was practically impossible to get off the island. As soon as a prisoner went missing, a flag was raised and a cannon fired to signal the water police on Fisherman Island. All the off-duty warders put out in boats and patrolled off-shore. The water police would arrive and the island was searched. Even if the prisoners survived without food, water or shelter — and it can be freezing over there in winter — they still had to get across the bay. The island's boats were securely under lock and key and any unauthorised boats approaching the island were fired on to keep them away. So it wasn't odd that William never got off the island. The strange thing was, that the last time he said he'd never left the prison at all. He certainly didn't show any signs of hunger or insect bites but, according to the reports, he literally disappeared for about eight hours. It was never explained and he was punished anyway.'

Sally bowed her head, imagining William's frustration. Wasting his life away within sight of the mainland, thwarted each time he tried to get home, angry that he'd been the victim of a gross injustice. Eventually the strongest man might lose heart.

'Then he hanged himself,' she said in a hollow voice.

'Yes, poor bugger.' James hesitated then got up and left her for a few minutes. When he returned he carried a thick leather bound book. It looked old but very well preserved.

'Look, I don't know why I'm doing this.' He put it in front of her. 'Take care of it, as you see, it's the original. The family gave it to me because of my interest. Normally I wouldn't let it out of my sight.'

She looked at him inquiringly.

'Take it home with you and read it. It'll tell you all about what happened. It's Rose Carew's diary.'

Chapter 19

W hy didn't I tell him about the letter? Sally wondered as she drove back to the city.

She touched the precious diary which, carefully wrapped, was on the passenger seat beside her. It had been generous of James to trust her with it. They'd spent an hour going over the details of William's family and his two years imprisonment and she now had a folder crammed with photocopies prepared for her by Carew to study at her leisure.

'You should drive up to Bell's Creek to see the family home,' he'd said as he farewelled her. 'It's now owned by a nice couple who are restoring it. They'd be delighted to see you. Name of Grant. Rose and Walter are buried on the property in the family cemetery. It's an interesting place.'

'I'll do that,' Sally had promised. 'I'd enjoy it.' An inexplicable sense of urgency gripped her. 'When could I go? I'll take time off work.'

'I'll give them a ring, ask when's convenient. I'll call you, and you can call me any time if you need more information.'

Pure instinct had stopped her from producing the letter. Anyway, she thought, he might have written me off as a crank who'd faked the whole thing to get attention. He'd have been suspicious if I'd produced a perfectly new letter telling him it was from last century. She played out the scene in her mind, thankful she hadn't had to explain it to James. He was perfectly nice, enthusiastic and helpful but that, she thought, would have strained his generosity somewhat.

'And I've got the diary', she chortled gleefully. 'Surely I'll get some clues from that.'

Clues to what? Her inner voice asked with some asperity. She heard Chris Young's voice. 'Best of luck in your search, dear.'

It's down to me, she thought grimly. I stuffed things up for William and he expected me to help him. All right, William O'Meally, if I can do anything, *anything*, I will.

Sally turned off the main road. She had another call to make before she tackled the diary.

Peter was getting out of his car in the driveway of the presbytery when she drove up. He walked down the front path to open the gate for her.

'Sally. Come in and have a cuppa. I've just been doing my hospital visits.'

The front door was open. He led her inside and put down his case, calling out, 'I'm home, Marcia; got a visitor. May we have coffee in the lounge room?'

A voice answered him from the back of the house. 'Okay, Father, coming right up.'

Sally sat down and watched Peter take off his dog-collar.

'I loathe hospitals, don't you?' He said cheerfully. 'They smell of disinfectant and disease and they're so noisy. I always wonder how the patients ever get to sleep.' He sat down. 'One poor woman in the bed next to my parishioner kept throwing up the whole time. I need a drink afterwards to get the taste out of my throat. Would you like a small whisky first?'

'Thanks, I'd love one. You look very official, in the uniform.'

'I don't wear it that often. Just a cross in my lapel does the trick. But the patients seem to need more of God's presence and the black shirt and dog-collar can be a comfort. Now,' he handed her a glass, 'you've come to tell me more about your ghost, I hope.'

'If you've got time, Pete.'

He grinned. 'That's nice. Only Jules calls me Pete these days. I'm glad you came.'

There was a knock on the door and Mrs Adams came in with the coffee on a tray. She and Sally exchanged a few pleasantries before the housekeeper left them.

'Now, let's have it.'

Sally turned her glass around in her fingers, wondering where to start. Then it all tumbled out, about her visit to James Carew and his loan of the diary.

'Is that it?'

'Yes.' She picked it up. 'I didn't want to leave it in the car, even locked. It's precious.'

'I'll say. May I see?'

She handed it over and he unwrapped it. 'Lovely handwriting.' He turned the pages. 'This will be fascinating.'

Sally put down the glass and collected herself. 'Pete.'

He looked up and immediately closed the diary. 'Is this confession time?'

'Advice time.'

'Sally — of course. If I can.'

'It's a bit of a religious question, really.' She hesitated, then blurted out, 'If I found out about all this, what the truth really was; if I knew for certain who shot William that night, could it possibly change anything?'

'Hmmm.' He put his fingertips together and tapped them against his mouth. 'You mean, could it change things for William?'

'I know he hanged himself, I've seen his grave; but I accidentally got in the way of something important and I want to know, can the past be changed in the present?'

There was a long pause, then Peter said slowly, 'Well, I believe it can — but perhaps not in the way you mean. I believe past events can be transformed, not the physical events but our interpretation of them. We can do this by present forgiveness and understanding, so that they lose their painfulness and hurt. And, in that way, we're set free.'

'If I found out the truth,' Sally persisted, 'if I did what Walter should have done, would have done if the letter had been posted, couldn't just that action help in some way? If we are linked somehow in our minds, could my knowing bring some peace of mind to William?'

Even as she struggled to voice her thoughts, Sally felt her face growing hot. She must sound completely mad. What she was proposing was nonsense. But Peter was listening quite calmly, his forehead wrinkled as he tried to follow her meaning.

'I'm in the miracle business as well as the truth business,' he said seriously. 'Possibly, Sal. If someone with a pure heart, pure intentions, with no vested interest or desire for anything but the truth for its own sake, undertook such a quest — who knows? It might free William from whatever torment you believe his soul to be undergoing.'

'But, would he know? Would he know I followed through, kept my promise?'

'Honestly, I don't know. I believe anything, literally anything, is possible. I really do believe in miracles, you know.'

Sally leaned back and smiled at him. 'Thanks, Pete, I'll have that coffee, now.'

Back home Sally carried the diary through to her bedroom. Tim looked up as she went past.

'Where have you been? I thought you were supposed to be resting.'

She stood in the doorway, watching him. His books were spread all over the coffee table and he'd been scribbling notes in his neat hand, spilling the papers across the sofa.

Sally went over and picked them up. 'You'll never make it as a doctor if you don't learn to write illegibly,' she joked. 'I can read this easily.' She pushed the papers to one side and sat down.

'Well, where did you go?'

She felt a sudden familiar antipathy. 'Out.'

'Obviously. Where, out?'

Sally's nerves tightened, shying away from his implied ownership of her. She'd tried a hundred times to understand the feeling
of entrapment that came over her when Tim questioned her movements. It had started after the engagement. She said quietly, 'When
we were just friends, sharing a house, you never asked me to explain my comings and goings.'

He leaned over and ruffled her hair. 'I didn't have any contol
over you, then.'

'You don't now.'

'We're engaged, Sally. Don't you think you owe me some explanation when you disappear for hours on end? I was imagining all
sorts of things. I thought you might have taken off somewhere.'

Sally's eyes opened wider. 'Why on earth would I do that?'

'Well, we're not getting on the best lately, heaven knows why.'

'Tim, that's ridiculous. Look around you; all my things are still
here.'

He said aggrievedly, 'I still think you owe me an explanation. I
was worried about you.'

She stood up, her eyes blazing. 'That's always your problem,
Tim. A little rational thought would have told you I'd be back eventually. I'm not in any way answerable to you, not now we're engaged, not after we're married. If I tell you where I go it'll be because
I want to share my life with you, not out of any sense of duty.'

'Keep your hair on. I only asked.'

'Do you hear yourself? You sound like Giles. You want to control my actions just the same way he does Ellie's and Amanda's.
Only with you it's passive, manipulative, not openly aggressive. I
won't accept responsibility for your worrying. It's entirely up to
you.'

She stormed back into her room and closed the door. Sitting on
the bed, still shaking with fury, she thought, It's just nerves. Getting engaged takes some adjusting. We'll settle down. How dare he
ask me to explain myself! Only, he's not really like Giles. When
we're married, it'll be better.

She wished she had someone to advise her, a close relative, not
just a friend. An only child, Sally's parents had died in a car crash

when she was eight and, until she was seventeen, she'd lived with her aunt. Aunt Felicia was a single parent, perfectly nice but always so busy with her own children and full-time job. There never seemed time for real conversations and Sally had never felt close to her, not enough to share the deepest secrets of her heart. Those were whispered in Juliet's receptive ear. As soon as Sally had found a job, the girls moved into a flat together. Normally her lack of close family never bothered Sally. But these weren't normal times.

She reached instinctively for her mobile phone, then stopped. Juliet was wonderful but Sally needed someone older, experienced in relationships and marriage. The only older woman she was close to was Tim's mother and she'd seen how Ellie handled her life.

'You need a cup of tea, a Bex and a good lie down.' The old phrase made her frown. Tim sometimes used it, jokingly, to soothe her when she became hostile. Hostile? I'm not hostile, I just get crabby now and then. It's nothing major.

Then why had the word jumped into her mind, causing her to clench her hands together and compress her lips to stop herself screaming with frustration?

Right now. This is going to stop right now. I don't need past life therapy or analysts or any other voodoo. I've been awful to Tim; it's perfectly reasonable of him to expect some explanation about my doings. I always told Jules where I was going, how long I'd be — or I'd leave a note. It's common courtesy and I never minded before. I only go ballistic with Tim. I'm going to change from now on. The decision made her feel better.

Although she knew she ought to go out and apologise to Tim, a strange reluctance held her back. What was the point of saying she was sorry when she had no idea why he triggered such uncharacteristic behaviour in her? He'd want to know why he'd upset her and he'd still be curious about where she'd been and why she didn't want him to know.

What's the harm in telling him? she wondered. It's not a big deal to say I was interested in the family history of a prisoner on Saint Helena. I'll go right now and tell him and apologise. She jumped to her feet.

No! A voice screamed in her mind. Don't tell him. Don't tell him about William. It's not safe.

Sally sat down again, stunned. What made her think that? She examined her feelings. She was panting, her palms damp. She closed her eyes and slowed her breathing. Why? She asked herself. Why not safe? Slowly from the depths of her mind the thought came. Not safe... to say...there's...another man.

Rubbish! She thought emphatically. Absolute rubbish. William wasn't another man. She was just interested to know more about him. A picture of William rose in her mind. She'd give the whole thing careful thought, work out how to tell Tim and say 'sorry'. Later.

'Meanwhile,' she said to the room in general, 'I have a job to do.'

She unzipped the inner pocket of her handbag and searched for the letter. Then she pulled out all of the compartment's contents. With a sickening jolt in her stomach, she upended the bag and spilled everything out onto the bed, turning the soft vinyl bag inside out and checking and rechecking the items on the bed.

'Oh, no. Oh, no! I've lost it! Dropped it somewhere.'

She forced herself to think rationally. She'd put the letter there earlier, she hadn't opened that inner pocket at all while she was out — unless...

She picked up her mobile and stabbed at the numbers.

'James, it's Sally Cooper. Sorry to bother you again but — I've lost a letter from my handbag. Did I drop it at your place?'

'Hang on, I'll have a look.'

She held her breath, her heart pounding. Minutes later he was back.

'Sorry, it isn't here. Anyway, I put everything away after you left and I'd have seen it if it had been here. Oh, Scott and Alisha Grant said Thursday would be fine and they'll expect you when they see you.'

'Thanks, James.'

Sally switched the phone off then thought, The car! She rushed outside. Tim's voice followed her. 'I suppose you're going out again.'

She heard the complaining tone and closed the front door with more force than she'd intended. She hunted through the car. Nothing. William's letter had vanished into thin air.

Tim knocked at Sally's door.

'Do you want dinner? I'll make it, if you like.'

She sat up, her eyes swollen, her face stained with tears. She hastily dabbed some make-up over the damage and opened the door.

'We're going out for dinner,' she announced, 'to a nice intimate restaurant where we can talk. I don't care if you've got to study. This is more important. This is us, Tim, and it has to be sorted now.'

He touched his wine glass to hers and drank, then set the glass down and said, 'Well, you called this meeting. Do you want to tell me why?

Sally grimaced. 'Is that what it feels like? I just wanted a chat over a good meal. We don't talk much these days.'

'I'm studying, you're working.'

'I know, but we should make time.'

'That's what we're doing now.' He refilled their glasses. 'I'm ready.'

'No big deal. I just wanted to tell you what I'm doing — as a friend, Tim. We're such good friends. I used to be able to tell you anything, like a big brother.'

As she heard herself say the words she thought, they were the best times with Tim. I really miss him, the way it used to be. She plunged on, 'I'm going away for a couple of days.'

'Oh? Where to, or is it a secret?'

'No, I'm going to a place called Bell's Creek, in the Brisbane Valley — Nanango way, I think.'

He frowned. 'That sounds familiar. Yes. Wasn't there a big gold strike there in the eighteen-nineties? A couple of Americans, brothers — the Andersons — found a rich seam. They'd come over from the California diggings years before and knew where to find good gold country. People thought they were crazy until they broke through to the main seam.'

Sally grinned. 'I haven't the faintest idea. The trivia you know always astounds me.'

'I read about it in school, wanted to go out and strike it rich myself. Apparently they pegged the best of it, cunning buggers. So there wasn't much left for anyone else and the whole thing petered out. It was a very concentrated field. The brothers got to be millionaires, though, and went back to America to live the good life.'

'You wanted to be a prospector?' She stared.

'No, I wanted to have a fortune in gold. I didn't expect to work hard for it. One or two pick strokes, then — bingo!' They both laughed and he asked, 'Can I come with you? It sounds interesting.'

'No.' Sally shook her head, wondering why she suddenly felt she was in some sort of danger. 'Not this time. It's a bit personal.'

'I see.' Tim toyed with his fork, his eyes downcast. 'Look, have you got another bloke? Is he going with you?'

'Is that what you think?' She asked coolly. 'Thanks for the trust, Tim.'

He looked squarely at her. 'Well, what am I supposed to think? You announce you're swanning off for a couple of days, it's personal, and your fiancé isn't welcome.'

The waiter chose that moment to bring their meal and they began to eat, Sally suppressing her annoyance. I'm supposed to be apologising, not starting another fight, she reminded herself. He's right. I owe him the truth, but only part of it. The way he's acting, he'd try to use the full story as an excuse to make me feel guilty.

'I was going to tell you, before you jumped to the wrong conclusion.' She delicately dissected a prawn and tried to ignore the small warning bell in her mind. 'I'm going to look at an old homestead. They're only expecting me and I don't know if they'd want extras. I got interested in the life story of one of the prisoners on St Helena and followed him up a bit. I met a descendant of his girl friend today. I'm going to see the house where the prisoner lived. The girl lived there later, with his brother. She married the brother after her boy friend was sent to St Helena. I'll go on Thursday and be back Friday afternoon.'

Tim's eyes narrowed. 'Does this prisoner have a name?'

'I doubt you've heard of him. William O'Meally. He...hanged himself on the island.' She tried to sound nonchalant.

Tim said, 'So he's my rival. A dead man.'

'Don't be an idiot, Tim. William died in 1882.'

'But there's something, isn't that right?' He looked closely at her. 'I bloody well felt it all along. You're right, it is a bit personal.'

'You're crazy. I'm interested, that's all — and you couldn't take two whole days away from your studies, so you wouldn't be able to come, anyway.'

'I wouldn't be welcome, anyway. Let's face it, Sal, you've got a thing for this William O'Meally. I heard it in your voice when you said he died.' He shook his head. 'You're losing all sense of reality. You refuse to sleep with me, you've become secretive, crying all the time. Classic symptoms. You're bloody obsessed by another man.'

'This is ridiculous.' Sally's voice was like ice. 'Grow up, Tim. You're making a fool of yourself.'

He pointed his fork at her. 'Grow up yourself, Sal. I may be a fool but at least I'm not obsessed by a dead man. If you ask me, you've fallen in love with William O'Meally.'

Chapter 20

'Have I?' She examined her face in the mirror. 'Have I fallen in love with William?'

She had admitted to Juliet that William was attractive but what made him so to her? He was physically handsome but so were other men she knew and she'd never been especially attracted to good looks, too often finding that they masked a shallowness of character. Was it simply that she felt sorry for him and was one of those women who fell in love with the helpless in a desire to rescue them? But she didn't think of William as being particularly helpless. He had an inner toughness and ability to stand up to his tormentors. She'd seen that — giving cheek with an impish pleasure, accepting the inevitable back-lash. She winced at the horribly descriptive term. 'Unable to be broken', James Carew had written. William's sense of humour had probably got him into trouble all his life but he bore the consequences with a surprising maturity, more concerned for others, herself, for instance, than his own impending severe punishment.

Sally thought that William, at twenty, was more mature than Tim would ever be. He accepted total responsibility for his actions but was undeterred from doing what he thought was right. She couldn't imagine William sulking because he wasn't invited on a trip. She thought, rather, he'd understand and respect her desire for space, her need for privacy. But then, William had his own personal quest from which it had been impossible to turn him, and he'd recognise that same need in another.

How do I know so much about him? We've never met; according to Chris he's not in my past at all. She reached out to the mirror's cold reflection. I'm not making it up, she thought. Somehow I know William like I know myself. It's fascinating.

Earlier, Tim had bitterly accused, 'You're obsessed by a dead man.' She'd denied it, but now, examining her feelings, she finally admitted it to herself. William had become an obsession. He was constantly in her thoughts. His strained young face rose continually in her mind, reproaching her for her untimely interference in his affairs. Guilt threatened to overwhelm her. She had to help him, she *had* to.

Peter's words echoed in her memory. "If someone with a pure heart, pure intentions, with no vested interest or desire for anything but the truth for its own sake." It made sense. If you were going to ask God for a miracle it had to be from the position of selfless, unconditional love because that was the only kind the Almighty recognised. So she couldn't love him, couldn't feel anything deeper than friendship. Anything more might destroy any chance she had of keeping her promise to him.

Sally frowned at her reflection. She'd never wanted to love William, never thought of him like that, so why did this recognition bring her a measure of relief. She had Tim. She was in love with Tim.

But she was determined to find a way to make good her promise to William, even if she'd given it without understanding. The thought of his despair cut like a sword at her heart. She imagined him patiently collecting scraps of fibre, making his rope night after night in his cell, with the single-minded determination she understood so well; hiding its growing length from the warders. She couldn't bear it. If there was a way to relieve his suffering, she had to do it. There was really no choice.

'All right, William,' she breathed, 'it's time to start.'

Escape from the Past

She turned from the mirror, a feeling of peace spreading through her. She'd asked for her miracle. If there was any justice in this world or the next... She sat on her bed, plumping the pillows up behind her back, and opened Rose Carew's diary. She was ready to begin her quest.

Sally turned the pages, chuckling now and then, absorbed by this intimate glimpse into the life of a girl of the eighteen hundreds. She decided, if she had had a sister, that sister would have been very like Rose.

She must have been quite a handful, Sally thought. Her poor father, he didn't have a prayer. More than one entry mentioned that: "Father wants me to go or to do such and such but I do not think I shall. I must persuade him otherwise."

At first, Rose had seen William as just one of the boys of the district. She was courted by various local lads and didn't seem to favour one above the other. The diary commenced on Rose's fourteenth birthday and was kept intermittently, being less a-day-to day journal of her activities but more a record of special events; although the details of life on her father's farm leapt from the pages in her vivid and lively accounts.

She's like William, Sally thought. Strong-willed and loyal, mature and sure of her own abilities. They must have been so happy until he was sent away.

Rose wrote of her father's disapproval of her relationship with the O'Meallys and how, in spite of his misgivings, she regularly visited Glendale Farm.

'Their home is less formal than mine,' she wrote wistfully. 'The brothers are not restricted and set about by all the rules of propriety with which father tries to restrain me. There is always singing and laughter, a happy, casual air, and I am warmly welcomed by Mrs O'Meally whom I love dearly. Her many kindnesses to me after the loss of my darling mama cannot be imagined. She, too, lost a beloved mother when she was a girl, and so she understands and feels for my position.'

On another occasion:

'Mrs O'Meally chased us all out of the house, saying that we were under her feet and she desired to spring clean. This was, I am sure, more a desire to be free of our constant chatter, as it is still wintertime! She had packed such a picnic hamper for us and we rode to Wallaby Creek and spread our tablecloth under the she-oaks. After our feast, the boys challenged each other to a race, and, when I cried out in protest at being thought too weak (being a mere girl), for such an exploit, William said I might join them. Whitey is very fast and I believe they were afraid that a *mere girl* might show them up; and said so! They were naturally put on their mettle. So we mounted and Walter gave the signal to start. You will be happy to know, dear diary, that, although William won by a nose, I was directly behind him and thus Walter came in third, claiming that Tara was tired. You can imagine how William and I laughed at that! What good friends the boys are and like brothers to me.'

Gradually the diary began to mention William more and more, describing how handsome he was becoming, that he was Rose's favourite partner at the bush dances, her pleasure in his company. Then, a sad entry:

'My father is determined that I shall not grow up a hoyden, as he likes to describe me, and so I am to sail to London to stay for a season with Aunt Alice. I cannot imagine what I shall find to do there; I shall be so bored, for, in England, the social season is winter, which, in Australia, is spring and summer and the most glorious time of activity on the farm. I will miss seeing the new-born lambs and the spring blossoms; the shearing, as well. I will be expected to sit decorously in Aunt's drawing room and receive morning visitors. How dull. She so disapproves of me, I cannot imagine how father persuaded her to consent to my visit. I cannot make him change his mind on this. How I will miss all my friends!'

It was on Rose's return from England that she realised her affection for William was deeper than mere friendship.

'How fine he is, how strong and handsome. Father is adamant that I should not encourage him and I am sure I do not, because I am not a flirt (which was one thing in my favour with Aunt Alice); however, William seems to need no encouragement. He often rides over to visit me, preferring, he says, to have me to himself, for when I am at Glendale, there is Walter and often other boys and Jack d'Arcy has always shown interest in me. William says nothing but is quick to be before Jack in asking me to dance and lifting me from the saddle, although I am well able to dismount without their aid, and did so for years before they decided I could not. How foolish boys are. And yet, there is a quality in William that fills me with admiration. I think of him far more than the others and am proud to be with him, whatever Father may say.'

'Oh, Rose,' Sally sighed, 'you are so right.'

Rose unfolded the story of her growing love for William with a delicacy and innocent charm. Then, on a page smudged with tears, she wrote that her father had chosen a husband for her and expected her to comply with his wishes. Sally had already learnt of the arrival in the district of Robert Leicester who, older and more sophisticated than the other boys, made sure of his friendship with Rose's father before openly courting her. He had been referred to once or twice as a business acquaintance of George Carew and one whom Rose found dull and tiresome. But then the blow had fallen, further exacerbated by the added dictate that she was not to see William O'Meally again and, if she did, her father would send her to England and make sure William suffered the consequences.

'I must convince father I mean to obey him,' Rose had written, 'until I can decide what to do. William has become so dear to me, if only I could tell him of my love. Surely I am not alone in my affection, because I believe he looks at me with a softness in his expression which he does not show to the other girls. How could I be mistaken? I am in duty bound to write to him that I cannot see him again. I have promised father that, while he is away in Brisbane town, I shall not try to see William; however, if he should try to see me? This was not precisely discussed. I will inform him that father will be away for some days and that will not be breaking my word, dear diary, for I did not promise not to tell him I am all alone, except for Mrs Moore, who sleeps in the other wing of the house.'

'Good for you,' Sally said. She knew, as Rose knew, that William, given the facts, would always find a way around any obstacle. Fascinated, she read on.

The next entry was undated. Waking from her night of love with William, Rose had evidently been in such a dream of bliss, mundane things such as dates had escaped her notice. She'd received an urgent note from William, asking her to wait in the garden, and he had come to her there. The story of that night was told with such passion that Sally felt her cheeks grow hot. All Rose's upbringing had been thrown out the window; she'd given herself joyfully to her lover and her life had been changed forever. As Sally read the impassioned entry she began to feel a pang of discontent. Why hadn't it been like that for her? There was nothing wrong with her sexual relationship with Tim — he was, as the saying went, good in bed. He knew all about foreplay and arousal and how to satisfy her physically. Then how did Rose, innocent, untaught, apparently given a horror description of the duty of a wife to her husband in those rigid, joyless Victorian times, manage to rise to such heights of passion and obvious sexual fulfillment the first time around? Sally felt like crying out that it wasn't fair. She felt life had cheated her and wondered, when she and Tim were married and had a more stable, certain relationship, could they create such ecstatic love?

No, because Rose, wise at seventeen, had given her the answer. She was a girl deeply in love and her passion was returned by William, who didn't need to bone up on technique. He adored her so much he knew instinctively how to be gentle with his virgin love, so there was only pleasure for her — and Rose had given herself in perfect trust that he would look after her.

'And you weren't disappointed,' Sally whispered. 'I want to be loved like that. Does Tim really love me or am I just convenient for him?'

She didn't think to ask herself if she loved Tim. She'd already told herself she did. She looked at her watch. It was past one; if she didn't get some sleep she'd be like a rag in the morning. She closed the diary and turned out the light but sleep was elusive and she lay for hours staring, dry-eyed and wakeful, into the night.

Next morning, Tim seemed determined to behave as if the quarrel of the previous night had never occurred. He chatted brightly over breakfast, determinedly ignoring Sally's monosyllabic answers. She told him she hadn't slept well. He assumed she'd been distressed over the evening's events and she didn't disillusion him. As usual, he'd put any unpleasantness behind him, preferring to believe that Sally's stress was causing her to over-react.

'Being engaged isn't always fun,' he said, echoing her own thoughts. 'We're going through a time of adjustment. We'll be fine, Sally, you said yourself that we've always been good friends. I'm not worried about your weekend, you go and enjoy yourself.'

Like a paternal blessing, she thought angrily, but didn't say anything. She hadn't the strength to start another argument. Tim would simply refuse to react, smiling at her as if she was being childish and neurotic and suggest she take something for her nerves, putting the blame on her. Then he'd look at her in that patronising way and say, 'I'm worried about you, Sal.'

She wondered where that had come from. Patronising. She'd never thought of him in that context before. Now she realised it was the perfect term. He was behaving like an older brother; protective, humouring her, *patronising* her.

Sally pushed her chair back. 'I'll be late for work. I'll do dinner tonight.'

What she felt like saying was, 'Why do you want to marry me?' Only she wasn't sure she wanted to hear the answer.

Chapter 21

'Phat!'

Sally almost shouted the word. There was a startled exclamation from the living room and Tim knocked at her door.

'Are you okay, Sal?'

'Yes, sorry Tim, I got carried away.'

His footsteps retreated. Sally put down the diary, her forehead wrinkled in puzzlement.

William was with Rose that night, she thought blankly. That was the night they made love and she forgot to date the entry. Why didn't they listen to her?

She picked up her mobile and rang James Carew.

'Sally. How're you getting on with the O'Meally clan?'

'I've been reading Rose's diary. The night of the horse raid, that got William imprisoned, he was with Rose. Her diary is explicit. Surely you must have read it.'

'Yes, and she did, eventually, bring that out when he was re-tried. However, she'd already told the investigating officer William hadn't been there that night. She did try to submit her diary later as evidence, which was a pretty brave thing for her to do, but it was pointed out that, as the entry was undated, it could have been the previous night. George had left the day before the raid so Rose had been alone for two nights. It was only her word, you see, the word of a young woman desperate to save her lover. Her father and Walter, as well as the sub-inspector, fought to keep her out of it and the Carew's housekeeper, Mrs Moore, was adamant that no one had been near the house on either evening. So it was believed Rose had invented the whole thing to save William's neck.'

'The entry couldn't have been made up and inserted later, though. The pages are consecutive.'

'Yes, but the fact that she hadn't dated the entry was damning. A pity she didn't think to date it before she took it to the authorities. I suppose she assumed her word was beyond doubt. Anyway, it probably wouldn't have made much difference. If she'd been allowed to go to court, a clever barrister would have made nonsense of her story. She'd have lost her reputation and all credibility. Have you read the sub-inspector's report and the evidence given at the trial?'

'Not yet.'

'It doesn't support Rose's story.'

Sally was about to cry out, But William said he was unjustly imprisoned for another's wrong, then caught herself up in time. That would have taken more explaining than she felt capable of at present. She thanked James for his time and rang off.

'Men! Anyone reading that entry and thinking Rose made it up to save William needs his head read.'

She stroked the diary's cover. 'Poor Rose,' she said softly. She'd read how George Carew had arrived home early, then Sub-Inspector Stapleton had ridden to the farm with the dreadful news of William's arrest and his injuries. Rose had hardly been able to control herself but, knowing both men to be watching her, had fought for her love in the only way she could.

Caught between a rock and a hard place, Sally thought. If she'd admitted she'd been with William she'd have been disgraced and sent to England and he'd have been hounded by her father — possibly accused of something else to get him out of the way. Even if she had told the truth, they'd have said exactly what they did when she finally spoke out, no longer caring about the consequences. That she'd made it up to save him.

Rose had written bitterly, 'Mrs Moore vowed that no one came to the house whilst father was away. She was sound asleep in her own room and could not have heard us, (indeed, we made sure of it, for how could we know what was to come?) but she must needs convince father of her perfect guardianship of me. I hate her for her lies. I have never disliked her so much in my life. She has not the courage to admit the truth, that she was oblivious to all, for she is so desperate for father's good opinion. So, William and I are to be sacrificed for her good name.'

'I believe you,' Sally whispered. 'William was with you and somebody waited for him and shot him on his way home.'

Who? She wondered. Who hated him so much? He believed it was Jack d'Arcy but Sally felt she could make a case against Robert Leicester, who must have known how Rose felt about William. Tongues were never still in a small community. And there was Rose's father himself, who had arrived unexpectedly that same night. He might very well have worried, knowing his daughter's strong will, and being suspicious of her miraculous compliance to his dictate, that she'd use the opportunity of his absence to see William. He could have ridden out to the farm, watched William leave, and ambushed him. And there were other boys who wanted their rival away from Rose. She wished she could see him again, get his version of events, find out exactly what had happened that night.

Of course, it had been d'Arcy who had betrayed him, going to the police instead of telling Walter of his brother's escape. Otherwise, Walter might have been able to help the lovers go away together, out of reach of the law and George Carew.

There was also the sub-inspector. He was obviously keen on Rose and seemed an overbearing, self-satisfied man with an overly high opinion of himself. Sally thought his handling of the case highhanded, refusing to let Rose testify but visiting her regularly during those terrible days, trying to win her over.

'He'd never get away with it today,' she muttered.

Rose had written that Stapleton seemed eager to please her: 'to show me that he is not a brute but has only my best interests at heart. They all say that,' she continued wistfully, 'whilst refusing to accept that my best interests lie solely in having my dearest William returned to me. Frederick...'

Oho, it's Frederick, now, is it? Sally thought.

'...grows more affectionate every time we meet and I am considering how I may best use his regard for me. William denied we were together that night and, out of love for me, asked me to do the same. But the case against him grows daily more desperate, in spite of Walter's attempts to make them believe he was with William at the time of the raid. So I have decided, if Frederick continues in his liking for me, I will tell him the truth and plead with him, for my sake, to speak for William.'

Oh, Rose, Sally shook her head. You were an innocent, weren't you? William might have done such an honourable thing but old Fred — couldn't you see he was determined to drop William right in it?

The poignant tale went on. Rose was trapped in her original lie which Stapleton preferred to believe, incurring her father's wrath for daring to say she'd spent the night with William. And then shamed by Mrs Moore clinging tenaciously to her story, making Rose seem a liar and a hussy into the bargain. Poor Rose, living in a nightmare, turned to William's brother and friends for help.

'Jack d'Arcy is such a comfort to me. Although he loves me and has no wish to see me with William, he has called on me daily to inform me of William's progress and will speak for him at his trial, giving him a good character. Jack is truly kind and worthy of the love of a good woman, which I sincerely hope he will find one day. He told me that, whilst his dear wish was that I might return his affection, as I cannot, he will no longer importune me but accept my friendship only; and, further, he will do everything in his power for William. It is at times such as these that one finds whom one's friends truly are.'

'Or who the snakes in the grass are,' Sally growled to herself. Now, was Jack d'Arcy genuine or trying to make Rose so grateful she'd reward him later if William didn't make it? She didn't know how treacherous the man could be, if William's right and d'Arcy betrayed him.

Walter had also gone regularly to see Rose. 'Father does not like it but, seeing my grief, has not the heart to refuse Walter's visits, although we are closely watched.' When William was sentenced to hang, Walter told her he'd appealed for a retrial and was determined to overturn the sentence.

'They did not believe his evidence,' Rose mourned. 'He strongly supported William's opinion that I should not give him an alibi but trust in the story Walter invented. However, distressed at the sight of his poor brother in the dock, (for which I cannot blame him), Walter broke down in court and did not give his evidence convincingly, according to Jack. Because of his hesitancy, some others who had agreed they had seen the brothers at the Squatters' Arms that night, became less sure of the date and were easily broken and made to look fools by the prosecutor. Walter was sick with shame and in agony for William's plight. He blames himself terribly and his mother will not even speak to him for letting William down. Walter has continued to plead William's case, writing to demand a fresh trial. If he is not successful, my beloved will meet his dreadful fate. I cannot write of it or allow myself even to think it. I pray daily that those whom God surely joined together in the purest love, cannot be put asunder by anything man may do. I must believe it with all my heart and trust in His Goodness. Anything else is unthinkable.'

Sally put down the diary and wiped her eyes. She'd been so moved by Rose's predicament, she'd shed a few silent tears. She related strongly to Rose's feelings. She was facing the same situation, wanting to help William against all the odds. If only Walter had received the letter, she thought. And how could I have been so criminally careless as to lose such a precious document? Despite her annoyance with herself, she smiled slightly. Perhaps someone had found it wherever she'd dropped it and mistakenly popped it into a post box. What a surprise for Australia Post! It might be an idea to make inquiries there, just in case.

I should look at the other papers, read the official reports. I'll be in Bell's Creek tomorrow. I'd like to be fully informed.

She pulled the folder towards her and began leafing through the photocopies. James had gathered as much documentation as he could, copying newspaper reports of the trial as well as court documents. *The Bell's Creek Chronicle* had carried the story in exhaustive detail. It was big news, locally. William was well known and obviously well liked. Many people wrote to the paper expressing outrage. *The Chronicle's* editor had kept the letters, they had been far too numerous to print, and Sally read through them all. Some claimed to have evidence exonerating William. She presumed these had been followed up and dismissed as good-hearted attempts to help him. One man said he'd met the brothers along the track earlier in the evening and that they'd been arguing about something. The writer had been called at the trial but his testimony hadn't helped because this had been before the raid and Walter himself had admitted remonstrating with William, trying to persuade him not to be a fool, but to go with him to the pub. The prosecutor pointed out that the man's evidence was irrelevant as William could easily have continued on to McIntyre's station from there in plenty of time to commit the crime.

Sally read the reports of the trial with mounting depression. The prosecution had put together an excellent case, despite the lack of physical evidence. Stapleton had been certain the two horses they'd been following were from the raid and no one disputed him, in spite of Sergeant Mallory's testimony.

'PROSECUTION: You say that you cannot be certain that William O'Meally was one of the men you were chasing. Equally, can you be certain he was not?'

'SERGEANT MALLORY: No, I cannot be certain either way.

'PROSECUTION: Therefore, I put it to you that William O'Meally might well have been one of those men.

'SERGEANT MALLORY: I cannot say that he was. There was no definite proof that he was.

'PROSECUTION: Kindly answer the question, Sergeant. William O'Meally might well have been one of the men.

'SERGEANT MALLORY: He might have been, but...
'PROSECUTION: Thank you, Sergeant, that will be all.
'JUDGE TIMMS (taking notes): He might have been.'

'Why didn't the defence pick up on that and cross-examine the sergeant?' Sally exclaimed in frustration. The O'Meallys hadn't had the means to hire a solicitor for William, the man appointed to defend him had done his job barely adequately and without passion. Sally felt he could have refuted more evidence, cross-examined more objectively. He didn't fight for William because he didn't believe him, she thought.

The Carews weren't called at all, there'd been no need. William had been determined not to involve Rose. His friends, including d'Arcy, could only swear he wouldn't steal horses and, given his other exploits, weren't believed. As Rose had mentioned, Walter proved a weak link, apparently so upset he wasn't able to sustain his alibi with any conviction. The prosecution made short work of his story.

Kitty O'Meally hadn't helped, being seen to have deliberately concocted several different stories, none of which was the truth. She'd become abusive and called the judge a 'blind old fool who had no sense of justice', which hadn't gone down well with the jury; although she'd probably won their sympathy, they didn't accept her evidence.

'It's not good enough,' Sally burst out impatiently. 'I need something else. William wasn't on the raid but anyone who was couldn't say so without incriminating themselves. I need to find out who waited for him and shot him. If it really was Jack d'Arcy, I want to know. That's the issue here. *Who shot William?*'

She saw the time and tidied the papers back into the folder. She'd take them with her to Bell's Creek, try to find something there. Perhaps, if she was in William's own place, she'd be guided to whatever she needed.

I can try, she told herself. I can only try my best.

PART THREE

Bell's Creek
1996

Chapter 22

B
ell's Creek lay between folded hills of flowing grasses, sun
bleached to gold, in the foothills of the Blackbutt Range.
The highway had long since by-passed it and Sally nearly
missed the small road sign that proclaimed Bell's Creek, 10 km.
She turned off down a narrow road which snaked through deep,
cool forest, thick with hoop pine, bunya and eucalypt, towering
above a floor of bright green bracken and fern.

The road emerged in the more open hills around Bell's Creek
and became the small town's main street. The buildings were a
mixture of modern brick bungalows on the outskirts, older timber
high-stilt Queenslanders, and the low-set brick and timber houses
of the district's pioneers. She pulled up outside the Bell's Creek
Hotel, a turn-of-the-century two-storey building with a wide upper
verandah and ornate lace-iron work. The shops along the main
road were of the same era as the hotel and lifted curved corrugated iron awnings over the footpath. The iron constantly cracked
and popped as clouds moved over the sun, sounding like the pat-
ter of hail or bursts of rifle fire.

Sally booked a room for the night and asked directions to
Glendale Farm. She drove slowly, trying to absorb the atmosphere,
thinking that it probably hadn't changed much since William's day.

She passed several forestry tracks with their attendant warning signs to campers to act responsibly in the forests, then pulled hard over to the extreme edge of the road to squeeze past a huge truck hauling timber, its load of pine logs securely chained to a long trailer.

At a fork in the track another sign pointed her to Glendale Farm and she finally came to cleared farm land, dotted with giant trees. The road ran along a barbed-wire fence; on a near rise she could see a low building with a steep pyramidal roof of the ubiquitous corrugated iron, with several tall brick chimneys. A five-barred gate carried another sign with the single name Grant and a track led over a cattle grid to the house. Beside the gate was a letter box with a short hollow log lashed to it for papers and a covered wooden shelter for milk churns and produce.

Sally got out of the car and breathed the country air appreciatively. It was wonderfully peaceful here with only the sound of the wind and a chorus from a pair of magpies on the greener grass under a stand of eucalypts. She opened the gate, drove bumpily across the grid then got out again and closed the gate behind her.

The Grants had heard the car engine and were waiting for her as she drove up to the house. They made her welcome and brought a late morning tea out onto the verandah.

'You found the place all right?' Scott asked, smothering a scone with jam and lashings of cream.

'Easily. They gave me directions at the pub.'

'Not the original building, sadly.' Alisha waved at Sally to help herself to more scones. 'Don't stint yourself out of politeness. It's our own, made here on the farm. The first hotel, The Squatters' Arms, burned down in 1885. There was a brawl between the police and the cellarman, Buck Buchanan, and a lamp got knocked over. They built a new hotel on the site of the old so the cellars are the genuine article, then later, it was extensively remodelled to what you see now. Buchanan's shack still stands out the back. He led a gang of thieves for years in various raids on local properties, stealing horses and cattle, you know. The law finally caught up with him, hence the brawl. He was in Boggo Road gaol for a few years then, after the United Kingdom and America signed their first ex-

tradition agreement in 1890, he was extradited to America for similar crimes.'

'After tea we'll show you the house and farm,' Scott said. 'James
tells us you're interested in William O'Meally. This part of the house
is all original, built by William's father, Thomas. The chimney bricks
were made here on the property and the timber cleared from the
paddocks and prepared on site. Lots of red cedar here then, and
tallow wood, iron bark...'

'The house was added to by Walter's sons,' Alisha put in. 'Michael
lived here with his family — he was killed at Gallipoli. The boy's
sister, Maggie, always lived here, a sort of perennial babysitter, and
Walter and Rose were here until they died in 1942.'

'James said Walter died then Rose just a few months later.'

'Couldn't live without him, they said. You'll see their graves,'
Alisha promised. 'Well, if we've all finishd, Scotty and I will take
you around. You'll stay for lunch, of course.'

'The kitchen is separate, you see.' Alisha led the way through a
small back garden to the next building. 'There was always the haz-
ard of fire from the wood stoves. Kitty O'Meally had her vegie and
herb garden here and I resurrected it. Maggie let it go to weeds
and she didn't maintain the house any better. The people she sold
it to only used it as a weekender to get away from the city. The last
owners weren't gardeners either — or farmers, for that matter. He
ran the local real estate office and she had a dress shop. Pardon
me, a boutique, I should say. They sold out last year to retire to
some canal estate on the coast. We were looking for something in
the country to escape the city pollution, a place to raise kids when
we come to that, so we snapped it up.'

Scott paused by a side gate. 'The road ran right past here, once.
Walter bought the neighbouring farm and joined the two properties. We're turning Glendale back into a working farm.'

'Scott has a mania for cattle,' Alisha sighed. 'He's got a herd of
Brahman. Spends hours with the boys from Primac discussing se-
men and artificial insemination, all very boring stuff and no fun at

all for the cows, I shouldn't think. Personally, those great beasts scare the life out of me, I don't mean the boys from Primac so I give them a wide berth. Come and see the kitchen.'

'Isn't it inconvenient, detached from the house?'

'We love it. It's so big and cool, and look at the size of the baker's oven. I bottle all my jams here in the kitchen.' Alisha opened a pantry door to show Sally shelves crammed with jars. 'I've got my own pet project, bringing the orchard back into shape and planting new trees.'

'I think the O'Meallys would be pleased.' Sally looked about her at the big room with its tiled floor and scrubbed wooden table.

'We've kept the original fireplace — found it behind some crappy modern shelving — and we've gathered a display of various cooking implements of the period, as you see,' Scott said. 'We're restoring the place as authentically as possible.'

'We use a proper electric oven, though.' Alisha grinned. 'The O'Meallys installed an oven when they got electricity out here, so why should we slave away over iron pots and open fires? The fire is lovely in winter, though. We do our toast over it.'

Sally was conducted all over the house which had little of the O'Meallys' energy left. William's niece, Maggie, had been the last O'Meally to live here and she'd left thirty-four years previously, taking her personal knick-knacks with her. Some of the furniture had belonged to the family but most had been deemed too old-fashioned by the following owners and had been disposed of.

'We're slowly finding suitable things,' Alisha said. 'We've got old photos of how the place looked, taken at family gatherings and so on, and we read anything in the way of letters and documents for any mention of furniture or personal items. I believe the kitchen table was Kitty's and we found a rubbish tip full of broken china and bottles and furniture, so that gave us a lot of clues.'

'Do any of the original families live in the area?'

Scott nodded. 'You should talk to Ma Drake in the cake shop next to the pub. Her family was here then. Her great grandfather was one of the first to settle in Bell's Creek. He was a timber cutter — used a hand saw and had a bullock team. Got speared twice by wild Aborigines.'

'Those were the days,' Alisha teased. 'Come on, Sally, we'll have lunch then walk over to the cemetery.'

It's interesting, Sally thought, but unfamiliar; it means nothing to me. I don't believe I was ever here.

She was curled up in bed, listening to the night sounds of the country town, the occasional voice raised in the bar downstairs, a motor bike in the road under her window, a mopoke's haunting cry. Her hotel room was furnished with chintzy curtains and chair covers and she had a double bed to herself which she'd covered with James Carew's photocopies. Rose's diary was in her lap. It had been far too important to leave behind. She wanted to finish it here, where Rose had lived and died.

On this very site George Carew had stayed the night William was shot. Buck Buchanan had worked here — she knew of him from the various police reports. He'd been entertaining John Francis in his shack behind the hotel. The O'Meally boys had looked in on their way to drown William's sorrows...

'But it was a lie,' Sally said. 'Walter was with Jack d'Arcy that night because William said so in his letter. They'd separated somewhere along the track, presumably near the Carew's farm, and Jack had lain in wait for William.'

She'd gathered the papers of the court proceedings into a neat file and flicked through them again, looking for d'Arcy's testimony, a picture forming in her mind.

D'Arcy gave William a character reference. In the police interviews Jack said he'd been with Limpy Patterson. I'll bet they were all in on the raid. Buchanan and Francis, because they were together...and Stapleton thought Francis had been shot. There was something about that; she hunted through a pile of newspaper clippings. Yes, here it is, 'Local Hero Saves His Friend'. Walter again and Johnny Francis. I think Stapleton was right.

Walter seemed very good at making up stories to protect his friends; pity he botched his evidence. Stapleton's report, she read it through again, was suspicious of Buchanan and, according to Scott and Alisha, he was later proved to be the ringleader. So, he must have led the raid that night. William should have been there but had received Rose's letter. He'd rushed off to see her instead, so the gang members all knew about it. Now; Buchanan wasn't one of Rose's admirers and he'd had his hands full with John Francis, anyway; Limpy didn't seem to have been interested in her and neither was James McLeod. He wasn't mentioned anywhere in her diary only that he'd once done some fencing on the farm and was a loner who preferred his own company. So that left d'Arcy. It was him, all right, but how could she prove it?'

She had a sudden wild idea of holding a seance and summoning the ghost of Jack d'Arcy, to explain itself, then shook her head, smiling at her insanity.

Well, d'Arcy lost Rose, anyway, she thought. He kept going around to see her, pretending to be her friend. No doubt gloating that William was out of the way and even making sure he didn't get back to her when he escaped. But it didn't do him any good. I wonder what happened to Jack? I'll check the local archives for him.

At least she knew what had happened to Rose and Walter. The Grants had taken her across fields of golden grass to a creek where large boulders made easy stepping stones. On the far side of the stream, with a view of the property and the blue ranges beyond, they'd led her to the cemetery behind its dry-stone walls. They'd gone through the gate and slowly walked along the line of graves.

The oldest belonged to Liam O'Meally, Thomas's father, who had been laid to rest with an iron fence around him, now in urgent need of de-rusting. Then Thomas, and Kitty next to him, with suitable biblical texts. There were children's graves. A baby, still-born, a toddler and another Walter, aged thirteen, all Rose and Walter's grandchildren.

'Young Walter died in a farm accident; run over by a tractor,' Alisha had said. 'I'm slowly cleaning up here, starting with the oldest graves, getting rid of the weeds and the lichen which seems to love the cemetery. You couldn't read Liam's headstone at all and

Escape from the Past

Thomas and Kitty's was a mess. I haven't attempted Rose and Walter yet. They're over in the corner under the camphor laurel which, unfortunately, Rose planted. It's such a pest and its berries mess up the graves. I should turf it out because it takes over the creek beds from the native species but — Rose put it there and I don't like to.'

Sally had knelt by the grave. The names and inscriptions were badly obscured by lichen and mosses — this must be a damp corner — and tall weeds flourished against the headstone. She'd just made out Rose's name and the W and LT of Walter's. The inscription was less difficult. It had been Rose's choice and grated on Sally as she slowly picked out the words. 'Devoted in death as in life. What God hath joined together, let no man put asunder.'

Which, Sally thought, was exactly what she'd said about William. So her devotion was of fairly short duration.

She'd remembered Alisha saying that Rose couldn't live without Walter. She decided she didn't like Rose very much, after all.

Chapter 23

S ally woke to the song of magpies and butcher birds, currawongs and kookaburras, interspersed with the harsh cawing of crows.

Like waking up in an aviary, she thought and stretched, yawning widely. Rose's diary lay where it had slipped from her grasp the night before. She remembered opening it, then nothing more until this morning.

'Must be the country air,' she decided. 'I just flaked out.'

She dressed and made her way to the dining room where breakfast was being served. As soon as she'd eaten she went out into the fresh morning which was sweetly scented with the soft tang of the Australian bush.

The cake shop also served coffee, tea and milkshakes and, set out under the awning, white plastic tables were already laid with stainless steel sugar bowls and ashtrays, to cater for early morning customers. Sally pushed open the wire screen door and went inside.

A sharp-faced woman, her hair in lacquered waves, appeared from a back room. Sally judged her to be in her late forties.

'Can I help you?' She smiled the impersonal smile of a shop

keeper to a potential sale.

'I was told to ask for Ma Drake.' Sally felt awkward not knowing a more formal title.

'You're the woman from Brisbane?' Her smile deepened.

'Sally Cooper. How did you know?'

'Alisha Grant was in earlier. They supply my milk. She said you'd be calling. Come through to the back.' She lifted a portion of the counter.

'I didn't know what to call her. Is it Mrs Drake?'

'Heavens, everyone calls Gran Ma Drake. She wouldn't answer to anything else. I'm her granddaughter, Mrs Bradbury.' She opened a door into the living quarters behind the shop and raised her voice. 'Gran, it's the lady from Brisbane.' She ushered Sally into the small room and said, 'You'll have to speak up. Gran's nearly ninety and a bit deaf but her mind's still sharp.'

Ma Drake had the same sharp features as her granddaughter. She was sitting in a chair by the glow of a single bar radiator with a cup of tea on a small table close by her. She scanned Sally with surprisingly bright eyes and waved her, with a claw-like hand, to the opposite chair.

'Sit down and you can turn off the heater — I'm cooking in here.'

Sally obediently flicked the switch and the radiator began to crackle into coolness. Mrs Bradbury nodded at Sally and went back to the shop.

'I like the fire in the mornings, though,' the old lady shot at her suddenly. 'It's always a cold place early and I'm up at five every morning. Never could lie in.' She cocked her head on one side like a predatory bird. 'What do you want, then?'

'I'm interested in William O'Meally, I'm doing some research on his life.' Sally thought this was the safest tack. Research had a solid, respectable sound and gave her a reason to be nosy about anything she felt was connected with William.

'William, eh? Young Billy. Didn't have much of a life to research. Alisha Grant told me what you were after.'

'She said your grandfather was one of the district's pioneers.'

'That's so. I was born ninety years ago next month. Grandad knew them all. My father was born the year William was taken away. He was two when Billy killed himself. What do you think, eh?'

'Marvellous,' Sally murmured. 'You sound invaluable, if you don't mind talking to me.'

'You a friend of James Carew? He come nosing around after William once. I'll fill you in, what I can. Yeah, my family was the first here. Bell's Creek was named after my granddad, Arthur Bell. He camped along the creek, further up the range. He cut timber in the Blackbutt Range in the eighteen-sixties. That's when he came here.'

'So I believe.' Sally hitched her chair forward and Ma Drake gave a short laugh.

'Got you interested, eh? No one wants to hear about the old days much, not any more. Most of them moved away; not much work for the kids, they all want to be in the city. What happens to them there? They live in cardboard boxes in the street, that's what I hear.' She nodded and was silent, lost in thought.

Just as Sally wondered if she should speak, Ma Drake gave her another of her sharp looks.

'All right, pet, get on with it. What do you want to know?'

Her notebook at the ready, Sally settled back to enjoy the old woman's reminiscences.

'They all knew he never did it,' Ma Drake remembered. 'He was courting Rose but never said, because of her father. Carew was an old bugger, according to my granddad, and times were different then. You didn't just go jumping into bed with whoever took your fancy, like on the telly. More than your life was worth. And Old Carew hated the O'Meallys. He must have had a fit when Rose married and moved to Glendale. Kitty would've been glad to have her, give her a happier home than her dad ever did. Old George married his housekeeper, Mary Moore. About time he made a respectable woman of her, Granddad used to say. George died before I was born but Mary was alive. Eighty-five she was then. I remember her when I was three. I thought she was an old witch out of a story book. She was bent double and talked to herself.' Ma Drake drew up her own straight back. 'She never saw ninety, though. I'll see ninety. I'll see a hundred, I reckon.'

'There was no proof William was with Rose,' Sally said. 'No one believed Rose and Mrs Moore said he was never there.'

'Old bitch,' Ma said unexpectedly. 'Coming all moral over Rose when everyone knew she was carrying on with Carew, the old hypocrite. Billy should've up and told them all and took Rose off somewhere. It didn't do him any good, keeping quiet, did it? Left the way clear for Walter.'

'Yes, I think he should have said,' Sally agreed. 'He was trying to save her reputation.'

'What good's a reputation? He'd have married the girl. It wouldn't have been the first time a man got his leg over *before* the wedding. Granddad used to say William was too much like his dad, head full of romantic stuff. The girls liked it, though. 'Round Billy like bees 'round a honey-pot, so Granddad used to say.'

'So the other boys would have been jealous?'

Ma snorted with laughter. 'What do you think? No need, though, Billy only wanted Rose. They all knew that but, with Billy himself saying he wasn't there and old Mary Moore backing him up, what could they do?'

'What about Jack d'Arcy? He was in love with Rose.'

Ma Drake gave her a quick, sideways glance.

'Done your homework, haven't you? My ma was cousin to the d'Arcys. Jack d'Arcy, "Wild Jack", they called him. My granddad and his dad were like that.' She crossed two gnarled fingers. 'Jack's dad made whips and Jack learnt it off him. Best whip maker in Queensland. I still got Dad's whip, somewhere, made by Wild Jack himself. Dad was given it by Granddad.'

'I'm interested to find out how William was shot.' Sally pursued. 'Who was in the vicinity.'

'You're a bit late, pet, it won't help Billy now. You're thinking it might have been Jack?' The old woman asked shrewdly.

'What do you think?'

'You're not the first to think so. Jack lost friends over it. He was the O'Meally boys' best mate but word was he turned Billy into the police later, when the boy got away from St Helena Island. I never could see that. Look, if Jack had shot Billy, he'd have done it face to face, in a fair fight. Granddad always said Jack was square, as square as they come and as good a mate as you could get. He wasn't one to sneak around in the dark and shoot you in the back. Granddad was older than Jack by eight years but they were mates and he reckoned Jack was all right. He said the police must have seen Billy, or some one else did, going up to the d'Arcy's, and dobbed him in.'

'Who'd have done that?'

'No one knew. Someone who hated Billy's guts, I reckon.'

'Didn't William know who shot him?'

'He told the police the man had a hood over his head. He was bigger than Billy, but so were half the blokes in the district. Granddad said Billy wasn't a big man and he was wiry.'

'Wiry but very strong,' Sally said half to herself.

'I heard that. I hear all right, sometimes. You sound like you knew the boy.'

'I read about him.'

'As strong as a bull, Granddad said. Listen pet, if you want to know who shot Billy, I can't tell you. I made my own guess a long time ago but it's just what I think. He went on to be an important man hereabouts, had a big property. So I can't see any sense in saying anything and hurting innocent people over what was just wild lads fighting over a girl. There's never been any proof.'

'But you don't think it was Jack?'

Ma Drake gave a knowing smile. 'If it was Jack, why didn't he stay and marry Rose? She liked him enough. He gave up his claim on her and pushed off. Went droving out west. Died of some fever he picked up six years later. You tell me, if he done it and nobody knew, why didn't he stay and take Rose off Walter? Eh? What do you think, pet?'

Sally nodded thoughtfully. 'I think you've got a point, Ma. Thanks very much. It's been marvellous to talk to someone whose family goes back to those times.'

Ma Drake was clearly delighted to have had Sally's rapt attention. Her cheeks were pink and her eyes gleamed with pleasure.
She said expansively, 'You come and talk to me any time, pet. Of
course, we weren't exactly here after Billy got taken away, but I've
got lots of stories about the old days.'

Sally jumped and her pencil jerked across the page, tearing the
paper. 'What do you mean, not exactly here?'

Her voice was sharper than she'd intended and the old woman
looked down, her face closed, and mumbled, 'There's no need to
take that tone with me, girl.'

'I'm sorry.' Sally bit her lip. 'I was surprised. It's... it's terribly
important to me, Ma. I really want to know the truth.'

Ma Drake gave her a sullen look. 'Pretty words, pretty winning
ways, they don't cut any ice with me. You come here, saying you
want to hear about those times, then jump down my throat. You
can clear off, then.'

'No, please, I'm really sorry. I didn't mean to offend you.' Sally
surreptitiously crossed her fingers. Surely she wasn't going to be
thrown out before she'd got the information she wanted. 'Do tell
me what you meant about not being here. I really am interested,
Ma. You've been wonderful and it's all so fascinating.'

She wondered if she'd overdone it and waited anxiously, the tip
of her tongue pressed between her teeth, her breath temporarily
on hold.

Ma Drake was mollified. She pursed her mouth and nodded
slowly. 'All right, pet, don't go on. What I told you was what I heard,
you see? After they took Billy away to prison, Granddad was that
upset. He said he'd never live in a place where a good man, and an
innocent one, mind, could be treated so bad. So we moved right
away.'

'But, I thought you were born here. You said you knew Mary
Moore when you were three.' Sally's heart was sinking rapidly. Could
it be that Ma Drake had just been leading her on, telling her what
she wanted to hear in order to hold onto an audience? She'd obviously loved having Sally drinking in her reminiscences so avidly. It

had made her feel important, wanted.

Ma's eyes were like flint. 'I wasn't fibbing, girl.' She snapped. 'I did know Old Mary then. She come out west, where we were, to stay with family. She was a mad old thing, mumbling all the time. Her mind was gone, see? She couldn't look after herself. I was scared of her. So don't you hold your nose in the air and say I'm a liar.'

'I didn't. I wouldn't.' Sally shook her head vehemently. 'And it's been fascinating, honestly. I just want to know what the facts were.'

'Oh, facts, is it? The fact is, Wild Jack d'Arcy come out west and he and Granddad went droving together. Jack never talked about those times. Some said it was because he had something to hide.'

'When did you come back to Bell's Creek?' Sally asked, trying to keep the urgency out of her voice.

'Must be near twenty years ago. My daughter moved back here and bought the shop. She died soon after.' Ma Drake sniffled and pulled a hanky out of her sleeve. She drew it over her eyes and wiped her nose. 'It's a terrible thing, to outlive your daughter. You expect you'll go first but it doesn't always happen like that. I come over for the funeral and Lee, that's my granddaughter, said I should stay here and she'd look after me.' She gave Sally a pathetic look. 'I'm an old woman. I can't look after myself. I should've died before my girl.'

'But you said you were going to live to be a hundred,' Sally said, trying to rally her. 'That'll be something. Mary Moore didn't see ninety.'

'That's the truth,' Ma Drake agreed complacently, her self-pity forgotten.

'Ma,' Sally said impetuously, 'what about the newspaper office here? They'd have archives going back to William's time.'

'No, pet.' Ma shook her head. 'There was a fire in the pub, not three years after Billy hanged himself. It spread to the buildings on either side, sparks flying, you see. One of them was the newspaper office. All the records were lost except for the ones before 1882. They'd been taken out a few days before to make more room. The editor stowed them in a shed out the back and they were saved. It's no good looking there.'

Sally put her pad and pencil away in her bag. She felt desolate. It seemed she'd come to a dead end.

Ma Drake looked at her closely, her sharp eyes glistening with sudden interest. 'You look like you lost ten quid and found a penny. What's it matter to you?' Then her voice changed and she said abruptly, 'Who are you? What's your business with William? You're up to something, I can feel it. You've got a strange look.' She shrank back, suddenly suspicious. 'I don't want to talk to you any more. There's something queer about you, girl. You'd better go, now. I'm not saying any more.' She called out, 'Lee, Lee. Come here.'

Mrs Bradbury opened the door. 'I've got customers, Gran, what's the matter?'

Ma Drake had hunched herself into the appearance of a decrepit old woman. She mumbled plaintively, 'I'm tired. This lady's going now.'

Sally got up reluctantly. Ma Drake's keen, triumphant stare hadn't escaped her notice. She bent politely to shake hands but was ignored. She could only thank Ma for a fascinating morning. Her words were greeted with a stony silence.

Sally gave up and obediently left the shop.

Chapter 24

'What do you think?' Tom Grogan hissed out of the corner of his mouth.

William shrugged and muttered back, 'They're buzzing around like bluebottle flies.'

'Keep your eyes to the front. It's none of your concern,' the warder shouted.

The work gang had been lined up, picks, hoes and other farming implements over their shoulders, when the row in the hospital broke out. Warders ran, shouting, whistles were being blown and the dispenser warder was frantically signalling his fellows to hurry.

'Quick march.'

The work detail moved out of the stockade into the fields. A warder ran after them and they were halted while the guards conferred.

'O'Meally, give Grogan your hoe. Superintendent Townley wants to see you.'

'Question is,' Tom growled, 'whether it's better to slave in the fields under this merciless sun or have an interview with that bastard.'

'You've whetted my curiosity.' William handed over the hoe.

'I'm interested to meet the new man.'

'Go carefully,' Grogan warned, 'he's a devil.'

'I'll give him your regards, then.' William winked and followed the second warder.

'What was all that racket at the hospital?'

'Prisoner Collins. Cut his throat.' The warder shook his head. 'Poor bugger bled to death.'

'Where'd he get a knife?'

'Had it with him. Made it himself.' The man shuddered. ' He was a gruesome sight. I tell you, O'Meally, I often wish my wife and children were not in this depressing place but I'd go mad without them. Those married men whose wives live on the mainland are in exile. They only see their loved ones every few months, then are torn away from them once again.'

'You're breaking my heart,' William growled.

'I know. You fellows are in a worse case — but you broke the law, after all, and must do your time. But, suicide, the worst sin of all.'

'A welcome relief, if you've nothing else to look forward to.'

'How could a man be in such despair? I cannot understand it.'

William grinned. 'You're a good fellow, Leighton. A pity more were not like you.'

They reached the superintendent's office. Leighton reported to the warder on duty and they were admitted.

Superintendent Townley looked coldly at William. He had a stern face and his moustache bristled under a jutting nose. His eyebrows were bushy and his thinning hair was parted in the middle into two waves and close cropped at the back.

Warder Leighton said, 'Prisoner O'Meally, stand to attention.'

'That's what I was doing,' William said and added solicitously, 'Am I standing at attention enough for you this time?'

'William O'Meally.' The superintendent's voice was even. 'Horse theft and manslaughter.'

'I didn't do either of those things, sir.'

'You've an unenviable reputation, O'Meally.' Townley's eyes bored into his. 'One might infer you are a troublemaker. So let me warn you, there is no room for troublemakers in my prison.'

William grinned. 'That's good news. Give me my civilian clothes back, then, and I'll be off.'

The other man's heavy eyebrows snapped together.

'I'd heard you've a clever tongue in your head. Keep it still in future or it'll be gagged.'

William was silent. The gag was a revolting instrument of torture. A short hollow piece of wood was inserted over a man's tongue and strapped into place by leather cords which fastened behind his ears and over his head. A chinstrap held it firmly in place and the man's hands were encased in thick leather gloves, belted around his waist, or worse, he was put into a stout canvas straight jacket, to prevent him removing the gag. The previous superintendent, John McDonald, had rarely used it and then only for brief periods on extremely violent prisoners. William felt this new man wouldn't hesitate to carry out his threat and use him as an example.

'That's better.' Townley nodded. 'I intend to put a stop to these constant escapes of yours. I will not permit you to give my prison a bad name, let me tell you that now. I believe in iron rule and strict discipline and you will quickly discover that I am serious in this. There will be an immediate upgrading of security, from more effectively securing the gun and ammunition locker to clearing the canefields. I maintain they are an open invitation for a man such as yourself to bolt into their cover and are highly combustible and easily fired by anyone spiteful enough to put a match to them. More scrub will be cleared and the warders will be even more alert than before.'

He drummed his fingers on the desk.

'I can assure you, O'Meally, your flights to freedom are at an end. You will be given no such opportunities again and I advise you not to make any further attempt.'

'There are other ways off the island, sir,' William said quietly, 'as William Collins has just proved.'

The superintendent's eyes flashed to the warder and he gave a snort of annoyance.

'It wasn't Mr Leighton. You cannot keep such a thing a secret. It will be all over the prison by now.'

'You'll have no chance to follow that man's example,' Townley said sternly. 'Warder, this man's cell is to be searched twice daily for illegal implements and a close watch is to be kept upon him at all times.'

William leaned across the desk. 'It is a worrying thing, is it not,' he said softly, 'that I might destroy your record?'

Townley smiled grimly. 'My reputation is quite secure, I promise you. I have an excellent record as police magistrate at Ipswich and before then. I intend to go far in my career and a jumped-up little rebel such as yourself is not going to harm me. I am a hard man, O'Meally. Don't try my patience.'

He held William's gaze with his own. 'You've had your first and final warning,' he said harshly. 'Your insolence today will be added to the charges against you. You'll answer to the visiting justice tomorrow. That's all, O'Meally, you're dismissed.'

As Warder Leighton took him outside, William let go a long breath.

'Phew. Now there's a right bastard.'

Leighton looked at him seriously. 'He is that, lad, so no more of your tricks or you'll be in hot water so deep you'll drown yourself.'

"I'll get away from here.' Meat-Axe Ludlow glanced furtively around the exercise yard.

'Talk's cheap,' Tom Grogan grunted briefly.

Meat-Axe flushed and pulled nervously at the faint blond hairs on his top lip. He turned to William. 'You've done it. Four times.'

William was keeping a watchful eye on the warders but they seemed more interested in discussing Collins' suicide than observing an illegal conversation between the prisoners in the yard. He imagined the screws had all been knocking back the grog to steady their nerves and were probably muzzy as owls. He nodded to Meat-Axe and replied, 'Aye, but it's not so easy. It's hardly a stroll in the country.'

'Still, you managed it all right.'

'With him it's a matter of will,' Tom cut in.

Meat-Axe stared uncomprehendingly. 'Who's Will?'

'Don't be daft, boy.' Tom cuffed him irritably, his eyes glaring at the boy from under their alarming brows. 'I'm only saying that Billy wants to escape worse than they want to keep him here.'

William laid a restraining hand on Tom's arm. 'You're like a bear today.' He turned to Meat-Axe who'd shrunk out of Tom's reach. 'It's not the escaping that's the problem, lad,' he explained kindly. 'One guard only to supervise a gang of men, close to the bush. Your mates can cause a ruction, get the screw to look away and off you go, into the scrub. The real task is getting off the island. Between them the warders and the water police have the place sealed up so tight very few make it to the bay.'

'And them that does often gets drowned for their troubles.' Dingy Bell, a convicted thief, who was squatting on his heels, gazing into the distance and scratching the ginger stubble on his chin, added his mite.

Meat-Axe ran his tongue around his lips eagerly. 'But, there's ways, ain't there?'

'It's been done,' Tom growled, 'but mostly they never get off the island and get hauled back, their garb cut to ribbons by the scrub, their bellies bawling with hunger and their skin red-raw from scratching pestiferous insect bites.'

Frenchy Le Fevre, serving four years for forgery, grinned, and his dark eyes twinkled. 'The sandflies here, they have teeth this long.' He measured the distance betwen finger and thumb. 'I would not care for a night in the bush. It is quite bad enough in the cells without nets to protect us, no?'

'And them that get to sea get drowned, just like Dingy said,' Tom continued. 'And them that make it to shore get recaptured, like Billy.' He saw Ludlow's face and said resignedly, 'Oh, go on, tell the eager young fool how you did it last time, Billy.'

William grinned. 'Sometimes a boat will come adrift from her moorings on the mainland and the tides carry her over and beach her here. That's why the guards carry out regular searches along the foreshore.'

'For driftwood, too,' Frenchy reminded him.

'Aye, if there are those fool enough to brave the sharks on a log.' William shuddered.

Frenchy gave a crack of laughter, hastily suppressd. 'Ah, *oui*, the shark, she has teeth *this* long.' He held his arms wide and Meat-Axe shot him a resentful look.

'Don't tease the lad,' William admonished. 'Why should he not plan to break free?' He continued, 'A few weeks back, two of the farm's horses got loose and ran off in the night. McDonald decided they might have been forced onto the flats on the south-east shore by the incoming tide. I grew up on a farm so he figured I'd be the man to bring them back. Me and Dopey Dawson.'

Tom took up the story. 'So Billy and Dopey goes off through the mangroves, all on their own, there being no screw available to oversee their little jaunt. And, lo and behold, there's a trim little row-boat lying adrift amongst the trees. Now, Dopey, he's as mad as a hatter and don't see the significance. But Billy hides it out of sight. They find the horses and bring 'em back and aren't they McDonald's white-haired boys?' He gave a derisive snort.

Meat-Axe listened avidly. 'So, how did you get back to the boat?'

Dingy Bell grinned. 'He told me and Tom and we set up a scheme. Next day we was working on the farm. When they brought us back I managed to leave a spade behind and Billy and I got sent back for it. Billy scarpered into the bush and I went back and told them he'd took sick and gone to the hospital. By the time they worked out he weren't there, it was dark and Billy was away in the boat.'

'There was a wild storm that night,' William remembered soberly. 'A severe one. Came up from the south-east, with hail and howling winds, sea like a cauldron. I barely made it to shore alive. Took all my strength to crawl into the mangroves so I could rest without discovery. I was eaten alive by mosquitoes with teeth as big as Frenchy's sharks.'

'Next day the island was searched.' Tom finished the tale. 'Then the boat was reported missing and they figured Billy might have gone further than the island. They searched the mainland shore and found the boat, nothing more than a wreck. They thought

Billy must've drowned but those bastards don't give up easy. They have the tenacity of the hounds of hell so they kept looking anyhow.'

'But they didn't find him,' Meat-Axe breathed.

'Watch yourselves, screws coming,' William hissed. He finished softly, 'They didn't find me then. I'd recovered my wits, stolen a feed and some clothes and was on my way home. Beware of false friends, Meat-Axe.'

'Get moving, you bastards.' The guard's breath stank of liquor. 'Back to your cells.'

William winked at the others and meekly strolled towards the cell block.

Chapter 25

Wwilliam clenched his jaw until the tendons in his neck stood out like cords. Sweat beaded his face which was white from the shock of the indecent pain as the lash fell with awful consistency across his back, striping his flesh with even, burning welts.

The punishment was being observed by the visiting surgeon, visiting justice and Superintendent Townley, who stood austerely with the others, watching with grim satisfaction as the sentence was meted out.

The surgeon moved uncomfortably and said in a low voice, 'If he shows signs of collapse, I shall stop this. Fifty lashes is too extreme.'

Justice Reynolds shrugged. 'The man is incorrigible and unrepentant. In my experience, those who have been flogged, rarely expose themslves to the lash a second time.'

Meat-Axe Ludlow was also prescnt and flinched with each stroke. His own sentence for attacking the warder was twenty lashes and he dreaded his turn. He licked his dry lips and shot a scared glance towards the officials.

Another man, awaiting the lash, growled contemptuously, 'Don't let them see that you fear it, man. Indifference is our only defence and gives courage to the rest. If you join the devil's own brigade, you must expect the devil's own punishment.'

A warder behind them snapped, 'Silence on parade,' and was treated to an insolent stare from the second man.

William tried to shut off the pain by pulling his mind away but the onslaught was all invasive, taking every ounce of his strength and courage to steel himself for each new stroke and deny them the pleasure of hearing him cry out.

Think of her, think of the girl, he told himself. Pray God she got my letter away safely. If Red can prove d'Arcy's guilt, perhaps Jack will take my place in this wretched prison.

The thongs of the lash caught him in the softer flesh of his armpit and he fought back angry tears. Not much longer now. He dreaded breaking down more than he feared the lash itself. If he could bear it without a single whimper, if he could walk away from here without assistance, the other men would respect, even revere him. He'd already made quite a name for himself through his escapes. He'd stand tall and get himself to the hospital unaided or die in the attempt.

The monotonous count went on. Thirty...Thirty-one...Thirty-two. Rage, as red and as hot as the bleeding cuts being inflicted on him, surged through his brain. A scarlet mist blotted out his sight and his temples throbbed. The bastard was enjoying this, enjoying striping his back with his neat trademark. He understood the torture — he'd been flogged once himself, so the story went — but still had no compassion for the men he inflicted it upon. It was his job and he did it above and beyond the call of duty, curse his stinking hide.

I'd like to kill him, William's mind raved. Get my hands around his ugly neck and squeeze every last drop of life out of the poxy bastard.

He strove to control his fury. Other men cursed the flogger, other men collapsed under the lash, screaming for mercy. The visiting surgeon might stop their torment but the escape was only temporary. When they were considered able to receive the balance of their punishment, they were tied back to the triangle and took the remainder of their strokes. Why put off until tomorrow what he could bear now? And bear it he would and stand upright and spit in the face of the smug, fat bastard.

The final blow seared into him, then came the shock of relief as the blows ceased to fall.

The surgeon stepped quickly forward. 'Get that man directly to the hospital and see to his wounds.'

William shook off the warder and turned around, forcing his trembling legs to do his bidding. Nearly collapsing from the pain he drew himself up, his eyes blazing with hatred. The flogger's lids flickered with understanding. He waited.

William stood rigidly, knowing all eyes to be upon him. His spittle landed on the man's cheek.

'You're getting soft, Annie,' he snarled. 'You couldn't raise a blister on your grandmother.'

He could hear harsh, terrified sobbing as Ludlow broke down. It almost unnerved him but he held the flogger's eyes with his own defiant gaze for a long moment before he walked stiffly, dragging one shaking leg to follow the other, towards the prison hospital.

Chapter 26

S ally paced up and down in her room.
This is ridiculous, she thought, it's only a tape and probably complete rubbish, just me making up a good story out of my imagination. It's not as if I have to believe it. I don't really have to listen to it at all.

She'd throw it away. It wouldn't tell her anything. She snatched it up, then paused, irresolute.

What if it really was important?

How could it be? She didn't believe in past lives. Well, she wasn't sure if she did or not. Perhaps she should at least hear it.

But the very thought of listening to the session with Chris Young, which lay like a black hole in her mind, made her want to cry.

Oh, for heaven's sake, what was wrong with her? Why couldn't she simply listen to it or chuck it out?

She slowly ran a finger around the cassette, as if outlining it. 'Well. It can't really hurt, can it?' She appealed to the empty room.

She pushed it determinedly into the tape recorder and pressed the play button, then sat nervously on her bed, clasping and unclasping her hands.

'What's your name?'

Escape from the Past

'Lottie.'

'How old are you, Lottie?'

'Ummmm — nearly five.'

'What year is this?'

A giggle. 'I don't know.'

'Where do you live?'

'In a house, silly.' Another childish giggle.

'Is your house in the town or the country?'

'It's in London, of course.'

'Tell me about your family, Lottie. Do you have any brothers or sisters?'

'My brother, Teddy. He is at Eton, but he is home, now.'

'Tell me about your parents?'

'My papa is dead.' The voice caught itself on a small sob.

'When did your papa die?'

'Just yesterday.'

'Do you know why he died?'

'He was sick. Mama says Teddy is the man of the house now. He will look after us so we must not worry or be sad.'

'What are you doing now, Lottie?'

Pause. 'Playing with my hoop. Teddy gave it to me but I must not go out of the gate. There is a blackbird in the garden, see?'

'Yes. What is your surname?'

A long pause. 'I have a pet frog but do not tell Mama. She says frogs are dirty. I kissed it but it is still only a frog.'

Sally listened with fascination to the voice on the tape. It was clearly recognisable as her own but with an artless, childish quality as if she was reliving a childhood of which she had no recollection.

'Do you know your full name? Your surname?' Chris Young's voice was patient.

'Teddy says that, if I am a good girl and mind Nanny and learn my lessons, he will give me a kitten.'

'Can you count to five, Lottie?'

'Of course.' The voice was scornful.

'I want you to close your eyes and count very slowly up to five. At each number you will become one year older. Do you understand?

Begin to count now.'

There was a pause as the tape burred softly around the spindles and across the heads.

'Are you still there, Lottie?'

'Yes.' The voice was less childish.

'How old are you now?'

'I am ten years old.'

'What is your full name?'

'Charlotte Maria Petersham.'

'What year is this?'

'The year is 1890.'

'Do you know who is on the throne?'

'Of course.' Surprise. 'Queen Victoria is our monarch. She has been queen forever.'

'Tell me about your family?'

'There is only myself, mama and my brother Edward who is at university.'

'Is that Teddy?'

Giggle. 'He says it is not manly to be called Teddy but I do it to tease him.'

'Tell me about Edward.'

'He is very kind to me and always brings me presents. He once gave me a kitten but it grew so fast. It lives in the kitchen now and kills mice.Cook cannot abide mice so she is pleased to have Sooty. Edward says I am his little pet and he will always take care of me. I have no father, you see, and mama is often poorly. She has never been strong and each winter Doctor Colby fears for her health.'

'Charlotte, close your eyes and count slowly to five. When you open your eyes you will be fifteen.' Pause. 'Are you still there, Charlotte?'

A sigh. 'Yes.'

'What are you doing now?'

'I have just returned from mama's funeral. It was a most moving ceremony. When I have removed my bonnet I must help Edward entertain our guests.'

'Tell me about your life now.'

'I am very happy. It would be wrong of me to be otherwise for I am loved and cossetted by Edward. He is my guardian now and has been since Mama became so ill two years ago.'

'Do you have friends?'

'I have two girlfriends. Sarah and Jane.'

'Do you know any boys?'

'Edward does not encourage them. He says I am far too young to be thinking of boys. I know that Reginald Harrison's father had often talked with Mama about my future.' Pause. 'Do not tell that I listened at the door. Mr Harrison paid particular attention to me so I was curious. I have met Reginald several times. Edward says he will not allow the plan. He does not care for boys to look at me. He says there is plenty of time and he could not do without his little angel to be with him and make him laugh. He says I am his own treasure. One day, of course, I must have a husband, but Edward will be very sad to lose me.'

'Charlotte, close your eyes and relax. You feel very peaceful and happy.' Pause. 'Think about Edward. Did you ever know him before, not as a brother, perhaps, but at any other time?'

There was complete silence then Sally's voice, heavily accented, spoke.

'Pierre is my 'usband. We marry only one year since. 'E rescue me from — *peste*! I cannot think of ze English — ah, *oui*, ze terror. 'E rescue me from ze terror.'

'The French Revolution?'

'*Oui*. I am thus grateful and I consent for 'im to become *mon mari* — you understand?'

'Do you love him?'

'What is zat to me? Pierre give me my life and I give it to 'im in return. 'E love me to despair, zat I know, and 'e risk 'is life for me. It is right, *n'est ce pas*, that I should marry 'im when 'e want me? Thus ze debt is paid.'

'What is your name?'

'I am Henriette de la Roche.'

'Henriette, I'd like to speak to Charlotte.'

'I am Charlotte.' The English accent had returned.

'Charlotte, did you ever see Pierre de la Roche again?'
'Yes, he is Edward, my brother. I hate him.'
'You used to love him.'
'I was vain and stupid. I did not know what he was. I did not know what love was.'
'What has happened?'
The voice was choked with tears. 'He has sent Charles away and I will never see him again.'
'Who is Charles?'
'My beloved. We met at a ball last year. As soon as our eyes met we loved each other. Edward was furious when he found out. He has grown so accustomed to having me all to himself, he cannot bear the thought of another man taking his place. I sometimes believe he would marry me himself if he could for he behaves more like a husband than brother and is so autocratic and demanding. It is unnatural for a brother to be so devoted to his sister that he denies all other men access to her.' Charlotte's voice rose indignantly. 'I told him so and he said, as he is my guardian, I will be obedient or I will not see one penny of my fortune and no man will wed a woman with no dowry. He is utterly hateful. I shall die an old maid for he shows no desire to take a wife himself, saying he loves only me. He has ruined my life with his insane jealousy. I shall never forgive him, never!'
The impassioned tirade stopped as suddenly as it had begun.
'Charlotte, did you ever see Edward again, at any other time?'
There was a little gasp and Sally's voice, sounding sleepy and distant, said, 'Tim's my fiancé. We're getting married soon.'
'Why are you getting married?'
'Tim wants to. I wasn't sure but I do love him and I suppose we should just go ahead. He seems to need the security. His father's been on at him about it.'
'Sally, is Lottie there?'
'I am Lottie.' Sally's voice strengthened.
'Did Lottie ever know the man that Sally knows as William O'Meally?'
'No.'

'Did you know William before then, at any time before Lottie?'

'No, I never knew William then.'

'Were you ever in Bell's Creek, Sally, or was Lottie?'

'No.'

'Do you know an island called St Helena, off the coast of Queensland?'

'Yes. It's a bad place.'

'Were you ever there?'

'I went with Juliet.'

'Relax, Sally, and think. Were you ever there before that?'

Pause. 'No. Never.'

Chris continued to probe gently, talking to what appeared to be various versions of Sally, but she could find no past connection between Sally, William or the island. Finally she relaxed the girl again and brought her back to consciousness.

Chapter 27

'Lad, lad, wake up.'

William groaned and a hand clamped hard over his mouth.

'Hush. It's Tom.'

'Tom!'

'Lie still, lad. The tale of your flogging's all around the yards.'

William struggled to roll over but the rough mattress, stuffed with corn husks, rubbed so painfully on his back, he stayed on his stomach, pushing himself up on his elbows and wincing as his muscles knotted under the raw lash marks.

'Lie still, young fool.' Grogan repeated. 'There's nothing to be gained from opening up the cuts.'

'What in hades are you doing here?'

'Severe stomach cramps, brought about by the filthy food. The bread was burnt and so sour it wasn't fit for pigs, and the sweet potatoes had been left too long in the ground before they were over-boiled for our dinner.'

'Sounds the same as they gave me and my stomach's well. Did you fake the cramps to see me?'

'I thought of it,' Grogan admitted softly, 'but there was no need.

Dingy Bell found some mushrooms in the fields and smuggled them into our mess. Like as not they were toadstools for the dramatic effect they had on us. I exaggerated my case and they could not say I was not ill. What happens to you now, Billy?'

'A week underground for my insolence.'

Grogan shuddered. 'The lash is more humane.'

'You'd not say so if you had my back.'

'Shutting a man up in a black hole, to drive him mad without a single gleam of light, as if he were buried alive — no, that's the devil's own invention. Then, to put him on bread and water into the bargain — the soulless bastards.'

'It's only a week. I thought I'd be facing a month at least except the surgeon, who is strongly against the dark cells, said he could not allow it. Townley was in a rage. He'd dearly love to bury me for a year.' William gave the ghost of a chuckle.

'Aye, lad, and still you laugh.'

'I've good reason. My faith's in a little fair-haired lass with a frightened face and a brave heart. She will fulfill her promise, I am sure of it. Even now, Tom, my brother will be seeking out Jack d'Arcy and he'll drag the truth from him one way or another.'

'Meanwhile,' Tom grumbled, 'my bed's got lice in it, my mattress is so full of lumps it's painful to lie upon and my blanket's so filthy the stench from it is enough to make me gag.'

'Well, and so is mine.' William grinned. 'The dark cells will be a welcome relief from the torture of a bed in the hospital.'

Chapter 28

'I see, now.' Sally told her reflection in the mirror. 'Yes, that's been the whole trouble.'

She'd been sitting for a long time, examining her face with a sort of detached curiosity. It was a cool day and she'd pulled on a blue light wool jumper. Her expressive eyes had instantly taken up the colour, enhancing the impression that she was observing a stranger. She pulled her fringe to one side then flicked it back. Had she always been blonde or had one of her other selves, Henriette, perhaps, been born with black hair and dark, flashing eyes?

Who was Sally Cooper, really? She wasn't sure any more. So much lay out of conscious reach, deep in her psyche, possibly awaiting its opportunity to rise up and inexorably alter the course of her life forever. Now she'd listened to the tape she could vaguely remember parts of the session, as if recalling a dream which drifted just below the surface of her consciousness. There was no doubt in her mind that she'd discovered the source of her growing unhappiness. As she'd heard the voice that claimed to be Charlotte, all the frustration and resentment she'd been experiencing for weeks seemed to expand in her until she felt like screaming with exasperation.

The debt was paid. She thought angrily. Edward had no right to try to hold on to Charlotte. Henriette had already balanced it out. She married him out of gratitude and to repay him for saving her life. But he kept on demanding payment, even in their next life — still protecting her, dominating her, trying to own her.

She'd felt it every time Tim worried about her, every time he asked where she'd been. When he'd put the engagement ring on her finger he'd seemed to think it gave him some sort of ownership of her. He'd said so himself: 'I didn't have any control over you then.' She'd experienced the same sense of distaste, of the inappropriateness of his claim of ownership that she'd felt as Charlotte. Deep inside her she'd known Tim was holding onto something that had been completed a long, long time ago.

It's the same feeling, she thought, pressing her hands to her stomach. That's how she knew it was true. She couldn't feel this so directly if it didn't involve her personally. At the same time, she recognised that she was equally to blame. She still carried a residue of Henriette's horror of what she'd been snatched from by Pierre, who'd apparently loved her so totally he'd risked everything for her. French history wasn't Sally's strong point but she'd read about the revolution, the aristocracy dragged in tumbrils to the guillotine, the shocking retribution extracted in blood by the peasants for their impoverished lives. She knew that the privileged of French society had lived in terror of informers from their own class who hoped to save their lives by betraying their friends. The people called the revolution the Terror. Henriette had been saved but those events had deeply scarred her. The horror had been so intense it had survived even beyond death. Sally sensed that, as a direct result of Henriette's gratitude to Pierre, Charlotte also bore deep within her a subtle impression that she should be grateful to Edward. Without knowing of their previous relationship, she'd rationalised this at fifteen by telling herself that, being so loved and cossetted by her brother, it would be wrong of her not to be happy. Later, this argument had worn transparently thin. An angry Charlotte, thwarted by Edward's possessiveness and ruthless domination, knew exactly what he was, too late. Once more, he'd demanded her lifelong devotion to him. What Henriette had willingly given, Edward demanded as his due.

It had to stop now. Sally had already felt what was happening but didn't want to admit it for fear of hurting Tim — and Giles and Ellie. But now she knew she was carrying the memories of Henriette and Charlotte. She watched her face set into determined lines.

He hasn't any right to keep extracting payment, even unconsciously, she thought. It would be awful for me and extremely bad for him, if we went through with the wedding. Tim's already confused and miserable and someone has to stop this pattern, this habit we've fallen into. It mustn't continue.

She got resolutely to her feet. 'At least I can put one thing from the past right,' she told herself and went into the living room.

Tim glanced up, a frown on his face. He pushed his hair off his forehead. 'Can't this wait, Sal? I'm in the middle of a paper on botulism.'

'How revolting. No, Tim, I need to talk now.'

'All right.' He put down the paper and took off his glasses. His face relaxed into a disarming grin. 'Anything for my woman.'

'That's what I want to talk about,' Sally said. He doesn't remember, she thought, he has no idea what he's doing or why, so go easy on him. She said, 'Tim, why do you want to marry me?'

He looked startled and slightly uncomfortable. 'I seem to remember mentioning that when I proposed, and you accepted,' he added with delicate stress. 'I never saw you as the type to need constant reassurance. I love you, Sal, you know that. For some reason you bring out my old-fashioned, chivalrous male instincts. Before you, I never met a girl I wanted to protect, to look after and watch out for. Don't laugh at me, I know it's not the role of a sensitive new-age guy.'

'I'm just not sure that that's a good basis for marriage. Sometimes I feel smothered by you.'

He looked concerned. 'Is that what's wrong? Why you said you needed space?'

'I think so.' Damn, she was ducking the issue again. This was extraordinarily difficult. 'I'm very independent, Tim. I'm glad you

love me but isn't the rest a bit of a cliché? I don't need you to worry
about me and protect me, I'm perfectly capable of being responsible for my own life.'

'I see. I come on too heavy.'

'Yes.' She was grateful that he was making this easy, then wary
of her gratitude. A worry nagged insistently at her. Edward hadn't
'come on too heavy'. He'd deliberately thwarted Charlotte, self-
ishly destroying her chance of happiness with the man she loved,
denying her a normal life with a family of her own. Sally recognised that this was why she'd felt so threatened by the strength of
Tim's devotion. He was already influenced by Giles and carried
Edward's feelings and memories, no matter how deeply hidden.
What if he reverted to his past behaviour after they were married ? Coming on too heavy would be putting it mildly.

Juliet warned me, Sally thought nervously, then her
commonsense reasserted itself. Most girls would adore having a
man like Tim. She loved him and she'd accept him and stop all this
worrying and just be happy with her lot. The line of a song flashed
into her mind repeating itself like a strange mocking chant.

Don't worry, be happy. Don't worry, be happy. Don't worry...
She noticed Tim was looking at her anxiously.

'I'll back off, but I can't promise not to want to keep you locked
up in a tower, all for myself, safe from dragons. I'll just try not to
mention it so often.'

Sally experienced a slight feeling of panic and said quietly, 'I'd
suffocate in a tower and I like to deal with my own dragons. Don't
try to control me, Tim.'

'Ah, we're back to that. Look, you were happy to get engaged,
or so I thought. I might ask you the same question. Why do you
want to marry me?'

'That's fair.' She sat back. 'Until we got engaged it was great
with you.' Then she remembered Tim's flawless, mechanical technique and Rose's passionate, undated entry and wanted to say, 'I
want to know exquisite joy, I want to be swept away and feel the
same fire she felt. I don't want to be owned out of gratitude.' She
knew it would hurt him immeasurably. The jangle in her mind

clarified to a single quiet thought and she finally faced the truth with a growing sense of dismay.

I don't love Tim.

She reared back, searching frantically for something, anything, to say to fill the awkward silence. She breathed deeply. 'You're one of my best friends, Tim, we've had such good times together. I thought that would be enough.'

'Is it sex?' He asked astutely. 'I thought we were good together. You come when I do, you said so. You don't fake it, do you? Is that why you don't want to sleep with me any more?'

Sally felt incapable of dealing him such a blow. She said, 'No, you're good; very good, in fact. It's just, lately, I've felt pressured, as if you want more from our relationship than I can give you.'

'I want to make you mine, Sally, it's natural. I want to marry you and know you belong to me.'

The awful truth still echoed in her brain. She had to get away, think it through. If she really didn't love Tim, if this wasn't just some highly strung over-reaction to all she'd been going through, she couldn't marry him. She said quickly, 'You should work on getting rid of any such idea.' She thought her voice sounded un-naturally high and tried to control it. Her hands were shaking and she clasped them restlessly. 'I don't belong to you, Tim, you don't own me. You never have. It's not healthy for either of us to think that way.'

'You're getting paranoid about this. It's just an expression.'

'It belongs in a sixties pop song.'

'Well, I think there's a lot more to this. I said it before, you're in love with someone else, or you think you are. You spend all your spare time chasing around after him, reading up about him. He's dead, Sally. Let him go because I'm sick of sharing you with a ghost.'

'It's not like that.' She swallowed. 'This is something I have to do, that's all.' She just stopped herself repeating William's words, 'To see justice done.' 'I made a commitment.'

'What, to a dead man?' Tim's voice took on an edge of irritation.

'Stop saying that.'

'It's true, but you just can't stand that he's dead, can you? You'd love it if he came alive so you could bugger off with him. You think he was more of a man that I am; maybe he was a real stud.'

He would think that. Sally gritted her teeth. Why did some men set such a store by sexual performance? She thought about trying to explain about William and Rose and her preoccupation with their lives, how important they'd become to her. She shook her head. Impossible. He wouldn't understand. In his eyes it would simply prove his point. She said shakily, 'Tim, please stop it. I made the commitment to myself.'

'Well, you also made a commitment to me, or don't you remember? To me, not to a dead man.' He flung the words at her. 'I'm holding you to that commitment, Sally. I'm telling you now, give up this obsession with the past or you can kiss goodbye to any hope of things getting better between us.'

Sally sat still, looking down at her hands. She'd been twisting the engagement ring around and around, listening to the growing ugliness in Tim's voice. Just like his father, she thought, over and over. Just like Giles.

She said quietly, 'I'm trying so hard to explain.'

He thrust his face close to hers. He was flushed, his hair standing up in points from his thrusting it back in desperation. He almost shouted, 'How come I'm always the one expected to change my behaviour. You're not prepared to give up yours. It's bloody unfair.'

Sally was suddenly released from the paralysis that had held her, stricken, to the sofa. She stood up, trying to soothe him with reason. 'You're absolutely right, of course. But it also isn't very fair of you to demand my total commitment to you and only you. I may commit to many things in my life. I have the right to ask for your understanding and trust.' She found she'd slipped the ring off her finger and looked at it mutely for a moment, her breathing hard. Then she held it out to him and said quietly, 'I think you'd better take this. It's not going to work for us, Tim. I've just realised I — I don't love you any more. I can't marry you.'

'No!' Tim rose swiftly, his face a mask of angry despair. 'I won't let you go. You keep asking me to trust you,' he grasped her arms fiercely. 'How can I, when you won't tell me what you're fucking well up to? I've got some rights. You're mine, Sally, and I'm not about to give you up to some fantasy. It's time you pulled yourself together, recognised your responsibilities to me. I'm going crazy.'

He pushed her head back, kissing her savagely, then began to press her breasts with urgent hands. His voice was hoarse, his breath hot against her face as she tried to twist away from him. 'I want you, Sally, I need you. Let me, please let me.'

She shuddered and pushed him violently. 'Get off me, Tim. This isn't helping.' The ring dropped from her hand and she heard it strike the coffee table.

He pulled her into his arms. She'd forgotten how strong he was, how fit. His eyes burned hotly into hers. Alarm bells began to ring in her head.

'I'll make you want me again.' He unzipped her jeans with one hand and began to pull them down, forcing her back on the sofa, one strong arm across her upper chest. She had the shocked thought that this couldn't be happening. She was about to be *raped*. The blood was pounding in her ears. She was suddenly violently angry and her fury overcame the fear which had frozen her. She wasn't helpless, she could defend herself.

Tim was panting with excitement, using both hands to force her legs apart, no longer holding her down. He groaned in an urgent, husky voice, 'Let me, Sal, let me. You'll like it, you'll want to, give me a chance to show you.'

'Tim *stop*.' She fought back, finally slapping him hard across the face. He gave a shocked grunt and jerked his body away from hers. Sally sat up, trembling. She pulled her jeans up, forcing back angry tears. She was safe. It was over.

'It's called rape, Tim,' she said in a quivering voice, 'whether we're engaged or not. I suppose you think that's one of your rights as well.'

'Sally.' He covered his face with shaking hands and began to cry in a harsh, uncontrolled way, gasping out between his sobs. 'I'm sorry — I didn't mean — I don't know what happened.' He gave a long shudder.

She got up, sick with loathing.

He dropped his hands. His eyes were ashamed, pleading. 'Don't look at me like that, Sal. I've said I'm sorry. Give me a chance to make it up to you. Sally, please, you have to let me explain.'

'I'm going to Juliet's. Don't try to ring me. I'll come back for my things later, when I'm ready.'

He blinked, then stared at her uncomprehendingly. 'You can't. You can't just walk out on me. You're my fiancée, for God's sake. You owe me, Sally.'

She looked back at him coldly. 'I owe you nothing, Tim. The debt's been paid.'

Sally went back to the house the next evening. Juliet had begged her to be careful and offered her a bed for as long as she wanted.

'You don't have to go back yet, Sal, I can lend you whatever you need.'

'I want to see him. He won't lose control again.' Sally sighed and admitted, 'It was partly my fault. I messed it up, Jules, and I was less than honest with him. He realised it was about William and I couldn't explain that I don't love William but promised to find out the truth for its own sake. How can I even start to say I believe I can help a man who died last century? Tim probably still thinks it's about his performance in bed. That was the first thing he thought of. And he was partly right.' She pulled at her jacket with restless fingers. 'I told him I don't love him any more but I chickened out of telling him I didn't feel enough passion for him when we have sex.'

'I notice you don't say, make love.'

'No.' Sally shook her head regretfully. 'It occurred to me last night that we never made love, we had sex. Good sex, great sex, fun and enjoyable and technically terrific, but he didn't make me feel like flying to the moon or writing love songs.'

Juliet smiled understandingly. 'You'd prefer a fumble with a bloke who turns your insides to jelly than a perfect screw with a great technician.'

'That's one way of putting it; and that was nothing to do with William. Perhaps, if I'd really loved Tim, he'd have been a real turn on. I should have made that clear. He thinks I have sexual fantasies about William. I don't. It was Rose's description of them together that made me realise what I was missing but I know that was their thing, not for me and William, even if it was possible, which it never will be. I just wanted Tim to trust me a little, accept that I couldn't explain and know it was all right.' Sally bit her lip then continued, 'Isn't that what a relationship's there for? The way we were, I'm better on my own. But I don't want to leave it the way we did. He was so guilty and I was in a cold fury. I want to say goodbye properly. We need to talk it out.'

But when Sally let herself into the house she found it deserted. She switched on the lights. The living room was unusually tidy. Her engagement ring was lying on the coffee table. A note next to it caught her attention and she picked it up, her heart pounding.

Dear Sally,
I've been doing some hard thinking. I don't know what made me behave like that. It wasn't me; I can't explain or excuse myself. I saw a jealous, manipulative, obsessive part of me and I don't like it. I don't know why you seem to stir up these feelings in me. No, I'm not blaming you. For once, I'm own-ing it myself.
You're right, it isn't healthy. You told me I was getting like Dad and I see it's true. I've decided to release all claim on you. It hurts like hell but I think it's the right thing to do. Consider yourself free, darling Sal, but hang onto the ring for a while longer, just in case.
I've gone to share with Barry. He's in the same year as me so we can study together. I'll phone from time to time, if that's okay, just to say, 'hello, friend.'
Forgive me, Sally, I hope you can. I can't bear to think of how terrified you looked and what I might have done to you. Perhaps one day, after I've done some growing up, we can

go out together — make a fresh start.
Lots and lots of love,
Tim.

Sally wiped her eyes. 'Oh, Tim, you made it,' she whispered. 'You broke the pattern and I failed again. I'm totally useless, I didn't even have the guts to tell you the truth. Now I've messed it up with you as well as William and I don't know what to do.'

She sat down heavily on the sofa. One day, she promised herself, she'd tell him. She owed him that much. They'd been friends as well as lovers and she couldn't just wipe away the memories. He'd be in trouble with his family, they'd think it was his fault. She'd go with him, help him break the news. When Tim accepted the break-up as irreversible, when he was willing to take the ring back, they'd talk. And she'd tell him the truth, all of it, in all its extraordinary detail.

Her heart felt like a lead weight in her chest but in the back of her mind was a hopeful glimmer of light. At least she and Tim were free of the past. Maybe there was still hope for William.

Chapter 29

T he dark cells were loathed and feared by every prisoner on St Helena. Reached by a small doorway underneath C wing, they were twelve in number, each measuring eight feet long by three and a half feet wide. They were poorly ventilated and totally devoid of light. It was, William thought, like being buried alive, as Tom had said.

The blackness crushed all sense of reality, driving men locked in the punishment cells for lengthy periods to madness from the all-encompassing dark against which their eyes strained hopelessly. Their health was further eroded by the bread and water diet which went with a spell in solitary. Bread of unreliable quality, baked by a warder with help from prisoners, in the bakery's two large ovens. Sometimes the bread was so badly undercooked it was not much better than eating raw dough; at other times, as Tom Grogan often grumbled, it was sour and inedible. Prisoners' complaints fell on deaf ears. The authorities were unsympathetic to claims that the food was rotten and the prisoners half-starved. Superintendent Townley had told the last man to complain that the food on the island was as good as he'd get outside. He'd irritably sent the man away with the promise that, if he didn't appreciate his dinner, his rations could always be halved so he'd have less of it to eat.

Dingy Bell had muttered under his breath, 'You lousy, tyrannical bugger,' but not quite loud enough for Townley to hear him.

William told himself he'd only be in the black hole for a week, which he could bear. He'd seen men taken from the underground cells after a month, in a shocking state, poor devils, looking like dead men, hollow-eyed with the blue-white skin of corpses and so dazed and confused they could hardly walk. The visiting surgeon abhorred this form of punishment and often spoke against it, preferring the decisive correction of the lash.

With his back still raw, but pronounced by the warder dispenser fit enough to complete his sentence, William was thrust underground and left alone in the pitch black to think over his sins. He'd been here before and had devised ways of surviving and passing the time which dragged relentlessly, there being no way of determining the hour except by the delivery of his daily ration of bread and water.

He'd found it helped to play games in his head, challenging himself to feats of memory or making up ditties using tunes he knew. He'd memorise songs which lampooned the warders and unpopular prisoners to share with his mates later, and set himself all sorts of puzzles to work out. And pray. That was a sort of comfort when he felt so utterly alone and abandoned.

He'd heard of men buried alive in mines, deep under the ground, and shuddered. He'd never be a miner — he loved the fresh air and light and the bush too much. Those men had survived by doing much the same as himself. Railing against his fate did no good and wore him down faster. By pretending that it was a pleasant change to have some time to himself to think about things, to not resist the dark but make it a friend, wrapping him safely around, giving him time to heal, that was the way to come out of this sane and whole.

Animals did that when they were wounded. They crept into a dark hole and didn't bother about eating, allowing their bodies to heal themselves, taking the respite they needed from the eternal task of daily survival. William would do the same, emulate a wounded beast, and return stronger than ever.

They couldn't drag him down, bend him to their will. They couldn't break him, William O'Meally — let them try their worst. He had a simple philosophy that kept him going day after dreary day. If he could get up again every time they knocked him down, then he'd won and was stronger than them all.

He thought about William Collins, dead by his own hand. What would cause a man to cut his throat? Suicide was a sin against God and Collins would be denied a grave in holy ground and his place in heaven. Or perhaps a compassionate God, seeing his suffering, would throw his arms wide and say, 'Come in, my son, it's all forgiven, for you were driven to it, I know.'

He, William O'Meally, would never contemplate such an action. He'd no need for despair, as long as he had Rose and she waited for him, as he knew she would.

It concerned him that he never heard from Rose. Every two months on the Sunday designated as letter writing day, he wrote to her, enclosing the letter with one to his brother, knowing that Walter would make sure she received his loving messages. It was only possible to write what the authorities would accept as 'legal', as each letter was read and initialled by the superintendent before it was allowed to leave the island. Still, it was better than nothing. Even the paper was supplied by the authorities and only for the two-monthly writing day.

Of course, there were other means of obtaining paper, illegally. And it was possible to smuggle notes off the island via released prisoners, if they could conceal the letters during the customary searches; and corrupt warders could sometimes be bribed.

William had begged Rose to write, through Walter. She must be too closely watched or she'd have managed to send him some word. As it was, all he had was hope and it glowed inside him, steady and unquenchable. Soon he'd be free and with his love again.

Chapter 30

Sally dressed hastily in the dark blue skirt and floral blouse which was the travel agency's uniform. She knotted a blue scarf around her neck, realised it was hopelessly uneven and fumbled urgently at the knot. At the third attempt she achieved a reasonably neat result. She ran a comb quickly through her hair, flicking at the ends to tidy them, noticing the dark shadows under her eyes. There wasn't time to redo her make-up, she was running late again. She'd have to skip breakfast. Her face was showing the strain and she grimaced. She couldn't keep up this pace for much longer. On top of everything, they were busy at work and, what was worse, she was beginning to make mistakes. She was short tempered, snapping at Fran, who'd looked concerned but hadn't said anything. She'd begun to skip regular meals.

I'll try to pace myself better, she thought, make sure I eat properly, and I'll get to bed early tonight.

Daily the fear that she was running out of time gnawed at her. The previous night she'd read the police reports of the initial investigation. She'd sat up till all hours, going over and over the papers, making notes, trying to work out what had actually happened that night in Bell's Creek.

When she'd finally gone to bed she forgot to set the alarm. She'd jolted awake with the sunlight pouring into her room, showing her how late it was.

She had tried to build the scene in her mind. Stapleton came out a positive hero in his own summary of events. Sally saw him very differently. As she hurried for the bus, she went back in her mind over the reports.

He didn't exactly fake the evidence, she thought, but he certainly read a *lot* into it to suit himself. It was all based on hearsay. There wasn't any proof against William other than circumstantial. It'd be laughed out of court today. It wouldn't even get to court because the police wouldn't have enough to take it that far. And the doctor's report, why wasn't that followed up? He clearly stated that William had a mark across his throat like a rope burn but no one checked to see who had a rope or how it might have been used. If he'd been riding, could someone have got it around his neck, or were they up a tree? If he was shot as he rode past, there couldn't have been a struggle. Doctor Evans was clear on that. First the struggle, then the shot. Possibly William had been escaping his assailant.

'If only I could ask him,' she wished aloud. A passer-by glanced suspiciously at her.

Did someone try to strangle him with the rope, or hang him? These days, forensics would have checked every rope in the district for evidence of skin tissue. In William's case it was conveniently forgotten or they simply didn't have the techniques available.

She also felt the sub-inspector's report glossed over the black trackers' role dismissively. Sally had always believed the trackers were exceptionally skilled but Stapleton had brushed their findings aside, not so much by what he said, more by what he had omitted from the report. Yes, there were too many loose ends. James was right. Stapleton had a body in the frame and he was going to make sure William was caught very tight indeed.

She passed the day in a worried dream. Fran spoke to her three times before Sally noticed. Some of the staff had begun to watch her anxiously. She pulled herself together and concentrated on her work.

On her way home she bought a kebab for dinner and, as soon as she'd eaten, she turned wearily to the reports of the second trial. She came across a comprehensive document of several pages, written in a close, cramped style and addressed to Mr David Thomas Seymour, Commissioner of Police. It was signed by Camp Sergeant Peter Horace Mallory. Sally read through the detailed report. Her suspicions had been correct.

A deeply concerned Sergeant Mallory had gone over the head of his superior, detailing his misgivings over the handling of the whole case and giving his opinion that William could be innocent of the charges against him. Mallory was worried that the sub-inspector had not accepted the validity of the native police findings. Stapleton seemed determined to build a case against the prisoner, he was personally attracted to the prisoner's woman and therefore prejudiced against the prisoner. The sub-inspector had seriously mishandled the whole affair. In the sergeant's opinion, the officer was not suited to the mounted police in that he did not understand the Aborigines or respect their abilities. Thus he was not qualified to be in charge of them.

He respectfully begged that Mr Seymour investigate the matter to prevent a serious miscarriage of justice.

Sally remembered Rose saying that Walter had written to demand a retrial. She shuffled through the documents. There was no sign of any letter from William's brother. She bit her lip, not wanting to be a nuisance to James, but there was no other way. She dialled his number.

'No', he said, 'if Walter did write there was no record of it. What caused the retrial was Sergeant Mallory's letter to the police commissioner. After the second trial, Stapleton was called to Brisbane to explain his actions. There was a closed inquiry into the whole affair. Mallory gave evidence and Stapleton was found unsuitable for the Queensland Native Mounted Police and dismissed. I believe he'd only got the appointment because his commanding officer in the British army pulled strings and called in some favours after Stapleton was disgraced over a duel.'

'What happened to him?'

'Ma Drake, you said you met her? She told me it was rumoured he went off exploring in the desert and didn't take advice about supplies. Didn't understand the danger. She remembers her parents discussing it and thinks it was probably in the newspapers. She reckoned a local tribe found him months later; he'd died of thirst. Apparently he saw himself as another Eyre, exploring Central Australia and coming back a hero.'

After James rang off, Sally went back to the reports but her mind kept drifting. It was uncomfortably quiet in the house. Not that Tim had been noisy, but he was usually there, studying in the living room, occasionally muttering to himself, calling out to her if he was making coffee. Suddenly the house was empty, and lonely.

'I should look for someone to share,' she mused. She moved her hand restlessly across the sofa's abnormally tidy cover. Tim had contributed some money to housekeeping and rent by working two nights a week at a local restaurant. Sally would need help with expenses eventually or she'd have to cut into her savings.

She'd think about an ad in the local paper. She began idly to draft it in her mind. She liked having someone else around the house but, at present, it might be more prudent to hold off for a while. At least until she'd put this thing with William behind her. She didn't want to have to explain her behaviour to a stranger. Yes, better to wait. She needed to concentrate on the task before her. She could manage financially for a bit longer.

'I'll put off buying the Porsche till next year,' she said, then remembered that was Tim's joke and fell silent. Talking aloud to herself made the silence infinitely worse.

She switched on the radio, stood the mindless chatter of the DJ and the constant advertisements for about ten minutes, then hunted along the dial for a station which claimed to deliver easy listening, without DJs. She found the station. They were playing a sixties pop song of the 'you belong to me and I'll never let you go' variety. She switched off the radio.

Perhaps she'd get a kitten. Even as she had the thought, she knew she couldn't. It would mean leaving it alone all day while she was at work. In spite of their seeming aloofness, she knew cats needed and enjoyed company and it wouldn't be fair to deprive it. She'd know it would crying and mewing in its little high-pitched mew and she'd feel awful. No kitten, she decided.

For the first few days after Tim had left, Sally vacillated between guilt and relief, remorse and self-justification. Unable to settle, she wandered restlessly about the house, finding a certain measure of relief in thoroughly cleaning every nook and cranny. She hadn't felt like reading any more of the diary, judging Rose as shallow and unworthy of William's trust. When she'd tried to concentrate on the other papers, her mind slid away from the long, wordy documents and the evidence which seemed so unfairly weighted against an innocent man.

Gradually a sense of rightness brought her some peace. However it had come about and no matter how lonely she felt, she knew it was for the best. Finally, on the fourth day, she'd gathered the papers together and spread them out on the coffee table, which reminded her painfully of how Tim used to work, covering the table with books and folders.

Now she counted on her fingers. It had been twelve days since her encounter with William. If he and she were still sharing the same passage of time, he would soon attempt to escape for the fifth time. That strange attempt that James had mentioned, when he claimed never to have left the prison.

He was winding them up, Sally decided. He'd enjoy that, watching them working out if he was serious about having been there all along. He told me he'd get away again.

That had been just over two weeks after they returned him to the island. There was very little time left. Only a few days after that, William had killed himself. She had to find an answer. Go through everything again.

Depression settled over Sally like a grim cloud. She wasn't at all sure she could deliver on her promise. She knew William was innocent but any evidence had long since vanished in a convenient thunder storm and a botched investigation by a biased, incompetent officer.

Chapter 31

S ally looked at the calendar, a sense of panic tightening her
chest.
'I can't do it,' she worried, 'there's just not enough information, not enough time.'

James had assured her there was nothing more to find; he'd
gone through all the available material exhaustively. She believed
him, he was a patient, painstaking historian. When she'd tentatively called him to check if he could have missed anything, he'd
invited her down for coffee and a chat and had outlined his research methods which she couldn't fault.

'If I tried to find out more?' She'd ventured.

He'd studied her in silence for a moment then shrugged and
said, 'Why not? Although I'm sure I covered the lot. I'll give you a
list of my sources; the archives and libraries, newspapers, organi-
sations, but they've only got what I've already seen and copied. I
can't think of any other source. I interviewed all the relevant people at Bell's Creek, even put an ad in the main national papers for
anyone connected with the area who might know more about
William.'

He hesitated, then said diffidently, 'Look, I know how easy it is to get a bit obsessive about research. It's frustrating trying to piece the past together, imagine how archaeologists must feel. Time just loses things, people's memories fade, documents go missing, old letters are destroyed. Probably just as well.' He'd chuckled. 'How would the world ever keep track if everybody kept everything from the past? We'd need archives as big as cities, and how about cataloguing it all?'

He'd leaned forward earnestly. 'What I'm saying, Sally, is — I think you're getting too involved with this. The simple fact is, we don't know who shot William. He didn't know himself. There was no technology then to match the bullet to the gun — and you can bet, if anyone had been suspect — they'd have dumped the weapon so fast the police would never have found it.'

'Someone must know,' she persisted.

'Someone once knew,' James corrected her, 'but whoever it was, the secret probably died with him. He'd never have said. It was most likely William's friend Jack d'Arcy. William thought it was Jack, you know.'

Yes, I know, she thought, but how did you? She said, 'Did William think that?'

'Yes, he told someone, I know I read it somewhere, and some of the old people up at Bell's Creek remember stories that Jack copped a lot of flak and left the district.'

'Why would he leave if he'd shot William to clear the way for himself with Rose? Why not brazen it out?'

'Rose sent him packing, didn't you know? She'd heard the story that he'd done it. That's where it is, of course! I've read so many documents, they get a bit confused sometimes. I gather you haven't finished the diary. Rose tells the story in there. Near the end, somewhere. So, it really seems that's as close as we'll ever get. I think you have to accept that Jack shot William, because we'll never know for sure, and be satisfied with that.'

But I'm not satisfied, she thought. If that's all there is then I haven't helped at all. It doesn't change anything for William because Walter never got the letter. William will escape again and be recaptured and hang himself and never know I tried. Rose will marry Walter and William will have nothing else to live for.

What did you expect? Her inner voice said caustically. That's what happened. You've got too wound up over the idea that you could change the past. Snap out of it, Sally. William's dead, the past is past and you've got to get your life back on track. Stop trying to play God.

She wished she could see him, just one more time, to explain what had happened. Would he understand or think her crazy? She remembered he had thought she was mad, the way he'd looked at her.

It didn't help to think of the way William had looked at her, concern for her sanity furrowing his brow. He was never going to look at her any way again.

Chapter 32

'Well, O'Meally, I hope you've learned a salutary lesson.'
'Yes, I have indeed, sir.'
'I don't believe you'll try to escape again.'
'Perish the thought, sir.'

'You look no worse for your punishment. However, the visiting surgeon thinks you unfit for hard labour.' Superintendent Townley prodded a paper on his desk. 'It says here you're a farm hand. Know about working in a smithy, do you?'

'Yes, sir, I've done work as a blacksmith on the farm.'

'Good. The smith's reported sick with a fever and is in the hospital. You can take his place in the blacksmith's shop until he recovers. Report to the smithy in the morning.'

Tom Grogan rubbed a hand across his balding head. 'Jaysus Christ, will nothing kill you, lad?'

'Nothing has, yet.'

'We'll not be seeing you in the pit for a while, in your state.'

'Unfit for hard labour.' William stretched his back muscles experimentally and winced but his gentle brown eyes held a gleam of humour. 'So they're putting me to work at the forge.'

'The man's a scoundrel. Doesn't he count that as hard labour?'

'It's probable he never did any such work himself. Brisbane Joe's in the smithy, he'll give me a hand. It suits me, Tom. It will be a change, making something with my hands again.'

'Aye, leg irons for your mates.'

'If it weren't me it would be some other. There's also shoeing to be done and mending the farm implements. It'll be like old times.'

'It's possible you'd find something good in hell to give you pleasure.'

'Moaning does no good, Tom.'

'Maybe you're right, Billy, but it helps to pass the time. You missed a treat down the black hole. Dingy Bell got into Townley's garden and removed from it some tomatoes and one or two eggs.'

William groaned. 'You lousy bastards, could you not wait until I was out?'

'A thief must take what he can when he has the chance. He's working in Townley's house at the moment. He's promised us treacle when he next finds himself alone in the kitchen.'

'Even their rotten bread would be palatable with a daub of treacle.'

'I've always said it, Billy, every mess needs a table-mate who is a thief by profession.'

'Cut the noise here.' A warder paused by the two prisoners. 'What was you discussin' so secretly?'

William grinned. 'Just saying how a bit of treacle would make the bread taste almost well-cooked and that's no secret.'

The warder gave a grunt of laughter. 'You may dream about it, but it's not likely ye'll come closer to it than that.'

'Very likely,' William agreed. 'I'll just have to dream, then.'

Chapter 33

He didn't want to be recognised, Sally thought, so he didn't just cover his face but his whole head, which means he was very familiar to William. She clicked her tongue impatiently. Doesn't help me, in a small town he'd have known everyone anyway. But who would have been sure he'd be passing that way and on that night? Or was it just an ambush on the off chance, by someone figuring out his likely movements? How could I find out? Only by talking to William.

Give it up, she advised herself. Tim had said she was obsessive, James said the same thing. Even Jules had begun to look at her sideways.

Thinking about Juliet made her remember she'd promised to keep Peter up to date. She rang his number. He was out, visiting a parishioner. She left a message with Marcia Adams.

Chapter 34

There was a great hiss and a cloud of steam went up as William plunged the searing metal into the water barrel. He lifted it out and Brisbane Joe inspected it, then gave a morose grunt and jerked his head towards the fire. William, handling the tongs with easy familiarity, returned the hoe to the forge.

Joe wiped his broad face and said, 'Bloody hot work.' His long black beard glistened with sweat beads.

'You worked in a forge all your life, Joe?'

'Yeah. When I was a little fella out on Bald Hill Station, used to help me dad.'

'You never went stock riding, like other blacks?'

'No fear.' He grinned. 'Better workin' on the station. Pretty women. No good livin' out in the bush; nothin' for a man there, 'cept other fellas.'

The metal began to glow red and William placed it on the anvil. Joe's great muscles rippled in his shining black arms as he swung the hammer.

'Boss's wife, pretty woman, hung around. All the time.' He grunted out the words between the hammer blows. The clanging drowned out what he was saying for anyone not standing directly beside him. Warder Dalton, on duty by the door, missed most of the conversation.

'She liked you, Joe?'

'I reckon she liked — the black boys, orright — watched me workin'. Said I was, fine figure of a man.' He put down the hammer and winked at William. 'That one's done, Billy, next one down there.'

William thrust the hoe into the barrel to cool, picked up the metal strip indicated by the big Aboriginal, and laid it in the fire. Brisbane Joe nodded almost imperceptibly to another prisoner who immediately engaged the warder in conversation.

'I'm near fainting with the heat, Mr Dalton, is it not time for a break?'

'You look well enough to me, man.'

The metal was laid, red-hot, on the anvil.

'What are we making, Joe?' William's voice was low.

'Knife. Not for the kitchen. Man feels better with a knife for his own.'

The hammer rang and William moved casually to block the anvil from the sight of the warder who was still explaining why it wasn't yet dinner time. Once more the tongs swiftly plunged hot metal into steaming water. The hiss covered over Brisbane Joe's soft words.

'That lady. One day I'm watchin' her in the garden and she says, "Joe, come over here, I got a job for you." You know what that job was, Billy? Seems she wanted a black boy up her. Took me into the house, into the bedroom, 'cause the boss was away, and took off her clothes.'

'Holy Mother!'

'Get back to work and stop your malingering. I'll tell you when it's dinner time.'

'Yes, sir, Mr Dalton.'

'Into the fire again, Billy, she's nearly ready.'

'What happened?'

'She got a black fella, all right, good and tight, as far up her as she could take 'im. She was moanin' and groanin' and screamin' out, like she was dyin' and I was drivin' away as hard as I could.' Joe licked his lips and his eyes gleamed. 'And the boss come back and caught us fair and square.'

He nodded to William who brought the knife blade back to the anvil. Brisbane Joe struck savagely at it then William returned it to the water.

'She starts really screamin' then and fightin' me like she's gone mad and cryin' out that I got her by force and tore off her clothes and raped her. I got a whippin' by the boss with his stock whip, then 'e calls the police. I got sent to trial and here I am, the white bitch.' He scowled. 'She wanted it, same as me, then she turns on me.'

He took the metal from the tongs and slipped it inside his shirt.

'Watch out for the women, Billy, they want it from you, real fierce for it, but they turn on you as soon as they've got it and then you're in real trouble.'

William manoeuvered the tongs to grasp the next piece of metal, a horseshoe.

Not my girl, not Rose, he thought. She's as true as I live and she'd not betray me. She's a wonderful girl, a rare, special one, and I'm lucky to have her waiting for me.

Chapter 35

T he phone rang and Sally quickly picked up the receiver. 'It's Peter. What's the news?'

He was a good listener. She could tell him precisely how she was feeling without wondering what he was thinking, if he was judging her. He gave his full attention, absorbing what you were saying so that you had no doubt that he'd heard you and understood. If he didn't completely follow you, he'd stop, go over a point again, probing with gentle questions.

Sally felt better just having the chance to sob out her feelings of inadequacy and inability to take her quest any further.

'You said you believed in miracles,' she flung at him.

'I meant it; but perhaps this wasn't the miracle. What God wants and what you want may not be the same here. Perhaps the real miracle was a healing from your past with Tim which was brought about by your meeting with William. That got you interested in exploring further, finding out about past lives. You'd never have done that if it hadn't been for him. What if you were never supposed to be William's miracle at all? Suppose he was meant to be yours?'

'I get what you're saying,' Sally nodded at the phone, 'but the link with him was so strong. You said that yourself.'

'We can only make our human judgements based on a very tiny data base. God has the whole programme running. You've done the best you can, Sally. Put it in His hands.'

'I don't feel right about it. I still think it's important that I help William.'

'I don't believe you can do more at present. Wait. If you're meant to take it further, you'll get the chance, I'm sure of that.' He stopped suddenly.

'Hello? Peter? Are you there?'

'I just had a thought.' There was a considering note in his voice. 'I wonder if William is part of your future? You were only looking at the past because you linked up with his life then, in 1882. We may have it all back to front.' Peter sounded excited. 'What if he came back from the future to help you.'

Sally couldn't think of anything to say. Something jogged her whirling mind. 'Future lives?'

'Why not, if all life is happening, past and future, at the same time? It's been documented by past life therapists. They can move people forward, beyond their current life, into the future. People claim to be in the year two thousand, three thousand, and so on.'

He paused, sensing her confusion.

'You're tired, Sally, and distraught. My priestly advice to you is this; make a cup of Milo, put a measure of whisky in it, go to bed and have sweet dreams.'

'Priestly advice?' She felt his smile through the phone.

'Well, it always works for me.'

Chapter 36

The prisoners were fed in the exercise yards, in messes of five or six men. They sat on benches at long tables fixed into the hard ground. Above them, a rough shed roof was barely adequate to keep out the weather. The yards were surrounded by massive block walls of blue-grey beachrock from the island's quarry. When first dug out, the gritty conglomerate was soft enough to be cut into large blocks and shaped with a spade or an axe but, exposed to the air, it quickly set to a rock-like hardness.

At dinner time William sat next to Tom Grogan who muttered, 'And how are you liking your spell from hard labour?'

William hungrily tore a piece from his bread. 'I'm working the tongs only. Brisbane Joe's doing the hard work and Dusty Miller's on the bellows.'

'Watch out for Joe, lad, he's a mad devil with the strength of ten men when he's roused.'

William, his mouth full, glanced around the tables. There was no fear of Joe's overhearing, for the the black prisoners messed and exercised in C Yard, but he didn't want the warders on duty listening to his comments. Aboriginals and Chinese were generally kept apart from the other prisoners, white prejudice being rife against the blacks, both Aboriginal and the unfortunate islanders 'blackbirded' to work the cane fields. And even more so against the Chinese who had flocked to the Queensland goldfields in the early years, causing huge resentment among the white miners.

'Brisbane Joe looks after me, takes the hard work upon himself. You're prejudiced, Tom. Joe's a good enough fellow and was badly done by when he was sent here.'

Tom peered distastefully at his own bread and dropped it back on his plate. 'Ah, he's told you that story, has he? And you think him hardly used. Let me tell you, lad, the black bastard waited until his boss was away, dragged the man's wife into the bedroom and savagely raped her.'

'He said it was not like that. He says she wanted it and led him on and only turned on him when her husband came back and caught them.'

'And you believed him.' Tom spoke through a mouth full of over-boiled mutton. 'That's your whole trouble, Billy, you'd believe good of anyone. Perhaps you think Satan himself was badly treated by the Almighty and did not deserve to be thrown out of heaven. I read the newspaper reports, lad. Joe bashed the poor woman senseless. He has a taste for white women, she was not the first. She nearly died from his cruelty and when her husband tried to intervene, Joe drew a knife on him and cut his face to ribbons. He always carried a knife. No, he likes to imagine it was the way he tells it but there's a cunning, mad glint in his eye when he talks about women. Don't trust him, my boyo.'

'He's got a knife now,' William whispered. 'I helped him make it this morning.'

'Jaysus! You don't know anything about a knife,' Grogan swore softly, 'and you didn't see him make it. It's none of your business, Billy. He's out for some mischief, mark my words. You and Albert Miller better watch your backs; Joe'd not hesitate to use that knife if he's planning a break.'

He stopped and glanced irritably across the table. 'What in the Lord's name are you about, Dingy? What's got into you, man?'

Bell had been trying to get Grogan'a attention by screwing up his face and making surreptitious little jerks of his head. Grogan said, 'He's finally gone barmy like so many poor buggers in this hell hole.'

Bell's pale eyes signalled caution. 'Will you shut your trap, Tom, and hand over your bread? You, too, Billy.'

Grogan stared. 'Well, praise be, the cunning devil's done the deed, Billy lad. Treacle's on the menu.'

Warder Dalton, on mess duty, walked past but Dingy Bell's hands were quickly out of sight. He gave the warder an obsequious nod, swiftly lowering his sandy lashes. Dalton's eyes searched the table but, finding nothing amiss, he moved on.

'Phew, a close shave. He's got eyes in the back of his head,' one man muttered.

'Not he,' Bell said scornfully. 'Saw me feeding the superintendent's chickens the other day and stopped to tell me all about ducks.'

'Ducks?' William asked.

'The man's mad on ducks. Says we should have ducks on the island. He's partial to the eggs, you see, and roast duck.'

'We're all partial to that.' Grogan's eyes gleamed. 'Think of it, lads, roast duck on the menu as a change from cursed hominy, sour bread, rotten meat and vegetables and bully tea.'

'No, listen, I'd taken the eggs, d'you see,' Bell persisted, 'and they was in me pockets and me shirt and bulging out and Mr Dalton never noticed.'

Frenchy Le Fevre, who had been quietly eating his way through the tasteless meal of bread, mutton and potatoes, nudged William. 'Eh, Billy, the Kate brought mail yesterday. There is a letter for you, from Bell's Creek. I was in the sorting room today.'

William's heart leapt. Perhaps it was from Rose. Perhaps she'd finally managed to get a letter past her father, to Walter.

Chapter 37

S ally hadn't meditated since the trip to St Helena. She felt disinclined to open herself to any further bizarre happenings, although Kaitlin assured her, her encounters with the past were not a normal result of meditation. Most people, she'd said, experienced only relaxation, a heightened sense of well-being, answers to problems and general life-enhancement.

'You'll have to do whatever you think is best,' she advised, 'but don't write it all off as a bad experience. Meditation may have made you more sensitive but I don't think you'll have that sort of trouble again, unless you particularly want it.'

'I didn't particularly want it then.'

'Perhaps you need more supervision. Would you like to work with a group? Or I could meditate with you sometimes.'

'I don't think I'm ready for it,' Sally said frankly. 'If you want the truth, the idea scares the daylights out of me.'

'I'd advise you to meditate on it,' Kaitlin said with a grin, 'if I didn't think you'd hit me.'

As Sally drove home from Kaitlin's, she thought about the conversation with a growing excitement. Kaitlin had said, 'unless you particularly want it.' But she did particularly want to see William again and hear his story.

She was suddenly overwhelmed by anxiety. It was all nonsense, wasn't it? Was she becoming dangerously obsessive, perhaps losing her mind after all? How come she was willing to believe the most insane things? The bruises on her arm had disappeared, she could almost convince herself they'd never been there, that it had all been a bad dream. And now she didn't even have the letter to verify the story.

Peter saw the letter, her inner voice reminded her.

Yes, well, I'm not so sure about him, either. All this rubbish about past lives and future lives and miracles. He's a priest, for God's sake, what's he doing dabbling in the occult, or whatever it is?

She turned into her driveway and ran the car into the garage. She liked this little house. It was handy to the shops, the city bus for work; there was a lock-up garage and a huge, spreading poinciana in the front garden. All summer it had decorated the lawn with orange-red flowers, their heady, acrid perfume filling the warm air. There were trees all around her and a park a few minutes walk down the road. She'd hate to leave here but she couldn't manage the rent by herself much longer. Also, the owner was making noises about possibly selling. If she did, new owners would increase the rent, for sure. Then she'd have to find someone to share — or look for another place.

Sally went inside. It was nearly lunchtime but Kaitlin had treated her to a huge morning tea and she had little appetite these days, anyway.

'I'm going to get rid of it all,' she said, 'take everything back to James and forget it. I must have been stark raving mad to have got involved at all.'

She marched to her room and bundled up the folder of photocopies and the diary, wrapping them carefully and placing them in a plastic shopping bag. She'd drive down to Wynnum this afternoon. It would be nice by the bay, with its sea breezes and mangroves. It was Sunday, just two weeks since she'd met William. Time to finish the whole ridiculous affair.

Perhaps Peter was right. Her experience had certainly helped clarify her feelings about Tim and face the fact that she didn't love him. She'd felt much more free, more alive inside, since she'd found out what games they'd both been playing.

She'd have to assume that was the whole point of whatever had happened. That, at least, made sense.

In two day's time, William will escape again, the thought nagged at her. And you never made any attempt to reach him, get his side of the story. You're a complete wimp. He trusted you. You were the last one he turned to. Jack d'Arcy betrayed him, Walter and Rose betrayed him and now you're doing the same thing.

'I can't,' she pleaded, 'it wouldn't work anyway.'

How do you know, if you don't try?

'I'm scared.' Her voice was a whisper.

Do you think William wasn't scared? He faced a lot worse than you ever did but *he* didn't wimp out.

She went slowly through to the living room. James Carew's booklet lay on the coffee table. She picked it up and opened it to William's photograph. Following a blind instinct, she went into the kitchen and brought back a pair of red, tapered candles she and Tim had used for special celebration dinners. Then she went back into her room and dug out some incense sticks she'd shoved in a drawer years ago and almost forgotten about.

She propped up the book, flanked with the candles and incense, which she lit. The candle flames were almost invisible in the sun-bright room so she drew the curtains. She sat cross-legged on the sofa in front of her impromptu altar and, not knowing a suitable prayer or incantation, bowed her head three times, chanting, 'Let me see William again. Let me see William again. Let me see William again.'

She closed her eyes and breathed in the spicy incense fumes, letting her mind drift, allowing the sounds of the quiet Sunday to grow in the still room.

William's voice was not one of them.

Chapter 38

There was no work on the island on Sundays. The prisoners were able to fraternise or enjoy the luxury of reading what ever material they could get. There'd been talk lately of providing a library but it hadn't eventuated. There were church services which the men were encouraged to attend and a room was set aside for that purpose at the end of B wing.

William sat on a wooden bench in the white-washed room, his leaden mind barely absorbing Superintendent Townley's bible reading. As usual, an ordained clergyman had failed to appear and Townley was providing religious comfort. The prisoners found this ludicrous and offensive, given his stern attitude and petty rules of discipline which he insisted, on pain of punishment, were obeyed to the letter. However, church was as good a place as any for a quiet read or a game of cards or dice, always providing you weren't caught, so a number of men were attending the 8 a.m. Catholic service.

Meat-Axe Ludlow was dealing the cards. He pushed a hand towards William but was ignored.

Tom Grogan frowned and fingered his beard. The lad had been behaving in a mighty peculiar way since yesterday, walking around in a daze as if life had dealt him such a painful blow he might not recover from it. His white face was not just from the week he'd spent underground, Tom guessed shrewdly.

Brisbane Joe and some other non-whites were at the back of the room in their own corner. Joe sat like a great black mountain, his strong arms folded across his chest, his long beard flowing over his shirt.

A warder approached him, which made Tom glance across with interest. Generally the warders, knowing Joe's erratic temper and vast strength, were wary of approaching him on what they judged to be fairly unimportant issues. This man, Warder Bagley, was new and still full of zeal.

'Here, you, Joe, how dare you come to divine service without your coat. Get along back to your cell and fetch it at once.'

Townley's voice petered out. Angry at the disruption, he was about to demand an explanation when Joe's deep voice rang out.

'Leave me alone, you bastard, or I'll do for you.'

'Don't answer me back. Go and get your coat right now.'

Warder Leighton approached and said softly, 'Have a care, man.' He said to Joe, 'Be reasonable. You've been given an order. The quicker you go, the sooner we can get on with the service.'

Brisbane Joe was surprisingly light on his feet for such a big man and was up and dancing into the aisle like a boxer. The two warders fell back as he shouted, 'Come and make me, you buggers.'

Townley called out, 'Restrain that man at once.'

Leighton had seen the blade in Joe's huge fist. 'Where'd you get the knife, Joe?'

'I made it myself and I'll kill myself if you try to get it — or I'll kill you, you bugger. I'll slit your bloody throat.'

The room hushed, all other activities forgotten. Other warders came up to reinforce their two comrades.

Joe suddenly went beserk, swearing and slashing with the knife. The first two warders jumped back but Bagley was a fraction slow. Joe's left hand shot out and pulled the man hard against his great chest, twisting Bagley's arm up behind his back. Joe's right arm lay across the warder's throat.

Some of the prisoners tried to talk him to his senses but he began to back down the aisle, dragging the terrified Bagley with him.

He reached the door and paused, his voice menacing. 'Keep off me, you bastards, I'll do 'im. I'll cut 'is head off. Now, open the door.'

White-faced and shaking, Leighton obeyed. Brisbane Joe said, 'Don't follow me or I'll do for the lot of you.'

Warder Bagley started screaming, a high-pitched wail of terror.

Joe growled, 'Stop that or I'll kill you now,' but the warder, mad with fear, continued the horrible sound.

Brisbane Joe's arm moved across the man's throat. The noise was cut off with a dreadful gurgle as blood spurted across those nearest to the two men. It ran down Bagley's body as it slumped in Joe's arms and began to stain the floor with a dark, sticky pool.

Brisbane Joe flung the lifeless body away from him and gave a maniacal laugh. 'Try and get me, you buggers, just you dare.'

He ran outside.

The room broke into pandemonium with prisoners yelling and trying to clean the blood off themselves; others getting as far away as possible from Bagley's gruesome body with its gaping wound nearly severing the head and still spurting blood. Warders ran, blowing whistles, organising themselves into some sort of order for the search.

Grogan looked at William, registering his glazed eyes and rigid body. The boy had been badly affected by the sudden, shocking violence.

'Look away, Billy,' he said calmly. 'The human body has a terrible amount of blood in it.'

The prisoners were being herded back to the yards. Grogan put his arm around William's shoulders.

'Come on, lad, let's get you out of this stinking place.'

William got to his feet and walked obediently outside with Tom guiding him.

What's wrong with Billy? The older man worried. It's like he's bereft of his senses. Dear God, I believe he's been broke at last with this final, dreadful occurrence.

'Come on, lad,' he said gently, 'not far to go now.'

Chapter 39

'What is it, what's got into you?' Grogan muttered. 'You can't crack now, Billy, you're one of those that keeps this lousy prison sane.'

William's eyes turned to his friend. Concern had softened Tom's normally hard, weathered face. He tugged at his grizzled moustache in a worried gesture and said, 'We're mates, Billy boy, share it with me. Perhaps I can help.'

'No, there's no longer any help for me.'

'What sort of daft talk is that? It's not like you. What's brought you so low? Was it Joe and Bagley, now? That new warder was as hard as nails and bidding fair to become another Townley. Surely you don't grieve for him?'

'No, for I've seen more brutality and violence here than any man should see in his lifetime.' William reached into his shirt and pulled out a letter. 'I think my heart's been broke, Tom, for all the life's gone out of it. My Rose, my blessed girl, she's finally written, after all this time.' His voice shook and he made a pitiable attempt to steady it. 'Not a word for near two years, and I'd put it down to her father's watching her too close, but now I see the truth of it.'

'What is it, Billy? Tell me, for the Lord's sake.'

'Rose writes that she is to marry my own brother.'

Grogan felt the shock hit him like a fist in his gut. He struggled to find some word of comfort but could think of none.

William returned the letter to his shirt and said simply, 'I don't blame her, Tom, for it was unfair of me to ask her to wait. There was never any real hope of my freedom and Rose is a young woman who deserves to be loved.' He steeled himself to continue. 'She says she knows that it will be impossible for Red to gain my freedom, for he's tried everything he knows. He is unable to bring d'Arcy to justice. At least he has saved Rose from that false devil. He showed her my letter and Rose has sent Jack away. She says she will always love me but, as she will never see me again, and as I asked Red to take care of her, she believes I might find some comfort in knowing she is in my own home with my mother and Walter to look after her.'

'It makes sense, lad, as you'd say yourself.' Tom gripped his young friend's shoulder in a gesture of unspoken sympathy.

'Yes,' William agreed bleakly, 'it will be best for Rose.'

'There are other women, Billy.'

'Not for me. It's the end. What use to escape if she is no longer free to go with me? She wonders why I never wrote to her and that has hurt her. I wrote faithfully, every writing day, and trusted Red to get my letters to her. Something has gone terribly wrong.'

'Aye, I told you before, you're too trusting. You're an honourable man and see honour in others where it's not.'

'Perhaps he could not get them to her, perhaps he was not permitted to see her alone.'

'If there'd been a way, he'd have found it, surely? Through a woman friend, or some such.'

'He must have done his best. He's my brother and knew well how it was between Rose and me.'

Tom didn't reply. They sat for a while, each occupied with his own dark thoughts.

Finally William said, 'I can see no point in this miserable existence. I must be free of it, Tom, one way or another. I cannot go home to suffer the sight of Rose and Walter as man and wife; I don't wish to live without her. I've seen how easy death is here, how the means of it may be obtained. I can forge a blade and do as Collins did or as Joe did to Bagley. It would be quick at least, not like this living death I'm forced to endure daily.'

'Lad, don't talk like that.' Grogan was alarmed. 'It's a bitter blow but, who knows, the truth may still be found out and you can make a life for yourself. You'll recover from this; you may not think it now, but it's true.'

'Thanks, Tom, you're a good fellow. You've helped me survive this hell and I'm grateful. But only the thought of Rose kept me going day after black day; she was the only light in my dreary existence and now I've lost even that. I wish Joe had done for me, not Bagley. That poor bastard was terrified. I'd welcome death as a kind friend.'

It had taken six warders to recapture and subdue the big Aboriginal and two of those had received deep knife wounds. The flag had been run up the mast and a telegraph sent to urgently summon the surgeon, and extra police to remove Joe to Brisbane. In the meantime Joe had been dragged to a single cell, cursing and reviling the warders with gruesome death threats and had been securely locked up to await his transfer. He'd immediately set to work to do as much damage to the cell as he could and his deep voice could be heard bellowing like a bull as he battered the walls with his night tub and tore his hammock to pieces with his bare hands, maintaining an unbroken stream of invective.

William jerked his head towards the noise. 'What did that gain Joe? He'll be locked up in Boggo Road and his life made more of a misery than before. At least he had some measure of freedom here, which is natural to the blacks. He'd be better dead. I believe we all would.'

Chapter 40

Sally uncrossed her legs and blew out the candles, feeling like a fool. What on earth could she have been thinking of, trying to summon William to her? The sooner she accepted that she'd tried to carry out an impossible task, that it wasn't her fault she'd crossed some sort of time barrier, and stop blaming herself and trying to make amends, the better it would be.

She picked up the bag of documents and went out to the car. Halfway down the street she turned around and drove back home. She carried the bag back inside and sat down. Hours later she still sat there, sick at heart, unable to work out what to do for the best.

All the next day she worked mechanically, still in a zombie-like state, until Fran decided she could no longer ignore the situation. Just before five o'clock she paused by Sally's desk.

'Sal, you're still not better, are you?'

Sally's head jerked up. She'd been so involved in her own misery she hadn't noticed the supervisor. She said sharply, 'I'm fine. Stop going on at me, Fran.'

'I wasn't aware I had been. Go home, Sally, and sort out whatever it is before you come back. You've been snapping everybody's head off for days. You're walking about as if your mind's light years away. It's unsettling for all of us.'

'I'm sorry, all right? I'm just tired. I'll be okay tomorrow.'

'If you're not, I don't want to see you. You've got your own personal black cloud hovering a foot above your head and we're all getting rained on. If you don't want to talk about it, that's fine by me — but get help, Sally.'

'I don't need help, thank you.'

'I've known you for four years and in the last couple of weeks you've become a changed woman. You're morose and moody. Off the planet most of the time. I'd say you do need help. Now I'm telling you, do whatever you have to, but stay out of the agency until you sort it.'

'I'm sorry,' Sally said stiffly. 'Sorry to have been such a pain.' She rose and began to put on her jacket.

Fran grinned. 'Yes, well, we're all sorry.' She gave her an impulsive hug. 'About Tim and about how obviously unhappy you are. You won't talk to us or let us help and we're your friends. So you don't give me much choice. Now, get out of here, Sally Cooper, and don't come back until you're totally better.'

Chapter 41

A t six a.m. on Tuesday morning, the stockade bell clanged, an insistent reveille which woke the prisoners every morning.

William groaned and opened his eyes. He'd been with Rose, just bending to kiss her. A moment later and he'd have tasted her sweet lips. He stared around the single cell he'd been allocated since his return in a move to isolate him from anyone sympathetic enough to aid him in future escape attempts. Prior to that he'd been in a ward with twelve other men. It had been cramped, only twenty-four feet by twelve, but the ceiling had been high and when the hammocks were slung in two tiers, there was room enough and companionship, too.

Once the men were locked in their cells for the night, they had an hour in which talking was permitted. At six-thirty *silence* was called and any further noise until the stockade bell rang in the morning was punished. But it was possible to continue whispered conversations, in spite of the constant passing of the warder patrolling the long corridors in cloth slippers to muffle his footsteps. William missed the gruff, somehow soothing voice of Tom Grogan and the camaraderie of his other cell mates. This single cell was the same size as the underground cells and his hammock took up all the space. He thought it little better than a dog kennel and felt caged, as restive as a trapped animal.

His eyes went to the place between the bricks where he'd hidden the knife he'd made the previous day. How long before they found it? His cell was being searched twice daily but he'd become adept at concealment. Nonetheless, he'd take it with him, just in case.

The clanging stopped. He had five minutes to dress, roll up his hammock and join the growing line of men filing out of their cells to empty their night tubs into the cess-pit in C Yard. The poor black prisoners had to exercise and eat there, with the stench of the prison's night-soil in their nostrils. He got quickly into his clothes, slipping the sharp blade into the lining of his boot, a place he'd made for it while there was still enough daylight last evening. He picked up his bucket and began to move forward when he stumbled and put it down again, rubbing his eyes and staring in alarm.

Something was wrong with the light in his cell. It was sparkling and shimmering in a strange, fluid sort of way and the walls themselves seemed to be melting into nothingness.

William gripped one of the iron rods to which his hammock had been fastened. *This had happened before*. He'd been talking with the strange lass by the blacksmith's shop and the air had begun shimmering and dancing. Then the smithy had melted away, leaving only a shell, and the stockade wall and most of the prison had vanished before his very eyes.

'Holy Mother of God, protect me,' he gasped.

'Come on, Prisoner O'Meally, we can't wait all day for the likes of you. Out of your cell, man.'

William could hear the harsh voice but his cell was no longer recognisable and everything familiar had disappeared.

'Hey, where's O'Meally? Did he come past you men?'

A whistle shrilled very close to him. He could have reached out and tapped the warder on the shoulder. He wanted to call, 'I'm here, you fool, can you not see me?' But suddenly he wasn't there any more. He was somewhere totally alien and completely unexpected.

Escape from the Past

On Monday night, Sally exhausted herself reading through the whole file of reports again, desperately searching for any little clue that would point her to the real culprit. When, defeated, she eventually staggered to bed, her thoughts were in such a turmoil sleep was impossible. She pulled herself wearily into a sitting position, her shoulders slumped with fatigue, her head aching, and tried to still her agitated mind.

As the clock ticked inexorably, counting the seconds towards William's fate, she gripped her hands together so hard that the nails dug painfully into her flesh. She cried aloud in a frantic voice, 'Help me, oh *please*, help me.'

It was a sort of prayer. The best she could manage in the circumstances. Tears poured down her face. It was a long time before she was composed enough to curl back under the covers, hugging a pillow to her for comfort.

Towards dawn, Sally finally fell into a deep sleep, blessedly untroubled by the horrors that had pursued her all night, through a series of fitful dreams.

The noise that jerked her awake was sharp and sudden and came from the living room. It penetrated the depths of her unconscious mind and, in her confusion she thought Tim had come back. She slipped quickly from the bed and opened the door.

The young man in the living room was holding several pieces of a china vase, a look of consternation on his drawn face. His dark curls were close cropped and his clothes were of a coarse dull-white cotton, patched and faded. He smelt dirty.

He looked up with wide, frightened brown eyes and awkwardly held out the shards. 'Forgive me, it was an accident. I meant no harm.'

Sally grasped a chair back, her legs trembling violently. '*William!*'

The air between them was shimmering and moving and his eyes widened, staring through the shifting light.

'Holy Mother of God. It's you! It's my angel!'

Chapter 42

Williams's startled gaze turned to one of shocked embarrassment as he became aware of Sally's short, flimsy nightie which clearly outlined her body, leaving absolutely nothing to his imagination. Even barefoot and in her nightshift, Rose had been well covered. He averted his eyes.

'William, thank God. It is you!' She reached out a hand.

'Please, ma'am,' he took a step back and forced himself to stare at the wall. 'You, you're indecent.'

She looked down at herself, gave a gasp, said, 'Wait there, don't you dare move,' and whisked back into the bedroom. She tore off the nightie, grabbed her underwear and dressed rapidly, choosing a long-sleeved blouse and calf-length skirt which she hoped would pass William's muster.

God, let him still be there. Oh, God, don't take him away yet. Praying under her breath she opened the door. William was standing where she'd left him, staring around him at so many unfamiliar objects.

Where do I start? Sally thought in sudden confusion. The TV, VCR, electric lights. Will he be too overwhelmed to deal with it?

His sour, unwashed smell wafted to her. 'When did you last have a — bath?' She just stopped herself saying shower. She wasn't sure if he'd understand.

'We wash our clothes each Saturday, ourselves on Sundays.' He seemed grateful for the ordinariness of her question.

'Then it's been two days since you washed?'

'There are no proper facilities, see? In summer we bathe in the sea, in winter we have a basin in the yards.'

'Would you like a hot bath?' Sally thanked providence that the house had a bath as well as a shower.

He gave her a quick smile, rapidly grasping the situation but taking no offence. 'That would be a luxury indeed, ma'am.'

'Come on.' She beckoned him through to the bathroom. He was still grasping the pieces of broken vase and she gently removed them from his hand. 'Don't worry about those, I never liked that vase anyway.'

He trod gingerly after her. She opened the door to the bathroom and he looked amazed.

'I'll explain everything later,' she said. 'Just have a good soak first. This is how you get the water. Hot tap, cold tap. They're marked with coloured tops so you know.' She put the plug in and turned on the taps. 'You'd better not touch anything you don't recognise for the moment.' She clasped his hand. 'I know it's all strange and you must be so confused but I promise you, you're safe with me.'

His face lit up. He was surprised at his pleasure in seeing her again. She might be the most unusual female of his acquaintance, but he felt instinctively that he could trust her. 'That is the one thing of which I am sure this morning. The rest,' he looked about him, 'is this how angels live? Am I — am I in paradise, ma'am?'

'No, and I'm not an angel, just a friend. Here's the soap. I suppose you use a loofah or something. I can run to a sponge and I've got a shower brush somewhere.'

She opened the cupboard under the basin. 'Here it is. Just throw your clothes onto the floor outside and I'll put them through... I'll wash them for you.'

He looked horrified. 'Ma'am, you cannot.'

'Yes I can and stop calling me "ma'am". My name's Sally Cooper. Call me Sally. You can't wear those filthy things.' She rummaged in the linen cupboard and brought out a couple of towels. 'Here. I'll leave you to get on with it, then. Have a nice time.'

She closed the door behind her and waited.

William stood gazing around him with fascination. Everything was so bright, so colourful. And there was a strange, stiff curtain, almost transparent, like glass, patterned with bright flowers and leaves. He touched it. Not glass, for it moved under his hand with a scraping sound and it was hung on hooks. He moved the plastic shower curtain experimentally and saw the tiled recess behind it and the shower rose. It was the most wonderful, elegant little thing. He guessed its purpose and that the taps in the wall would operate it. On a shelf were hard, shiny bottles, strangely shaped, in all the colours of the rainbow. What material were they made from? Not glass, not porcelain. Some heavenly substance, perhaps.

He remembered Sally, waiting for his clothes, and flushed with embarrassment. She'd had a determined look on her pretty face. He felt she'd not hesitate to wrest his garb from him. He gave a wry smile. Rose had that same determined streak. He knew very well it was useless to argue with such females, once their minds were set on a thing.

He stooped and unlaced his worn boots, then removed them, placing them gingerly by the bath. He unbuttoned his shirt and trousers and slipped out of them, then hesitated. He was as naked as a new-born babe. He'd just open the door a crack, and keep himself well out of sight behind it.

The door opened tentatively and William's prison shirt and trousers slid across the floor. Holding them at arms' length Sally headed for the laundry. They give me the creeps, she thought as she filled the washing machine, putting in extra powder and a dash of disinfectant. I'll have to get him something else to wear.

Tim had taken all his clothes. Sally thought of the nearby shops. There was a St Vincent de Paul's; perhaps she could get something there. She judged him to be about a small men's in size.

In the meantime, until the shops opened, he'd have to manage with a towel or her dressing gown which might just stretch around him.

She wondered what he'd like for breakfast. He looked half-starved. She glanced at her watch. The corner store opened at seven. In an emergency she could go around the back and the Indian owners, who lived on the premises, would serve her. She'd hardly anything in the fridge, what with not worrying about proper meals and grabbing take-aways on her way home from work. Without Tim to cook for she'd let the shopping go.

She started the washing cycle and went back to the bathroom.

William, having thoroughly scrubbed himself with Sally's lavender scented soap, luxuriated in the tub of hot water, his mind puzzling over his situation. He rubbed a hand along the rim of the bath. It was solid and real. He'd always imagined heaven as ethereal, cloud-like. And the girl, she'd said this wasn't paradise, nor was she an angel. That must be true, because everyone knew angels were incapable of falsehoods. His reasoning was a little muddled on this point, but it made a sort of sense.

If she wasn't an angel, then how did she appear and disappear at will, and transport him through space to a world that had many similar things to his world, but made of a magical substance, and in such colours? He'd once thought her a witch — or a devil. He chewed the end of his moustache thoughtfully. There was nothing evil in her, he'd be prepared to swear it on the bible. She'd thanked God when she'd seen him so she was in league with the Almighty, for sure.

A strange, insistent memory kept nagging at him. There was a familiarity about this place and these objects around him, but he could not, for the life of him, think where he could have seen them before. In a dream?

At that moment, there was a tap at the bathroom door. Sally called, 'William, I have to go out for a while. Will you be able to manage?'

There was a startled exclamation and a surge of water slopping onto the floor. The door opened and her arm was held in a vicious grip.

'Oh, no, ma'am, I was taken in by that ploy once before.'

Sally looked at his naked, dripping body, lather running from his hair.

'Who's indecent now?' she asked wickedly. 'I told you, you're safe with me. I'm not Jack d'Arcy.'

His hold tightened, making her wince. 'You know about Jack? You cannot have read my letter, it was private. I trusted you.'

She held his gaze steadily. 'Trust me now. You said you knew you were safe with me. I promised I'd explain everything. I'll be back in ten minutes, fifteen at the latest.'

His eyes burned suspiciously into hers, then a reluctant smile flickered, transforming him from a savage and dangerous man to the intelligent, gentle boy she knew him to be. He let go her arm.

'I'll wait for you, ma'am. Tom Grogan says I'm too trusting for my own good. Perhaps it will be the death of me, yet.'

'Not from me, it won't.' Sally gave him a little push. 'For goodness sake, get back into the bath.'

She took her handbag and car keys. Normally she'd walk the short distance; today time was of the essence. She had no way of knowing when William would be whisked away again.

Then her eye fell on the calendar and understanding flooded through her. Today is the day he disappeared off the island. They thought he'd escaped although he said he'd never left the prison. In a way he was right and how could he have explained this?

She felt giddy and sat down. What's happening? That was a hundred and fourteen years ago and he's here, now! Was I back or is he forward? Does time really work both ways, as Peter said?

Her heart slowed as she remembered reading that he'd been away from the prison for eight hours. She had enough time after all. She went to the front door then came back and unplugged the telephone. Better to not force too much technology on him all at once. She tapped at the bathroom door again.

'I'm leaving now. I'll lock the door on my way out so no one can get in. See you soon, William.'

Once outside she ran to the car and, driving well over the limit, sped to the shops.

Escape from the Past

The door was just opening as she arrived at the Seven to Seven
'You're an early bird.' Nanni Shastri let her in. 'Where's the
fire, Sally?'

'No fire; I'm just completely out of food. I'd better stock up.'
She went to the fridge. 'Milk, and sausages, bacon, eggs — bread.'
She chose a country style loaf, thickly sliced, and dived across to
the vegetables. 'Tomatoes, ah, butter.' She returned to the fridge.
'You must be hungry.'

'A friend just dropped in for breakfast. I'll have a tin of baked
beans as well and a jar of marmalade. That ought to do him.'

'Aha, him? You got a new man already? Fast work.'

'No, honestly, just a friend. From the country. He's used to big
breakfasts.' She handed over the money. 'Thanks, Nan, gotta rush.'

Back at the house the bathroom door was still closed. She called
out, 'I'm back, can I come in?'

The door opened to release a cloud of warm, scented steam.
William stood there, looking shamefaced, a towel draped around
him.

'I'm sorry. You took away my clothes. I have no other.'

'Use this.' She unhooked her dressing gown from the back of
the door. 'It's not too girlish and at least it'll cover you.'

He took it awkwardly. 'This belongs to you? You're very kind.'

'Your clothes are still wet and anyway, for a few hours at least,
you can be free from prison gear.'

His eyes lit up. 'Free.' Then he rubbed a hand across his chin.
'I, I need to shave. There was no time before I was brought
here.'

'Use my razor.' Sally went past him and picked up her dispos-
able. Amused, he took it from her.

'This little toy?' He chuckled.

'It'll do the job. It's closed, you see? A safety razor. It's so you
can't cut yourself. Use the soap for lather, I don't have any shaving
foam.'

'You — shave?'

'Yes. Girls do these days. Don't worry about it.'

He turned towards the mirror and she saw the shocking scars

on his back.

'William!'

He swung back in consternation. 'Lass? What, ah, a sample of Annie's work. I told you what they would do to me.'

The tears ran down her face. He touched her wet cheek gently.

'Don't waste your pity on me. It was no great thing and nearly healed.'

'It's horrible, barbaric.'

'Do you think I'd not pay that price and more for a taste of freedom?'

'You shouldn't have to. You were innocent.'

'Aye, of some things. Leave me to shave, ma'am. I am very well, I assure you.'

'I told you, it's Sally.'

'Very well, lass; Sally it is, then.'

'When you've finished, I'll be in the kitchen, cooking breakfast. It's through there. Just follow your nose.'

William leaned against the kitchen door frame, watching Sally bustling about. In this room, too, there were many familiar objects, but others were totally foreign. Even the ones he recognised were quite different in style from those he knew. The oven, for instance. Where was the fire? What made the strange metal spirals glow red with heat? And what was the tall, shiny white box with doors, whose inside lit up magically when Sally opened it? There were bottles inside and jars, and coloured boxes. She'd taken the butter out of one of the boxes. Did the tall white contraption keep things cool?

He found it hard to think about anything. A frying pan sizzled on the stove and the smell of bacon and eggs frying made his stomach ache from hunger.

'On the island they give us hominy for breakfast,' he ventured, 'porridge, which is tasteless and grey; only sometimes it's blue with mould. This is a very welcome change.'

Sally bit her lip. She couldn't burst into tears at every disclosure, appalled as she felt. She briskly pulled out a chair.

'Come, sit down. Here's the bread and butter, you can start with that. And there's marmalade.'

He fingered the plastic bread wrapper curiously but made no comment. She opened the oven and brought out a dish of sausages which had been keeping warm and put it in front of him, then piled bacon and eggs on his plate. She served herself, feeling properly hungry for the first time for days.

'Is that all you eat? You ladies must always be watching your figures. It's not enough to keep a bird alive.'

'It's plenty. This is a huge breakfast for me.'

She watched him ravenously shovelling food into his mouth.

He saw her gaze and tried to chew politely but the food was making him desperate to get as much of it inside him as he could before it all melted away as dreams did always. He swallowed and said, 'If this is a dream, it's a tasty one.'

'It's not a dream. Would you like coffee, no, tea, right?'

'Tea would be very good.'

Sally opened the fridge and took out a carton of milk. She turned her back to William and poured some into a glass jug but his quick eyes had noticed.

'You keep milk in a *box*?'

Sally grinned. 'Yes, and fruit juice and custard and cream and, oh, lots of things. It's all right, William. They never leak.'

William sipped his tea appreciatively. 'That is wonderful. Better than the bully tea they tend to serve us; and I've not seen anything like these little bags. It's a clever idea.'

'Bully tea? What's that?' She had a vague idea of billy tea.

'Well, they brew it from the leaves that have already been drawn. It's little better than hot water.'

'Is the food very bad there?'

'My friend Tom curses it daily. It's not so bad but meagre for some, being strictly rationed and often poorly prepared. We have a thief at our table who supplements our fare by his cunning. From the superintendent's own garden if he can smuggle it past the warders. The vexation is more the monotony of it, day after day, and it does no good to complain. It changes nothing.'

'Well, you can eat as much as you like here. I'm just going to hang out your clothes.'

'I owe you more than I can say.' He looked at her earnestly.

'What, for giving you a decent breakfast?'

'For that and the bath and this pretty gown.' He pulled it closer around him, a twinkle in his eyes. 'It's to be hoped the lads never find out. No, Sally, for sending my letter to Walter.'

'But — ' She blinked.

'Aye, it was a brave and clever thing you did. There is a lot I can't fathom about you, you are certainly not the prisoner I thought you, for if this is the female prison, there'd be women lining up to be admitted to its luxury. I don't know who or what you are, or where I am, or if you're a dream or some miracle, but you have my thanks. I will always be in your debt.'

'My name is Sally Cooper, I'm not a prisoner and this is my house, well, I rent it. I don't understand how the letter got to Walter. There's a lot we need to talk about, William, after breakfast.' She wondered how on earth she *could* explain and added, 'Well, I'll do my best. I don't understand it all myself. But we've got time; hours, yet.'

'You know this?'

'Yes. You're in the middle of your fifth escape attempt — and I'm going to see you enjoy every bit of it.'

He raised an eyebrow but didn't question how she knew. He said suddenly, 'The bath! I was afraid to pull out the plug for fear of the water pouring over the floor.'

'I'll fix it. It's quite safe. The water runs away down a pipe and out into a sewer.' Sally remembered he still had to negotiate the flush toilet and wondered what his reaction would be to that.

Outside the door she went back to the laundry and hung out the spun clothes.

What did he mean, she'd got the letter to Walter? And James said Rose had found out about Jack and given him the push. Did the letter get through, by some miraculous chance, and had Walter taken it to Rose?

She closed the washing machine and leaned against it, feeling wobbly again.

Walter got the letter, her heart sang. You made it, Sally, you made it. Somehow, by just making the commitment, you crossed time and space and the letter disappeared because it went to Walter.

She felt like singing and dancing, laughing and crying. It was coming out right at last and William was going to be okay.

Humming a bright tune she went back to talk to him.

Chapter 43

W illiam stood by the window, watching the cars in the street outside. A slight frown creased his forehead.

After breakfast, Sally had taken him into the living room and, after one or two false starts, took a deep breath and managed to stumble through the whole story. The difference in their time zones, her trip to St Helena, his incredible appearance in her time, how desperately she'd sought to discover the truth for him. She left nothing out that applied to the events up to the present moment. She had wondered with concern how much she should say. She was sure it would be wrong to mention events which, for him, were still in the future. She glanced anxiously at him from time to time, wondering what he was thinking behind his closed face.

She waited for William to say something, express shock or disbelief. Clad only in her chenille gown and his boots, which he'd insisted on wearing, he still had a quiet dignity and aloofness which she found disconcerting. She wondered when the warm, outgoing, fun-loving youngster of Rose's diary had turned into this self-sufficient, quiet introvert who wrapped loneliness and despair around him like an impenetrable cloak to use as a shield against the world.

He turned towards her, showing no special emotion.

She said quickly, 'It must all sound crazy to you but it's true. I'm not lying.'

'I know that, lass. All these things,' his comprehensive gesture embraced the street as well as the house. 'If it's not a dream, and I can only accept your word that it is not...' He hesitated then continued slowly, 'Since I met you I have had strange dreams about a place like this. I could no more explain them than I could speak of them. I wondered if my mind had become unhinged. I seem to know things that are beyond my knowing. For instance,' his eyes went to the candles she'd left on the coffee table, 'in this world you've no need of candles to give you light. You simply do this.' He walked over to the light switch and flicked it on. Startled, Sally watched him from the sofa. 'I cannot explain how I know these things but if, a long time ago, I was here, the memory must have remained.'

'We still use candles,' she said quietly, 'in churches, at celebrations, for intimacy and comfort. A live flame is sometimes better than all this artificial light. There are many things that are still the same as in your day.'

He switched off the light and came to sit beside her. 'One thing that has not altered is the loyalty of a true friend.' He took one of her hands between both of his.

She felt his warm, calloused skin and shivered.

He said quietly, 'I noticed you no longer wear your pretty ring. Have things gone badly for you, also? Have you lost your own love?'

Sally allowed her hand to rest in his. She felt immeasurably comforted by his sympathy. She shook her head. 'I didn't really love him, I just thought I did for a while. We were better friends than lovers. I broke off the engagement, it was the right thing to do. I'm all right, William. It's you I'm worried about.'

He squeezed her fingers gently. 'What will happen now?'

She couldn't help herself. 'You're not in the prison. They'll assume you've escaped again and they'll punish you. I'm sorry.'

'It's not your fault, lass, how could you have prevented this? We are both caught in some great scheme we cannot fathom and must take each moment as it comes. You believe I will be here for some hours?'

'Yes, so history says.'

'Then we'll trust history.' He released her and asked pensively, 'Do you think I will live in this world of yours some day?'

'I don't know.'

'Perhaps, if it is true we are reborn, I'll come here again. This life seems very good to me.'

Sally forced a light note into her voice. 'Yes, come and see me.'

'I'll do that. Write down your direction and I will come and drink tea in little bags with you.'

They laughed together then she blinked rapidly to force back the tears and asked, 'What will you do now?'

'There's nothing left for me. Perhaps you do not know. My Rose, my sweet girl, has accepted my brother in my place. They are to be married next month. Red showed her the letter and, whilst she has turned from Jack, she has accepted Walter. The only comfort I can find is that she will be away from that devil Carew and cared for by my mother.'

'Does Walter love Rose?'

'I did not think so. Perhaps he is doing this for me, thinking I would never return. There's no use in trying, now.' His eyes hardened. 'I have made up my mind not to stay on the island and there's no place for me elsewhere. I am determined to end it, for once and for all.'

'William, no! You have to fight.'

'For what? My life is over. Don't you be sad for me; it will be a blessed relief.' He bent down and slipped the thin, sharp blade from his boot. 'I made it myself, forged it in the smithy. It will be a quick and painless way to leave this sad life.'

'You can't, you can't.'

'You are thinking I'll be damned in the sight of God? I am damned already. My life is cursed. If I live it will be in perpetual torment, knowing Walter is in my place.'

A small seed of suspicion took root in Sally's mind. She interrupted impetuously. 'Do you trust Walter?'

'He's my brother.'

'So were Cain and Abel brothers.'

'You think Red ...? No, it is impossible. He fought for me, made up a story for the trial, moved heaven and earth to have them acquit me.'

'He broke down in court and it was Sergeant Mallory who got the retrial. Now *he's* marrying Rose.'

'A cruel trick of fate, no more. If he'd been able to get my letters to her, she never received them although I wrote, and it made her despair. She could not write to me and thought I did not write to her. It was a sad misunderstanding; surely no one is to blame. Now it is too late.' He stood up. 'I should dress, Sally, I cannot remain wrapped in your gown, charming though it is.'

'I'll get you some other clothes.' She jumped up. 'Will you wait for me?'

'Well, I cannot go with you. Even in your world I think this would not be respectable garb.'

'Definitely not. Make yourself some more tea, I'll show you how the jug works. I'll be back before you know it.'

Sally made the trip to the shopping centre again, finding a parking spot near the op shop. She hunted through the clothing, selecting a pair of trousers and a long-sleeved flannel shirt she thought William would find familiar enough. There weren't any trousers with button flies. Would she have to spend the whole day explaining modern living to him?

Underpants? she wondered, he didn't have any. And does he wear singlets?

She paid for the clothes and dived into Coles. They had men's underclothing and socks. She hesitated between boxer shorts and Y fronts, chose the shorts and waited anxiously in the fast lane which seemed even slower than usual. Glancing impatiently at her watch she finally reached the check-out, then she was free.

All the time she was shopping her mind worried back and forth.

He'll kill himself, she thought dismally, he's given up and I don't blame him. What an appalling life. What will they do to him when he goes back? They've half-killed him already. Maybe he's right to end it.

No! I can't just let him die. I love him. I love him.

Shock waves pulsed through Sally. She stumbled to the car and unlocked the door, nearly dropping the key from her shaking fingers. She slumped onto the driver's seat. That was why she'd fought so hard for William. No wonder the sight of him in her living room had set her pulses beating madly. No wonder she'd wanted to sing and dance with joy. Oh, God, what was she to do now?

She bowed her head at the awful realisation. Tim had been right. He'd felt threatened and his jealous mind had leapt to the correct conclusion. She was in love with another man, a man she could never have, a dead man from a different time who had his own love. Even if they'd been in the same life together she knew, without a shadow of doubt, that William would have remained steadfastly true to his Rose and she, Sally, would have had no chance with him.

She lifted her head, her expression bleak. Well, there it was. She and William were both in a hopeless position. She couldn't have him, he couldn't have Rose. They were both doomed to remain unfulfilled.

The trouble was, in spite of all her intentions, she'd had an unspoken, until now even unformed thought that, if she could help William, change things for him, he'd turn to her in gratitude and they'd somehow be able to stay in the same time zone, be together always.

You're not in Brigadoon, she told herself. You had the hide to tell Tim to grow up. Like he said, grow up yourself, Sally Cooper. And anyway, the after-thought struck her, I wouldn't like to live in his time and he would be totally lost in mine.

No, if she was going to help William it couldn't be for herself — for her own underhanded and impossible desire. It had to be for William's sake, and Rose. He belonged with Rose and Sally had no right to ask that time be tampered with for her gratification.

She pulled herself together and started the engine. She'd been miraculously granted one day with William. She'd accept that and then let him go. She would. She'd find the strength, for his sake. And she wouldn't stop trying, wouldn't let him down. She'd find something. There *had* to be something.

She knew there wasn't. The historical fact was that, in two days time, William would hang himself.

What about Walter? She asked herself as she drove home. I've been too much influenced by William's trust in his brother. Ma Drake said he left the way open for Walter. Did that mean Walter was in love with Rose? And he was with d'Arcy that night, right on the spot. What if d'Arcy went home and Walter stayed to ambush William?' She shook her head. William wouldn't accept her arguments. Family loyalty made it impossible, in his mind, for Walter to betray him. Suddenly Sally wanted to know more about big brother Red.

When Sally arrived home, her heart jumped at the sight of William. She felt herself blush and hid her face, rummaging through her shopping.

'Here.' She pulled the clothes out of their bags. 'Shirt, trousers — zipper. Instead of buttons. You grasp this bit and pull it up, see?'

He frowned. 'Is it not...dangerous?'

'Dangerous? Oh! Not if you're wearing underpants. Here, best I could do. And socks. Enjoy!'

'You're very kind, Sally, but you should not spend your money on me in this way.'

'It's my pleasure.' She pointed to Tim's room. 'You can change in there.'

When he came out he was smiling. 'It is good to feel socks on my feet again although I fear the skin is so rough it will rub holes in them.'

While he'd been dressing, Sally had taken a firm grip on her emotions. Now she faced him and asked seriously, 'William, tell me about that night, the night of the horse raid.'

'It's private, Sally, I have never told. I made a vow to keep Rose from scandal.'

'Which she broke. I know all about it, anyway— no, I can't tell you how. I just want to hear your side of the story.'

He sat down and said quietly, 'It is true we were thieves. Don't think too hard of me. We were all wild, untamed lads who thought it a lark to run rings around the authorities. All lads are like that.'

'They certainly are these days. Go on.'

'Buck Buchanan was our leader. He had the experience. The gang was myself, Red, Jack, Flash Johnny Francis, a brave lad of sixteen, Limpy Patterson and McLeod, the Scotsman. Seven of us. We thought it a daring thing, to take cattle and horses from under the very noses of the squatters, and gold, too. I was one of them who robbed the Andersons on their way down from Cooyar Creek. I have a bag of their gold put aside for emergencies. Men like Ned Kelly were our heroes. He died two years since, in Melbourne Gaol; perhaps you heard of it? Brought down by Queensland blacks. He was a great man, a reformer. He had a cause for which he fought, against the injustice of the British law. We were but wilful boys, ripe for danger and excitement. I should have been with them that night but I went to Rose instead and we, we lay together as man and wife.' He cast a quick look at Sally, wondering if she'd be shocked by this revelation. It was hardly fit talk for a well brought up lass. He was relieved that she didn't shrink from him but continued to listen calmly.

She's a rare one and no mistake, he thought gratefully and continued, 'We vowed not to tell as her father, George Carew, is a strict, religious man and disapproves of me. He forbade her to see me. He'd have made her suffer, forced her to marry a man of his choosing, and made sure I was got out of the way by some means or other; he has powerful friends. To save her, I refused to say where I was.'

'But she admitted it later.'

'Aye, and brought all the trouble in the world down on her sweet shoulders. She must have suffered greatly.'

'What happened after you left Rose?'

'I was riding home, dazed with happiness. I rode straight into the trap. A rope was stretched across the track and caught me hard against my throat, dragging me from my horse. My assailant was on me before I could draw breath and it was a deadly struggle, him being bigger and stronger. I thought I knew him but could not see his face and he gave me no chance to recover from my surprise. I broke from him, using a trick I learnt against Red when we wrestled together. I was going for my rifle when he shot me. That is all I remember until I woke in Doctor Evan's surgery. Of course they did not believe me. Would you?'

'I believe you with all my heart.'

'You are my friend; you and Tom Grogan may be the only true friends I have in all the world.'

The warmth of his smile made her catch her breath.

He said sadly, 'So you see, I never did what I was accused of but I did other things against the law, so perhaps this is God's punishment. But I swear, if I had my life to live again, I'd be as honest and upright as any judge and the Lord knows it's true.'

Sally wanted to fling her arms around him and comfort him. She cleared her throat and held her voice steady. 'Tell me about Walter.'

'Red? He's a big, strong, handsome fellow, with hair like flame. The same as our father, who also bore that nick-name. Mother used to say how the sunlight glinted from his hair, so bright it was, like new minted guineas.'

'He was on the raid?'

'Aye, and he tried to persuade me to go. He argued that I should not go to Rose but stay with my mates. I insisted they could do the thing without my presence and we parted on bad terms. The boys were ambushed and, well, you say you know the story.'

'You love your brother very much?'

'Our family has always been close. He's more than a brother to me. He's been father and friend also.'

'And so you trusted him with your letters to Rose.'

'Of course. But Carew is canny. He must have prevented him from passing them on. I could not write to her directly; he'd have intercepted my letters and burned them.'

'But Walter was seeing Rose. Couldn't he simply have told her he had letters? That you'd written? Couldn't he have left them somewhere for her, given them to someone her father wouldn't suspect?'

'Tom talks like that.' He glanced at her sharply. 'Would you have me doubt my own brother?'

'Wasn't Rose supposed to give Walter her letters to you?'

His eyes met and held hers. She let him read the growing suspicion in them.

He finally looked away and muttered, 'I cannot think such evil of Red. You would find me hard to convince, believing as I do that Wild Jack was the cause of my betrayal. To accuse Walter — no, he would never betray me. What proof do you have against him?'

'None.' Which was true. Only a niggling suspicion that bore further investigation. She stood up. 'Let's drop it. We haven't got much time and I want you to enjoy what's left. I went to the butcher while I was out. Do you fancy steak for lunch?'

'Steak?' His eyes gleamed. 'Sally, you are a wonder. Boiled mutton is the only meat we get and often so old the stench would turn your stomach.'

'Come and talk to me while I cook and after lunch I'll run the iron over your prison clothes. You can't turn up in those.'

'I'll keep the socks, though, for we are not issued with such incidentals and these are good and warm.'

'Wool. I got the toughest I could find.'

Sally tried several times to broach the subject of Walter's loyalty but was deflected each time by William's refusal to believe ill of his brother. As the clock hurried them towards his leaving she gave it up, contenting herself with making sure he was well fed and that his clothes were ironed and as presentable as she could make them.

Towards the end they sat on the sofa, hardly speaking, each aware of the coming moment when they'd be torn apart, and the realisation that this may be the last time they'd ever see each other.

William sensed her despair as the hour wore on and wished there was something he could say to comfort her. 'You mustn't be concerned about me any more. You did your best and I'm grateful. I should not have asked you to help me but I did not know the situation.'

'Of course you didn't and don't you dare apologise. I wanted to help. I'm not going to give up; I'll keep looking for a way.'

'There is no way. I told you, Sally, I'll not live without my girl.'

She swallowed and asked baldly, 'Would it be so bad? Is she so important?'

'She is to me.' He smiled bleakly. 'If only you knew how I love her and the pain of being without her. I gave myself to her, you must understand me. With all my heart and soul I gave myself.'

'There are other girls.'

'I know; loyal, beautiful, like a certain fair-haired lass I have also grown to love.'

Her eyes flew to his face. He was looking at her tenderly and she didn't trust herself to speak.

He nodded. 'You feel it as well, this bond between us. Perhaps you think it unreasonable of me to cling to the memory of Rose.'

'No.' Sally shook her head. 'I... I love you, that's true, but I know it isn't right. I make no claim on you, William O'Meally, even if it was possible. Whatever I've done was for you and Rose, not for me. I know you belong to her.'

Somewhere in her mind she heard the echo of Tim but knew it wasn't the same. William didn't want to manipulate or own Rose. He recognised the simple fact that they were paired for life, like wild ducks or wolves. He wouldn't try to hold onto her against her will but, if he lost her, he wouldn't take another mate.

He said softly, 'It's a fine, understanding woman you are, Sally, and I wish it could be otherwise between us, for you are very dear to me.'

He opened his arms and she went to him, letting him draw her close to his heart, feeling it beat strongly under the soft flannel of his shirt. She felt his lips brush her hair and closed her eyes, accepting whatever affection he could give her, resisting the urge to clutch at him, to beg him not to let her go.

After a while she gently disengaged herself. 'We're running out of time.' Her voice was calm. 'You'd better change your clothes.'

His eyes anxiously searched her face. 'You'll be all right, lass?'

'Yes. Don't worry. But, please, don't do anything without thinking it through.'

He grinned. 'You promised to write down your direction. Let me have it, if you please, so I can come and drink that tea with you.'

She smiled through her tears. 'Right, now that's a promise.'

When the moment came she stood close to him until the strange shimmering melted him from the room.

'Goodbye,' she called through the void. 'I love you, William, please don't forget me.'

PART FOUR

St Helena
1882

Chapter 44

Superintendent Townley dipped his pen into the ink well and frowned. He waited, regimenting his thoughts, while the ink dried on the nib. Finally he shrugged, re-inked the pen and began to write with a firm hand.

To the Comptroller-General of Prisons, Brisbane:
Sir:
Following the successful recapture of escaped prisoner William O'Meally, I submit the following report:
The prisoner was securely locked in his single cell on Monday evening as usual, having occupied single accommodation since his last escape from the island. This was done to isolate him from fellow prisoners who make a hero of him and cannot be depended upon not to aid him in further escape attempts.
When Warder Rolland released the prisoners at six a.m. on Tuesday, O'Meally was absent from his cell. There was no visible means of escape and, under my instructions, the cell had been thoroughly searched twice daily to prevent concealment of weapons or other aids to escape. The warder assured me it was impossible for O'Meally to slip from his

cell unnoticed and equally impossible for him to leave during the night. As is customary, the warders carry a small time-clock which, at regular intervals, is placed into the type-box at either end of the corridor, an impression being printed onto paper inside the clock. The warder must imprint the paper every half-hour, requiring him to constantly patrol the corridor between the cells. Upon examination, Warder Rolland's clock imprint showed he was alert throughout his watch. Warder Rolland is a reliable man, not known to take a bribe or be under the influence of spiritous liquors.

Regretfully I can give no reasonable explanation as to how O'Meally left his cell. The fact remains that, on Tuesday morning, he was not in it. When the matter was reported I took every precaution, raising the flag, firing the cannon to alert the water police and sending a telegraph to Lytton to inform them of the emergency. I instigated an immediate search of the prison and the island, which was joined by the water police on their arrival from Fisherman Island. No trace of the missing prisoner was found.

Townley paused and stared morosely at the paper. O'Meally had threatened to destroy his reputation; the comptroller-general would think he'd run mad, submitting such a ludicrous report. He'd be rid of O'Meally, one way or another; but how the devil had he contrived to go missing in such a singular manner?

Damn you, O'Meally, how dare you make me a laughing-stock. What trick did you use and will you play it again, just to see me turning the prison upside-down? Not if I can help it.

He turned back to his task with a sigh. It had to be reported and O'Meally was going to regret this latest action for the rest of his life. He dipped his pen in the ink and continued.

At two p.m. on Tuesday, the prisoner startled warders by strolling from his cell. He would not say by what means he left it or how he managed to return. There is no place of concealment anywhere in the cells or corridors. O'Meally showed no visible signs of exposure to the weather, or having been bothered by the many stinging insects. He was not hungry, despite missing two meals. Indeed, he looked extremely fit and well. His clothes had been freshly laundered, although he had not been near the laundry all day.

I can only assume he cleverly concealed himself, possibly in a roof of one of the workshops, and stole enough food to last the day, also a change of clothing. He must have planned to wait until the hue and cry had died down, then make his way to the shore and effect his escape.

When closely questioned, O'Meally denied having left the prison confines, and claimed not to have left his cell at all. He persists in this ridiculous story, making a mockery of the warders and the prison's stringent security measures.

I have put the prisoner on shot drill until Thursday when the government steamer Kate returns with the visiting justice, who will review his case.

Sir, I respectfully submit that St Helena is not the place for this prisoner. He is a disruptive influence on the other inmates and, in spite of regular and severe punishment, continues to make a nuisance of himself by his constant escape attempts. I request his immediate transfer to Boggo Road Gaol where he will not have the freedom and scope for his activities and will be more constantly watched.

Townley signed the letter, read it through, blotted the ink and addressed an envelope.

'That will fix you, O'Meally. They'll put a stop to your little games in Boggo Road. You'll live to regret you ever crossed swords with me.'

William picked up the cannonball, staggered to the opposite end of the exercise yard, dropped it, turned around, picked it up again, and carried it back to the other end. He'd been doing this for nearly two hours and it was amazing how heavy a twenty-four pound ball of lead could become.

The warder assigned to oversee the shot drill punishment called out, 'Rest.'

William dropped the ball and sank to his knees. Shot drill was usually only given for an hour and a quarter daily to those who'd got themselves into trouble. Townley had extended the time for William, forcing him to go for an extra half hour. He's determined to break me this time, William thought blackly.

His back felt near to breaking, his legs could barely support him. He was exhausted to the point of collapse and the dreariness of the punishment totally depressed him. Warder Leighton stared into the distance, seemingly absorbed by a string of birds flying over the island, giving him time to recover.

William pulled himself to his feet with a mighty effort and stood, swaying, but reasonably upright. Leighton brought his gaze slowly back.

'Ah, O'Meally, you'd better get back to your work, then.' As William lurched past the warder muttered, 'It gives me no pleasure to supervise your punishment. Why do you persist in your disobedience, lad?'

'You'll never understand,' William grated.

'You young fool. He'll send you to the mainland, to Boggo Road, where there are no open fields and pleasant scenery. He is adamant that you will be transferred. I know your hatred of being shut away from the sun and fresh air. You are doing yourself considerable harm.'

'If the other warders catch you talking to me you'll be put on report yourself. You cannot help me, Leighton, so you may save yourself the effort.'

Leighton shook his head. 'I'm sorry to hear it. Come on, then. If you can keep on your feet, I'll hand you over to Mr Dalton. But, think over what I've said. You will die of suffocation in Boggo Road.'

'I will die soon enough, anyhow, I think,' William snapped, 'and maybe I'll see you all in hell.'

Chapter 45

Some hours later, after Sally had composed herself, she rang Peter and poured out her story.

He plied her with excited questions and ended wistfully, 'I wish I could meet William. I don't suppose it's possible.'

'I never really expected to see him again,' Sally admitted. 'I was so exhausted and felt so impotent, I just called out for help. I knew I was beaten but I wasn't prepared to accept it.'

'It's called letting go,' Peter said. 'The best way to make space for miracles, I always think. Do the best you can and trust things to work themselves out.'

'Well, all I know is, I'm still in there pitching for him and I won't give up.' She faltered, then added, 'I *can't*. Peter, it's Tuesday. He hanged himself on Thursday. The day after tomorrow.'

His voice was grave. 'Sally, take care. Originally your only idea was to give William peace of mind. Now it sounds as if you want to change history itself, stop him taking his life. I'd say that was ego talking, and pride. You're walking a dangerous path if that's your intention.'

'You said you believed the past could be changed in the present,' she challenged him.

'I never said the physical events. I said we could change our interpretation of them, rob them of their power over us, see them differently.'

'I don't care,' she said defiantly. 'William's in trouble and I'm the only one who can help.'

'I think your emotions are too involved,' Peter countered gently. 'I'd be a very poor friend indeed if I didn't warn you of the danger. You'll end up hurting yourself. You sound utterly weary. Are you looking after yourself properly? How are you coping financially?'

'I've taken paid sick leave. Fran insisted. But I'll have to go back to work next week. If... if I can't help William, it'll all be over by then, anyway.' Her voice broke.

'Sally, don't. You're worn out. I'll come over — or I could ring Jules. She's been worried to death about you. She'd come and stay the night.'

'No, I don't want anyone,' Sally said quickly. 'I just want to be alone.'

The next morning Sally returned to Rose's diary, impatiently turning the pages, looking for the entry James had mentioned.

'Mr Stapleton has left Bell's Creek, recalled to Brisbane, and it is to be hoped, dismissed,' Rose had written, 'for it is quite clear he never meant to help William and only used him as an excuse to continue to visit me. I will not care if I never see him again. I must now depend entirely upon Walter to save his brother.'

Sally grimaced. Some hope! Rose now mourned the loss of William and spoke with ever increasing despair of Walter's efforts on his brother's behalf. Sally couldn't understand exactly what Walter was supposed to be doing and Rose didn't elaborate. He seemed to be spinning her a plausible story which she was swallowing. She continued to count Jack d'Arcy a friend, mentioning from time to time his grief at William's imprisonment.

As the months dragged on, Rose wrote less and less frequently and the pages lacked the sparkle and gaiety of the past. Sorrow had matured her; she waited patiently, praying for William's release.

She was clearly concerned that she'd had no letters from him.

'For he promised to write regularly, whenever he was permitted. He could not send letters here, for father would have burned them, but we agreed to correspond through Walter. He writes to his family, and Walter gives me such news of him as he can, so why has he deserted me? Is it from shame? Surely not, for each time I write, I assure him of my loving devotion and beg him to let me have word soon. He seems not to realise how he is neglecting me. Is it possible the prison authorities are censoring his letters and not allowing them to be sent to me? Walter has promised to make inquiries. Sometimes I fear that William has forgot me, but then I remember our love and cling to my memories as though they were a life belt.'

He wrote to her, she wrote to him — the go-between was Walter. Sally touched the page thoughtfully. Granted, George Carew had kept a close eye on them, Rose had said so. But Sally couldn't accept that Walter hadn't had a chance to whisper to her. Rose must have had girl friends visiting. Walter could have used them to pass messages. And she wasn't incarcerated at home. She was out and about. He hadn't made any effort at all that Sally could see. Another black mark against him. She made a mental note. She didn't believe William's brother was afraid of Carew. Walter had been one of a daring gang of thieves. He'd have enjoyed fooling Rose's father, passing William's letters on under his very nose. Hadn't William said they thought it was a lark to run rings around people?

She continued to search for the reference to Jack. The entry she was looking for was nearly at the end of the diary. Rose described her shock at the news, brought to her by Walter — good old Walter, Sally thought caustically — that William had escaped and had sought help from Jack d'Arcy.

'We knew nothing about it, but a letter has arrived from William, telling Walter that, rather than riding to him, Jack went to the police and betrayed William to them. Walter is most shocked to learn his brother was so near and he not able to assist him. I could scarcely believe Jack such a traitor. I faced him with his treachery and he denied it, as he was bound to, but I have seen William's letter and have sent Jack away. I refuse utterly to have anything further to do with him. When I asked him, in the face of his denial, who else could have betrayed William, he could not answer me but fell silent, guilt and confusion writ all over him.

'Walter fears it is the end for William. He has done all he can for him but now the guards will watch him closely, and he will have no further chance to get away. He says he will always do as William asked and look after me. I am afraid I will never see my beloved again.'

Sally pulled a note pad towards her and began to write quickly, jotting down points as they occurred to her. When she'd finished she read through the list, nodding slowly.

It all fits, she mused. No wonder Jack couldn't answer Rose. He must have guessed the truth and been shaken to the core. Walter was his friend, William's brother, Rose's comforter; totally above suspicion. Jack probably couldn't think of a way to tell Rose without looking as if he was trying to shift the blame. As far as Rose was concerned, the sun shone out of Walter's —.

She chewed the end of her pen. How do I prove it? William is adamant old Red's a saint. I'll need evidence. She paused. Even if she found it, there was no guarantee she could get it to William or that it would make any difference. She turned back to the diary.

'I am so unhappy. My father is to marry Mrs Moore and I cannot continue here with that woman in the place of my dearest mama. Walter believes, in spite of all his attempts to free William, that it is impossible and we will never be together. Walter has been so good, so kind. He has confessed to me what I have known for many months, that he loves me. Being the gentleman that he is, he would not have told me had there been hope of reuniting me with William. He feels that, as William has asked him to care for me, we should be married. Thus I would have sanctuary in William's home, with his darling mother, and a good husband who understands my position, and loves me with all his heart.

'I am deeply grateful for all he has done and surely he deserves me to reward him with my hand in marriage. He does not mind that my heart is given to another and I believe William would want to know I was safe and well cared for. If I cannot have him, at least I can bear his name, and join with his family.'

Ah, Rose, never marry out of gratitude. Sally groaned and turned the page.

'This day I have consented to become Walter's wife and must write to William to inform him and to say goodbye. Father is furious but will not stop me. Possibly, as Robert withdrew his suit as soon as he heard I lay with William, he believes I am ruined beyond all hope, and is glad to get any husband for me. Mrs Moore, no doubt, has persuaded him it is for the best. She would certainly not want me in the house. I must put the unhappy past behind me and be a good wife to Walter, the most deserving of men. I pray that God will comfort William and that he will learn to be happy without me.'

There was a break of a year in the entries as if Rose, weighted down with sadness, couldn't bear to commit her dark thoughts to paper. The last page was dated the twenty-sixth of June, 1883, and was very short.

'The inquiry is finally over. It is found that he died by his own hand. What a terrible time it has been, especially for Kitty, whose remorse knows no bounds. However, I believe she is growing to accept what happened as God's will and is easier in her mind.

'In spite of the grief that his brother has caused us, we have put the past behind us, and my darling husband and I grow daily in contentment, man and wife, until death us do part. In my heart, I know that death himself has no power to separate us and, in due time, will face even that grim reaper without fear. For surely, whom God has joined together, not even death can put asunder.'

'Well, at least you got over it all right. You played into Walter's hands, got rid of Jack and stayed about as loyal to William as — as!' Sally couldn't think of a suitable example of disloyalty and relapsed into bitter silence, thinking, how could she, after all her protestations? How could she have fallen in love with Walter? Was he so plausible?

At least she knew the truth now, or thought she did. She closed the diary and carefully rewrapped it. James could have it back. She didn't want it around any more, reminding her that, if Rose had failed William, so had she.

A thought flickered in the back of her mind. Hadn't the inquiry into William's death taken a very long time for a simple suicide? Were the prison officials so incompetent? She dismissed it. It hardly mattered now.

She looked gloomily at the calendar. It was Wednesday. To-morrow was William's last day and there was nothing she could do about it.

Chapter 46

There was an imperious rapping at the door and Sally went to answer it. The mail contractor grinned at her and handed her a package wrapped in brown paper.

'Sign, please.'

Sally signed the form and the girl said, 'See you later,' and went briskly down the path to her van.

Sally carried the package inside, turning it over to see who on earth had sent her a registered parcel. The address was firmly printed in black marker ink.

'Mrs Lee Bradbury, Sugar'n'Spice Cake Shop, Bell's Creek, Queensland.'

Sally pulled off the paper to reveal a large shoe box securely taped then tied with string. She broke through these defences and opened the box. The contents were also carefully wrapped and taped in brown paper. Like 'Pass The Parcel', Sally thought, intrigued.

An envelope, addressed to her, lay on top and she quickly prised it open.

Dear Miss Cooper,
We were having a clean out of some of Gran's old papers and

came across these. Gran says she's never seen them before. She must have stored them without ever reading them. She insisted I send them to you for your research. As they are family documents of historical interest, I'd appreciate it if you would take every care of them and return them to me by registered post as soon as possible.
Yours faithfully,
Lee Bradbury.

'Absolutely,' Sally murmured. 'What's in here, then?'
She carefully lifted the tape and opened the packet. Inside were letters and documents, mostly faded and obviously very old. With her heart racing she began to sort through them.

They seemed to have belonged to a Mr John Bell. Letters, newspaper clippings, all dated in the eighteen-hundreds.

'Ma Drake's grandfather,' Sally exclaimed. 'Jack d'Arcy's friend.'

She arranged them in date order. There were a number of newspaper reports of William's trial — she'd already seen these; it was the letters that excited her immediate interest. She began to read them, reverently picking up each paper and placing it back in the box after she'd read it.

The earliest letters were from friends John had met as he travelled as a timber worker, giving him news of his mates and their families. There were several love letters from an Elizabeth Brown, then a sepia photograph of Elizabeth and John on their wedding day in 1875. There were letters and notes from family and friends, congratulating John and Elizabeth on the births of various children, including a son, Matthew, born in 1880; Ma Drake's father.

Then Sally began to find letters written from someone called Jack, with vague addresses such as 'Up the Condamine', 'Drovers' Camp', "Along the Diamantina' or 'The Swede's Hut.'

Jack d'Arcy! She felt almost euphoric. She began avidly to read his letters. He wrote mainly of droving, the country he travelled through, mates he met up with on the track; sometimes he asked if there'd been any news of friends in Bell's Creek. Sentences leapt out at Sally. 'No one writes to me from home. Have you heard if

Rose is in good health, and does Red make her happy? If you get word he does not, or ill treats her in any way, tell me and I'll come back, I swear, and kick his head in... I still love the dear girl. I think I always shall... In the lonely watches of the night, I remember happier times, dancing with Rose and swinging her around in the country waltz.'

Then, in 1888, a letter was addressed 'Western Downs Station' and read, 'I've not been well. Took sick up along the Maranoa with a fever and feeling pretty low. Mrs Eden and her girls look after me day and night, bless them.'

Some months later John Bell received a letter from Mrs Claire Eden, Western Downs Station, Via Mitchell, Queensland.

Dear Mr Bell,
I am sorry to have to bring you the sad news of the death of your friend Mr John d'Arcy. He asked me to send his things on to you which, respecting his last wishes, I have done, including this letter he said was private and I must get it to you. He is laid to rest on the property here, on a hill under a tall blue gum, with a view across to the west. It is a very beautiful spot and if you were wishful to come to visit his grave you would be assured of a warm welcome.
Yours faithfully,
Claire Eden.

Poor Jack. Sally fingered the letter. All he wanted was to be happy with Rose but he ended up in a lonely grave in the west, as far away from her as he could be.

She picked up the letter which had been enclosed with the note from Mrs Eden. It was Jack's last message to his friend. As Sally read it, little shock waves flowed through her body.

Dear John,
They tell me I'm dying, old friend, and I'm not sad to go. So weak now and often delirious, but clear-headed today and must write this so I can go easy. It's preyed on my mind for

many long years and I must tell someone. Only, it's a secret, John, and I bind you to keep it, for our friendship's sake. Never tell a living soul, for I won't have Rose find out. What good would it do now?

It wasn't me shot Billy or put the police on him. It was his own brother.

I knew it! Sally thought.

Red wanted Rose for himself. He let it slip one night. I think he hated Billy, his voice was so bitter. Red tried many times to win Rose, but she looked on him as a big brother, which infuriated him. He always did have a temper. The day after the raid, Red's face was damaged, like he'd been in a brawl. He said he got that way from riding into low branches whilst escaping. I knew it was a lie because we'd rode together and he never had such an accident, nor would he after I left him at Carew's fence, because his track home was well travelled and clear, as you know. He bore the marks of having been in a fight. I thought he and Billy must have fell out over Rose, but could not bring myself to believe Red shot him in the back, like a coward. I reckoned maybe they fought it out and Billy was found and set on by thieves whilst he was too weak to defend himself.

Sally exclaimed aloud. Walter had fooled everyone by acting as though he was trying to get William off, but he'd always meant to see him hang. He'd tried hard to stop William going to Rose that night. He couldn't bear the thought of them together, so decided to do his brother harm. According to Jack, Kitty must have known, for she gave up speaking to Walter and never trusted him again.

Sally shook her head, appalled by Jack's verification of her suspicions. She read on, her thoughts racing. When William escaped from prison two years later, Jack hid him and went to Walter! Of course, he still thought Walter was trustworthy. Jack thought the police must have spotted William and followed him, just an unlucky chance, and William thought Jack had given him away. He never did! Sally compressed her lips with anger. When Walter received William's letter, telling him Jack had betrayed him, he took it to Rose, and pretended it was the first he'd heard of William's escape. But it wasn't. How *could* he! Walter must have hated Jack visiting Rose, doing what he could for her. What a vindictive man! As bad, Sally thought, as Rose's father. Jack's letter was clear.

> Rose asked me if I had done what Billy said and I saw how cunning Red had been, and that it was him all along. He never meant to help Billy, and was afraid to let him reach Rose. Rose said I never went to Red because he'd not known Billy was free until the police warned him his brother was back in the district. He lied about that, as well. I asked questions then, and discovered Red was seen talking to Sergeant Mallory just after I told him Billy was at my place. Red made no attempt to go to Billy, but rode straight home.

Sally's heart was in her mouth. Jack wrote that Rose sent him off and wouldn't relent, although he tried to tell her he'd gone to Walter, not the police. Jack had been totally confused. If he said Walter had betrayed his brother, Rose would despise him and it would break her heart, and William's too. They had sufficient troubles to bear. Jack couldn't prove Walter's guilt and he saw Rose had more chance of happiness with Walter and Kitty than with George Carew and Mary Moore. He decided to keep silent as long as Walter was good to Rose and she never found out what he'd done. Then he left the district.

He must have loved her so much to sacrifice himself for her happiness! Sally thought. She read the final page.

> There's not much more now, and I'll write it down, then it's done and off my conscience. A tinker passed through some days after Billy was shot and he did some work at the O'Meallys'. I met him out west along the road three years

later and we were having a pint and reminiscing. He said one night he saw Red burying something out by the shed. It looked like clothes, but it was none of his business. He left next day and thought no more about it. Some months later he came back through Bell's Creek and heard the rumours. Then he got mighty curious. He dug around at the spot until he found some clothes, all dirty and ragged; he reckoned they'd been hidden because of the blood on them, they were all stained brown. And there was a canvas hood with two holes cut for eyes, which Red had worn when he shot Billy. That's clear evidence and still there, as far as I know, because he reburied it. He was afraid to involve himself. I reckon he'd done a bit of thieving around the district and wanted to avoid the law. By the time I heard of it, the tale had reached me that Billy hanged himself. It was too late to get justice for him.

You know it all, now, and I'm so weak I can hardly write. You keep it quiet, as I've done, for Rose's sake; but watch out for her, and if Red ever does wrong by her, use this letter as you see fit.

We'll not meet again in this world, John, so I'll say farewell and take my leave. All my sorrows will soon be over and I thank God for it.

Your friend,
Jack d'Arcy.

Sally touched the faded brown writing which, towards the end of the letter, had lurched and meandered over the page.

'If only I'd known when I saw William.'

She'd begun her quest with a driving desire to know the truth in the hope that by her knowing, William's spirit might be set to rest. She sat back and closed her eyes, conjuring up the image of him as he'd sat right here on the sofa, next to her. She felt the warmth of his rough hands clasping hers and in her imagination she looked into his eyes and said over and over, 'I know the truth, William, I know the truth and I can tell you.'

After a while it occurred to her that she should tell James. He'd want to copy the letters.

Not now, later. Tomorrow is the last day and I want to be with William, help him through his ordeal, if only in thought. Tomorrow is the day of his last escape.

Chapter 47

'Is this the final day?'
'Yes, I think so. He hanged himself on this day in 1882.'
'What will you do?'
'Just stay at home, be with him in spirit. What else can I do?'
'Would it help if I came over?'
'No, Peter, I'd rather be by myself. Thanks, though.'
'I'll pray for you, Sally.'
'Pray for William.'
'Yes, of course. Try to have faith that there's a purpose in all of this and it's good.'
'If you say so.'

Sally stood by the window, watching the autumn rain running down the glass. Perhaps, she thought, if he'd known the truth, William would still have hanged himself. He might have chosen to say nothing, like Jack; to keep it from Rose and give her a chance of happiness. Protecting her was natural to him. In the long run he might have felt she was better off with Kitty and Walter. I don't expect Walter was really evil or that he'd ever do anything like that again. He was jealous and desperate, he was only twenty himself when it happened. Boys go off the rails emotionally, it's testosterone or something.

She stared bleakly at the grey rain curtain. Would William have chosen to pay the ultimate sacrifice for Rose? That would make him some sort of saint. To her he was just an unhappy boy. Well, now she'd never have the opportunity to find out.

Oh God, be with him and comfort him and I'm sorry I haven't been in touch very often but I really need some sort of divine intervention now. I'm not asking for myself, I just want to know whatever happened was divine will. I don't have Peter's strong faith and, frankly God, I'm not convinced people hanging themselves is your divine will, if you don't mind my saying so. I'd have thought you'd prefer us to be happy and fulfilled. Amen.

The rain had set in against a leaden sky. A chilly wind rattled the panes. Sally remembered the knife William had shown her, forged by his own hand, honed to a wickedly sharp edge. She winced. Which was a better way to die? To slash yourself across the throat, if you had the extraordinary strength of will to do it, or to drop from a tree and risk slowly strangling to death? She turned away from the depressing scene outside and sought refuge in the kitchen. Over coffee she thought of William sitting opposite her, wolfing his breakfast, starved for a taste of eggs and bacon and marvelling that she ate so little compared with him. At least she'd been able to do that much for him. Would he remember her? Think of her at all before he died? Recall one small bright spot in his dismal life, the good food and the care she'd given him?

Can he remember me? Or did his memory wipe away when he went back? Was that why he'd recalled his time with me only in shadowy dreams?

He'd called her his angel. The thought warmed her. They'd had a miracle. The letter had got through. She hadn't failed; she'd promised to get it to Walter and somehow that had happened.

She hadn't let him down. It was Walter. He'd used the letter for his own purpose. He knew Jack was innocent and got rid of him through Rose. She hadn't failed William.

You can hardly take the credit for that. You didn't post the letter.

But she had made the commitment and carried out her intention not to do it for herself.

Sally went back into the living room. There was a small fireplace; she and Tim had enjoyed curling up in front of the fire on winter nights. The house had a dead, dank feel about it and she wanted the comfort of live flames.

'A live flame is sometimes better than all this artificial light.' She'd said that to William.

She shivered. The fire had been laid some weeks ago during a brief cold snap at the beginning of autumn and she tapped on the logs to warn any spiders to shift themselves, then lit a spill of newspaper and thrust it into the kindling.

The flames crackled and ran up the logs. Sally hunched on the thick sheepskin rug by the fireplace, nursing her coffee. She reached for James' booklet and hugged it to her, staring into the leaping fire.

'I'm here, William,' she whispered. 'It's all right, I'm here.'

Alisha Grant paused by Scott's chair and dropped a kiss on his head. He looked up in surprise.

'You're not going out in this?'

'It's not that heavy. Thank God for the rain at last.' She glanced down at her mackintosh and gum boots. 'I'll keep dry. I just had a really strong urge to clean up Walter and Rose today. Anyway, the weeds will pull up better now the ground's had a good soaking.'

'Do you want a hand?'

'No, you sit and contemplate your acres, oh lord of the manor. And think about how you're going to stop that leak in the dining room ceiling.'

Alisha pulled a rain hat firmly over her hair and, armed with a bag of gardening tools, trudged across the wet fields to the creek.

Chapter 48

'Sally, Sally, wake up.'

'William, it's all right, I'm here.'

There was a familiar chuckle. 'So am I, it seems. Wake up, lass.'

Her eyes flew open and focused uncomprehendingly on the man who knelt on the rug beside her, calmly placing more wood on the fire.

'William!'

He caught her in his arms. 'Aye, but don't screech at me like that, lass, you near scared me to death.'

'I was dreaming.' She hugged him, oblivious of his dirt and sweat. 'I thought you were a dream.'

'I'm real enough.' He looked down at her. 'You were dreaming of me?'

'I've been worried sick about you.' She let him go, suddenly embarrassed, and scanned his face. 'I thought you were going to kill yourself.'

For a moment he concentrated fiercely on the fire. Finally he looked back at her. 'Aye, I've thought of it. I've wanted to, but I cannot reconcile it with my conscience. They have always drummed it into me that to take one's own life is a mortal sin and — I'm afraid.' There was a sad resignation in his eyes as he continued, 'I see no purpose for my life; but, if it is God's will, surely I'll be damned to hell for eternity if I end it.'

'I don't believe it.' Sally said warmly. 'I don't believe in hell and any God worth the name wouldn't condemn anyone to such a terrible place. If there is a hell, we make it ourselves in our minds.'

His eyes searched hers. The dancing flames cast strange shadows across his taut face. 'Do you truly believe that?'

'I do. I don't want to have anything to do with a God who's so mean-spirited and unforgiving He wouldn't understand how awful life can be sometimes.'

'I thought that myself. When William Collins cut his throat two weeks back.'

She became alarmed. 'I didn't say it to encourage you. I don't want you to kill yourself. I've got news for you, you won't like it, but it's true.'

'Then tell me quickly for I fear we've not much time. The Kate will be here within the hour, bringing the justice. He is bound to punish me for my day with you, which neither of us could help, but I'll not be able to explain that, now, will I?'

'Walter! My own brother? I cannot believe it's true.'

'I'm sorry.'

'There has been some mistake. It's a black lie. How came you by that story?'

Sally clenched her fists. She couldn't say she had a letter from Jack d'Arcy. He'd demand to see it. And he'd read that Walter married Rose and William hanged himself. Suppose he took that as proof that his case was hopeless, even saw it as encouragement to end his life?

Peter's warning had shaken her, although she hadn't admitted it to him. She was tampering with something beyond her understanding. She was totally out of her depth, rushing headlong into a frightening abyss, instinct impelling her crazily forward. That instinct had already warned her not to tell William about future events. She'd slipped up once, but only given him a glimpse a few hours ahead. She didn't want him to know of Jack's unhappy death and that he'd kept his secret so long out of love for Rose. It was private, between Jack and his friend John Bell, seeing as he'd chosen to share it with him. It would grieve William and perhaps make him lose heart.

He was still frowning at her, waiting for her to explain. She'd have to convince him without Jack's letter. 'I can't tell you. You *have* to trust me. Look at the facts. Walter knew where you'd be that night and he was on the same track home. He gave you an alibi by telling an unsustainable lie which he couldn't possibly expect everyone in the pub that night to agree to; it would have meant a massive conspiracy. Then he fluffed his evidence convincingly enough so that it looked as if he was grief stricken, seeing you in the dock. In fact, it guaranteed his story wouldn't hold up.'

'Stop, Sally, you go too fast and I cannot always follow you. These are arguments which could easily be disproved.'

'I haven't finished yet. Walter botching his evidence made the others back down as he'd known they would. He also helped stop Rose going to court. He kept visiting her, I'll bet you didn't know that, hanging around her, trying to get her to turn to him. He told her he got the retrial when it was Sergeant Mallory's report that swung it. Walter never made a move to get you off. He was after Rose and the last thing he wanted was you coming back. For heaven's sake, William, as soon as he got your letter about Jack, he took it straight to her, knowing she'd kick Jack out.' She paused for a moment to let it all sink in. 'He didn't try to prove Jack shot you because he already knew he was innocent.'

William was silent, watching the fire, his face grey with shock. Sally's heart went out to him but she went on relentlessly, 'The man who shot you didn't just cover his face but his whole head. He had to hide those bright red curls your mother was so proud of. They'd have given him away in an instant. Think, William. Wasn't it Walter who wrestled with you that night? Wasn't that why he was so familiar?'

She saw a muscle jump in his cheek as his jaw clenched. His throat moved but he said nothing. 'I can prove it was Walter,' she said gently. 'A travelling tinker did some work at your farm just after you were shot. He saw Walter burying some clothes by the shed one night. He didn't think any more about it then, but he came back months later and dug them up. The clothes had blood on them and there was a canvas hood with eye-holes. Your attacker wore a canvas hood, didn't he? How come Walter was burying those things if he had nothing to do with it?'

William bowed his head, tugging at his moustache with a trembling hand. Sally reached out to touch him and found his whole body shaking. She rubbed his shoulder soothingly, giving him time to control his pent-up emotions.

'My own brother.' William's voice was hoarse.

'He was in love with Rose. Don't ask me how I know that, but it's true. The clothes are still there, buried by your shed. That's all the evidence you'll need, if you could get someone to look.'

He turned towards her, his expression so grim she drew back.

'You write it down. All of it. Just like you told it to me, and sign it. Say you have information, you are a friend of the family. You can trust me to do the rest.'

He stood up and pulled her to her feet. 'Hurry, before I'm taken back. I will live to see justice done, yet. Red shan't have my Rose if I can stop it. Be quick, lass, or it will be too late.'

It was there in the booklet, in black and white. Today, Thursday, the last Thursday in April, 1882, William O'Meally hanged himself from a tree on St Helena. She'd seen the tree, stood under its branches; his grave was there in the island cemetery for all to see.

She laughed mirthlessly. What had she expected? For the print to suddenly change on the page to say William had been released? If she'd thought about it rationally from the beginning, she'd have realised you couldn't stop history from happening just the way it did. He obviously didn't succeed in convincing the authorities because, if he had, the information she'd given him would have been documented and appeared in the official accounts of the story.

He'd been so optimistic, snatching the paper from her, eyes glowing in his exultant face.

'I can never repay you. I'll remember this all my life and I will pray for you and bless you every day.'

He'd kissed her then, scarcely noticing, his mouth warm on hers, probably already imagining he was kissing Rose.

What on earth had happened when he'd found himself back in prison, brought before the visiting justice? What had caused him to plunge into such despair that he'd hanged himself just a few hours later, and what had become of the information she'd given him?

You're an idiot, she scourged herself. Who said that William's knowing the truth would make a difference, anyway? What an appalling hide to imagine you could have made one speck of difference. Next time you decide to save someone by changing history, go and get yourself committed to the looney bin.

When the realisation came it was horrific enough to send her to her knees by the sofa, her face buried in the cushions.

It must have been me, she thought, dismayed. If he'd never known the truth he wouldn't have been so devastated. I gave him such a burst of hope that, when he wasn't listened to, when no one would go and check for the clothes, knowing that Walter had set him up must have been the final blow. If he'd never known about Walter he might have resigned himself to Rose being with him. Oh, God, it's my fault. If only I hadn't been so stupidly, determinedly arrogant, pushing ahead on a senseless mission to find out the all important truth. If I hadn't interfered, he might have lived. Perhaps he was never meant to know. Jack didn't tell him, he had more sense than I did because he wasn't thinking of himself at all. He was willing to take the blame, to say nothing. He could see beyond his ego and think about someone else.

She raised her head. The clock ticked steadily on. It would be all over now, anyway, and William would finally be at peace. She just didn't know how she was going to live with the knowledge that she had driven him to his death. One hundred and fourteen years ago, she reminded herself. If he was alive today he'd be one hundred and thirty-four.

She put another log on the fire. William was better at placing the wood than she was. Hot tears started to her eyes, then overflowed in a torrent of misery.

It's all over. Oh, God, he's dead, *he's dead.*

When the deluge of pent-up frustration and self-recrimination had finally quietened to the occasional hiccupping sob, she dried her eyes and went to the wine rack.

She was going to celebrate William's memory in true Irish fashion, as befitted an O'Meally. She planned to get good and properly drunk.

Towards one o'clock Sally began to feel hungry. She wasn't the type to deliberately drown her sorrows with drink so she'd half-heartedly managed about three quarters of the bottle which had only made her slightly muzzy. The call to eat grew more insistent and she concentrated her efforts and strolled, in an almost straight line, to the kitchen.

Half-way through a cheese and pickle sandwich something jolted her memory.

William made a *knife.* How did he have time to make a rope? Last thing he talked about was some poor sod who'd cut his throat.

She sought for an explanation. Perhaps he didn't make the rope himself. Some other prisoner could have made it and William nicked it. But why didn't he use the knife? Did he lose his nerve? It's a bit cold-blooded. Perhaps he thought a rope would be easier.

She continued to sit there, her mind going around in an unhappy reverie.

Chapter 49

A lisha hung up her hat and raincoat and struggled out of her gum boots. She found Scott up a ladder in the dining room.

'Any progress?'

'Didn't anyone tell you you can't mend a leaking roof in the rain? It's coming from right where we found that old metal box. Perhaps something came loose when I dislodged it.'

'Can you fix it?'

'When it dries out, yes. Is that why you married a handyman?'

'Why else? It wasn't for your cows. Fancy a coffee?'

'Sure.' He came down the ladder and they went out to the kitchen, dodging through the rain.

'I've had the oddest morning.' Alisha spooned coffee into the beaker.

'Tell me.'

'Well, I'm cleaning up Walter and Rose, working at all that lichen and — it isn't Walter in there at all.'

'How come?'

She switched off the electric kettle and filled the beaker. 'I can't explain it. We were told it was Walter so we've always read his name there. The W and L, and the last letter did look like an R. The whole thing was so indistinct; anyway, why would we query it? So, I'm scrubbing away and scraping it down and it isn't Walter Thomas, it's William James. William was sent to St Helena, wasn't he? Unless there was another William, a cousin or something.'

'Are you sure?'

'Am I sure! Of course I'm sure. I've just spent two hours cleaning it up. The historians have got it wrong, that's all.' She moved restlessly around the kitchen. 'It's infuriating, sometimes, trying to get the O'Meallys clear. It's almost as if there's a conspiracy of silence. And what about the extraordinary lack of documents, except for that old box? Where have they all gone to?'

Scott nodded thoughtfully. 'It certainly doesn't help, having practically no one here from those times. What with people leaving when the gold ran out, then the town nearly dying in the drought, when so many farmers just walked off the land.' He smiled at Alisha's frustration. 'Stop prowling about. We should contact James Carew about the grave, and that girl in Brisbane, Sally Cooper, let her know. She was researching William.'

'It must be the same one. They wouldn't have had two William Jameses, and we never heard of cousins out here.'

Scott shrugged and pushed the plunger down in the coffee. 'Interesting. We certainly thought Rose married Walter.'

'Then she's got no business going to the afterlife with his brother.'

Chapter 50

S ally lay back in the bath, scented foam up to her chin.

He's everywhere. He sat in this bath and shaved with my razor. I'm never going to be free of him. And the worst is, I don't think I want to be. Tim was right, I'll end up a weirdo, living with a fantasy.

There was a distant knock at the door.

'Damn!'

Don't answer it.

It's probably Jules or Peter checking up on me.

It's probably market research or Jehovah's Witness. You'll get to the door and they'll have given up and gone.

Shut up!

She got out of the bath and hastily dried herself, pulling on the robe William had worn. She went through to the front door and opened it the length of the safety chain.

A man stood wetly on the top step, his jacket collar turned up against the rain. His dark hair was flattened on his head and water dripped into his eyes.

'Yes?'

'I'm sorry, is this an inconvenient time?'

'Yes. Do I know you?' She thought he looked vaguely familiar but the dusk and steady rain had made the late afternoon gloomy and the outside light had stopped working weeks ago.

'I don't think so. I'm looking for a family who used to live here, years ago. Last century, in fact.'

'This house wasn't here last century. Sorry, goodbye.'

'No, wait. Was there another place built here?'

'I haven't a clue.'

'I'm looking for a family by the name of Cooper.'

Sally blinked. 'My name's Cooper but I've only been here a couple of years.'

'Look, can I come in?'

She hesitated. 'I'm in the middle of a bath. I'd rather you didn't.'

'I don't want to be a nuisance but I'm getting drenched out here. I promise I won't attack you.'

An odd tingling sensation began to spread through Sally. There was *something* about him. Instead of closing the door as she'd intended, she said lightly, 'Yes, well, I expect all attackers say that.'

He considered the justice of this, an amused glint in his eyes, then shook his head. 'I doubt it. They probably don't waste time pacifying their victims — they'd just pounce, don't you think?'

She peered at him, her eyes adjusting to the gloom. His eyes were brown, his features... 'Are you sure we haven't met somewhere?'

'If I was an attacker, that would be my line. I'm sure we haven't met. My name's O'Meally; Michael O'Meally. Christ!' He stared at her in consternation. 'Are you all right?'

Sally leaned weakly against the door but managed to slip the chain off. 'No, I'm not all right but you'd better come in.'

Sally switched on the heater and hung her unexpected visitor's jacket over a chair in front of it to dry. Bewildered, she turned and studied him, her breathing uneven. His resemblance to William was strong enough to make her sink into a chair, her knees trembling. Under a vigorous towelling his hair had fluffed into a mass of dark curls with a reddish tint. Michael was about twenty-seven,

Sally guessed, older than William. He wasn't a big man but under his cream pullover, his body was well muscled. She could see that, although he was clean shaven, his humorous mouth and firm chin were William's own. His eyes too! She caught her breath. Wide set, gentle, the same warm brown.

He brushed the last drops of rain from his damp trousers and opened a brief-case, pulling out some papers.

'It's an extraordinary coincidence. The Coopers I'm looking for had a daughter named Sally and must have lived at this address in 1882.' He looked up. 'You're not going to faint again, are you?'

'I didn't faint before. I've had a traumatic day and you're the last straw. *I'm* Sally Cooper.'

He put down the papers and frowned. 'Is there something going on I don't know about?'

Sally picked up the St Helena booklet and opened it at William's photograph. She handed it silently to the man who was enough like William to be his older brother.

'Ah, you know about William? He's my great-great grandfather.'

Sally gasped. It wasn't possible. William hadn't been married. Unless...could Rose have been pregnant? After that one night, and never said, never even mentioned it in her diary? Was that why she was so willing to marry?

Michael gave her a quick, understanding smile. 'No wonder you looked odd. I'm supposed to look like him.'

Her head reeling, Sally forced herself to reply, 'It's a very strong resemblance.'

'Well, you can't really tell from old photos.'

'Believe me. You're older than he was then but you could be brothers.'

He shot her a puzzled look.

Sally shivered, although the room was warm. 'How did you know where to find me?'

'I wasn't looking for *you*. I'm trying to trace a woman William met when he escaped from St Helena. You're not old enough.' He grinned. 'It is extraordinary, though. This is the address and you're Sally Cooper, and,' he picked up a paper and read, '"a pretty, slim lass with short hair the colour of ripe wheat, and a strange manner of speech." Except for the strange manner of speech, he could have been describing you.'

She reached out an unsteady hand and took the letter, nursing it to her. Strange to him, he kept telling me to slow down. Oh, William.

Michael said carefully, 'I'm the one in the family who's particularly interested in our history. So, when some papers were found in a strong-box they were sent to me. You're very pale, do you want a drink?'

She shook her head. 'Just tell me.'

'Our family home's owned by a couple —'

'Scott and Alisha Grant.'

'You know them?'

'We've met. I — I'm interested in William.'

He paused. 'Look, I'd better start at the top. I'm not sure what's going on but it's par for the course at the moment. Until last week, I thought I was Walter O'Meally's great-great grandson. William's brother. Walter was engaged to Rose, the banns were called, notice in the paper, the marriage certificate had Walter's name on it. I can only assume, in all the confusion, the priest wrote his name because, until the last minute, it was going to be Walter. There must have been a huge drama. I guess no one remembered to change the name.'

Sally blinked, trying to make sense of all this. She asked urgently, ' *What* confusion? Why was there a drama?'

Michael looked at her for a moment, surprised by the wave of pleasure that flowed through him. She was leaning forward, the soft gown wrapped around her, her fair hair dishevelled. Her grey eyes were wide and dark shadowed in her pale face. He had the impression she'd either been ill recently or under a huge strain. He resisted the impulse to reach across and take her hand. Good God, he'd only just met her. Why did he have an overwhelming desire to pull her into his arms and hold on to her. He felt an inexplicable sense of relief just to be here with her and looked surreptitiously at her clasped hands. She wasn't wearing a ring. He found himself fervently hoping there wasn't a bloke in her life.

Sally was watching him impatiently. He smiled warmly at her and continued. 'There's always been a strange lack of information about the past in our family. For some reason, documents have gone missing. Official files were lost, misfiled probably, but never found; although, I put it down to a lack of bureaucratic interest. My great aunt Maggie had a lot of papers but she went a bit batty. Let everything go to seed, including herself. She just threw all the documents away.' He grinned. 'We call it the O'Meally curse. We reckon it's a devilish plot to keep us from knowing about an old pact with Satan himself.'

Sally made a strangled noise in her throat and Michael's expression quickly sobered. Why was she staring at him with such painful intensity?

He said gently, 'Sorry, I'm rambling. Scott and Alisha were doing some restoration work last week and found an old strong-box wedged in the ceiling. It was locked and there wasn't a key. They didn't like to open it and as it had William's name on it they sent it to me. You know, it's the oddest thing, but all the time I'm telling you this, I get the feeling you know something I don't.'

Sally said baldly, 'Yes.'

'Do you want to tell me?'

'No. Go on.'

He shrugged. 'I opened the box and found papers from William, including that letter.'

Sally turned the letter over. William's strong, flowing script filled the page.

Glendale Farm,
September 24th, 1882.

To Whom It May Concern:

There is a debt I owe a woman in Brisbane town which, for reasons I cannot explain, I am not at present able to repay. I charge my descendants, whomever shall inherit my estate, to carry out my wish, as follows:

They should go to Brisbane town, to the suburb of Red Hill,

number 2 Acacia Street, and find Miss Sally Cooper, a pretty, slim lass with short hair the colour of ripe wheat, and a strange manner of speech. She rendered me a great service when I escaped from prison in April, giving me shelter and finding out the evidence by which I was set free. Tell her I have not forgot her, nor shall ever, that I think of her with gratitude and great affection. She was my angel when I needed a miracle. You may wonder why I have not gone myself. I believe she is not to be found at this address at present and will not be returning to it for some years, by which time I shall not be able to honour my debt.

The enclosed package is for her. Tell her I've no need of it and want her to have it. She is not to mind how I came by it, but to enjoy it. Tell her, if I ever can find the means to do it, we will meet again.

William James O'Meally.

'You see why I'm anxious to find her. As soon as I read that, I felt William was talking directly to me. Any clues you can offer would be much appreciated.'

'He was set free.' Sally felt stunned. 'I... I always thought he hanged himself.'

'So did I. There's obviously been some mix up.'

Sally leaned back in her chair, aware of Michael's close scrutiny. She felt comfortable with this man, she could let down her defences with him, tell him the truth. She thought suddenly, *He's nice. I feel I've known him for years.*

She smiled at him and saw the warmth of his expression. She knew she was blushing and asked quickly, 'Do you know James Carew?'

Michael nodded. 'Yes, I gave him all the documents I had when he was researching William's life. We're some sort of cousins. I gave him all the stuff on the trial.'

'That came from you?'

'You've read it?'

'There was nothing in any of James' material to suggest William was released.'

'I know. Apparently the woman, your name-sake, Sally, helped him. I've got it all here. She discovered information which William presented to the visiting justice who authorised a new inquiry into the whole case. William was released a month later. There were a number of documents in the box; reports from the visiting justice, William's release papers. Presumably the official records were lost or destroyed and the true story along with them.'

Sally pulled her dressing gown more closely around her and took a deep breath.

'Michael, there's something I have to tell you. It's extremely involved and I won't blame you if you don't believe a word of it and think I'm crazy.'

'Why wouldn't I believe you? You look sane enough to me. Let me take you out to dinner and we can talk.'

'Yes, please, I'd like that.' She got to her feet. 'I'll go and change. Give me ten minutes.'

'I'll just use your bathroom, if I may. I must look a wreck.' He rose and crossed the room to the corridor that led off to the bathroom and laundry. Sally stopped.

'How did you know where it was?'

He looked startled. 'I just... I just knew.'

'You are serious.'

'Why do you suppose he couldn't come himself and expected his descendants would still find Sally as he'd known her? Or that he knew she wouldn't be at that address yet? He was a bright, intelligent man and he believed me.'

'And your priest friend can verify all of this?'

'He saw the letter; and Jules can tell you that I met William on the boat and again on the island. You can talk to Kaitlin or Chris Young — or my ex, if you like. He'll tell you I was behaving like a fruit loop.'

'I don't want to talk to your ex. I'm just glad he is your ex and not your current.' He was concentrating on his food, not looking at her.

William's trick, she thought. He's so like William, not just in looks. He's warm and sensitive and he listens with all his attention. I... I really like him. She was aware of the sudden charge of energy that passed between them as he finally glanced up and met her eyes. For a moment they sat, smiling at each other. Then she looked away, breaking the contact. She wasn't ready to commit her emotions so soon and so she tried to push down the strong sense of attraction she felt for Michael. She could drown in those deep brown eyes, and enjoy it. 'What did William leave for me? That I was to enjoy without asking questions?' Sally asked.

'I'll give it to you but don't screech.'

'He said that. Not to screech at him. Does that mean you believe me?'

'I don't have much choice.' He reached into his jacket pocket and pulled out a small leather pouch which he pushed across the table. Sally took it, fingering it wonderingly. It was heavy. She opened the corded neck.

'Just look inside, don't tip it out.'

She peered into the bag and was stunned into a long silence while Michael continued his meal.

She cleared her throat. 'It's gold!'

'Gold dust and nuggets. I imagine it's worth a small fortune.'

'This is the gold he took in a raid on the Anderson brothers. He told me he'd put it by in case of need. He could have used this to buy a top barrister. He'd have never been sent to St Helena.'

'He couldn't. As soon as he produced it he'd have signed his death warrant, proved beyond doubt he was one of the gang.'

'That's true. But it's stolen.'

He grinned. 'I knew you were going to say that. The Andersons made a fortune, they wouldn't miss one small bag. Now, do as William said, enjoy it and don't mind how he came by it. He became a reformed character, apparently, and went straight for the rest of his life; according to his papers, anyway.'

'It makes me an accessory after the fact.'

'So, report it. It's a hundred and eighteen years after the fact.

See if anyone cares.'

Sally's heart leapt with excitement. She'd accept William's gift. He'd wanted her to have it and it had come at the perfect time. 'I can buy the house. I can get the Porsche this year.'

'Porsche?'

'Joke.'

'You can take me to dinner tomorrow night.' Michael suggested.

She looked questioningly at him, her heart racing. He liked her. He wanted to see her again. She took a deep breath and tried for a casual tone. 'Do you want to?'

He reached across the table and took her hand in a familiar warm clasp, looking at her with William's eyes.

'Yes, I want to. Do you think, now I've finally found you, I'm going to risk losing you?'

Chapter 51

S ally and Tim sat on a bench in the park near Sally's house. He looked at her earnestly, his eyes magnified by his glasses. 'Thanks for coming with me, Sal. Dad would've hit the roof if you hadn't been there.'

'He was put out, wasn't he?' She grinned. 'At least you're in the clear. He was far more inclined to blame me. Called me a flighty little miss.'

Tim smiled slightly. 'He was disappointed. They all were.'

She patted his hand. 'They'll get over it. In time, they'll see it really is for the best.'

'Yes, I know that now. To tell you the truth, I'm not sure I could cope with the weirdness you seem to attract. I have to believe your story because you've never lied before, but, honestly, Sal, it's a bit thick.'

She smiled to herself. Tim couldn't see the wonder of it all. He hadn't once marvelled at the miracle, clearly preferring to distance himself from what he judged as aberrant behaviour. Not like Michael. She said merely, 'I know. Weird is the word.'

'And Peter, egging you on. Not very priestly, if you ask me.' He looked away from her, gazing across the manicured grass to a line of trees along the fence. 'Thanks for returning the ring. I suppose you're going to marry this new bloke?'

Sally hesitated. 'He's asked me but...' Then she smiled and nodded. 'Yes, Tim, I'm going to marry Michael.'

Peter poured coffee for the three of them. 'Is it William?'

'I don't know. I keep wondering; if he'd been a few years older, born to a different generation, William could very easily have been like Michael. The same sense of humour, the expression in his eyes, the romantic streak.' Sally smiled reflectively. 'He says things, unconsciously, that sound as if he'd known me once, but he doesn't remember. He seems to instinctively know things about me. He knew his way around the house. It could have been a lucky guess but it was odd that William wasn't much fazed by twentieth-century life; he said he had dreams about it. When I went to Chris, we were looking for a connection with the past because that's where I met him, but I said on the tape that I didn't know William then, implying I knew him later. The link wasn't with the past but with the future.'

Juliet, curled up on the presbytery sofa said, 'With Michael? Chris could find out for sure.'

'I don't care. I don't really want to know. He said he never married before because he always knew I'd come along, one day. So we're getting married as soon as possible to make up for lost time.' Sally gave a happy sigh. 'Remember what you said, Jules, about a man who turned my insides to jelly? It's worse than jelly. More like soft ice-cream, all gooey and shivery. He's wonderful. This time it's absolutely right.'

Juliet grinned. 'Well, you're certainly glowing. I agree. I think Michael's a hunk. You're a lucky girl, Sal.'

Peter said, 'He's a lucky man. You'll ask me to perform the ceremony, of course.'

'Of course. And I'll buy the house and we'll live there.' She stretched luxuriously. 'William got his Rose and I'm going to have my house and Michael and we'll probably produce lots of little

O'Meallys with red curly hair and everything in the garden is suddenly very lovely indeed.'

She reached for her cup and looked wonderingly at Peter. 'Tim said it was weird, and it is. Michael's been contacting the rest of the family. Suddenly, out of the blue, all sorts of old documents are turning up. In the backs of drawers, hidden away in odd places, like that box in the ceiling at Glendale. All verifying William's story. The Parks and Wildlife Service rang Michael yesterday. They've just found a missing file from 1883 and there's a letter from the prison superintendent, referring to William. They're posting a photocopy. Michael keeps looking at me sideways. He says I must be a witch and I've broken the O'Meally curse. The strangest thing was when he dropped in to see Ma Drake. She was quite upset. She said it was all my fault and she'd known I was up to something.' Sally shrugged. 'Weird, indeed.'

Juliet sipped her coffee and frowned. 'I wonder if we'll ever know why on earth the records said William hanged himself?'

Chapter 52

In July of 1883 on the island of St Helena, Superintendent Townley was at his desk, composing a report. He laid down his pen, blotted the ink and read the paper through.

To: The Comptroller-General of Prisons, Brisbane.
Sir,
It has been brought to my attention by the Under Colonial Secretary, that an error has been made in the official records concerning the death by suicide of the prisoner William O'Meally. I have carried out a full investigation and am now able to clear up this matter.
In April of 1882, the prisoner brought fresh information concerning his case before the visiting justice who carried out his own investigation of the events which led to O'Meally's conviction. Certain evidence came to light which not only proved conclusively the prisoner's innocence, but also the guilt of his brother.
William O'Meally was released from St Helena on May 21st, 1882, and his brother, Walter, was incarcerated in June of the same year.

The error in the records came about owing to the similarity of the brothers' initials, being WJ and WT O'Meally. It was Walter Thomas O'Meally who hanged himself in April of this year, 1883. The confusion arose due to the poor handwriting of the warder making the report. The '3' in the date being mistaken for a '2', and the prisoner's second initial being read as 'J'.

I can thus definitely confirm that it was Walter O'Meally who hanged himself in April of this year. William O'Meally remains, to my knowledge, hale and hearty on his farm at Bell's Creek.

In reference to the aforementioned death of prisoner Walter O'Meally, I must regretfully close the file on this matter. After exhaustive investigations, and in spite of my personal belief that his suicide was questionable and that O'Meally was in fact most foully murdered by a prisoner, or prisoners, in revenge for the injustice done to his brother, I can find no evidence to support my theory. All prisoners uphold the suicide claim in what I believe to be a conspiracy of silence. William O'Meally was one of the most popular prisoners on St Helena, and became something of a folk hero to the other inmates.

Meat-Axe Ludlow glowered at Tom Grogan across the table.

'You bastard, Tom, I've just worked it out. It was you stole my rope.'

'What d'ye need a rope for, lad? I had a better use for it.'

'It took me months to gather enough yarn and to spin it. I was going to use it to break out.'

'It was a fine rope, lad. You should speak to Townley, offer your services as an instructor, teach the lads about the art of rope making.'

'You callous bugger. T'weren't your rope.'

'Ask Dingy to steal you another, from Townley's shed.'

Bell shook his head.'Sorry, I'm being assigned other work.

Townley thinks he has made the connection between the poor performance of his chickens and my presence in the fowl yard. No more eggs for us.'

The others groaned. Frenchy said, 'They have me working in the new library. I will see what I can find, some paper, eh?'

'Can't eat paper,' Dingy pointed out.

'Perhaps Meat-Axe can make a paper rope.'

'Oh, you are all very humorous. Months I spent on it and now it's gone.'

'Claim it back from the superintendent. Walter's finished with it.'

Dingy Bell said softly, 'You did a good job, Tom, with that bastard.'

'Aye, he looked natural enough, swinging there. I made a promise to Billy, see? He wanted justice done.'

'To my mind, it's been well and truly done.'

Tom Grogan gave a satisfied nod and muttered, 'Amen to that, lad, amen to that.'

The End

Author's Note

The idea for setting a story on St Helena came to me some years ago during a visit to the island. At the time we purchased a booklet by Jarvis Finger, entitled *The Wild Men of St Helena*. Reading the stories of the prisoners and their exploits, the thought came, there's got to be a novel in here!

I have a great fondness for our colonial past, due to many years as a singer and researcher of traditional folk music. To my mind, you can't beat a bush band pouring out gutsy bush music, concertinas flowing in and out, bows dancing across fiddles, a tea-chest bass booming out the rhythm and a line of couples bobbing and weaving, their boots and shoes shaking the old timber flooring of a wool shed or country hall.

I chose the Brisbane Valley for the fictitious township of Bell's Creek, remembering a collecting trip some friends and I took up there in the seventies, when we followed the stock route outlined in the song 'Brisbane Ladies'. The cemetery at Glendale Farm is copied from the walled cemetery at Taromeo Homestead.

The Queensland Native Mounted Police came into the story from the pages of a booklet, *The History of the Native Mounted Police*, issued by the Queensland Police Department. They would not, in reality, have been camped so near to the Brisbane District; they were stationed further out, in places like Goondiwindi, the Condamine River, Roma, the Maryborough District, Taroom, Gladstone and Rockhampton. They travelled vast distances and were responsible for maintaining law and order across huge areas of the growing colony. Their story is colourful and fascinating and deserves a mention as part of Queensland's colonial history, so I have used 'author's licence' (why should it be reserved for poets only?) and given them a place in my book.

As well as my own knowledge of the times, I drew upon other sources, as listed below:

A Pictorial History of Bushrangers by Tom Prior, Bill Wannan and H Nunn, published by Paul Hamlyn Pty Ltd, 1969.

Complete Book of Australian Folk Lore compiled and annotated by Bill Scott, published by Ure Smith, 1976.

Information re the convict ships *Surrey* and *General Hewitt* and the subsequent inquiry, also the Eureka trials, came from: *A Concise History of Australia* by FLW Wood, MA, Victoria University College, Wellington, NZ, published by Dymocks Book Arcade Ltd, 1953.

Journals of Expeditions by Edward John Eyre is in *The Australian Collection* by Geoffrey Dutton, published by Angus and Robertson Publishers, 1985.

Some of the characters and incidents on St Helena are drawn from similar stories in a series of booklets by Jarvis Finger. William's smart remarks are taken from the story of Thomas 'The Mouth' White, who never knew when to keep quiet, and was constantly charged with bad language and 'spirited exclamations'. William's question, 'am I standing at attention enough for you this time?' is a direct quote from Thomas White. Brisbane Joe was inspired by Aboriginal Albert, who was sent to St Helena for fifteen years for the rape of a white girl. Albert was 'insolent and disorderly' and the warders were 'extremely wary' of the huge man whose violence ultimately led to his transfer to Brisbane.

The faces of the prisoners, as Sally experienced them, can be seen in *The Wild Men of St Helena*. The reference to William Collins cutting his throat and bleeding to death while in the hospital is factual.

In 1882 the superintendent of the St Helena Island Prison was, indeed, Captain William Townley, who replaced John McDonald in April of that year. His oppressive rules and rigid discipline created strong resentment among the prisoners which led to a rebellion in 1886 over a petty dictate which all of the prisoners disobeyed. A month later a petition circulated secretly among the inmates, outlining the prisoners' grievances, and an official parliamentary inquiry was set up. However, the authorities supported Townley's management methods and no action was taken.

The other factual character is Warder Michael Dalton. In October 1882 he was put on report for 'bringing ducks on to the island without informing the superintendent'. This alerted me to his probable interest in ducks which I then embroidered to suit the story.

By the way, the prison library was established in 1883 — too late for William to enjoy.

The artifacts of which Sally saw photographs on the ferry to St Helena, including the gambling chips, dice, dominoes, playing cards and canvas belt, are on display at the Queensland Historical Society's headquarters in the Old Comissariat Stores, William Street, Brisbane.

The Commissioner of Police in 1880 was Mr David Thomas Seymour, as mentioned in Sergeant Mallory's report. Other historical characters are the Governor of New South Wales, Governor Macquarie, Charles Thatcher, the 'minstrel of the goldfields', Sub-Inspector O'Connor and, of course, Ned Kelly and Queen Victoria.

Jarvis Finger's booklets were an excellent source of information. The titles are, *The Wild Men of St Helena*, *True Tales of Old St Helena*, *More True Tales of Old St Helena*, *The Escapes From St Helena* and *The St Helena Island Prison In Pictures*. They are published by Boolarong Publications, Bowen Hills, Brisbane, and are currently in print.

The story of Matthew Manning's ghost can be found in his book, *The Link*, published by Colin Smythe Ltd, Bucks, UK, 1974.

Apart from those listed above, all other characters are fictitious and are not intended to represent any persons, living or dead.

Anne Infante
Brisbane 1997